Arcadia's Daughter

A Novel

By

Charles Griswold

To my wife Lynn without whose encouragement and loving dope-slaps this work would not have been completed

The Prey

"I had not expected to die so young.
I had my whole life ahead of me, but as it turned out,
I would not change any of the events that befell me."
– Abigail Johnson, 1872

New York City, May, 1872

Frank Robinson didn't know this would be his last murder. He'd killed countless men, women, and the occasional child. Frank felt nothing when killing—his heart didn't race, his breathing remained steady, his face placid. He'd learned his trade in the Union Army and continued in civilian life after deserting seven years ago.

He waited in the alley with the stench of last winter's trash rising in the warm spring air. He saw his victim approaching, a small, rotund, jovial man in a frocked coat and derby hat. The man smiled and walked with a spring in his step. His wife had hired Frank to kill him. He didn't know why nor did he care; only that she had the money. Frank followed him for two days, learning his habits and deciding on the location to fulfill his contract.

The victim cut through the alley as usual on his way home. Frank stepped out of the shadows and grabbed the man from behind, covering his mouth with his large hand to muffle his scream. The man struggled but was no match for Frank's massive size. He slipped his knife into the man's chest, sliding it along the rib until he felt a slight twitch as the blade entered the heart. The little fat man went limp, falling face down beside the carcass of a rotting dog in the muck and filth. Frank stooped to wipe the blood off his knife on his victim's pants before walking calmly out of the alley toward the saloon a few blocks away.

In the saloon, Frank claimed his usual spot at the end of the long mahogany bar where he could keep an eye on who came and went. The crowded noisy room smelled of stale beer, tobacco, and puke. His imposing size and icy demeanor usually ensured his solitude. An old man in ragged clothes, bent and walking with a limp, approached him with hat in hand.

"Frank, I've been lookin' fer ya." The old man showed a toothless smile.

"What do you want, Smitty? Can't you see I'm drinking?" His gaze made the old man cringe like a dog expecting a beating.

"Well, there's this man, you see. He's been asking around. He needs a job done, some young girl, won't say where, but says it pays well. Yup. Pays *right* well, he says. He gave me this address. Said he'd be there ta'marrow noon, he did." Smitty extended his hand at arm's length and handed the paper to Frank.

He took the address and put it in his pocket without looking at it. "You see this guy around before?" He stared straight ahead toward an unseen place and continued to sip his whisky.

"No, Frank, ain't never seen 'im before. He's a dandy, dressed all smart and such. Asked for you by name, he did, like you's old friends. He gave me a dollar to hand you that address."

Frank glared. He didn't like it when anyone knew his name. Frank had no friends, no drinking buddies, and no female companions. He had no need for such society. Frank was a specter, anonymous, a stranger in the crowd, always blending in, never showy. Other than his enormous size, which Frank tried to hide as best he could, he was only another face in the mob.

"By name you say? And you sure you ain't never seen 'im?" His voice drew the attention of others at the bar.

Smitty took a half step back. "No, Frank, honest, he ain't but a stranger. But like I said, he asked for you by name."

"Umph." He downed his shot of whiskey.

Smitty stood cowering, holding his hat with both hands, trying to smile. Frank glanced at the old man, then reached in his pocket and flipped a buffalo head nickel to him.

"Thank you, Frank," he said stepping backwards. "I'll see y'es around." He turned and quickly hobbled out of the bar.

The next day, Frank walked through the crowded streets of Five Points, intent on his destination. He wondered who this man was that knew his name, and if he'd have to kill him. The address he'd been given was a squalid tenement on Orange Street. The acrid smell of piss and garbage assaulted his nose when he entered the dark stairway. A baby wailed, and a man's angry voice resounded from a second floor apartment. He knocked on the door of the third floor apartment noted in the address.

"Come in." The apartment was empty except for a table and chairs. A solitary patch of sunlight shone through a tear in the curtains illuminating swirling dust. A man sat at the table with only his outline visible in the semi-darkness, face obscured by the low brim of his hat. Frank noticed his shoes in the patch of light. They were new, shiny, and made of expensive leather. Men who wore shoes like that could afford to pay for what they wanted, Frank thought. So he stayed to hear him out.

"You're Mr. Robinson, I trust?"

Frank nodded slowly, wary of the man shrouded in

shadow.

"Please have a seat. My employer, Mr. Anon, wants you to kill someone, a young girl. I understand that this is your line of work, Mr. Robinson." The stranger's voice was high and lilting, and it grated in Frank's ears. It didn't sound natural. He pulled the chair farther away from the table and sat. Feeling a chill, he pulled his coat closed.

"I don't discuss business till I know who I'm dealin' with. I didn't catch your name, stranger."

"My name is of no importance."

Frank shifted in his chair. His usual client was a greedy business partner or desperate wife. He couldn't size up this stranger in the shadows.

"I don't come cheap. You got money?" he quipped.

"Yes I do. This is a simple job for a man of your talents, a young girl. After all, how much trouble could she be?" There was slight snicker in the man's voice.

"Where does she live?" asked Frank.

"She is an only child who lives on a remote farm north of Boston."

"That's it? That's all you got?"

It sounded like a wild goose chase to Frank. He stood to leave when the man slid an envelope and a dagger across the table. The dagger had a black wooden handle fastened with brass rivets. Its blade was crude and discolored. Frank picked up the envelope first. It contained a thick stack of bills, more money than Frank had ever seen.

"There's a thousand dollars."

"Alright, you got my ear." Frank resumed his seat facing the form in the shadow.

"There will be another thousand when the job is

done. What you do with the rest of the family is your business."

He had killed for as little as twenty dollars. For a thousand dollars more, he would gladly kill the whole family. He'd kill his *own* mother, too, if that's what the man wanted.

"Well, okay, sure, but you've not given me a lot to go on. Might take months to track down every one-horse farm north of here," said Frank holding tight to the money.

"Pick up the knife," commanded the man.

Frank didn't like being ordered about, and he especially didn't like not seeing the man's face. He wanted to kill him and be done with it, but the thought of another thousand made him think better of it. He picked up the knife. It was cold, lighter than he expected, almost weightless in his hand.

"Point it to the north," said the lilting voice.

Frank did as he was told. The knife grew noticeably warm in his hand, like the handle of a coffee pot. Frank stared at it as a chill run through him and, uncharacteristically, his heart began to race.

"Ah, you felt it, didn't you?" The stranger's insidious voice held a hint of satisfaction.

"Yah, it's some kind of trick, ain't it?" Frank said as an accusation. He thought he was being fooled, and he didn't like it.

"Yes, but a useful trick. The knife will lead you to your quarry. When you point it in the right direction it will become warm. The closer you are, the warmer it will be. It will glow when you face the girl. When you find her, you must stab her in the heart with the dagger."

"I'd rather shoot her, if it's all the same to you."

"It's not." The voice in the darkness became loud and threatening, catching Frank off guard and causing him to flinch. "It's this knife in her heart if you want your final payment. I will know if my wishes are not carried out. Am I clear?"

"Hey, you're the boss. We'll do it your way." He stood up, sliding the knife though his belt and pocketing the envelope. "How do I get in touch with you when I'm done with the job?" Frank's voice rose as he sought to reassert himself.

"Send a telegram to Mr. Anon at this address. Your money will be waiting here when you return. Now go." The stranger silently pushed himself further back blending into the shadows.

Frank left the apartment, took the stairs two at a time, and spilled onto Orange Street relieved to have some distance from his strange, disagreeable employer. It was a cockamamie job, but the money was too good to pass up. Frank boarded a train for Boston that night with the dagger pointing the way.

Perfect Sorrow

"And all the winds go sighing, for sweet things dying."
– Christina Rossetti

Central Maine, May 2001

Sarah and David were driving back from Waterville on a cool spring day with their two dogs, Abe and Louie. They had been married for two years. Sarah was eight years his senior, but that difference hadn't mattered to either of them past the first date. They differed in every measure. He was six foot two; she was five foot four. He was athletic; she was a book worm. David worked as a cabinetmaker; Sarah was a college professor. He was impulsive and spontaneous; she was thoughtful and cautious. She didn't make a move without a plan.

At the end of their first date four years ago, they knew they were opposites, but they filled in each other's voids. David brought spontaneity into her orderly life by taking her on mystery dates or doing things on the spur of the moment. Sarah helped David focus. She saw when he became scattered and, in her own gentle way, would reel him in with a few well-chosen questions. They shared a love of music, art, and cooking, as well as a strong physical attraction. David made her laugh, and Sarah anchored David in his sea of hyperactivity. They were better together than apart.

They'd spent the morning hiking on cross-country ski trails at the now deserted ski area. The forest smelled of last fall's decay and new spring growth. Patches of snow lingered in dark spots under low pine boughs. Sap surging from the roots driven by warm days and cold nights had turned the maple buds red. The trees were tapped with bright orange plastic tubing, which collected sap into large plastic tubs set beside the road.

When David was a boy and the farmers still used pails to collect the sap, he would dip his fingers in the buckets and let the sweet sap drip into his mouth. Abe and Louie were wet and exhausted from bounding through the woods, following the forest inhabitant's scents, and eating things Sarah would rather not know about. The car smelled like wet, muddy, happy dog.

"Honey." Sarah's voice startled David, and the taste of maple sap he'd been savoring vanished. "It's a junkshop, let's stop."

David braked and the tires skidded on the gravel as they stopped in front of the Fairfield Antique Mall. Calling it a mall was a pretentious exaggeration. It was a series of long rambling sheds connected together and resulting in a rabbit warren of trash and occasional treasure. There was not much worth looking at, but a lot of it.

The front room was clean, well-lit, and smelled like furniture polish. The best antiques were staged here where they were certain to be seen. Further back were old books and magazines, less desirable furniture, and collectables of dubious quality. Sarah and David quickly passed over the expensive items in the front room and moved to the rear of the building that contained the contents of houses cleared out after the owner died, and either the relatives didn't want the stuff or there was no one left. Old mahogany furniture that had once been someone's prized possession, given a lifetime of care, was now dusty and forsaken. Most personal of all were the old family albums filled with pictures of stern looking relatives and babies who had long ago grown up, their identities and stories lost. The photographs were a mute testament to lives that had passed into obscurity.

"David, come over here and look at this." Sarah knelt beside a dusty box of discarded photographs. A hand lettered sign said *25 cents or 5 for a dollar.* "Look at all the poor lost relatives. There are husbands, wives, uncles, and cousins, all forever anonymous. It's kind of sad, somebody's loved ones cast aside in this dusty box." She glanced up at her husband.

"This one looks like four sisters on a summer day standing under a tree in front of a house. What do you suppose they were doing that day? They look happy," she said. "Maybe they were having a family reunion after not having seen each other for years, or a casual summer get-together?" Sarah's voice trailed off.

David had a less romantic view of the photographs than Sarah's, but found the buildings and the peoples' clothing interesting. He tried to place the time period by what they were wearing—seemed like early 1900s by the length of the hemlines.

"Oh, David, look at this one. It's a young girl, a teenager I think, in a white dress with pretty smocking on it and a big bow in the front. It's adorable, looks handmade."

"Sarah, I'm sure all the dresses back then were handmade."

Sarah chuckled. "I'm sure you're right. She's holding a bouquet and looks like she's half awake. That's funny. Why would they take a picture of her looking like that?" asked Sarah.

"Can I see that?" Before she could answer, David snatched the photograph out of her hand and went to the window to get a better look in the daylight. The young girl was positioned on a love seat but at an unnatural angle. Her hands were placed on the bouquet rather than clutching it and her face was oddly sunken with her jaw slightly open. An older woman seated beside the girl looked stricken as though her body could not contain her grief. A weathered looking man with a trim beard stood behind the settee with one hand on the girl's shoulder and a large book held in the crook of his arm. He looked grim, as though no emotion on Earth would ever break through his facade.

David called to Sarah, "You gotta see this. I've read about these photographs, but I've never actually seen one before."

"I don't see what's so special about a dozing girl." Sarah sounded puzzled as she joined him at the window.

"Sarah, she's dead!"

"Oh, my God, are you sure?" Sarah leaned in. "You're right. That's really creepy. Why would anyone do such a thing?" Sarah pulled back as though the photograph had an unpleasant odor. She looked at David in anticipation.

The photograph captured a perfect moment of sorrow, the parents' grief from the loss of their child, and their complete devotion to her even in death. Her mother's face reflected pain that would last all her days. David gazed at the image, wondering who this young girl was. What was her   story?

Abigail

"Sometimes you have to kind of die inside in order to rise from your own ashes and believe in yourself and love yourself to become a new person." – Gerard Way

China Maine, May 1872

It was springtime. The world held the promise that comes after the stillness of winter. Abigail's life of nineteen years was nothing but dreams. She ached for a life beyond the isolation of her family's farm in the Maine wilderness — of adventure in distant lands, of romance, of love, of family. She dreamed of a rich life well lived.

Abigail's day began with the excitement of a small adventure when her mother sent her to town for supplies at Mr. Small's store, a journey of only a few miles, but one that offered a welcome respite from the monotony of the farm. The road home followed the river, which ran full with the spring snow melt and threatened to overcome its banks. Water rushed over the rocks and shone with a white luster highlighted by the bright spring sun. The roar of the cascading water drowned out the sound of Moses pulling the wagon on the rocky road. He knew the way home and was in no hurry, nor was Abigail.

The day was warm and bright, a relief from the knife-edge cold and darkness of the past few months. Abigail and her parents were sentenced every December to confinement in the house, and to days of boredom. Spring was their parole from the captivity of winter. Last season's snow was visible under the low pine boughs in the forest. It would last into June hidden in the cool, dark shade. Maple trees lining the road had red halos from the swelling buds. They had been tapped and set with covered buckets to collect the surging sap.

"Whoa," She called out to Moses, giving him a short tug on the reins. He appeared perplexed why they'd stopped, but made no complaint. Abigail climbed down from the wagon and went to a sap bucket hanging from its tap on a maple tree. Using her fingers, she dripped the cold sweet sap into her mouth. She wanted to lift the bucket and drink deeply, but that would not be ladylike, so she contented herself with several more small tastes, one of her secret joys of spring.

Abigail stood alone beside the road, her fingers wet and sticky with maple sap, and closed her eyes, imagining she was on a great adventure, a journey to a distant land, riding in a fine coach approaching a bustling city with a great castle visible over the next hill. In the evening, she would dine in a great hall filled with royalty and foreign emissaries all dressed in the rich costumes of their lands. She was the much sought-after visitor from America. For an instant, the vision was real, the excitement palpable. When Abigail opened her eyes, she was still confined in Maine with only Moses seeking her attention, wondering when they'd resume their journey home.

Standing beside the maple tree, Abigail looked up the gently sloping field that led to the Farrington house in the distance. The stately two-story brick house had chimneys set at each corner, an extravagance reserved for the wealthiest homes. The Farrington farm was the largest, most prosperous in China, Maine.

Jacob Farrington came to mind and a deep ache rose within her chest. She missed him. They had played together as children, and stayed friends. Their friendship had grown into something special, unspoken of, but understood between them. Jacob had marched off with his four older brothers to fight Mr. Lincoln's Great War to save the Union. Jacob died in the Battle of Little Round Top, by all accounts a hero. His brothers died of typhoid fever. Little was said of the brothers, other than they had died preserving the Union.

Occasionally Abigail saw Mr. and Mrs. Farrington in their buggy on their way to the Baptist church on Sundays. They were a testament to sacrifice and sorrow. One could not speak with them without experiencing their pain. It defined them. Their very stature seemed diminished under the weight of their grief. Looking up from the road, the house itself appeared to mourn.

Abigail's Father said the Farrington's loss was God's judgment for the sin of pride and for working on the Sabbath. Father kept his opinions to himself when anyone in town mentioned the family. Mr. Farrington was well-respected in town, and the family's loss was seen as a noble sacrifice. Abigail believed Father had his own sin to repent for—the sin of envy.

Moses and Abigail continued their drowsy pace until they came to Weeks' gristmill. The rushing water formed a wide arch as it overflowed the dam and crashed onto the rocks below. The sluice gate was closed and the water wheel still. Mr. Weeks was one of the ten men who did not return after the end of the southern rebellion. He fell at the Battle of the Seven Pines, and his remains were never found. Mrs. Weeks placed a head stone in the village cemetery so people would remember him.

As they rode up, Isaac Weeks was spading the family garden. He was her age, nineteen, and the eldest of five brothers. Isaac had been nine when his father fell. Mrs. Weeks had struggled to keep the mill going early on, but now Isaac had taken over the running of it.

"Morning, Isaac."

Isaac walked over to the wall and took off his hat.

"Good morning, Miss Johnson, how are you this fine day?"

"Isaac, why are you speaking to me so formally? We've known each other since we were children. You have no cause for such formality with me."

"Well, Miss Johnson—I mean Abigail, well—you see, you and I are both older now, more adult, and I thought I should address you proper like. That's all." Isaac was not what you would call a good-looking young man, and not tall as one might like. Mother described him as having a pleasant look. He had left school early to help his mother. As Abigail looked at Isaac leaning on the stone wall, he seemed much more a man than the boy she'd grown up with.

"Abigail will be fine between you and me when we're alone. You may call me Miss Johnson when we are in polite company." She rather like the idea being addressed in a more adult manner, and bristled when her former school mistress, Miss Crommett, called her "Abby" at the store today. Abigail believed herself to be an adult, to have reached the age of reason, and competent to make her own decisions about her life; but she was trapped, held prisoner by her father and her circumstances. Abigail felt a sudden rush of anger at the injustice of her situation and feeling so powerless to change it.

"Abigail, are you alright? You looked angry. I meant no disrespect."

"No, no, it was nothing you said. I was thinking of something else." She smiled at Isaac to reassure him.

"Abigail, I'm wondering if you were planning on going to the GAR charity dance next weekend. If you are, I hope you'll have a dance with me." Isaac looked down at his feet. The veterans were raising money to build a Grand Army of the Republic fraternal hall. They had a charter from the Congress of the United States granted in honor of the service and sacrifice of the town.

"Yes, I am going. Mother has made me a new dress for the occasion. And, yes, I will have a dance with you, Isaac. You come and make your manners like a gentleman and I will accept."

"Why, yes. Yes, I will." Isaac smiled.

"Well, I'd best be going, Isaac. Father will be angry if he thinks I've been wasting my time. Give my regards to your mother."

"Bye, Abigail, see you at the dance."

As Abigail rode away, she realized that Isaac was sweet on her. He could easily ask Father for her hand in marriage, which to Abigail seemed merely trading one confinement for another. She imagined herself with three children at her feet and one on her breast. The Weeks were a prosperous family, and while they were not Quaker, Father would easily put aside religious differences in favor of getting her married off, and removing the burden of her upkeep. The commandment said to honor thy father and mother. If Father commanded, she must obey, for without her family's support, she had none at all.

Once Abigail left the grist mill, the spring day quickly turned windy and cold. Dressed in her summer coat and hat in anticipation of a warm, bright day, she felt chilled to the bone. Abigail shivered and gave Moses an extra shake of the reins to urge him into a reluctant trot. Threatening black clouds swirled across the sky. A large dark curtain of rain raced across the field like a band of highwaymen pursuing her.

Abigail's Death

"Has this world been so kind to you that you should leave with regret?
There are better things ahead than any we leave behind."
– C.S. Lewis

China, Maine, May, 1872

Abigail arrived home shivering, soaked to the bone, as the setting sun illuminated the retreating dark clouds with a pink glow. Father came out of the barn when he heard the wagon approaching. She expected a stern lecture for wasting her time. Father had no need to socialize and thus saw no value in it for Abigail or her Mother.

"Father, I'm sorry to be late getting home. There were a great many people out today and everyone wanted to talk. I couldn't be impolite."

"Never mind that now. The Sabbath is beginning; go in the house and warm yourself while I put the horse away." Her Father took the wagon to the barn to unhitch Moses without a further word. She was thankful Father was in a hurry.

Abigail's Mother had dinner cooking, and the strong fire in the stove warmed the kitchen. The smell of last season's potatoes, carrots, and turnips with a good measure of barley filled the air.

"Abigail, where have you've been? You should have been home hours ago." Her expression turned to concern when she saw Abigail. "You look chilled to the bone. You're soaking wet. Go get out of those clothes and I'll get you some mint tea and honey."

Abigail changed into her flannel nightgown and returned to the kitchen to sit beside the stove. The heat felt wonderful. She'd envisioned sitting here while shivering during the ride home in the cold rain. The heat revived her as she sipped her tea, but when she stopped shivering, she realized that she didn't feel at all well. Her body ached and her throat hurt.

"So why are you so late? I worried when it started to rain," said Mother.

"When I got to Mr. Small's store, the entire town was there. It was such a nice day; everyone was out enjoying the sunshine. I saw Miss Crommett, she was there along with her sister, Celestia. She said that they were moving to St. Cloud, Minnesota, to live with their brother. He'd gone there after being mustered out."

Abigail raised her voice. "Miss Crommett kept calling me 'Abby' like I was still a schoolgirl. I wanted to correct her, but didn't think it was my place to do so."

"She was your teacher for many years; you were right to have held your tongue."

"Miss Crommett went on at length about Mary Cunningham and her new position as a teacher in Portland after she'd matriculated from the Women's Seminary." Abigail's mother knew this was difficult news for her to hear, as this was the position she'd wanted, but which her Father would not allow. He did not hold with the freethinking Congregationalists. Neither of the women dwelled on the subject.

"I also saw Isaac Weeks turning over his vegetable plot. I stopped and spoke with him a while. He asked if he could have a dance at the GAR charity social. I told him he could if he made his manners."

Mother smiled. "I'm sure many young gentlemen will ask you for a dance. You have a beautiful face, fine delicate features, wonderful auburn hair with red highlights, and best of all, those gray-blue eyes. I don't know where you got those from—not from my side of the family nor your father's." Her Mother put her hands on her hips and looked Abigail up and down. "You're a fine young woman, mighty fine, and a good catch for any man." She turned back to the stove.

Mother speaking of her as a "good catch" reminded Abigail of the question she longed to hear the answer to.

"Mother, when are you going to speak to Father about my going to live with Grandfather in Augusta? I would like to go this summer."

Her mother didn't meet Abigail's eye when she answered. "I don't think we can discuss it until after the harvest. You know how busy it is, we need every hand."

Abigail stared at the floor. Mother had already spoken to Father and he had not approved. This was her way of postponing the decision.

"I think what we should do is have Grandfather ask." Mother glanced at Abigail as though she was a schoolgirl whispering in class. "After the harvest, we will go to Augusta to visit Mother and Father. We've gone every year since your father and I were married. This year won't be any different. I can speak to Mother and she will have Father make the request. Your father has always respected your grandfather, being a deacon in the Society and all. He will not be able to refuse his request."

"Oh, Mother, what a wonderful idea!" Abigail tried to smile, but the growing ache in her throat made her wince. Swallowing was hard despite the soothing tea.

"Abigail, are you ill? Let me feel you." She put her hand on Abigail's forehead and the back of her neck. "You have a fever, child."

Father came in, took off his coat, and saw his wife

hovering over Abigail.

"Is she ill? It's no wonder, out all day in a summer coat, getting caught in the rain. The weather changes quickly this time of year, you know..."

"Alfred." Mother cut him off in mid-sentence. "She has a fever. We don't need a lesson on changeable weather right now."

"Humph," Father replied. Mrs. Johnson almost never countered her husband, deferring to him on most subjects, but Abigail was her reason for living. The reason she endured the hardships of rural farm life with a dour, joyless husband.

"Come, Abigail, I'm putting you to bed. I'll bring you some broth later."

Her mother brought up a brass bed warmer and ran it under the covers to warm the cold bedding. Abigail fell into a deep but fitful sleep. She awoke before dawn drenched in sweat and feeling worse than ever. She called for Mother, who changed her sheets and placed a cool cloth on her forehead.

When Abigail awoke again it was daylight. Her Mother sat beside her on the bed with a basin of water, wiping her face and arms.

"How are you, my child?"

"My throat hurts terribly, my whole body aches. I feel quite weak. What time is it?"

"Oh, it's mid-afternoon. You've been sleeping since yesterday evening." Her Mother wiped her brow bringing her daughter a moment's relief as much from her touch as the coolness of the moist cloth.

"I sent your father to fetch Dr. Harris. He's been gone a while. I expect him back presently. You shouldn't talk, just rest."

Abigail was worried that Mother felt the need to send for Dr. Harris, and even more worried that Father had consented. Her body ached and her mouth was parched. Her Mother gave her a sip of water which felt good in her mouth but the pain of swallowing was almost too much. Abigail's Mother never left her side. Her Mother stayed by her side comforting her daughter by singing her favorite hymns until she fell back to asleep.

Abigail awoke shivering in the night. The flickering lamp on the nightstand lit the room. Mrs. Johnson, exhausted by her vigil, rested her head on the bed. Her husband sat in a chair behind her reading his Bible.

"Did you bring the doctor? What did he say?" Abigail asked, straining to speak in a whisper.

"Dr. Harris has gone to Boston for two weeks. Don't worry, dear, you'll feel better tomorrow. The Lord is watching over you. Father and I have been praying." A shiver shook Abigail to her toes. She didn't remember ever feeling this sick. Merely turning her head was an effort. Her Mother held Abigail's hand as her Father droned on from Ecclesiastes. Abigail drifted in and out of consciousness.

At dawn, Abigail returned to consciousness. There was a soft light in her room. She couldn't focus, but she could hear her Mother and Father speaking.

"Alfred, I fear that the Lord is calling Abigail home. She's been delirious for two days. She is so still, so very still, barely breathing."

"Louisa, there is nothing we can do. It's God's will. If this is her time, then we can only pray that He will call her to His heavenly multitude."

"God forgive me, Alfred, but I find little comfort in that notion. A mother should not have to bury her daughter.

Abigail has been my joy all these years. If she leaves us, there is nothing for me but to wait till the Lord decides it is my time to join her."

Abigail heard her and wanted to speak, to tell her Mother not to be sad, but she couldn't move. Every moment of consciousness drained and sapped what little strength remained within her. She slipped into unconsciousness again.

Abigail heard her Mother calling her name from a distance as though she was calling Abigail in from the fields. She struggled to focus. Mother sat by the bed and Father stood behind her holding his Bible. Abigail felt the sickness had left her. She tried to rise up to speak, but was unable to move or utter a sound. Oddly, this didn't bother her. She was happy to see her parents. Her Mother looked drained like she hadn't slept in days with eyes red and her hair askew. Abigail wondered why her mother couldn't see that she felt better. Her fever must have broken, and she was sure she'd be well in time for the dance. Her Father looked stoic, more somber than usual. Behind him Abigail saw her new dress hanging up. It was so pretty with the smocking and the lovely pink satin bow. Abigail was so looking forward to the dance, even to dancing with Isaac.

Everything became still and quiet. Abigail's body had no sensation at all. She floated, rising to a great height where she could see her family's entire farm and all that lived there. She saw China Lake, the Farrington Farm, and Mr. Small's store. Abigail saw her Grandmother sitting in her parlor in Augusta. Moses was in his stall looking at her. The cows in the field awoke and looked at her as well. The spring chickadees roosting in the tree outside her window watched. Even the mice in the hayloft stopped their search for seeds to watch Abigail.

The earth stopped its rotation about the sun, and all

life paused for this moment. Abigail smiled at her Mother as she felt herself being swept away into darkness by a great silent wind.

Abigail awoke slowly without thought or understanding; all was dark and silent. She was alone, unaware if it was day or night, not knowing if she'd slept a day or a year. Pictures formed before her as though projected on wisps of smoke, coming into focus and then dissolving slowly. Abigail recognized the transient images. They were her own thoughts and memories, her desires and hopes, her fears and uncertainties, all that she was carried on the wind, swirling before her as though seen from the center of a whirlwind. Abigail couldn't tell if these pictures were moving or if she was. She was broken, shattered, by some terrible force and cast into a tempest. A force controlled her that she could neither see nor stop. Abigail tried to pull the pieces together before they were lost in the chaos. Terror gripped her. She feared she'd be scattered, never whole again.

Why was this happening to me? I would not be violated in such a terrifying manner. She'd lost control of her person, and wanted to fight whoever or whatever caused this horrid illusion. *Stop it! Stop it!* She screamed again in silence. *I will not abide this!* She yelled again at her unseen tormentor. Anger turned to fury, rising within her, and became her salvation.

The swirling tempest calmed, drifting away like a storm vanishing on the horizon while Abigail willed together all the shattered pieces, her thoughts, her memories, her desires, back together. What had been shattered like a broken mirror flowed together with each shard precisely fitting to the next with Abigail's mind as the glue. Abigail was whole, and alone in a silent void.

Where am I? Is this my room? Even on the darkest night Abigail could see out the window past the tree to the fields beyond. *Where were Mother and Father?* She remembered her mother holding her hand, she'd been crying. Her father looked grim standing behind Mother, clutching his Bible to his chest. Abigail wanted to run down the hall to their bedroom and tell them she was alright. But the room was too dark. She couldn't see, hear, touch anything, or move. *Where was the door? Where was I?* The darkness closed in her.

Why had I been abandoned? Mother, Mother, come here! I'm afraid! I need you! Father, it's me, Abigail. I'm lost, Father, come find me! Father, I'm scared! Help me, Father! No word of comfort came.

Abigail felt pieces of her began to drift away as her being became undone once more. Her focus lapsed, panic returned. And anger followed the panic. *I will not allow myself to be rendered asunder on the wind.* Abigail drew the anger to her embracing it and she grew stronger, willing herself whole again. The fragments of herself came back together, faster and stronger than before. She felt more whole, more solidly joined.

Abigail's mind raced while she floated in the dark, desperately searching for anything familiar, any sight, any touch. She imagined she heard Mother in the kitchen cleaning up from breakfast, and Father coming up the stairs in his heavy boots.

An eternity passed while Abigail prayed for someone to rescue her. Slowly, almost imperceptibly, the formless void became lighter like the twilight before dawn. Something moved. Shapes came into view. Abigail strained to bring them closer, into focus, hoping to grasp something solid, to latch on to a piece of flotsam in the void. The shape became the outline of a person shrouded in a gray mist. He or she beckoned Abigail, called to her, but the mist muffled the sound. *Was this my rescuer?*

Exhaustion overtook Abigail. She'd held back the chaos for such a long time. She imagined she was drowning, swept out to sea by a powerful current as the safety of the shore slipped way. All the while, a shadowy figure on the shore urged her to safety.

Terror gripped her as she felt herself breaking apart once more. *Would I ever be whole again? Why had Mother and Father forsaken me?* Abigail was spent, too tired to hang on. She felt herself slipping beneath the ocean of chaos.

Abigail flew apart.

The One That Got Away

"The last enemy that shall be destroyed is death."
– 1 Corinthians 15:26

Boston, May, 1872

Frank Robinson reached Boston after a day's travel by train. Standing on the platform, he held the knife, pointing it in the four cardinal directions. As before, it felt warm when he pointed north, but now a cold biting ache crept up his arm. He cursed the knife and quickly returned it to his belt.

He spent the night in a seaman's hotel by the waterfront, and planned on setting out to the north again the next day. He almost got into a fight when a man bumped him, causing him to spill his beer. He'd killed men for less. Frank rose to challenge him, but remembering the next thousand dollars, he sat down and finished his dinner, not wanting anything to get in the way of winning his prize.

The next morning he made his way through Haymarket Square to the Boston and Maine station, and took the train to Portsmouth, New Hampshire. The knife was warmer, still indicating north. Each time he held the knife his arm arched and a rage grew within him. When he'd killed before he'd experienced nothing, a cool mechanical act. Now when he held the knife he felt desperate to plunge the knife into the heart of the girl. He wondered how much farther he'd have to go. In Portsmouth, he booked passage on a paddlewheel packet boat that steamed up the coast. It stopped in Portland, Maine, then up the Kennebec River to the Hallowell docks south of Augusta. The passage was expensive, but he was in a hurry, anxious to satisfy the demand of the knife.

During the voyage, Frank kept checking the knife. It continued to feel warm when pointed north. In Portland, it still pointed north. It wasn't until the packet boat navigated up the Kennebec River that the knife grew warmer and suggested a change to the east. First only a few points, but when the boat docked in Hallowell, the knife was hot to the touch and pointed decidedly east. His heart raced as he felt the knife. His anticipation grew. He was almost gleeful, knowing that his prey was closer.

Frank hired a horse and rode hard for a day, not sparing the beast. He knew he was close. Each time he'd checked the knife it felt warmer, and now it made his arm ache something fierce. The little man in the shadows hadn't said anything about that happening. This was surely the devil's doing, he thought. Each time he held the knife, he was overcome with desperation to find the girl. He imagined his satisfaction when he thrust the knife into her heart.

He found himself beside a lake approaching a crossroads with a Baptist church and a store. A sign read *China Lake General Store*. He took the knife from his belt to see what direction to go next. No matter which direction he pointed the knife, he felt nothing. The knife remained inert in his hand, and no longer caused his arm to ache. His heart no longer raced. Whatever power the knife had to point the way to his quarry had vanished.

Frank didn't know what this meant. The last time he'd checked the knife was hot, not merely warm. He was sure he was close. His thoughts went to the strange unseen man who had sent him off on this wild goose chase to the backwoods of Maine. Frank Robinson didn't like being denied. He'd come all this way, and he felt like killing someone. He wanted the final payment of a thousand dollars.

He inquired at the general store. The proprietor, a yokel named Small, said there was a young girl, Abigail Johnson, an only child, who lived on a farm down on Neck Road. Frank rode off toward the Johnson farm hoping to find the girl, hoping that the knife would return to life and confirm his kill.

When Frank came to the farm entrance, a large box-like wagon turned onto the main road. Painted on the side in elaborate lettering was, *Clark Photographic Mobile Van*. A solitary driver sat in front, a rotund man with a fat face topped with a bowler hat; large mutton chop sideburns made his face look rounder still.

"Good day to you, sir," said the man.

"I'm looking for the Johnson farm. Is this it?" Frank asked.

"Yes it is. I just came from there. You come to pay your respects to the bereaved?"

"Who died?"

"The daughter—buried her not an hour ago. Very sad. She was a pretty young thing, barely nineteen. She came down with scarlet fever, and was called home to the Lord. The family wanted a picture of her before they laid her to rest."

"They've already got her in the ground, you say?"

"Yes. She is in her final rest now. Are you family?"

"No, not family," said Frank in a low voice, seething with anger that his hunt had come up short.

He'd spent days searching for this girl, going where the now silent knife had taken him. No sense trying to dig her up to see if the knife glowed. He'd have to kill the family to do it. Too messy. Messy was never good, always led to trouble. Frank would never know if this was the girl he was supposed to kill. He turned his exhausted horse and rode off in the direction he had come from, leaving Mr. Clark wondering who this disagreeable fellow was.

Frank Robinson raced back to Augusta. His exhausted horse collapsed east of town. He left it lying beside the road near dead, and walked the last few miles. He sent a telegram to the Five Points address saying that he'd completed his job and was returning to collect his money. When boarding the packet ship to return to Boston, Frank reached for the knife, but it was gone. He thought he'd lost it during the ride back to Augusta. His employer probably wanted his knife back, and now it was gone. If he made a stink about it, he'd kill him, but only after he'd gotten his money.

Frank Robinson returned to Five Points three days later, consumed by greed, and quickly made his way to the dilapidated tenement on Orange Street. He bounded up the stairs to the third floor apartment. He caught his breath, took off his hat, and knocked on the apartment door.

Two days earlier, outside a bar on Bayard Street, a well-dressed man wearing a black fedora pulled low over his face had approached Black Dog Bourke, the leader of the Dead Rabbit Gang, one of the two street gangs that ruled Five Points. The stranger handed Bourke an address written in precise handwriting on fine linen stationary. He'd told Bourke that a man would arrive at the address in two days carrying a large sum of money. Before Bourke could ask him any questions, the stranger disappeared into the crowd.

"Come in," said a muffled voice from inside. Frank, obsessed, didn't notice that the voice was different, not the high pitched, singsong voice he'd heard at the first meeting.

He entered the dark apartment and was immediately set upon by three club-wielding men. The first blow stunned him, breaking his nose and left eye socket. He fell to his knees, bewildered. His last thought was of the thousand dollars he'd been promised. A second blow across the back of his head knocked him unconscious. Bourke delivered the third and fatal blow, crushing Frank Robinson's skull.

The Heretic

"The heretic is always better dead.
And mortal eyes cannot distinguish the saint from the heretic."
– George Bernard Shaw

The whirlwind subsided fading like a storm moving away, and Abigail easily willed herself together. She found herself in a small, featureless room dimly lit by a flickering lamp on a rough-hewn table. A worn, leather-bound book rested beside the lamp. Her body felt whole, stronger, familiar but not entirely so, different in ways that she could not explain. Abigail stepped toward the chair set beside the table, thinking it would be calming just to sit after the frightening chaos, an experience she didn't understand and one she hoped would never return.

"You have returned, mademoiselle. I feared we'd lost you like so many others before."

Startled by the voice, Abigail gasped and pivoted to face the sound. There stood an old man with a slight build, a little shorter than her, dressed in a gray robe tied about the waist with a rope. As he came toward her, she saw in the dim light that he was more weather-beaten than old, as though he'd had a life of hard farm labor similar to her father. Abigail stepped back.

"Who are you?" she moved to put the table between them." And where am I?"

"This is almost too good to be true." The old man clasped his hands together and smiled at her. "Do you know how long it has been since I've had an unblemished soul appear? And a *talker* – you move, you know where you are, and you speak to me. Most souls appear briefly, and then dissolve away like smoke in the breeze. I say breeze, but there is no wind of any kind in this forsaken land." He twirled his hand in the air.

The man paused, staring at Abigail, continuing to smile, as if some long lost relative had appeared on his doorstep. He chattered on, "Once in a very long while, a *walker* appears. They don't drift away, they stay whole, but they are lost within themselves. Their eyes don't see, nor do their ears hear. They wander in no particular direction and then they are gone, *c'est fini*. We may never see them again." The old man paused once more, seeming to calm.

Abigail thought the man was exceedingly strange, possibly mad. She had no idea what he was carrying on about, but he appeared harmless enough, and not very sturdy. Abigail believed she might be able to fend him off if need be.

Straining to keep her voice calm, she stood up straight and asked again, "Please, tell me who you are and where is this place? I need to get home. My parents are going to be worried."

He stopped smiling and touched the book on the table with his fingertips. "Well," he said in a measured voice, as though choosing his words carefully, "there is a lot to tell, and then there is a lot not to tell because I do not know myself. I am like Gershom in Exodus, a stranger in a strange land, although this place is neither Egypt nor Israel. That being said, I'm sure I can ease your fears a bit, but what I have to tell you is not a joyful tale." He pulled out a chair.

"This may take some time to explain. Do you mind if we sit?" he asked, tilting his head and waiting for her reply.

Abigail sat and noticed she wore her new white dress with the pink bow; the one Mother had made her for the GAR dance. She thought it quite odd she should be wearing her dress, as she had no memory of putting it on. Mother had taken weeks to make it and wouldn't have let her wear it any place other than the dance.

"Have you abducted me? Have you stolen me from our farm?" she shouted, realizing she had no idea what day it was, or how she'd come to be in this cramped room.

"No, no, no, mademoiselle. I found you. You are lost, and I will do all I can to help you. Please be at rest."

They sat in silence for a moment. His voice was reassuring, and Abigail came to think he meant her no harm. She took in his full appearance. He had a round face with a gray pointy beard, dark, deep-set eyes, and a ring of gray hair surrounding a bald pate. His smile appeared kindly. Abigail seemed to be the object of his fascination. He stared like a man seeing something of immense value, which made her nervous. "Mademoiselle, if you don't mind, can we begin with who you are and where you are from?"

Abigail thought it would be impolite not to respond. "My name is Abigail—Abigail Bidner Johnson. I am nineteen years old, the only daughter of Alfred and Louisa Johnson. We live on our farm in China, Maine."

He shifted in his chair. "Abigail, this is the name of Nabal's wife in the Bible. This isn't a name that is common to me, but it has a pleasant note to it. Do you mind if I call you Abigail?" He continued without waiting for her reply. "There is little formality here, you must call me Jacquis. In another time, I was called Jacques la Perfecti, but my Catherite title, Perfecti, has no meaning here."

Abigail had no idea what a Catherite was, but didn't interrupt his excited chatter.

"You said you are from China? In Maine? I know of China, but not of this Maine of which you speak."

"Maine is north of Boston and south of Canada in the northeast United States." Abigail looked at him, wondering why he didn't know where Maine was. He appeared to have no understanding at all.

"I'm sorry, my child—Abigail—but I haven't ventured more than a few weeks' journey from the town where I was born, Ax-les-Thermes in southern France near the Mediterranean Sea. Is the place you speak of near Germania or Saxonia?"

"No, I don't think so." Abigail knew where France was and thought maybe he was speaking about Germany, but she'd never heard of Saxonia. "The United States of America is on the North American continent across the Atlantic Ocean from France."

"Ah, yes, I had heard tales of lands across the great ocean, but these stories were never believed. Who is king of these lands? Who is your sovereign?" he asked in quite an everyday manner like it would be common knowledge.

"We don't have a king; we have a President, President Ulysses S. Grant. Have you heard of him?" Abigail could not make sense of the questions he was asking her.

"I have not. I am not familiar with the title of president. Is this like an emperor?" He glanced at Abigail and then continued, "It is of no matter. You can tell me of your president and the other nobles of your land at some later time. Please continue with your recent memories, think back to what you last remember and tell me." His voice was steady and reassuring in a fatherly way, engendering her trust. Abigail thought she must trust him, at least for the moment.

Jacquis sat back in his chair waiting for Abigail to continue. "Well, it was late May, springtime. I had been badly chilled when the weather turned on the way home from Mr. Small's store. I took ill, and Mother sent me to bed to rest. I slept the whole afternoon and awoke in the night feeling terrible and covered in sweat."

The old man leaned forward, hanging on her every word.

"I was in bed for a long time drifting in and out of sleep. My throat hurt terribly, and I couldn't eat or drink. The last thing I remember was waking up from a long sleep. I was very tired and couldn't speak or move, although I didn't feel sick anymore. Mother held my hand. Father stood behind her reading his Bible, but I couldn't hear what he said. Then I fell asleep again. That is all I can remember till I woke up in that terrible whirlwind, and then here with you. How I came to be here I do not know."

"Yes, I see, Abigail. Is that all? Nothing else? Nothing you remember from that moment? "asked Jacquis, leaning forward, tilting his head again, appearing intent on her answer.

"No." Abigail wondered why he pressed her on the point. It came to her that she had told this stranger, Jacquis, much more than she probably should have. She felt naïve.

"Again, sir, I ask you. Where am I and how do I get home?" Abigail tried to sound as formal and authoritative as she could. Her tone stopped his sharp gaze, and he looked down collecting his thoughts.

"Ah, yes, where to begin?" Taking a deep breath, he continued, "Let us start with what is easy and then move on to that which is not so easy, *n'est-ce pas*?"

"What I am going to tell you is confounding to the mind. You will think me a lunatic or a liar, perhaps both, but all I'm about to tell you is the truth. My name is Jacquis Autier. I died on April 10th in the year of our Lord 1310. I was burned at the stake for heresy by Satan's true servant, the Dominican inquisitor Geoffrey d'Ablis, sent by the Church of Rome, the synagogue of Satan, to crush all the Perfecti, the priests of the Catherites." Jacquis pounded a clenched fist on the table. Abigail recoiled; her face displayed her shock at his sudden anger and her utter disbelief in what she heard.

"Died? In 1310? Burned at the stake?" Her heart raced, and her eyes darted about the room. The door was bolted and the windows were shuttered. She saw no easy escape. She was trapped, alone in this small, dark room with a madman.

The old man's face contorted as he recounted the events. "Yes, Mademoiselle Abigail, I died. I was imprisoned for four years, starved, tortured for days, and then finally, burned at the stake in front of the demon inquisitor, all for being a Catherite." Jacquis' face contorted in rage. Abigail pushed back from the table distancing herself from his violent outburst.

"The inquisitor demanded I accept the Eucharist as true transfiguration into the body of our lord Jesus Christ. I could never accept such blasphemy. We Catherites don't believe that God would allow himself to be touched by the hand of man."

Jacquis looked up and saw the terror on Abigail's face. Pausing, he breathed deeply, his face returning to a milder expression as he continued. "Oh, my child, I know this is beyond your comprehension. I have said too much too quickly, you must excuse my ranting. Let me stop my discourse and answer your questions so as to ease your spirit." He settled in his chair with a smile and raised eyebrows.

"How do I get home? I just want to get home, please, please. Can you help me?" Abigail pleaded, feeling more lost than ever. She desperately wanted to return to her life as it had been, to the bright, warm days of springtime in Maine, to her family, to preparing for the dance, all of which now seemed more terribly distant as the minutes passed.

Jacquis spoke in a soft, halting voice as though it

pained him to speak. "I am sorry to tell you that you may never leave here — few souls ever do. When they do, I know not where they venture."

"What? Are you imprisoning me, holding me against my will?" Panic rose in her chest. "You said you'd found me. Why can't you help me to get home?"

The room closed in on her. She wanted to flee, but didn't know where to run. Then it dawned on her that Jacquis implied something else, something too terrible to be believed.

"Why do you refer to me as a—a soul? You—you speak like I'm dead too!" The breath left her body, her heart pounded. Abigail rose, knocking over her chair and feeling as if a bolt of lightning had passed through her.

Abigail's mind raced. *I had my whole life ahead of me. Was everything I had ever dreamed of now lost? Was I now condemned to spend eternity in this dreary place with no expectations of a life, of marriage, of children, with no one to love me? This wasn't right. It wasn't fair. What had I done to deserve such punishment? Was God smiting me for some unknown offense? Father was fond of reading from the Old Testament. I'd always thought God was quick to anger, capricious even, always punishing his people. But why me — why me?*

Abigail's mind was frozen, unable to conceive of what this odd little man had told her, what her eyes beheld. She was lost, lost in a wilderness for eternity. Her bones ached with despair. She was truly forsaken.

Jacquis picked up the chair and held it for her. "Please sit. I am not your jailer. You are free to go wherever you wish. My only desire is to help you at this terrible moment."

Abigail slowly sat down, frozen, barely breathing, staring at her hands folded in her lap. Jacquis sat facing her. He leaned forward on the table, folding his hands in front of him. He spoke in a soft voice, "I'm sorry to upset you so. The truth must be told, yet it gives me no joy to do so."

Jacquis extended his hand. "That was your moment—the moment you died. Don't you see? I think you know that I'm right." He searched her face for understanding.

Abigail sat for a short eternity. Her mind frantically tried to make sense of her situation as the enormity of it settled like a crushing weight. She was dead. Deep inside she knew this was true. The experience of the whirlwind was still fresh in her mind. But she felt alive. She was still Abigail, although her body felt different, ethereal in an odd way, like an image of her, somehow not solid as she remembered.

"Can this be true? Am I dead?" Abigail whispered, barely able to utter the words. *What else would explain all this? I must have died from the fever, perhaps from scarlet fever.* Her classmate Josiah Burke died of scarlet fever the previous year. One day he was in school and three days later he was gone.

Jacques met her eyes. "Am I in heaven?" Abigail asked, desperately hoping that all Father's lectures on a heavenly reward had come true.

"No." replied Jacquis, looking around the barren room. "This is assuredly not heaven, and I'm not sure if it's hell either. It is called Gehenna. I cannot tell you exactly where we are. It is not in my theology, to be sure." Jacquis moved his chair closer and took Abigail's hand.

"For reasons unknown to me, unblemished souls appear here every now and then in various states. Many dissolve—poof!" he said with a gesture of his hand. "A few unblemished souls re-form into recognizable people but neither speak nor hear. Fewer still, like you, can speak and hear as a mortal person. Why this happens I do not know. It confounds my understanding."

"What do you mean, unblemished?"

"Most souls belong here. Their souls are not clean; some are black to the core. They walk in from the mist that surrounds the town and take up their residence here. Their deeds have drawn them to this place. They belong here in Gehenna"

He looked at Abigail intently as though trying to divine the reason for her appearance. "Others like you are unblemished. There is no cause for them to be here. They appear out of nowhere as you did."

He studied Abigail as though trying to divine a reason. "Ah well, 'tis another mystery."

He clasped his hands together and prattled on about his early experience. Abigail didn't listen, but she found his voice soothing. She felt numb thinking about all that she'd lost—her family, her friends, her room, and the books she loved so much.

Jacquis fell silent, stood quickly, and then spoke in a loud voice which focused her attention. "Mademoiselle Abigail, that book." Jacquis pointed to the table where there was now a second book. The book itself seemed to frighten him. "Did you bring it? Did you carry it on your person?" he asked.

Curious, Abigail picked it up, *The Tale of Two Cities* by Charles Dickens. It was her favorite book, exactly like her copy from home. Holding it made the memories of her life come rushing back again, stronger than ever. She could almost smell Mother baking bread in the kitchen, hear the sounds of the cows in the pasture, and see Father in the distant field with his plow team. Abigail felt as though she could reach out and touch them.

"What is this doing here?" She asked Jacquis. He stared at Abigail and the book. And in an odd reversal of circumstances, he looked afraid of her. Abigail opened the book and read aloud, *"It was the best of times, it was the worst of times..."*

These were surely the worst of times and Abigail feared the best of times were lost forever.

Ehyeh

"In eternity there is no time, only an instant long enough for a joke." –
Hermann Hesse

In a dark forest clearing, a woman sat on a straw mat contemplating the flame rising from a small stone pyramid. Above her, galaxies coalesced from dust clouds and swirled into existence, stars flickered to life, and planets formed. Life rose and fell across countless worlds. She listened as voices from an untold number of planets sang an unending aria of joy and pain, of hope and despair, of love and hate, of life and death. She watched the great cosmic opera play out the story of creation. The woman moved her hand over the flame which rose to swirl between her fingers, and the cosmos danced on her fingertips.

I am the leopard that moves in the night, patient, waiting, moving unseen in the shadows. I have labored in secret for hundreds of years, guiding, planning for when the living and the spirit worlds align. The Owari board is set. The beads have been placed. The opening moves have been made. The ancient spirit, the Huntress, has arrived and is growing stronger. I have guided the Speaker to the right place and time. He may not have the strength to succeed, but the middle game has begun and must play itself out.

The weight of my hand must not be felt by the Evil One or the game will be lost. I will wait, as I have always waited, patiently, like the leopard, lying invisibly on the high tree branch watching.

The woman removed her hands from the flame and rested. She watched and listened as her children's game began anew. The souls of Arcadia sang songs for the warrior. Galaxies collided.

Lost, Found, and Busted

"Was it really some other person I was so anxious to discover...or was it only my own solitude that I could not abide?" – David Markson

It had been months since Sarah and David visited the Fairfield Antique Mall. The picture of the dead girl still captivated David. Sarah said it was creepy and didn't want it in the house. So for the first day, David kept it in the truck's glove box. On the second day, he secretly moved the dead girl's photograph to a shelf in his cabinet shop.

Her image drew David's attention every morning while he drank his coffee. Other times, he found himself staring at her during the day, transfixed, as though in a daydream. Sometimes without realizing it, he found himself holding the photograph. *Who was she, where had she lived, what happened to her parents?*

David knew the situation was out of hand when one day he thought he saw her in his workshop. He'd been holding the photograph, running his finger along the edge, and zoning out. The hum of the florescent lights faded, and for an instant he saw her standing in the corner. Her image wavered like a mirage. Then Abe barked, and the apparition vanished. The sound of the lights returned. The dark corner was empty. David wondered if Abe's reaction was because he'd seen her also, but the thought was too weird.

After that episode, his interest in her grew stronger. If he wasn't working, she was all he thought about. David dreamed of her some nights, always the same dream; the unknown girl standing alone on a hilltop searching for something. Why did a girl, dead for over a hundred years, hold such a fascination for him? The Twilight Zone music played in his head.

Maybe it wasn't weird, maybe just David being impulsive—again, a recurring theme in his life to date. In fifth grade a soft-spoken lady had given him tests in a room by himself, followed by a conference with his parents. David didn't know what the meeting was about, other than it was about him, which wasn't good. His father had taken off from work, which he never did, looking serious in his tie and coat. His Mother sat erect in her best coat with her purse on her lap. She held husband's hand and looked upset. David heard phrases like, "lack of attention" and "poor impulse control." His sister had always excelled in school. After that meeting, there were no such expectations for David.

The McCaskey kitchen order had kept David working flat out for weeks. The construction required careful attention to detail, fine cuts and precise joints, but sanding and finishing was mindless. His thoughts always drifted back to the girl in the photograph, and he formed a plan to discover her identity.

David had three clues. First, the picture had been taken in the late 1800s when photographing the dead was briefly in vogue, Second, he guessed that it had most likely been taken within some proximity to Fairfield where we'd found it. The third and most useful clue, written in faded ink on the back side, was the name of the photographer: Clark Photographic Studio, 27 Main Street, Biddeford, Maine. A Google search showed no Clark Studio in Biddeford, and 27 Main Street was now a bank. No help there. He'd found the Biddeford Historical Society on the town home page, listing its hours as ten till two on Thursdays, weather permitting. David decided to play the long shot.

On Thursday, David had a break while waiting for the final structural framing in the McCaskeys' house, and more importantly, Sarah was away for the day at an ancient history symposium. With luck, David could go to Biddeford and back without her knowing, and without having to explain himself. David thought he was acting foolish, and Sarah would surely think he was childish. He told himself he would make this one effort, for one day only, and then sell the picture on eBay as he'd originally promised Sarah.

The next morning, as soon as Sarah left, David loaded Abe and Louie in the car and drove to Biddeford. He parked in a shady spot, and left the car windows slightly open for the boys. David entered the library just as it opened at ten.

"Hello," he said. The girl behind the main desk looked up. She was not the librarian David expected—no high collar blouse, long skirt, or sensible shoes. Rather, she was young with bushy hair, a T-shirt with a shaggy scarf around her neck, jeans, and striking multicolored floral tattoos on her left arm.

"Can I help you find something?" She seemed eager as only people new in a job can be.

"I'm here about the Historical Society Archives. They open at ten?"

"That's right, they do—well some days they do, depends if Mrs. Cunningham comes in or not. And—I think you're in luck," she said looking past him. "Here she comes now."

Through the door came a trim, gray-haired woman in a striped dress, white handbag, and a large cloth shopping bag over her shoulder.

"Etta, you've got a customer. This man is interested in the archives."

She extended her hand. "Hello, I'm Mrs. Cunningham. I'm in charge of the Historical Society's Archives. What can I help you with young man? Mr.—?" She spoke formally, distinctly, so as to correct the young girl's familiarity.

"Austin, David Austin. I'm researching a Civil War

era photograph that came from Biddeford." He made a point of saying "Civil War" so that his interest would not seem so ghoulish.

"Well yes — yes I may be able to help you with that. Please, follow me downstairs and I'll open the vault." She gestured to the stairs. She seemed pleased to have a visitor, someone she thought she could help. The vault was merely a basement room with a gray metal door. Mrs. Cunningham switched on the lights, revealing a long room with file cabinets and shelves along one wall and display cabinets along the other. There was an old metal desk missing its drawers. The top was a precise arrangement of paper, pens, and a small, wooden index card box.

"I'm the retired head librarian. Katie upstairs is my replacement." Mrs. Cunningham's tone was dismissive. David guessed there was more to the story, but he didn't want to divert her attention. "When I retired, they put me down here with all the other antiques." She took off her coat and sat at her desk, motioning David to take the chair beside it.

"So you say you're researching a photograph. Do you have it with you?"

"I do. It came from Clark Photographic Studio in Biddeford. I think it was taken in the mid-1800s."

"Yes, yes. I think we have something on Clark's. Give me one second." She got up and went to a filing cabinet, returning with a folder labeled "Clark Photographic."

"Here is a picture of the Clark's Studio." The picture showed an old storefront with the name in large letters on a sign above the door. A man, presumably Mr. Clark, stood beside a horse and wagon. The wagon was a large box, big enough to stand up in. Painted on the side was, "Clark Photographic Mobile Van."

Mrs. Cunningham peered over her glasses and read from a typed page on yellowed paper. "The write-up says that Mr. Clark was formerly a school teacher who enlisted in the 12th Maine Regiment at the start of the Civil War. When he returned, he opened a photographic studio. He had an itinerant photographic route covering the state from York Harbor to Augusta. His mobile darkroom was a copy of that used by Mathew Brady in the Civil War. Humph, imagine that, the same as Mathew Brady..." Her voice trailed off, and she looked at David for a sign of recognition. David made a mental note to Google Mathew Brady when he got home.

"I'm sure there is a lot more to the story, but that's all we have. These write-ups were not done by real archivists — no one professionally trained — just some willing amateurs, you know," she remarked sounding embarrassed by the quality of the archives she presided over.

"May I see the photograph please?" she asked.

David handed it her. "It's a little macabre."

She studied the picture for a few seconds and grimaced.

"My goodness." Mrs. Cunningham peered at David incredulously over the top of her glasses. "Is that poor young girl dead?"

"Well yes, I think so." David explained the history of post-mortem photography to her.

"I've heard of these photographs, though I've never chanced to see one." She handed the photograph back pinched between two fingers as though it were something unpleasant. "I think we've established that Mr. Clark took the picture sometime after the Civil War and no later than 1889 when he died. What else would you like to know?"

"I hoped to identify the family, to find out where they lived and possibly find their graves."

"I don't believe I can be of any help to you there. Your only hope is to go see Swanson at the Kennebec Historical Society in Augusta. He's the best historian in all of Southern Maine. This photo could have been taken anyplace from York Harbor to Augusta, that covers a lot of territory. If anyone can set you straight, he can."

"Here's the address," she added, handing David a note card with the name and address written in precise cursive handwriting. "The society is open till two. I think you can make it if you leave now."

"Thanks. You've been most helpful," David stood up moving towards the door.

"If you don't mind my asking, what are you going to do if you find her grave?"

'Nothing I suppose. I read a poem once that said a person is never dead if someone says their name. Maybe that will be enough."

Mrs. Cunningham stared at her visitor and then smiled slightly. David couldn't tell if she approved or was simply glad the oddball with the creepy photograph was leaving.

"Tell Mr. Swanson I sent you to him. He'll remember me." She held up a finger to add emphasis.

The drive to Augusta went quickly, guided by the female voice of the GPS. David arrived a little after one at the Kennebec Historical Society on Winthrop Street, a wide street that sloped easily up hill, lined with Victorian and Federalist era homes, most having seen better days. The house, a late Victorian, was quiet when he entered. All the rooms on the first floor were empty, except for some paint cans and tarps in the corner. The oak floors gleamed, and the rooms smelled of fresh paint.

"Hello? Anyone here?" David shouted.

"Upstairs," a distant voice replied.

In a small upstairs room, jammed with boxes and papers in no apparent order, David found a tall, thin, elderly man. His bald mottled pate was circled with short white hair. He had "old man" ears that seemed too big for his face, and a sharp nose. His eyes looked keen and piercing, like he didn't miss a thing. He turned away from an old computer screen, the kind David had thrown out in high school.

"Sorry about the mess; we're renovating the downstairs. What can I do for you?"

"Mrs. Cunningham in Biddeford sent me. Are you Mr. Swanson?"

"Yes I am, just call me Bert. How is that old bird? Etta is the last of the old school librarians. They don't make them like her anymore. I used to see her quite regularly when she was the head librarian, before they fired her."

"Oh, she said she retired."

"You could call it that. The town fathers in their wisdom realized they could get rid of her and replace her with someone half her age and at half her salary. Anyway, you didn't come here for a civics lesson."

"Yes, well, I have this old photograph I bought at the Fairfield Antique Mall, and I'm trying to track down the family in the picture." He handed the elderly man the photo.

"Where's my magnifying glass.' He searched the clutter on his desk, and finding it, he studied the photo.

"Woo-hoo. You found one of the dead ones, didn't ya?" He looked at David with the smile of a five-year-old boy. "Let me show you my collection." He rose stiffly, hanging on to the desk like he'd been sitting too long, and shuffled to one of the many file cabinets, returning with an expandable folder. He laid out fifteen photographs, all dead people: people in coffins, two sad pictures of mothers holding dead babies, and one blurry photo of a dead girl sitting up with a penciled note on the bottom, *dead nine days.*" Burt sat down again at his desk and surveyed his photos.

"People have brought me these over the years. They didn't want them but didn't feel right throwing them in the trash, so they found their way to me. Collecting them has become a bit of a hobby. I'm hoping to write an article about them for our journal, though I'm not sure the editors are interested in such a morbid topic. Let me see yours again." He studied it once more with his Sherlock-Holmes-sized magnifying glass.

"Yup, yup, here you go." Bert positioned the magnifying glass so David could see. "See this book the man is holding? It's a Bible, and it's got a double overlapping star on the binding. That's a Quaker Bible," he said, clearly pleased with himself. "The only sizable number of Quakers around here came from either Vassalboro or China, so most likely this family was from down there. That isn't too far afield from Fairfield where you found your picture, so that kind'a fits, don't it?"

"That's great. It narrows the search to a couple of towns." David hadn't really thought he would find out anything about the girl, but now he just might. He felt a twinge of excitement.

"Yup, yup, it does," said Bert. "Now, all the records from Vassalboro were moved to China in the 1930s. So if you go to China, Carol at the town hall might help you find the death certificate for the girl." Bert tapped his index finger on the desk to proclaim his correct solving of the mystery.

"I got another tidbit that will help you narrow your search. Clark was pretty well known in his day. He had a regular circuit he traveled every spring and fall. He started doing the circuit in 1869 and stopped in 1875. By then he had enough business at his studio that he didn't need to ride the circuit any more. So your young lady there probably died sometime in that range, either in the spring or fall, assuming this picture was taken during one of those circuit trips."

David stood excited by the prospect of a fresh trail to follow. "This has been very helpful. I didn't think I'd ever find out who she was, but now with your help, I think I might have a chance. How far is China from here? And Carol? Do you have a last name?"

"It's about thirty minutes out Route 202. Carol Hoffman is who you're looking for. She knows everyone who's ever lived there for a hundred years, and if she doesn't know, she knows someone who does. She'll be there till four unless she decides to go home early, so you'd better get a move on."

"Thanks, this has been great." David took the picture and dashed down the stairs two at a time.

Thirty minutes later, he turned off 202 onto Weeks Mill Road, which ran beside a river filled with spring runoff crashing over the rocks flowing back toward Augusta and the Kennebec. The road was old and bumpy, populated with dilapidated mobile homes, each with old rusting cars and other unwanted possessions strewn about the front yards—typical rural Maine. David found the town hall on Lake View Drive which, in stark contrast, was lined with expensive summer homes facing China Lake, a long, thin body of water stretching the length of the town. Pontoon boats cruised lazily in the afternoon sun.

The town hall was a single-story prefab building— what the locals called a double-wide, two mobile sections bolted together. There were no cars parked in the lot, and he hoped Carol had not gone home early, but the door was unlocked and the lights on.

David entered and stood at the counter. "Hello?

Anyone home?"

"Yes, be right there, just making a cup of tea." From around the corner came an old lady with a cane in one hand and a New England Patriots' mug in the other. She moved slowly, slightly stooped with a heavily wrinkled face, wispy white hair, and a light blue sweater over a striped dress.

"What can I do for you, young man?" David could see she was trying to place his face, to distinguish local from outsider.

"Bert over at the Kennebec Historical Society sent me to see you."

"Oh, how is Bert?" She brightened immediately, changing from unsure to friendly. "He came to the ladies club meeting last year and gave a very nice talk about shipping on the Kennebec River. Nice man."

"He seems quite well and he sends you his best." A little schmoozing couldn't hurt.

"Oh, yes, Bert and I go way back. So you must be here to look up some names, I expect? We get the occasional out-of-town visitor researching family genealogies."

"Yes, I am, sort of." David went through his long explanation of the photograph, his trip to Biddeford, the details that Bert had added, and ended with showing her the photograph punctuated with a forced smile.

"Oh, that is sad isn't it? The poor mother, she looks so distraught. And the father, he looks like a tough old turnip." She let out a short sigh. "Well, you better follow me to the back room. I can't lift those old books by myself."

David followed her to a windowless room lined with gray metal shelves which held old ledger books. Handwritten labels listing the town and date were taped to the shelves. The room smelled of musty old paper. She bent over, examined the bindings, and then pointed at two books.

"Let's start with these." She pointed with her cane. "Put them on the table for me."

The first book was for Vassalboro, the town adjacent to China where the Friends Meeting House was.

"Vassalboro was not very big, so we can easily check all the deaths between 1869 and 1875, looking for a young woman in her late teens or early twenties." Carol carefully turned the pages, running her finger down each line, peering through the bottom of her bifocals, and stopping on each name. David held himself back from taking the book and looking for himself. She had her process, and David wasn't going to change it. He settled in his chair and allowed her to proceed.

"No help there, no young women died in Vassalboro during that period. Lots of older people and a number of young children but no one in their teens or twenties. Let's check China. Put these back and bring me the census books from China, it's those four on the other shelf."

David brought the four books she asked for, and her process began anew with her ancient finger moving slowly down each page. For forty minutes, Carol examined every death in the first three books. David was ready to burst, desperate to take the books and search for himself, having all the patience of someone raised on Google.

"This might be her. It's the right age and all. We'll have to check the other books to make sure there are no other young women. Yes, this could be her.

David stood, bent over her shoulder, and looked at where her arthritic finger pointed. "Abigail Johnson, died May 21, 1872, scarlet fever, age nineteen, next of kin was Alfred Johnson, father, Louisa Johnson, mother." The name of the cemetery was blank.

The name Abigail rang like a bell. "Yes, I think we

found her." He'd been thinking of her for months, and now he'd found out who she was. His heart thumped. He was electrified. Oddly though, leaning her name hadn't curbed his fixation, it had strengthened it. His chest tightened. David swallowed and looked back at the yellowed page.

"It is certainly the right age, and scarlet fever makes sense given how good she looks in the photograph. Scarlet fever can kill quickly without any disfigurement. Why is the name of the cemetery blank?" he asked.

"That means that the person was most likely buried in a family plot. Many farms had a family graveyard on the property somewhere. It was quite common back then."

"Can we look up Alfred Johnson to see where his farm was?"

Just then a woman's husky voice shouted from the front office. "Hello, Ma, you there?"

"Back here, Joselyn, doing some genealogy."

A rotund woman in her fifties walked in. She wore sweatpants and a flowered print blouse that did little to hide her bulk, and toting a large Gucci handbag which, given that she was dressed in Walmart's best, was certainly a knockoff. She held a lit cigarette and looked slightly out of breath as though moving her bulk strained her. She was a poster child for bad habits.

"Hey, ready to go?"

"This is my daughter, Joselyn. She's come to drive me home." She turned her focus to Joselyn. "Joselyn, dear, give me another five minutes. I got one more thing to look up for this gentleman."

"Okay, Ma, but I'm running late. Jimmy don't like it when his supper isn't ready." She continued to stand in the doorway so it was clear she was ready to go. David was apparently invisible to Joselyn.

"Those red books over there are the tax records. Bring me the book that covers 1872."

After another few minutes, Carol's finger found Alfred Johnson's tax payment, $107 covering house, barn, property, and stock on Neck Road.

"Neck Road? Is that all? No house number? "David asked.

"No, I'm afraid not. House numbers are a fairly modern contrivance. I don't think we had those in China till the 1920s, and only then because the state legislature told us to."

"I saw Neck Road on the map, it's five or six miles long. It could take a while to find anything there."

Carol stood up from the table. "Would you mind putting these ledgers back? I have to get my coat."

David was pissed that Joselyn had shown up and was in such a hurry to get "Ma" home. Carol was a wealth of information. He might have learned more without her daughter's interruption. Nonetheless, He'd accomplished much more in one day than he'd thought possible. He'd found her name — Abigail Johnson. David's excitement grew as he readied to leave.

"Young man," said Carol, standing by the front door with her coat on and keys in hand. "You might go speak with Ethel Nadeau. I took over for her when she retired. Her family has lived here since the 1700s. She knows everybody and their brother in China. She lives at the Lake Front Nursing Home. It's a few miles further on this road."

"Is it too late to try and see her today?"

"No, you'll be fine. The people there are happy when anyone comes to see one of their residents. Just explain to Ethel what you want, give her a minute to find her thoughts, and she most likely can tell you what you'd like to know about the Johnson family."

"Thank you very much, Mrs. Hoffman, you've been more than helpful." Joselyn had her mother by the arm now, hustling her out the door and into an old red Chevy Impala.

Joselyn sped away with Carol to fix Jimmy's dinner, and David let the dogs out to do their business. He had been remarkably lucky today, impossibly lucky — too easy, too many coincidences, all connected by the thinnest of threads, like a row of dominoes arranged to fall in unison. A chill passed through him. Was he one of the dominos?

Simply finding out her name had not satisfied him. His desire to learn about Abigail was still there, stronger than when he'd begun his search today. He'd expected that once he'd learned her name, his compulsion would've waned, that he could happily sell the picture on eBay and be done with it. Not so, the closer he got to her — to the girl named Abigail — the greater the attraction. David felt like a meteor being pulled ever faster to Earth by gravity. He hustled the dogs into the back seat and jumped in the front, eager to find this Nadeau woman and learn what else she might tell him about Abigail.

David' phone rang. Sarah was calling from their home number.

"Shit.   *Busted."*

Graveside

"They shall grow not old, as we that are left grow old:
Age shall not weary them, nor the years condemn.
At the going down of the sun and in the morning,
We will remember them." – Laurence Binyon

"Hi, hon," David said, answering the phone.

"Hey where are you? Out walking the boys? I got home early, the symposium was kind of a bust, off topic from what I expected."

"Well, yes, I am out with the boys actually."

"Can you come right home? I got Indian takeout."

"It may be a while—I'm up in China." There was a pause on the other end as he waited for the interrogation to begin.

"China? That's up by Augusta. What are you doing there?"

"Sarah, I found her, the girl in the photograph. Her name is Abigail Johnson. She died in 1872 of scarlet fever." His voice betrayed his excitement. He'd not mentioned the photograph for weeks, and had no idea how Sarah would react.

"Really?" A scolding pause followed. "I thought you got rid of that creepy photograph. You haven't spoken about it for months." Sarah's exasperation carried through the phone.

"It was on a shelf in my workshop. I'd forgotten about it, what with the McCaskey project and all. I found it this morning when I was cleaning up. So I thought I'd take a day off and see what I could find out." David was trying to make light of the situation, but the unspoken truth was that he was embarrassed and hadn't wanted her to know.

"Kind of a spur of the moment thing, huh?" Sarah wasn't buying it. David's trip to Maine in search of the identity of a girl in a photograph was the last thing she would ever do, and considered it immature on his part, although she never said so explicitly.

"Yeah, you know me, Mr. Impulsive."

"Okay — so — when are you coming home?"

"I have one more stop to make to see a Mrs. Nadeau who lives in a nursing home just down the road. She might know something about the family. I'm going to stop and see her, and then I'll head home."

"Alright, I'll leave the outside light on. Try to keep the dogs quiet when you come in. I'm sure I'll be asleep by then. Good luck with Mrs. What's-Her-Name."

"Bye, dear. The boys and I will be quiet when we come in." When Sarah took this businesslike tone with him, he knew he was in the shit house. It would take several nights of cooking supper to work his way out of this hole.

David walked into the nursing home at little past five, doubting whether the visit would be worthwhile. Carol was as old as Methuselah, and now he was going to visit her predecessor.

"I'm here to see Mrs. Nadeau." The young girl behind the desk looked up from her teenage vampire book, and without saying a word, she escorted David to Mrs. Nadeau's room. She walked in without knocking.

"Ethel. Wake up, honey. You have a visitor," the aide shouted. Ethel was a diminutive woman dwarfed by the large chair she rested in. She had white, wispy hair, thin to the point of balding. She wore a loose housedress which hung on her meager frame. A crocheted afghan covered her lap. She stirred from her nap, and the aide left the room with no further introduction.

"Yes? Hello, have we met before?" She struggled to focus on his face.

David moved closer. "No, we have not. My name is David Austin. Carol Hoffman at the town office sent me to see you."

"Carol, you say?" Ethel spoke softly, appearing to orient herself.

"Yes, Carol Hoffman at the town hall. She said you used to be the town clerk."

"Oh, yes. Carol, she took over when I retired. What did you say your name was again?"

"David Austin. I'm doing some family research, and Carol said you would be able to tell me about a family named Johnson. They lived in China in the late 1800s, had a farm on Neck Road." David spoke in a loud voice as clearly as he could.

"Did you say Johnson? Why do you want to know about them? Are you related?" Ethel came alive, filled with renewed energy from some unknown source. She straightened herself in her chair and leaned forward, eyes alert with all remnants of sleep banished.

"No, I'm not." David explained the entire story of the photograph and how he'd happened to be there speaking with her. She listened intently as he spoke.

"I was sure someone would come asking after the Johnsons. I'd almost given up hope, but here you are."

"You can't mean you were expecting me?"

"No, I didn't expect you specifically, but someone—it just happens to be you. Did you bring the photograph with you?"

"Yes, I have it right here." David handed it to her. She

put on a pair of thick glasses. Holding the photograph in one hand, she stroked it lightly with her finger and smiled slightly as though remembering a distant, warm memory.

"This photograph came from my house." Ethel searched his face to make sure David understood both what she said, and more importantly, what she implied. David's being in her room was no coincidence. Some external force had brought them together.

"Are you sure? This photograph?" David got the words out as his heart thumped wildly.

"Oh yes—it had a frame before, but yes—this very one. There couldn't be more than one of these, you know." She tilted her head with an impish grin. "You see, a year ago, I had what you might call—an episode, a little heart flutter—and I fainted. After that, my son—he lives out of state—decided in his wisdom that I shouldn't live alone, and he moved me in here. Well, before I knew it, he'd sold my house and all my belongings, had to do with Medicaid, he said. I asked my son about this picture, but he said it was long gone. I guess it just needed a little journey of its own to find its way back to me."

"How did you come to have the picture?" David asked.

"When I was a girl, my grandmother went to an estate sale at the Johnsons' farm after old man Johnson passed away. There were no living relatives, so the state sold off everything. Grandmother knew the family—Abigail, Louisa, and Alfred. She told me that Abigail died of scarlet fever at nineteen. Louisa was never the same. She grieved for five years and then died. Mr. Johnson, Alfred, became a recluse, living alone well into his nineties."

"Mr. Austin, David—do you mind if I call you David? Go to my closet there and bring me the box on the top shelf."

David brought her a tattered cardboard box and placed it on her lap. She opened it and handed a large book to him. It was old, worn at the corners, and printed on the cover was, "Holy Bible, the Society of Friends." In the center were two overlapping stars.

"This is Mr. Johnson's Bible. Grandmother bought it at the estate auction along with the photograph. This is the Bible that Alfred is holding in the picture."

David's breath left his body. He was electrified to have something tangible from the photograph. It took him a few seconds to start breathing again. The Johnson family were no longer anonymous, ethereal people in an antique photograph. They were real. If Alfred had walked into the room and asked for his Bible at that moment, David wouldn't have been surprised. This tiny, frail woman, lost in her oversize chair, entranced him. David waited for her next revelation.

"My grandmother had a special way about her. She knew things, things other people didn't, though she never made a fuss over it, just kept it to herself. When men were killed in the war, she knew before the families received their letters. She had a real sense of who was good and who was not, like she could see into them." Ethel looked at David with her milky eyes and continued.

"After Abigail died, Grandmother went to see Mrs. Johnson, to pay her condolences. The visit disturbed her. She wouldn't talk about it other than to say that Abigail was in trouble. We never knew what she meant. I mean, the poor girl was dead after all. If the Lord had put His hand on her, how much trouble could she be in?"

"Was your grandmother a psychic?"

"You mean palm reading, tarot cards, and the like? No, nothing like that. Where was I? Oh yes, Grandmother came home with the Bible and the photograph from the estate sale. She said that someone would come for them. The family thought she meant in a few days. She put them in a closet and, well, we all forgot about them till Grandmother entered her decline. She asked my mother to take the Bible and photograph home and keep them, again saying someone was coming for them. Grandmother died a few days later. My mother passed them to me, and I've had them all these years waiting for someone—for you I suppose—to come for them."

Ethel looked at the photograph again. "Don't you find there is something compelling about this photograph? I mean it's very sad, poor Abigail there. The photographer happened by the day after she died. Mrs. Johnson wanted a picture of Abigail before she was buried. I've always been attracted to it in some way I can't explain. I used to take it out of the closet every now and then to look at it. Peculiar, don't you think?"

"Peculiar - maybe. But I know what you mean. I've been looking at it every day for months. It's what drove me to find you."

"Yes, indeed. Abigail has brought you home to China to visit me."

Ethel focused on David again. He sensed Abigail's presence. They both did.

"Yes she has…" he whispered. Some minutes passed as they took in the moment.

"Open the Bible, there is a letter inside that was never mailed. It's a strange letter." Ethel wagged her finger at the Bible.

The letter inside the front cover was written in a precise, fluid hand, the paper yellowed with age.

My Dearest Sarah,

The Lord has called my dear Abigail home. I've lost the

reason for my life. My days ahead are dark and joyless. When the kitchen door opens, I expect to see her standing there. I think of her walking in the fields just over the hill, out of sight but still present. I hear her voice on the wind. I know in my heart that Abigail still lives.

I pray that Abigail is with Him in His kingdom but I am not certain she is, and the pain of such a thought is more than I can bear. I grieve for her daily and pray for the day when I can join her. I know if I call to her, she will answer and show me the way safely to my reward.

Alfred is lost within his Bible and neglects the farm. He reads Leviticus daily. He recites aloud the passages about the Canaanite children offered as burnt sacrifices in Gehenna to Baal. I fear the farm will fall to ruin.

As I write this letter, I see an owl through a window. I see it there daily. Each time I sit by the window, it waits for me. I fear it. Owls are harbingers of evil deeds. I feel I must destroy it to prevent the unseen evil from coming to pass.

I hope this letter finds you and finds you well. If you have a care, remember me and pray for me. My time is short. I hear the footsteps of the Ammonites coming close. We shall rejoice together in the Babylon Woods when Abigail is triumphant once again.

"Who was Sarah? David asked looking up at Ethel.

"Mother didn't know, the letter was never signed, and there was no envelope. We found it in the Bible after Grandmother died. The letter carries on in such an odd way. The family assumed that Louisa wrote it and died before she could mail it. Grandmother said Louisa had a troubled death; that she died before the Lord's time. I think she meant that Louisa took her own life."

Ethel had sunk back into her chair. The stress of speaking had exhausted what little energy remained in her frail body.

"Mrs. Nadeau, you look tired. I ought to be going. Do you want me to put the Bible back in your closet?

"Oh no." She held up her hand. "Take it with you. It's yours. Our family has waited over a hundred years for you to come. I have a comfort in knowing that it has found you. It's a relief really, a duty I feared I would not live to complete."

If Ethel felt relief from giving David the Bible, he felt its weight transfer to him. It bound him closer to Abigail, and his compulsion, verging on mild desperation, grew stronger. David would not leave China today till he'd found Abigail's grave.

"One last thing, Mrs. Nadeau, do you know where the Johnson farm was? I was hoping to find the family graveyard."

"Well, it's on Neck Road. You drive down there till you see a large brick house with four chimneys set on a hill, then a short way past you'll see two granite posts on the right. That's the road to where the farm was. It's all gone now, torn down, mostly grown over with trees, but I think you can find the family plot if you walk in a ways. Alfred, Louisa, and Abigail are all there. Thank you for coming. I hope you don't wait so long to come see me again." Her impish smile had returned.

David shook Ethel's thin, skeletal hand, thanked her for everything, and told her he would return sometime, a small lie. He didn't think they would meet again. Ethel had sunk in her chair with her eyes closed, appearing smaller than when he'd entered, but now more at rest.

Davis went back to the car where Abe and Louie waited patiently. He sat with the Johnson family Bible on his lap. The situation was more than he'd bargained for, and way too strange. What had started as a curiosity had taken hold of his life. He was torn between bolting for home and forgetting the whole business, and continuing his quest to find Abigail's grave. The momentary illusion of Abigail standing in his workshop seemed real, not just fatigue from a long day. Now, with Ethel and her family keeping the Johnson family Bible in trust for over a hundred years, tracking down the girl in the photograph was no longer a casual adventure. David had a habit of rushing headlong into situations without thinking, of regretting his actions, and here he was again.

David looked at the photograph once more. Ethel was right. There was something about her that drove him. He had to push on and find her grave, but there was barely an hour of daylight left. He had to hurry.

Neck Road joined Lake View Drive at the north end of town. Minutes later, David drove past the majestic Georgian style brick house with chimneys at each corner and found the granite posts that marked the road to where the Johnson farm had once been, and where he expected to find Abigail's grave.

The road was obscured as Ethel had said, entirely grown over with trees. Stone walls marked the edges where the road had been. As David walked into the dark woods, he heard mourning doves cooing their sad song, crows calling in the distance. *Sent over by central casting to complete the mood*, he thought and chuckled.

After he'd walked for a few minutes, the stone walls ended. The foundations of the house and barn must be close. Abe and Louie were happy following their noses through the trees, but were no help in finding the gravesite. David walked in a series of ever larger concentric circles until he found the house foundation and the family gravesite several yards to the side.

The plot was marked with four granite posts which had iron angles that had previously held wooden railings, now long since gone. There were three grave stones, Abigail's in the center, flanked by Louisa's and Alfred's. Small trees had grown up on the plot, and the headstones were askew, tilting badly. In several more generations, the forest would reclaim the site entirely. Abigail's headstone inscription read,

Abigail Bidner Johnson

Beloved Daughter

Died May 21, 1872, Age 19

"We shall meet again sweet daughter,

In a brighter time than this,

Where the anguish of this world of ours,

Is lost in deathless bliss."

David stood in front of the graves for several minutes until a tremor ran through him. Today was May 21st. *Jesus. What strange twist had brought me to Abigail's grave on the anniversary of her death?* He breathed deeply to subdue his desire to bolt for the car.

The forest had become dark as twilight set in. The woods were still. The crows and mourning doves he'd heard earlier were silent. Abe and Louie had stopped their roaming, and uncharacteristically lay at his feet. David thought about Abigail's death at a young age, Ethel's inference that Mrs. Johnson had killed herself, and Mr. Johnson's joyless submission to religion. This forgotten gravesite was a desolate, mournful place, a monument to three unfulfilled lives, and the hurt and sorrow that had passed here.

David took out the photograph to look upon Abigail's face once more; even in death she had a quiet beauty. He found himself touching, caressing the photograph as Ethel had. Why had her image fascinated him for months? Why had he driven frantically across the state following a gossamer thread of clues? And why had the Nadeau women waited for more than a century for him to come and claim the Johnson family Bible along with strange letter? Who was this young woman?

The woods had grown still darker, noticeably cooler, and unusually still, like the world had stopped spinning on its axis. David looked up from the photograph, and a woman wearing a white flowing dress stepped out of the shadows and walked toward him, her face veiled by the fading light. David heard the sound of her feet in the dry leaves, and the hem of her dress moved in the sudden rush of a twilight breeze. He was startled that anyone else would have joined him on his lonely vigil. She stopped, facing David across the graves. A sudden chill shot through him, the air rushed from his lungs, and the hairs on his arms stood up. David staggered backwards as he recognized who stood across from him. His heart pounded sounding the alarm with each beat.

David struggled to speak, the name refusing to form on his tongue, finally managing, "Abigail?"

"Good evening sir. I need your help." Abigail smiled and extended her hand.

Nicholas Eymerich

"Innocence eroded into nightmare.
All because of very bad touch.
Love, corrupted." – Ellen Hopkins

Spring 1377

Nicholas Eymerich rode on horseback behind Pope Gregory the Eleventh's papal carriage. He was seventh in the procession as his title, Chaplain of the Pope, dictated. The entourage had set off from Avignon a week earlier. It would be six more weeks till they reached Rome.

"My Lord Inquisitor, how long will we travel this day? This saddle has rubbed me raw and the pain is something horrible," said Monsignor Verde, Eymerich's aide. He was a small man with a pointy nose and a weak chin. His family had purchased his position with the hope that he would become the Bishop of Catalonia or even a cardinal. The monsignor's lack of political talents and predilection for altar boys had stymied his family's ambitions.

"José, you have done nothing but complain since we departed Avignon," barked Eymerich. "I suggest you silence yourself, and offer up your suffering as a penitence for your sins." The monsignor whimpered and turned away.

Eymerich had his own pain to endure. He had left the subjects of his inquisitions behind, and it would be some time before he could resume the sacred work in which he took such pleasure. He had returned the last five young witches to the Lord. Such beautiful girls. He could still see their adoring faces, and hear them as they begged his forgiveness. He had packed the pilliwinks, the witches bridle, and several irons which could be quickly heated in a brazier. If fortune smiled on him, a witch or a heretic might be discovered on the journey.

His thoughts went back to Sister Constantine at the convent in Girona where he'd been raised as an orphan. Her instruction in the ways of the godly had been brutal and unyielding. When he had turned twelve and was showing signs of manhood, Sister Constantine and two other nuns had taken him to the convent cellars. They tied him to a wall and stripped him. Then they'd removed their wimples and scapulars, and after dropping their robes, the three women danced naked in front of the young Nicholas and sang to the Angel Aamon.

They began to touch each other, and Nicholas experienced sin, an erection. At each sign of an erection, the women lashed him. This process was repeated for weeks until Nicholas could sin no more at the sight of a naked woman. The good sisters had purged his demons.

Nicholas had learned more from the good sisters than they'd intended. He found that he enjoyed instructing sinners through pain. The sin of fornication had been vanquished by the pleasure of pain. When he was fourteen he caught another orphan abusing himself in his bed. He had taken the boy to the stables at night, bound and gagged and whipped him. The experience had been exhilarating. It excited him still as he remembered the boy's muffled screams and the sight of the flesh peeling from the young sinner's back. Nicholas's body swelled with pleasure as he remembered. He had taken a lock of the boy's hair before dragging his body to the river. The sisters had taught him well. He was free of the sin of fornication, and he experienced God's own reward whenever he drove a demon from a sinner.

He prayed he would find a sinner, a heretic, or a

blasphemer during the journey. Tension rose within him from a burning desire to do the Lord's will. He needed the release.

"My Lord Inquisitor, the Jew you interrogated, Astruc Depieva, did he confess knowledge of the other members of the satanic brotherhood?" asked Monsignor Verde.

"No, the demon within him was too strong. I instructed him for days that he might free himself. I used every instrument at my disposal. His feet were blocked until his bones broke and he could no longer stand. I applied the pilliwinks to his fingers till his bones broke through the skin, to no avail. I had him imprisoned until we could return from Rome and resume our instructions, but King Peter of Aragon sent his guards and released him."

"How will we uncover the other members of this cult?"

"This secret brotherhood has been working for centuries to thwart the will of God. The Angel Aamon came to me one night and revealed this to me. The brotherhood moves in the shadows. They whisper in the ears of the righteous, turning their devotions to corruption. We must redouble our efforts, my brother."

"Yes, My Lord Inquisitor," replied the monsignor, and then muttered, "Once we get to Rome and are freed from these beasts."

Nicholas Eymerich prayed silently to the Angel Aamon as he rode. Aamon had appeared in his chambers late at night five years ago accompanied by a beautiful woman dressed as a queen. Her touch had filled him with grace and power. Aamon had instructed him to search out the members of the brotherhood and destroy them. There would be much to do when he reached Rome.

The Castaway

"My soul is bereft of peace; I have forgotten what happiness is."
– Lamentations 3:17

Abigail died in one world and was reborn in another, one she didn't understand or know friend from foe. She was a newborn alone in the jungle, naive, afraid, and defenseless. Gehenna was mysterious. The way her body felt, the look and touch of everything, the appearance of her Dickens novel, and Jacquis himself were all mysteries. Abigail needed to learn the ways of this land quickly if she was not to be its victim.

Jacquis took her to another room with the same gray walls, but with a window and door that opened onto a walled courtyard. A wood-framed cot, laced with thick ropes and topped with a hard mattress without sheets or blankets, stood against the wall.

"This room is for you, Mademoiselle Abigail. Please use it as you will. You should rest for a while. I'm sure this has been a trying experience. I need to go to the castle and arrange your audience at court. I will come for you later, and we shall speak more."

She stepped in front of Jacquis, blocking him as he moved toward the door. "Castle? You didn't mention a castle or court before." Jacquis casual statement about arranging an audience was another revelation filling Abigail with a myriad of questions.

"Ah, yes, the court." Jacquis smiled and tapped the side of his head. "Please excuse me, mademoiselle. The unexpected making, eh, we have not discussed making as yet. Let's just say the appearance of your book took me quite by surprise; I meant to tell you."

He backed up and took a more authoritative tone. "Gehenna is ruled by Queen Lilith and her court. It is her commandment that all new arrivals, especially fully conscious souls, be presented at court as soon as they arrive. Queen Lilith is all-powerful, and I have no wish to displease her."

Jacquis cocked his head to one side and then returned to his more familiar demeanor. "Your face tells me this concerns you. I would not worry, mademoiselle, a mere formality. You simply bow when she enters, tell her your name, answer any questions the queen might put to you, and then we will return. *C'est fini.*" Jacquis wiped his hands together so as to indicate the end. "I will return shortly, so please wait for me here."

Abigail wanted to know more about the queen, but Jacquis was already at the courtyard door, intent on his errand. "Thank you, Jacquis. Before you go can you tell me what time it is? When is sundown?" Abigail had lost track of time since her arrival.

"Ah, yes, time. Time is a mercurial thing here. There's no sun, no moon, or stars either. There is nothing in the heavens, just the constant gray that one sees. Step into the courtyard with me."

She followed Jacquis into the courtyard. The two-story house was topped with a red tile roof with a row of windows on the second story, each covered with a pair of crude wooden shutters. A large tree dominated the center, and there was a small wooden door with a rounded top at the far end. The walls of the courtyard were the same featureless gray as the house and interior rooms.

'You see." He pointed to the monotone sky, if indeed it was a sky. "There is nothing, just gray, nothing to mark the passage of time, so we think very little of it." Jacquis took a step backwards toward the door in the wall as he continued to speak.

Abigail stared at the featureless gray above. She missed the billowy clouds of August in Maine.

"Time varies by person. I may experience it faster sometimes or slower than others. And your perception will most likely be different from mine. Don't try to understand; it is a thing best ignored. Soon you will adjust and think nothing of it."

Abigail could think of nothing else.

Jacquis took another step backwards toward the door in the wall and forced a smile. His voice rose in tone and volume. "Also, you will find souls that come from all different ages and appear in no particular order. As I said, I came from the 14th century, and you, mademoiselle, are from the 19th. I have met souls from the 22nd century. As I told you, many things here are confounding."

"Wait. I have more questions."

Jacquis held up his hand and briskly walked to the small door. "Please, you should rest. We'll talk more when I return." He disappeared through the door.

"Thank you," she said to the silent courtyard. Her head was spinning. *How could time not be constant?* This was too much to think about, and she resigned to do as Jacquis suggested, and rest.

She sat on the cot in the barren room with her arms wrapped around her legs. Yesterday her world consisted of their small farm with once-a-year trips to Augusta. Even then, she'd stayed in her grandparents' house, never venturing out into the city. She'd lived a cloistered existence.

Abigail was friendless except for this strange monk, Jacquis, in whom she had little trust. The child in her wanted to succumb to despair, to cry, to wrap herself in self-pity and hope some adult would sweep away this nightmare.

This thought angered her. *I'm Abigail, an adult woman of nineteen years, perfectly capable of taking care of myself.* Caving in to despair was as much a threat as the whirlwind that had brought her here. She feared her emotions would consume her if she didn't resist. She could fall prey to the mercy of all who lived here, no longer the mistress of her fate. This she would not abide. She had conquered the whirlwind, and she vowed to conquer her fears. Lamenting could wait till later. Now she must learn how to make her way in this land, this Gehenna.

Like Jacquis, she too was a stranger in a strange land, but not for long.

Abigail left the room and stood under the large tree. When she'd first met Jacquis, she thought everything looked and felt ethereal. Now, standing in the courtyard, Abigail noticed all the colors were muted. The tree leaves were green, but a dull faded green like a washed out watercolor. Light seemed to come from every direction. The only thing that wasn't dulled was her dress. In contrast to her surroundings, the pink ribbon was vivid, and the white dress itself almost shimmered, one of many things she didn't understand.

The house was silent with no sign of any presence, but she heard voices through the courtyard door. Abigail tried the latch. It gave easily with a light touch. She bent down, stepped through, and found herself on a street filled with people. They wore all manner of clothing, some in simple leggings and tunics made from plain cloth, others in elaborate outfits of embroidered silk, a seemingly endless variety of styles and cultures.

Abigail had dreamed about visiting different peoples. Now here they were, parading in front of her. She laughed at herself. Her wish had come true. She merely had to die to realize it.

The cobblestone street was lined with houses and shops as varied as the people. Some buildings were Tudor style; others were brick Victorians similar to buildings in Augusta. One building was made of metal and glass in a manner she hadn't seen before. The street curved uphill such that Abigail could not see to the end. In the distance at the top of the hill, the walls and central keep of a large dark gray castle dwarfed the town. This must be where Jacquis had gone to arrange her audience, the thought of which filled her with dread. She laughed at herself again. She was dead and had lost everything she loved. How bad could it be to meet a queen?

Abigail stood for some time taking in the parade of people and costumes. It seemed like a carnival staged for her amusement.

A woman emerged from a small thatched cottage across the street. She watched Abigail for a few moments then strode over. "Hello dearie, I 'av'nt seen you before. Are you staying with the friar?"

"Do you mean Jacquis? Why, yes I am. I'm new here."

"Oh, I can see that by looking at your face. You look as lost as a newborn lamb." She laughed, shaking her hefty bosom which was barely contained by her laced-up bodice. She had a full skirt, a small apron about her broad waist, and a shock of auburn hair held in place by a scarf. "Why don't you step in for a cup of hot cider? We can talk a bit if you like."

"I think that would be very nice. Thank you ma'am." The invitation was a welcome moment of normalcy.

"Now, dearie, you can call me Philberta if that's alright with you. And what might your name be, if I may ask?"

"Abigail Johnson."

"Well, come with me, Abigail Johnson." Philberta smiled and wrapped a big soft arm around me. Abigail felt comforted for the first time since her illness and the horrible experience of the whirlwind. She smiled back at Philberta, thankful to be taken in by her.

They walked through Philberta's sparsely furnished cottage to a small English style garden. A stone walkway lined with flower beds led to a table and benches at the far end. There were a few plants set about but none in bloom, and all displayed the same muted colors as the tree in Jacquis' courtyard. Abigail sat on a bench, and Philberta excused herself and returned with a tray bearing two earthenware mugs.

"You've 'ad cider before haven't you, Abigail?"

"Yes, I have."

"Oh, that's good, so you'll be able to taste it."

"Sorry?"

"If you didn't taste or smell something when you were living you can't taste or smell it here. Funny it is, but that's how it works here. If you don't mind me asking, what year was it when you died?"

Abigail caught her breath slightly. The relief she enjoyed from having cider in Philberta's garden had taken her off guard and being asked about her death shocked her. "It was May of 1872."

"Oh. For me'self was 1551. Good Queen Bess was on the throne then. I was hung right outside the Tower, I was. Had a good crowd too, I did. I gave them a little curtsey before they put the noose around me neck. Had a big cheer for that, I can tell you." Philberta spoke casually as she sipped her cider with a slurping sound.

Abigail's stomach knotted up, and a chill passed through her. Her moment of normalcy had turned dark and scary. All the adults in her life had been quiet, godly people. Polite conversations ranged from the weather to crops. Crimes were unheard of in China. Father had spoken about the spawn of Satan that inhabited the big cities to the south. What crime had Philberta committed to warrant a public hanging? Abigail wondered if she in danger, but she was dead, after all; what could she do to me? Abigail swallowed hard, doing her best to regain her composure.

"Mine was a bad fever. I was gone in a couple of days." They discussed their respective deaths as one would the weather, and the casual nature of this conversation, more than anything, brought home the reality of Abigail's situation. This was no dream. She wasn't going to wake in her bed with only the memory of a nightmare. She was dead and having hot cider with a woman who had been hanged outside the Tower of London three hundred years before Abigail was born.

"Now dearie, 'ows your cider? Are you sleepy? Just a bit, perhaps?"

"Fine, thank you." Philberta appeared pleased to have a guest. "No, I'm not a bit sleepy. I'm so unnerved by all this, I don't know when I might sleep again."

"Pity." Philberta scowled briefly but then forced a smile.

"Can you tell me about the castle on the hill? I've never seen one before. Who lives there?" Abigail wanted to hear Philberta's complete description.

"Well you are new aren't you? The Friar 'asn't taken you to meet our Queen Lilith yet, 'as he? I'm sure he's planning to presently. Queen Lilith insists on meeting all new arrivals, soon as they come."

"I've never met a queen."

"Queen Lilith is our *maker*. We wouldn't have

anything without her."

"I don't know what you mean, *maker*?"

"You see that cider you're drinking, where do you think it came from? We don't have orchards full of apples, you know. This house, my furniture, that seat you're sitting on, it's there because I made it. What I mean is, I simply pictured it in my mind and it was there."

Philberta looked at Abigail chuckling again. "Close your mouth, dearie, it ain't becomin'." Then she continued, "When you was alive, unless someone carved a stone or cut down a tree, you couldn't make anything. Here, if you 'as the talent, all's you need to do is picture something in your mind and there it is. Nothing here is quite real. All sorts of things just come and go. If I don't think about something for a bit, then it disappears when I'm not lookin'. I've had a devil of a time keeping me cottage furnished, I can tell you." Philberta chuckled, rocking back and forth.

"Some people can't make anything at all; others make big houses, palaces really. Now don't ask me why it works that way. It just does. We all make do as best we can."

"I made a book," She said thinking about her earlier incident. "Do you think I have the ability to make other things?" This was an exciting prospect. "How do you do it? I was thinking of my books when one appeared."

"Yes, kind of—its 'ard to say really. No one taught me, it kind'a came to me bit by bit. Now I don't give it no mind. I can make enough for me. I don't seem to be able to make anything much more than this small cottage and a few belongings. Some poor souls can't make anything, and they usually become servants for those that can, those that are good at making. You'll notice that the closer you get to Queen Lilith's castle, the bigger the houses get. The stronger makers live closer, the weaker ones farther away.

"Do you make your food, or are there farms here?"

"Well, you know, that's funny too. You won't ever get hungry here, and you don't need to eat, nor sleep for that matter. Most people do eat, like you and I is 'avin' cider now, but it's all make believe. It makes things feel more normal, like when we was living."

Philberta spoke for a while about her life in London, a life filled with hunger, filth, and disease and ruled by a drunken husband. Abigail couldn't help but think she was better off dead. At least here she wasn't hungry, or sick, or beaten by a brute.

"So, Philberta, does anyone ever leave here? Is there anything beyond this town?"

"No one leaves this place that I've heard tell about. We are here forever, as far as I know. And beyond the town is only mist. A few folk have set off exploring, but they've never come back."

"Is that it? No one ever dies?" Abigail caught herself. "I mean, goes to heaven or some other place? Is everybody here forever and ever?"

Philberta nodded, leaned in, and gave a sympathetic smile. "Forever and ever."

Forever and ever sounded like such an awfully long time.

Philberta spoke in a whisper. "Now some people go and live in the castle, and we don't usually see the likes of them again. It's a bit of a mystery really. Us commoners don't talk about such things. What goes on in the castle is the queen's business, not ours."

Abigail finished her cider in silence. The taste was a welcome diversion.

"You know Philberta, I should go find Jacquis. I

didn't tell him I was going out, and I don't want him to worry. You've been very kind to spend so much time with me." Abigail stood with her hands clasped in front.

"I'm sorry you have to go, dearie." Then, with one swift movement, Philberta pulled a long knife from her skirts and lunged at Abigail. The blade barely missed her throat as she jumped backwards.

"Come on, dearie, this won't hurt at bit. I've dispatched many young girls such as yourself. I put opium in your cider like I did when I was living, but it doesn't seem to work here. It's a shame really. It used to be so much easier." She had a wide-eyed grin, and her tongue stuck out of the corner of her mouth.

She swung the blade back and forth as she stepped toward Abigail who screamed and grabbed a chair, holding it up to keep her attacker at bay. Even so, with her greater size, she pressed Abigail to the garden wall.

"Stop, stop! Why are you doing this?" Abigail screamed.

"I'm saving you, dearie, like I saved all my girls. There are so many wicked people. They might hurt you, but you'll be safe when I put you with my other girls." She slashed, just missing Abigail's throat. Philberta second thrust sliced deeply into Abigail's arm. She cried out. A searing pain shot through her like a lightning bolt.

Along with the pain came the anger she'd felt when she was trapped in the tempest. From deep within her, she sensed the rage boiling to the surface like a building explosion. As Philberta slashed at her again, Abigail dropped the chair and grabbed Philberta shoulders with both hands. A bolt of energy shot through Abigail's fingertips. Philberta's head snapped back, and she collapsed in an unconscious heap.

Abigail stood over her, trembling. Philberta lay with her arms and legs splayed, unmoving. Her skin was pale, grayish. Her clothing had also lost its color, appearing drab and washed out. Abigail didn't know what had happened and worried about leaving Philberta where she lay, not knowing if she was alive or dead. But, of course she was dead. Everyone here was dead.

Abigail looked around wildly. Was there anyone else here? Had anyone seen their struggle? Did Philberta have accomplices? Abigail ran from the cottage and flew across the street, stopping by the relative safety of the garden door, ready to jump inside in case Philberta awoke and wanted to finish "saving" her. The masses of moving people provided some relief.

Abigail collected herself, still shaken from the ferocious attack. She looked at her arm, expecting to see a deep wound and flowing blood. There was nothing, no wound, no blood, not even a mark on her dress. She didn't understand. She'd felt her knife cut into her. Now there was no mark whatsoever. The lessons of Gehenna were coming fast. Even the most casual of circumstances might quickly become threatening. Clearly there was much more she needed to learn.

Abigail watched the people as before, but now with new eyes as though seeing reality for the first time. Some passersby had large festering sores on their bodies. Others appeared not quite human, with horns emerging from their heads or back, and walked with a plodding gate. A man dressed in dark clothing with blood stains passed by, pulling two naked children by a rope tied to their necks. She wanted to rush out and save the children from the horrible man, but thought better of it. She'd been easily taken in by Philberta and decided to wait until she understood Gehenna and its dangers better.

Abigail backed up, pressing against the wall, hoping to hide within it. Her head twisted rapidly from side to side lest some other kindly citizen approach her with devious intent. She was alone in a crowd, no friend in sight, and no one she could trust. Abigail felt infinitesimally small.

School Begins

"Learning is not child's play; we cannot learn without pain."
– Aristotle

Abigail pressed her back against the courtyard wall while watching the parade of the glamorous and the gruesome in the street. A man wearing the blue uniform of the Grand Army of the Republic, and with a rifle slung over his shoulder, studied her from across the street. She wondered if he was one of the walkers that Jacquis had mentioned. He didn't move or change his expression, but his static gaze was fixed on her.

She stepped toward him, trying to make out his face. Her heart leaped. It was Jacob Farrington. She ran to him, pushing her way through the crowd. Abigail threw her arms around him and buried her face in his chest. It had been years since he'd marched off to war with the other volunteers.

"Jacob, Jacob! You don't know how happy I am to see you. I never thought I'd see you again."

She pulled back to take him in, still clutching his arms. He was motionless, his arms by his side, staring straight ahead with no expression on his face, not a hint of the joy Abigail felt.

"Jacob, what's wrong? Don't you recognize me? It's me, Abigail, Abigail from China." Jacob remained frozen like a statue with only his lips moving.

"Beware the queen. Do not reveal your powers to her." Jacob intoned in a warm, soft voice she remembered from years ago, but now flat, deadpan, without a hint of emotion.

"Jacob, what's become of you?" She looked into his eyes, but they remained empty as though his soul had been drained.

"My name is Ranger. I was sent to warn you. The heretic is on his way to take you to the castle. Beware, beware the queen." Jacob turned and disappeared into the flowing crowd. A passerby jostled her as she stood dumbfounded. She'd savored such relief at seeing a familiar face, a savior, someone she could trust that would keep her safe in this mysterious and frightening place.

Abigail wanted to run after him, to hold him, to never let him go. *What did he mean by "powers?" Why should she fear the queen? Should she not trust Jacquis?*

"Ah, here you are, mademoiselle," said a voice behind her. It was Jacquis. Abigail gathered her composure and turned to face him.

"I was looking for you. I feared you'd become lost."

"No, I was watching all the commotion in the street. I had no idea there were so many people here."

"Yes, there are a great many souls here, are there not?" He glanced at the stream of people. "I came to take you to your audience if you are agreeable?"

"If you say so, but I am a little anxious about meeting the queen." She was terrified, and certain Jacquis would take her whether she was agreeable or not. The castle sounded like someplace people like her—a commoner if ever there was one—should avoid, a feeling reinforced by Jacob's warning. Despite a thin veneer of normalcy, nothing in Gehenna was as it appeared.

Jacquis had taken her under his wing. She'd thought of him in a fatherly way, but now she wondered if he had unspoken motives. He treated this meeting with the queen much too casually, it seemed. Then there was Philberta, who had appeared friendly but then attacked her, and how had she knocked her out with a touch of her hand? Abigail needed to be on her guard and decided not to mention Jacob or his warning to Jacquis.

"Not to worry, these meetings are quite routine. This way." Jacquis set off at a brisk pace toward the castle.

Jacquis spoke very little as they walked, appearing intent on their destination. Abigail purposely stopped to look in shop windows several times to slow him down. She wanted time to think, to prepare herself. Whenever he noticed her dawdling, he would walk back and urge her on.

"Is there a specific time we are due for my audience?" Abigail remembered as soon as she said it that time was a little-used concept here. "Sorry, I forgot. No one worries about time here."

"No, there is no specific time. However, it would be better if we were there when the queen is ready to see us. It is not good to keep one's sovereign waiting."

"What can you tell me about her? Is she young or old?"

"The queen is young and quite beautiful, always dressed in the finest of fabrics. She loves children and is always surrounded by them. She is kind and provides for all her people. When you meet her I'm sure you will like her." Jacquis offered no further embellishments regarding the queen.

As they progressed uphill, the buildings lining the street became larger and more ornate, some with elaborate facades as Philberta had said. They passed a theater and several large restaurants filled with raucous people. The street now had proper sidewalks and street lights, which Abigail thought odd as Jacquis said it never got dark. Houses approaching the crest of the hill were mansions surrounded by high walls.

The castle was a massive, dark structure dominating the top of the hill. Its walls were at least fifty feet tall and surrounded by a foul, black moat. A drawbridge shouldered by two round, towering gatehouses provided the only access. The central keep behind the walls was an immense round building with multiple stories resembling a colossal wedding cake topped with a golden dome. The drawbridge was guarded by soldiers wearing black uniforms with red sashes, each holding a pike. Jacquis continued across without breaking his stride or offering a word of explanation. Abigail felt dwarfed by the castle's immense proportions, and a sense of foreboding swept through her as they entered.

Once inside the ward, they walked directly to the keep's elaborate arched portico, passing tall black iron doors cast with scenes of people making sacrifices in temples, and further down, scenes of people in pits of fire. At the top of the arch was a figure of a man resting his head on his hand, deep in contemplation.

Not very auspicious, she thought.

They stepped into a cavernous central hall with a vaulted ceiling supported by stone columns. Looming over them in the center was a massive black owl statue as tall as the family barn in Maine. Before it was a golden throne set on a wide stepped dais. Broad staircases on either side led to the first of six galleries. Five iron candelabras with twelve tiers of candles hung from the ceiling, lighting the expanse. More uniformed soldiers stood guard every few paces around the hall like statues, completely immobile, with deep set eyes like black holes.

Jacquis stopped at the entrance and looked around, rapidly scanning the vast empty chamber.

"I thought someone would meet us here," he said

softly to himself.

Abigail looked up. People dressed in regal costumes were silently filling the galleries.

"Ah." He turned to Abigail and spoke in hushed voice. "You are in luck, Mademoiselle Abigail, the queen is coming. I thought you would have your audience later, but she and the entire court are here now. Jacquis walked her to the center of the dais a few yards from the throne. "Please stand here and wait for the queen to address you." Jacquis bowed slightly and moved to stand in the shadow of one of the columns. Abigail stood diminutively in the center of the immense hall.

The guards moved to block the entrance. The people in the galleries above her murmured, some pointed toward her, some laughed, while others looked on menacingly. She was the center of attention and didn't like it. She'd imagined meeting the queen in some small room with a few people, not hundreds in this massive, gloomy cavern. It was all she could do not to flee to the relative security of the town, but her escaped was blocked by the guards. If there was a time to be brave this was it. She stood as straight as she could, and took a deep breath.

I am Abigail Johnson, a woman of uncommon strength. She repeated her mother's words to herself, needing to believe they were true. Her mother had told Abigail that her strong will was a curse for a woman, but now Abigail was glad for it. At this moment, she needed all the energy she could muster.

The crowd in the galleries grew quiet. From the darkness at the top of the stairs, a slender figure approached, a tall, beautiful woman dressed in a flowing, silky white dress with a golden sash about her waist. Her long black hair was pulled into an elaborate braid. On her head rested a golden crown resembling flames. She glided down the stairs with silent fluid movements. A slight smile grew on her face as she drew closer. Her eyes were inky black in stark contrast to her alabaster complexion. Children followed her, three boys and three girls, all barefoot and dressed only in knee length gray tunics made of coarse fabric. They moved without expression as though in a trance. A seventh boy, a head taller than the others and dressed in a simple black shirt and pants, walked beside the queen. She positioned herself on the dais with the boy close behind her. His eyes locked on hers.

"I am Queen Lilith. Welcome. I am the mistress of this realm and your sovereign." Her voice was deep and resonant, almost masculine, in stark contrast to her feminine appearance. Her words resounded throughout the vast chamber.

The queen's body began to glow, lighting the area around her. Her presence was more than visible. Abigail sensed her radiating, pulsing against her like a gusting wind, although the hall was completely still. It was beyond her comprehension that a person's body could shine from within or that an unseen force would pulsate against her. The queen's eyes were wide, focused on Abigail intently as though searching for her deepest secrets, dissecting her soul. Abigail felt her cold thoughts penetrating her like icy tendrils.

The queen was revealing all Abigail's innermost thoughts and secrets to the crowd. She would not allow this violation, and by resisting her, grew stronger. Standing straight, she clenched her fists and pushed back against the pulsating force. Strength rose within her. The crowd above whispered rapidly. Abigail wanted to look to see what had excited them, but she dared not take her eyes from the queen.

The queen's emanations ceased though her eyes

remained fixed on Abigail. In order to break her stare, Abigail curtsied as best she could. "My name is Abigail. I'm pleased to make your acquaintance, Your Majesty."

"Yes, dear child, the Perfecti has told us of you." The queen glanced at Jacquis in the shadows. "I am pleased you have come to visit us." Lilith stepped off the dais and moved to Abigail's right side, accompanied by the boy who walked beside her, clutching her flowing skirt and never taking his eyes from Abigail. Lilith made no sound as she walked, but Abigail heard the patter of the boy's bare feet on the stone floor.

"Where are you from, child? What ill fortune has brought you to my realm?"

"I am from Maine, in North America, where I lived on a small farm with my parents. I died of a fever." The queen had circled behind her and was now facing the statue. Abigail turned slowly to remain facing her and the boy.

"We have others from this place you speak of, this North America. I have visited places there myself on occasion. What year was it when you came to us?"

Visited? How could she have visited anyplace? Philberta said there was no way to leave. Abigail had a multitude of questions but no time to form them; right now she had to control herself. The queen's presence was almost overpowering, and it took all Abigail's concentration to maintain her composure.

"It was the year 1872, in the month of May, springtime."

"Ah, so long ago. We've had many arrivals since then. I think you will not bring us any news of the living. Pity."

Lilith continued to circle her slowly, unnerving Abigail like she was being stalked by a predator.

"You have the light, the light of a great maker. Do

you see how your dress, your very body glows?" The queen gestured to Abigail with her hand and surveyed the faces in the galleries. A murmur erupted from the crowd above as the people pointed at the diminutive girl on the floor.

Abigail's body was illuminated, shining as though lit from within. She's been so intent on watching the queen she hadn't noticed. The more she'd summoned her energy, the brighter she glowed. *Was this what Jacob meant by "powers?"*

"I sense you are an ancient soul. Your will is strong. Yes, very strong. You have great potential. The Perfecti has done us a great service." The queen smiled at Jacquis, and he acknowledged her with a low bow.

"Perhaps, in time, when you have fully realized your talents, you can join the other members of my court." Lilith raised her hand in a sweeping gesture pointing at the people in the galleries above.

"Would you like that?" Lilith had completely circled her and stood on the dais in front of the menacing statue. The boy resumed his place behind the stately queen.

"I would be most honored, Your Majesty," She lied. She had no desire to remain there another minute — the queen and her court terrified her — but she was torn by the desire to understand this power that emanated from her, and how she might control it. This was clearly the key to her new existence.

"We should appoint a teacher worthy of your talents. Someone experienced in the ways of the court." Her voice trailed off as she looked to the figures lining the galleries above.

"Who should it be? Ah yes, Lord Eymerich would be a fine selection. He is a learned man with a fondness for teaching young women, and he knows the ways of our realm well." Lilith pointed to a figure on the third gallery.

"Lord Eymerich, come here and take charge of our ward."

"Yes, my Queen," came a distant reply.

After a few moments, a man, dressed in a floor-length crimson robe with a matching cloth hat that draped down his back, descended the stairs. He was an imposing man, more than a head taller than Abigail with broad shoulders. His round, boyish face seemed too small for his body. He appeared middle aged. He knelt on one knee in front of the queen waiting for her to speak.

"Lord Eymerich, I desire you to take charge of training our ward, Abigail. I see much strength in her."

Lord Eymerich rose and nodded slightly in Abigail's direction.

"Yes, Your Majesty, I will begin at once."

"Yes, yes, very good. We shall be pleased to hear of your progress."

With that, the queen left the dais and ascended the stairs with the same gliding movements as before, her small, sad entourage trailing behind. The people in the galleries erupted in conversation after the queen departed. Jacquis stepped out of the shadows and approached.

"I think that went very well, mademoiselle. You impressed the queen."

Abigail's emanations had ceased. She nodded, too overwhelmed to speak and with no understanding of what had transpired. She needed to get away from the castle and find time to think. Maybe Jacob could explain what had happened, if she could find him. He had known her meeting with the queen would be more than the simple introduction Jacquis had suggested. Abigail feared the mysterious glow had revealed too much.

"Jacquis, you may leave now." Lord Eymerich spoke

without looking at Jacquis as though dismissing a servant.

Jacquis bowed. "My Lord." Then turning to her, he added, "Mademoiselle Abigail, I hope to see you again when your training is complete." Jacquis turned and briskly left the hall. While he seemed glad to be done with the queen and her court, Abigail was sorry to see him go. She didn't know if he was friend or foe, but he was a familiar face.

Lord Eymerich displayed none of the fatherly concern of Jacquis; just the opposite, he appeared devoid of compassion. He looked Abigail up and down in a way that made her self-conscious, small, and vulnerable. She thought again about escaping through the main entrance, but no escape appeared feasible. It would not be wise to anger this man or the queen unnecessarily. She was trapped.

"I'm honored that the queen has put me in charge of your training. It has been a long time since I've given instruction. I shall enjoy being the teacher again." Lord Eymerich's smile didn't ease Abigail's fears.

"The queen has declared you her ward, and as such you are to remain here with us. I will provide you with rooms in the castle. Follow me." He walked briskly to a low door in the rear of the hall, his boots echoing in the now silent hall. A small Negro page stood erect by the open door as they hurried past.

The passageways and stairs they traversed were low and dark, lit only by narrow slits in the wall. After a few minutes, Abigail was lost beyond all hope of ever finding her way out. The stone floors were uneven. She tripped in the gloom several times as she struggled to keep pace with her teacher's stride. He came to a wooden door with an iron latch and entered, with Abigail several paces behind. The room was cramped and barren with gray stone walls. A small balcony looked out toward the town many stories below.

Lord Eymerich stopped in the center of the room. Abigail ran to catch up and came to a halt beside him feeling flustered. With one continuous movement, he turned to face her and, without warning, struck Abigail a fierce blow with the back of his hand, which sent her flying through the air, crashing against the wall, and landing on the floor in a disheveled heap.

"Your training has begun," his voice resonated in the small room.

He paused to examine his handiwork, chuckled, and left the room with his boots again resounding on the stone floor. The suddenness and ferocity of his blow left her cowering on the cold floor, bewildered and in tears. The iron latch locked from the outside with a metallic clank.

Rebirth

"Death is many things, including the beginning of something new."
– Dawn Akemi

Abigail lay on the floor of her cell sobbing. The pain from Lord Eymerich's blow radiated across her face. The pain from Philberta's knife had vanished with the wound, but the pain from Eymerich's hand remained as though part of him lingered, inflicting more misery and fueling her despair.

She'd imagined dying was the worst fate that could befall her, to be ripped away from all that was familiar and the people she loved. This was worse. Abigail was a prisoner in the castle, waiting for a horrible man to return and strike her again. She'd never been hit in her life. Now she'd been dealt a blow that hurled her across the room. And while Abigail realized that she couldn't be killed twice, she could be hurt. Pain was just as real here, and possibly without end. Abigail saw no way of escaping or any way of returning home. Desolation filled the room.

Her crying subsided, and Abigail sat up resting against the wall. She stared at the gray stone wall across the room. In her despair, a new understanding came upon her. Lord Eymerich had taught her a vital lesson, not the one he'd intended, but a lesson Abigail could not have learned any other way. Abigail Johnson from China, Maine, was dead. Her body along with all her hopes and desires were buried in a distant place.

She was now Abigail of Gehenna, reborn in this land of tortured souls with no idea of what god or demon had damned her to this existence. She'd been cast away and washed up on some evil land. For her entire life, she'd been imprisoned because of her sex, and her father's rigid adherence to religion. In this new and hostile land, Abigail was determined not be subjugated again.

Pulling herself from the floor, she walked to the balcony surveying the town laid out beneath her. It was not as big as she might have imagined. In a short, steady walk you could easily reach the outskirts where the gray sky merged with the distant mist. Abigail wondered if anything lay beyond this castle and the surrounding town.

This was now her town, but the word "home" didn't fit. Home implied comfort, and there was no comfort to be found in Gehenna. It was merely the place where she existed. The queen had spoken about the powers Abigail possessed saying she had great strength and the ability to be a great maker. Abigail's body had glowed when the queen challenged her with her emanations, an effect confirmed by the reaction of the assembled court and by Jacquis' fearful expression. She needed to understand the extent of her powers, to master them quickly before Lord Eymerich returned for another lesson. It was time to practice.

Philberta spoke of making by envisioning an object in her mind. Abigail had accidentally made a book by thinking of her small collection in Maine. She had a vivid memory of her mother's rocking chair and side table from the parlor. She'd always enjoyed sitting on the chair Sundays when Father read from the Bible. Abigail closed her eyes and envisioned the chair and side table. Nothing. She tried harder to visualize the rocking chair and table. Nothing, again. This was harder than the casual effort that Philberta had spoken of.

Abigail wondered what to try next, when she heard a sound that filled her with dread, the sound of heavy boots on the stone floor outside her room. The latch moved and the Lord Eymerich entered.

Abigail moved to keep her distance as he strode to the

center of the room and removed his gloves. "Ah, yes. I see you've recovered from our last lesson and you are ready to continue, I trust?"

A small wooden table and stool materialized beside him. He sat down, placing his gloves on the table. Abigail suspected the demonstration was meant to impress her. It did.

"Where shall we begin?" he asked with the smug satisfaction of a man in total control.

"Tell me, should I expect all my lessons to be like the last?" Abigail said with her hands on her hips.

Lord Eymerich laughed loudly. "I simply wanted to have your focus. I find it makes the teaching go that much better when I have my student's devoted attention."

He stood and began pacing, his head swiveling to keep his gaze fixed on her. "Let me introduce myself, I think you should know the illustrious personage who is your teacher. I am Nicholas Eymerich, the Inquisitor General, formerly of the Crown of Aragon where I died in 1399. I am the author of the *Directorium Inquistorum*, my opus describing witches and how to entrap them. I understand my book was used by later inquisitors for centuries after my death. Perhaps you've heard of it?"

"No, I've not." Abigail said flatly.

"Ah yes, that was well before your time, I suspect. I am, or was, a member of the Dominican Order. My vocation was to search out heretics, blasphemers, and witches. I was really quite proficient. I enjoyed my service to the Lord and His Holiness, the Pope." He paused and stood erect, as though striking a pose for having his portrait painted.

He resumed his pacing. "My powers of persuasion were formidable, and creative. For example, take blasphemers; I would have their tongues nailed to a log before sending them out to walk the streets. See how clever that was? They were unable to blaspheme anymore, and they served as an example to others. Yes, very clever, don't you agree?

Abigail remained silent trying not to react to the horror of what he seemed so proud of.

"I've uncovered many witches. The young ones were especially resistant to my methods, but in the end, none could resist. They all confessed and begged for my mercy. Sometimes it would take days of careful persuasion to unlock their demons before they learned absolute obedience to me as God's messenger. Doing the Lord's work can be so fulfilling, don't you think? You know, I think those women all came to love me. They all offered themselves to me freely, willingly. They pleaded for my attentions. They all were grateful to have me as their confessor and for their final purification by fire before they went to the Lord's judgment.

He walked toward her. "You remind me of those lost souls I helped return to the Lord."

Abigail backed up as he approached, until he pressed her flat against the wall, looming over her, his massive body covering hers. He stroked the side of Abigail's face with his finger. His touch was like ice, and his breath foul. It disgusted her.

"Yes, you remind me very much of those young witches. I think you need to learn obedience as well."

He placed his hands on her hips and ran his finger up her body till he cupped her breasts and squeezed. Abigail gasped, thrown completely off guard. She'd never even kissed a boy, and now this horrible man groped her, caused pain and humiliation. Panic filled her throat.

Abigail would not be violated by this man. Blinding anger filled her, a flash of energy erupted within her, and with one mighty push, she sent Lord Eymerich staggering backwards crashing into the opposite wall. His face flashed with surprise quickly followed by anger.

"You keep your hands off me," Abigail screamed, her body glowing momentarily as it had with the queen.

Lord Eymerich quickly recovered his composure, returning to his superior, condescending demeanor.

"Yes, the queen was right about you. You are strong, stronger than I suspected. But you must learn obedience to your superiors and, most importantly, to the queen." He slapped his gloves on his hand in cadence with his words.

He returned to sit on the stool, and continued. His voice grew cold.

"You remember the tempest that brought you here? The queen has the ability to send you back, to push you so far into the chaos that you will never emerge. It is worse than death, trapped for eternity in the dark maelstrom between the living and the spirit realms. A fate Dante himself could not have imagined. You keep that thought in your pretty head as you contemplate the meaning of obedience."

"I understand, and I also know that the queen sent you here to teach me to be a maker. I think you better get on with it before I report to the queen your lack of attention to your duties." Abigail was not going to be intimidated by this sadistic monster, despite his imposing size and formidable powers. It took all her will to steady her voice.

Lord Eymerich's face grew fierce but then relaxed. Abigail imagined him considering the queen's reaction. So even he feared the queen she realized

"Yes, of course you are right my pretty, let's get on with it." Lord Eymerich stood. "Making is about having absolute belief that something is there. Wishing it was there, or halfheartedly believing something exists will not work. The table and stool I made when I entered, for instance, I had no doubt they would be there when I needed them. I barely thought about it at all. These were items that were convenient for me, so there they came to be, nothing more."

He took his gloves off the table and stepped to the side. "I can as easily remove the things I have made." As he said this, the table and stool dissolved into a mist. He used his abilities effortlessly without as much as a deep breath. "It is easiest if you start with an object that is most familiar to you, something that you vividly remember. Can you think of something?"

"Yes, when you came in I was thinking about a chair and side table that belonged to her mother. I remember it very clearly."

"Good. Now turn and face the wall." He pointed at the far wall.

Abigail was not about to turn her back on him after her first lesson. "No. I don't trust you. I'm not turning my back on you. Stand over there while I try." He smiled, bowed slightly, and moved to the far end of the room.

She kept her eyes open. This time Abigail assumed the chair and table were there, that they had always been there. She walked to where she expected the chair to be. Then, as she approached the center of the room, forming like wisps of smoke coming together, her mother's mahogany veneer chair with a red velvet seat, and its matching table materialized.

Abigail sat in the chair and began rocking. The rockers made noise on the uneven stone floor. The chair was absolutely real right down to the scratches on the left arm she'd made when she'd knocked into it as a child. Abigail was excited and rather pleased with herself. She'd performed her first conscious making. Abigail of Gehenna was learning.

Next, she turned to the wall expecting to see Mother's framed sampler, "Bless this Home." There it hung on the stone wall in the dark wooden frame with carved leaves at each corner. Abigail marveled at her making. The possibilities were exciting. She thought about creating a cottage like Philberta's and wondered if her abilities would allow her to create a larger house like those closer to the castle.

As Abigail reveled in her new found abilities, a sliver of hope returned — hope of not being at everyone's mercy, hope of mastering this new world. Her new existence presented possibilities that her previous life had not. She was on a mysterious adventure filled with very real dangers and unknown opportunities.

"You have done well, an adept student" said Lord Eymerich, though his face looked more concerned than pleased. "Most new arrivals don't learn this quickly," he muttered with a sidelong glance.

Abigail stood realizing that she'd dropped her guard again. A sudden weakness came over her. The making had drained her. Abigail suspected that developing her powers would come slowly. She was a newborn in this land and needed to gain vigor as she tested her new muscles.

"You are fatigued. Learning how to make is a tiring activity. It will pass with practice." Eymerich moved toward the door. "I have other matters to attend to. We will continue your training later." Without so much as a fare-thee-well, he left, closing the door and locking it. His footsteps trailed off in the corridor. Abigail was relieved to have him gone, and her tension drained away.

She went to the balcony and looked out over the town, which was a hive of activity, crowds of people in constant motion with no apparent purpose she could perceive. Surprisingly, Abigail found it invigorating to watch the people. The energy renewed her as though she'd awakened from a long, restful sleep. The more she watched the stronger she felt, a curious sensation, another mystery to uncover.

Abigail heard the metallic sound of the door lock, and the page from the great hall entered, skipping as he walked. Abigail had not paid attention to him when she'd dashed past him earlier. He was a small Negro boy, skinny, about ten years old, wearing a red tunic squared at the shoulders with a crest displaying a chalice of flames, sandals, and a crimson turban on his head.

"Hello, Abigail."

"Who are you? Did Lord Eymerich send you? Time for another lesson?" She was on her guard, and suspicious of everyone now.

"No, I came on my own. My name is Panya. I came to see if you were alright."

"You're sure no one sent you?"

"No, no. Panya goes where he likes, does what he wants. Lord Eymerich is not a nice man. He enjoys hurting people. Panya wanted to make sure you were not hurt."

"I was a bit earlier, but I'm all better now." *Better than before*, she thought.

"Are you part of the queen's court?" Abigail asked.

"No, no. Panya is only a page. I'm not important to them. I have no power they can draw on."

In a flash, Panya was on the balcony precariously dancing on the railing, oblivious to the great height. He moved with such speed Abigail barely saw him move, just a blur.

"Can you come down from there? You're making me

nervous."

He stopped in mid-dance, smiled, and hopped down, leaning against the railing with his elbows.

Panya smirked, displaying a certain self-satisfaction. "I know everything that goes on in court, maybe even more." He twirled on one foot and, in another blur of motion, appeared sitting in the chair rocking vigorously, smiling as he did so. Abigail's first urge was to caution him not to break it, but then she realized that her concern didn't matter here. She doubted the chair would break, and if it did, she could make another.

"Have you been here a long time?" Panya's ability to move so fast fascinated Abigail, and she enjoyed his impish nature.

"Oh Panya doesn't know how long he's been here, a very long time. Mawu, the moon, would have made her journey across the sky more times than Panya could count. Panya has been here almost as long as the queen herself."

"Where did you come from? I mean when you were alive. I lived in a small village on a farm myself."

"We didn't have a village. When our cousins, the wildebeests, followed the rains to the new grasslands, my mother, father, sisters, brothers, and all my relatives would pack up our *hena*, what you call a tent, and move with them. I died during our tenth journey with the wildebeests. I was playing in the trees with my brother when the evil green spirit that lives in trees found me. He was hiding, stretched on a limb. When I reached up, he bit me, sinking his fangs into my hand. I remember it hurt very badly. I ran home to my father but he could do nothing. I was dead before the sun went to his *hena*. I came through the great wind and here Panya be."

In her past life, listening to how a child died would

have brought Abigail to tears. Now his description was merely small talk.

"What can you tell me about the queen, the court, and the castle?"

"Panya knows everything, all the secrets. I see everything, but no one sees Panya. I have no strength, so everyone ignores Panya." He jumped off the chair and turned to look at the sampler on the wall.

"Tell me about the queen, and the children that follow her. Who are they?"

"The queen is the greatest maker. She is stronger than anyone. She can pull strength from all the court."

"What do you mean, pull strength from others?"

"Everyone here has some power, some a lot, others a little. The ability to pull energy from others is what makes you a strong or weak maker. The people at court are all the strong makers. The weaker ones live in town. The strongest makers can control other makers making them stronger or weaker. This is why she is queen, because she can control all the other makers."

"And the children? Are they her children?"

"Panya doesn't know, but she is never without them. They follow her everywhere. They never speak or smile or play. The queen has her favorite. The boy that is always closest to her." Panya sprang up, sat cross-legged facing Abigail, and looked about rapidly.

"Panya has to go now." He jumped to his feet in one impossibly fast motion.

"Wait, can't you stay and talk some more?" Abigail asked but he was already at the door.

"Panya will come back soon. Ehyeh, the mother of us all, wants to meet you."

'Wait!" but before Abigail could get an answer, the door swung shut and locked. *Who was Ehyeh?* Her questions had to wait until Panya's return. Abigail looked forward to his next visit. He was a spark of joy in an otherwise bleak existence, but she wondered if he could be trusted. Trust was a scarce commodity in Gehenna.

A Thread of Hope

"They say a person needs just three things to be truly happy in this world: someone to love, something to do, and something to hope for." –
Tom Bodett

Abigail waited locked in her barren cell for either Panya or Lord Eymerich to return. One visit she looked forward to, the other she dreaded. Abigail dragged herself to the balcony and stood transfixed by the wandering crowds in the town below. Their motion mesmerized her. Fixated on them, she lost track of her surroundings. Again, energy flowed into her, filling and warming, leaving her both revitalized and perplexed. Panya had said that strong souls in Gehenna pulled energy from other souls. Was she sapping the strength of others?

Returning to her chair, Abigail pulled her legs under her and shut her eyes, hoping to block out Gehenna's bizarre uncertainties. The room became silent, and a profound stillness surrounded her as the view of the room seemed to fade. Abigail leaped to her feet, fearing being engulfed by the chaos of the whirlwind. Panic rose within her closing her throat.

In front of her, a small dot of sparkling light appeared which grew quickly into a thin circle as tall as she was, and filled with swirling mist. The mist cleared to reveal a passageway, and inside Abigail saw a man standing in a brightly lit room. He was young, tall, handsome, and well-built with sandy brown hair and a kind face. Abigail was sure she'd never seen him before, and his attire was unfamiliar, but she was drawn to him like a long-lost friend whose name she'd forgotten. He looked like a carpenter, surrounded by half-finished cabinets and woodworking tools.

Abigail feared this was another test staged by Lord Eymerich to gauge her abilities. But then Abigail became overwhelmed by a compulsion to go to him. Her legs moved by themselves, carrying her into the circle where a sudden chill took her breath away like a dive into a mountain lake on a hot summer day. Her feet touched the hard floor. She felt grit beneath her feet. The room smelled of fresh cut wood, and air moved in and out of her lungs. Tears rolled down her cheeks. She was back among the living. The man standing in front of her was alive.

Some unknown force had returned her to life. Abigail prayed that this kindly man had been sent to take her home. He looked up. His eyes went wide, and then looked down at the small piece of paper he held. His eyes darted back and forth. She sensed that he'd been thinking of her, and although a stranger, she believed he recognized her.

As Abigail reached for him, there was a sudden blur of motion, and both the man and the room disappeared, leaving her gasping and facing the blank wall in the castle once more. The entire encounter lasted just seconds. She'd crossed over to the land of the living. Abigail had no understanding of what, if anything, she'd done to cause it, why it ended so abruptly, or if she could ever return.

Abigail took solace that a reality other than Gehenna was possible. This man, a living being, knew she existed. Abigail didn't know his name, but, in a way that she didn't understand, they knew each other. He was a friend, a lifeline to the living. Up until this moment she'd believed herself doomed to a bleak eternity in Gehenna; now she had a glimmer of hope that she'd not passed permanently into oblivion.

Abigail thought she must have appeared as a ghost

like some lurking specter, a vapor scaring children and adults alike. She wasn't pleased with this prospect but if this was one of her undiscovered powers, she had to master it quickly, lest she found herself drifting randomly between the living and the dead, an unpleasant state of existence.

The encounter exhausted her. Whatever she'd experienced took every drop of energy within her. Abigail instinctively returned to the balcony, arms by her side, eyes closed and imagined energy flowing to her. A new surge of energy rippled through her like a torrent, filling her in matter of seconds, restoring, and leaving her strong and vital once more. Abigail sensed an inkling of mastery, a minor measure of control over her existence. She returned to her chair feeling not so lost as a few moments ago.

Home to Meet Mother

"Masks camouflage the faces of both good and evil.
Keeps hidden what is a truth and what is a lie."
– Patti Roberts

Abigail sat thinking about the man she'd encountered. He was attractive with a strong, kind face. She liked his broad shoulders and physique. He was the image of a man she'd daydreamed about marrying. Abigail longed to see him again, to talk with him.

The lock clanked, the door swung open, and Panya bounded into the room. Abigail jumped out of her chair.

"Panya," she exclaimed putting a hand to her chest.

"It's time for you to meet Ehyeh. Are you ready to go?"

"Eh, yes, I believe so." An alarm sounded within her. Was she making another mistake in trusting Panya too easily? She'd trusted Philberta, and that hadn't turned out well. But Panya's innocence seemed genuine.

"But what about Lord Eymerich?"

"He won't miss you, no, no, he won't. He won't even know you've gone. He is busy with the countess and other members of the court. I heard him say he would leave you locked up for a long time." Panya's light lyrical words came almost as a song.

Her hesitation melted away.

"How can we get out of the castle without being seen? There are so many guards."

"It's easy. Panya can bend time. This is my secret. Not even the queen herself knows of this."

"I don't understand, bend time?"

"Let me show you." Instantly, Panya stood on the other side of the room grinning at me. "Did you see Panya walk over here? No, you didn't because Panya slowed time. Then I walked here and let time resume its normal journey."

Panya giggled. "This is why Panya sees everything in the castle but no one sees Panya."

It was too fantastic to be believed. Jacquis had said that time was different here, and she'd seen Panya move at incredible speeds before, so why not believe that little Panya, the humble page, could vary the passage of time? Abigail studied him. Did she trust him, not completely, but neither could she let herself be ruled by fear.

"Okay. I believe you. How am I going to get out of the castle?"

"You need to hold my shoulder and follow me. If you're touching Panya when Panya bends time, it will bend for you. When we are outside of the town you can let go."

Abigail put her hand on his shoulder, and they walked down the same dark corridor where she'd previously followed Lord Eymerich. They passed various open rooms where members of the court were frozen in the middle of some activity, like some giant museum diorama.

"Panya, do these people know we're here?"

"No." He looked over his shoulder and smiled at her. "For them, the time it takes us to walk out of the castle is less than a beat of your heart. Now you're a mouse like Panya." Abigail found Panya's smile enchanting.

They walked through a long passageway, then down the sweeping stairway into the now empty great hall, and stopped before the menacing owl statue.

As Panya looked up at the giant owl, fear spread

across his face.

"This is where the queen has her vision time." Panya whispered as though he didn't want the statue to hear.

"And what's vision time?"

"Oh, the vision time, the vision time, it is a scary time, the vision time," Panya sang. "Panya doesn't like to talk about it." He looked at his feet, avoiding Abigail's eyes.

"It can't be so scary. You can tell me. I won't tell anyone you told me. It can be our secret, just you and me."

"Just between us, okay?" Panya said with complete trust and innocence.

"Yes Panya, just you and me." Abigail knelt down on one knee to be at his level, still holding on to his shoulder.

"The vision time is when the queen speaks to the other side, to her children that are alive, where the sun and the moon still travel across the sky. It takes the strength of the entire court."

Panya pointed to the empty galleries above. "They assemble here. She stands in front of the statue and talks to people on the other side. She tells them to do evil things, bad things. Many people on the other side have died because of Queen Lilith." Panya grimaced at the events that had passed here, and validated Abigail's foreboding when she'd encountered Lilith.

"What kind of bad things?"

"To fight, to kill people, to have great wars, to cause great sickness, to build terrible fire bombs—Panya doesn't like to talk about it."

"Does she do this often?"

"More and more. She talks to men standing in a forest. They speak about places and people Panya doesn't understand."

The owl statue looked more sinister than a moment ago, an embodiment of ancient and lingering evil. Abigail's perception of the great hall changed from a regal palace to a pit filled with maleficent souls. She had a premonition of powerful forces at play moving toward, as yet unforeseen cataclysmic events, with her at the center

"Panya, let's go. I think we need to hurry."

They continued through the town, passing people frozen in mid-stride. It was all very strange. The pair quickly reached the edge of town and continued out across the featureless plain. Abigail looked behind. The town and the castle were gradually being obscured by the drifting gray mists, like a dense fog rolling in. There was nothing before them but the pervasive gray sky, an eerie nothingness surrounded them. They were in a wasteland for as far as Abigail could see. She trusted, hoped, that Panya knew his way.

"You can let go of my shoulder now," said Panya. "We're clear of the city and there is no need to hide anymore. Time will remain frozen till we return."

"How do you know where we're going? It's gray in all directions. There are no roads or signposts or landmarks of any kind."

"The sentinels mark the way. See, look ahead in the distance. There is a sentinel standing there."

Abigail made out a shape ahead. As they approached, she saw it was a walker, an old woman dressed in a Roman toga with a blank face and vacant eyes. She had been standing motionless facing the direction they were walking. As Abigail and Panya passed, the old woman fell in walking behind them. In the distance, was another motionless sentinel appeared becoming visible out of the mist.

"How did these walkers get here?

"Ehyeh sent them."

"I thought no one could talk to them."

"Ehyeh can." Panya winked at her. "And you can. Ehyeh sent Ranger to warn you about the queen."

"You knew about that?" Abigail stopped short and looked at Panya.

"Yes, but Ranger didn't have enough time to explain how to hide your powers from the queen, so you shone too brightly during your meeting. Now the queen knows you are powerful. That's why she wanted Lord Eymerich to test you, to learn how strong you are." Panya's face showed a child's concern of adult affairs, of worry without understanding. "Ehyeh told me to bring you right away."

The recent events now made sense. The queen had deliberately challenged her to provoke a reaction. And Lord Eymerich's attack was also meant to make her drop her guard and display her powers. Abigail felt like a child, embarrassed, angry with herself for being so easily manipulated. She vowed not to be taken in again.

Abigail and Panya continued through the void passing a dozen more sentinels who joined their march forming a silent procession. After they'd been walking for a long time, the gray mists thinned and parted revealing an immense lush forest. Unlike the few trees and plants in the castle town, this forest was bright green with dense foliage, a broad hill covered with grassland rose in the center.

"We're almost there," said Panya with some glee and quickened his pace.

Abigail too shared his excitement at the inviting vista ahead. It filled her with comfort, as if she had returned home from a long journey. She had no memory of this place, but rather a sensation, a feeling of familiarity like walking into a room for the first time and yet knowing where everything was. With this feeling came an absence of fear. Since being caught in the storm returning from Mr. Small's store in what seemed a lifetime ago, she realized that she'd been afraid, constantly on edge. Now as they approached the lush forest, the absence of impending danger highlighted how afraid she'd been.

Abigail saw that the forest was lined by a stand of immensely tall trees forming an impenetrable wall stretching as far as she could see in either direction. Two giant men magnificently built with rippling muscles, possibly ten feet tall, stood guarding a small passageway, and much to her embarrassment, each was completely naked. Abigail averted her eyes. She'd never seen a man naked before. Growing up on a farm, she certainly understood sex, but seeing men in such full and unabashed nudity shocked her. Her face felt scarlet.

The walkers entered the passageway through the wall without breaking their stride. Panya ran into the passageway behind them.

Abigail peered into the passage. The tree branches formed a long round arbor way. The leaves of the trees were luminescent. A light, cool breeze moved the branches and caressed her face. Abigail's body shivered. She entered and the light within the tunnel enveloped her like a rain shower washing away an invisible layer of soot and grime left over from Gehenna which had clung to her like a malignant crust. Abigail emerged feeling lighter, cleaner, and almost transparent, as though she might float away on a breeze.

Panya waited for her to transit the passage. Abigail eyes went wide as she emerged. Before her was a wide grassy plain which sloped gently uphill. Patches of trees, lush flowering plants, and a few rocky outcroppings dotted the landscape. Cottages and small huts were set about. The sweet scent of flowers carried on the breeze. A small babbling stream trickled down beside the path and ended in a pond. Large golden fish swam to the surface and splashed like pets greeting their owner. Bright, multi-colored parrots flew overhead. A pair of giraffes walked in the distance, eating leaves from the treetops. Most stunning of all were the drifting and billowing white clouds set against a deep blue sky like a summer's day in Maine. It was a land of pastoral beauty, a paradise.

Panya patiently waited while Abigail acclimated. She felt like a prisoner who been released from a dungeon into a bright summer's day, which was not so far from the truth. She nodded to him, signaling she was ready to continue. He turned and walked ahead along a curving, uphill path with her lagging behind, continually distracted by the myriad of people. Unlike the castle town, all the people, plants, and houses here were brightly colored and radiant. An old man wearing an orange robe sat cross-legged beside a small hut. He glanced at Abigail, smiling slightly as she passed, his face shining with an inner light. Further along the path two nuns walked arm in arm. They wore large, starched head coverings of white cloth folded upwards like wings. They stepped aside as Abigail approached, bowing slightly to her.

A man wearing a long black coat made of shiny cloth and a broad black hat trimmed with brown fur approached. He had a beard and ringlets of hair beside his face. "Shalom aleikhem azak uvarukh." Abigail had no idea what he said but he seemed genuinely happy to see her.

"Good day to you, sir," was all she could think of for a reply. The man nodded and watched as Abigail continued.

Another man dressed in Japanese robes approached her, bowed low from the waist, and said "Konnichiwa, Astarte-Sama."

Again, his words had no meaning for her, but she hesitantly returned his bow and continued up the path. Like Gehenna, there were people of every shape, size, and era, but unlike Gehenna, each person glowed with a special radiance.

People lined the path greeting her in languages Abigail didn't understand, others nodded or bowed. All the people we passed were similar—all serene, and all smiling. Abigail had no idea of where she was, but it appeared as though everyone knew her.

As they climbed higher, Abigail saw a vast land stretching as far as she could see. At the crest of the hill, a simple grass hut was set in the middle of a wide lawn. A large spreading tree with broad shiny leaves shaded the area. The people who had followed them up the hill formed a circle on the edge of the lawn. On the left of the hut stood a tall man dressed as an ancient soldier. His hands rested on a gleaming sword in front of him. He wore a leather shirt and skirt trimmed with gold, and a golden breast plate covered his chest; large white wings were visible on his back. He was immensely tall, easily nine feet, beautiful, angelic, and his body had a distinct glow. His face radiated warmth. Abigail was sure she knew him, but could not remember from where.

"Have we met before?" she asked.

"Yes, Abigail." He smiled as he said her name. Then, from his back, the two broad wings covered in white feathers extended and momentarily wrapped around Abigail, giving her a tingling caress, as a warm sensation rippled through her. His wings made a soft rustling sound as they moved. Abigail felt a soft breeze as they returned to his back.

"I am Michael. We have known each other for a very long time. I am pleased to see you once again."

Abigail was face to face with an angel, and the only thing that seemed remarkable was that it didn't surprise her. Intuition told her that she was speaking to a dear and trusted friend. She touched his hand, and energy, like warm water, flowed between them.

"Abigail, Ehyeh is waiting for you." She glanced at Panya standing beside the hut entrance.

"Are you coming?"

"No, this is your time with Ehyeh. I'll wait outside for you. Don't worry, Ehyeh is nice. She takes care of everyone here." The spirit of the place filled her and she knew she had nothing to fear.

"Does this place have a name?

"Ehyeh calls it Arcadia." Panya took my hand and gently directed her to the door. "You should go in now."

Abigail parted the rough cloth covering the doorway and entered the darkness within. As she stepped through, a shudder passed through her, changing her body. In an instant her perceptions become clearer with heightened color and clarity, more precise, shaper as though a veil had been lifted. Abigail was more aware of her hands, her legs, even of how her hair brushed against her ears.

Abigail was no longer in Arcadia, nor was she inside the hut. She found herself in a clearing in a dark forest. Above her, a clear night sky revealed stars, planets, and galaxies in gentle, constant motion. Her perception reached farther than she thought possible, as though she could reach out with her thoughts and touch stars at vast distances. A spiral galaxy spun overhead, and her vision zoomed through it, passing individual stars and planets as though her body, her consciousness had no boundaries. The entire universe was a living thing. Abigail sensed its breath, its pulse.

"Abigail," called a feminine voice, strong and clear, instantly returning Abigail to the confines of her human form. She looked down and saw a woman, naked except for a thin grass skirt, seated on a low cushion. Her skin was light brown, and her hair was dark and full. She wore a simple strand of colored beads which draped over her breasts, and golden bracelets on each wrist. Her face was oval, with a slightly broad nose, full lips, and soft green eyes that appeared to glow slightly in the low light.

The woman's face was familiar. Abigail knew her. She'd known her for a very long time. In her face, Abigail saw the likeness of every woman she'd ever known—her mother, her grandmother, Mrs. Cunningham, Mrs. Small, as well as a myriad of women's faces from every time and place. Her face didn't change, it remained constant, but Abigail's perception changed the longer she regarded her, as though looking at images being transposed over one another. Ehyeh's face reflected every woman's face.

"Please sit." The woman gestured to the cushion opposite her. Between them, a flame rose from a small, gray, stone pyramid which lit her figure with a soft, flickering light. The trees in the surrounding forest were silhouetted against the night sky. Visible within the trees, Abigail saw faces of animals and people; some she recognized and others were alien. They slowly moved in and out of the darkness, coming into focus and then fading away as new images took their place.

A soft, warm breeze blew through the trees, filling the clearing with hundreds of different smells, each distinctive, and each carrying its own vision. She smelled trees after a rain, the ocean, freshly plowed earth, animals of every kind, and people. The scents and the accompanying visions crashed over Abigail like a giant soft wave of experience enveloping her in a view of Earth and all that lived on her.

Behind the woman, suspended from a tree branch, was a tapestry woven from coarse brown fiber. On it were scenes of antelope running on a savannah. As Abigail watched, she realized that the animals were in motion. Each time she glanced back at it, the figures and their locations had changed.

Abigail's gazed returned to the woman before her. "Are you Ehyeh?" Abigail had an overwhelming and inexplicable desire to lie down with her head in the woman's lap cry. She was happy merely to be in her presence, content to stay there forever. Abigail's body pulsated softly with light in the semi-darkness. A slight breeze blew her hair. The antelopes on the tapestry ran and leaped in silence. For the first time since her journey through the whirlwind, maybe for the first time in her memory, she was home.

"Yes, I am Ehyeh. It is good you have arisen from your slumber, my daughter."

Things My Mother Told Me

"No man is poor who has a Godly mother."
– Abraham Lincoln

"Slumber? I wasn't sleeping. I lived on my family's farm in Maine. I was alive. I was happy," Abigail replied to Ehyeh.

No place could be more foreign to her experience nor feel as comfortable as where she was now. She'd gone from living with all its tangible reality to being stripped down to her barest consciousness in the whirlwind. She'd experienced the harsh mysteries of Gehenna and the serenity of Arcadia. Now she was in yet another place, a place where her being, her perceptions had no boundaries. In Ehyeh's presence, reality was fluid, a kaleidoscope of realities flashed by. Abigail's consciousness began to drift among the many visions before her.

"You were resting in the land of the living in a wakeful slumber, hidden from the evil that searched for you like a spotted fawn in the forest shadows safe from predators."

Her soft, clear voice called Abigail's thoughts back to the forest clearing. Why did she think she'd been hidden? Her family's farm was isolated perhaps, but she hadn't hiding. Abigail had no reason to doubt her, but she couldn't grasp what Ehyeh was telling her.

"I'm sure I know you, but I have no remembrance of you." Her mind raced. She felt farther from Maine than she could imagine. There were too many mysteries, too many questions, too many sensations coming at her too quickly. She was drowning.

Ehyeh touched Abigail's knee, and a wave of calmness washed over her, relaxing the tightness in her chest.

"When you crossed the void between realms, parts of you were lost, leaving you with many questions." Ehyeh moved her hands over the flame and it grew brighter. "Let me answer your questions."

"Who are you?" She asked.

"I am the guardian of the land of the living, and of the spirit realm." The flame from the stone changed to a soft blue.

"What is this place?"

Ehyeh gestured with her hands toward the sky and the dark forest. "This is where I am."

Her answers were spare but somehow sufficient, which puzzled Abigail most of all.

"I was in Arcadia, on top of a hill when I entered your hut. Then a change washed over me, and I found myself standing in front of you."

"Just as Arcadia is beyond the land of the living, this place is beyond Arcadia. It is beyond place, beyond time."

Her description was more than Abigail could comprehend. Wherever they were, it was boundless as if she could reach out and touch the farthest star.

"After I died, I awoke in Gehenna, a terrible place filled with horrible people and ruled by Queen Lilith. I feel as though I'm being punished for some sin of which I have no knowledge. It is a fate I do not deserve."

"You are not being punished, Abigail. I sent you there," said Ehyeh.

"You sent me there?" The tightness in her chest returned. "Why? What errand can I possibly perform? I'm a simple farm girl."

"I need your help to defeat the Evil One."

The forest around her seemed to fall away, leaving only Ehyeh's deadly serious face. Abigail had been subservient to all the adults in her life. How could she battle some evil soul?

"You must have mistaken me for someone else. I'm not capable of defeating anyone, certainly not the evil soul you speak of."

"There is no mistake. You are the one. You have always been the one. It is within you to defeat the Evil One."

Abigail had never felt so tiny, so ill prepared, or so incapable. It was as though Ehyeh were asking her to stand single-handed against Pickett's charge at the Battle of Gettysburg.

"Who is the Evil One? Is it Queen Lilith who rules Gehenna?

"Lilith is Adam's first wife. She refused him and mated with the Evil One. They spawned a race of children known as the Lilim in the land of the living. They appear human but are not. The Lilim are drawn to evil, and gather like a swarm of locusts in the presence of the Demon of all Demons."

"How will I know this demon," she asked.

"The Evil One's present form is not known, but I feel it moving in the shadows, marshaling its forces, preparing to strike. It has taken many forms, both male and female, and is always disguised, hidden, never who it appears to be."

"Does this devil know of Arcadia? Of you?"

"Arcadia and Gehenna both exist in the spirit realm, but Arcadia is hidden from the Evil One. I have surrounded Gehenna with mists that obscure everything beyond its boundaries. And yes, this Prince of Darkness knows me very well." Ehyeh looked at the flame, her face having gone blank.

"Is Arcadia heaven?" Abigail retained hope for the heavenly reward that Father had spoken of so often.

Ehyeh smiled at her question. "There are no pits of fire or angelic choirs. Living souls make their own heaven and hell. Some create their own demons and are mired in pain and despair. They exist side by side with souls who walk with angels surrounded by beauty and serenity."

Ehyeh moved her hands playfully over the stone pyramid. A flame rose in a twisting intricate braid of red, yellow, and blue light which vanished when she removed her hands.

"Arcadia and Gehenna don't feel real to me," Abigail said. "I was able to create a table and chair by thinking about them. I have the sense that I could reach through a wall if I wanted. It's like everything might dissolve into mist at any moment."

"Each realm, the living and the spirit, sings its own song, its own note, just as different bells have their own tones. The note is carried by everything—every soul, every creature, every stone—in that realm. It resonates within and throughout the realm. The different notes keep the realms apart and hidden from each other. These notes cannot be heard, but you can feel them as you move between realms."

All that Ehyeh told her sounded true, as though Abigail was remembering lessons she'd been taught a long time ago.

Ehyeh continued, "The song of the land of the living is high, strong, and clear, which makes the boundary between energy and substance almost unbreakable. This is why there are no makers in the land of the living. The song is too strong. In the spirit realm, the song is low and quiet.

There is little difference between energy and substance. Strong souls can change energy into substance and back again."

"This was how I was able to create objects, why the queen called me a maker?" Ehyeh nodded. Abigail sensed a new confidence as Ehyeh peeled back the layers of mysteries.

"What was the whirlwind I came through?"

"Like the meeting of two great oceans, the boundary between realms is turbulent and violent."

Ehyeh motioned with her hands and streams of light collided in a chaotic jumble that then faded away.

"Within the boundary, the notes from each realm mix and become discordant. There is no force to separate energy and substance. What you saw was energy and substance changing rapidly from one to the other, chaotic and uncontrolled. The strongest souls can control the chaos and come through without loss; weaker souls cannot."

"It felt like I was in a powerful, chaotic whirlwind, a horrible feeling of being flung apart."

"Yes, parts of you were changing rapidly from substance to energy and back again." Ehyeh looked as though Abigail's experience pained her.

"Being in the whirlwind made me angry, and when I became angry, I found I could pull myself together."

"Yes, because you are strong, one of the strongest souls in all of Arcadia." Ehyeh leaned toward her. "Your anger is a manifestation of your will. It revealed and then focused your strength in the chaos, allowing you to come through with your soul almost intact. Others come through, but are terribly wounded. You have seen the walkers. They have lost almost everything of what they were. When they arrive here they're empty vessels without thought or purpose. We find them and bring them to Arcadia, where we try to restore their souls as best we can."

"Is that what happened to Jacob?" Abigail asked.

"Yes, and more. Jacob is also an ancient soul, as old as you. He is a mighty warrior who has battled evil for millennia. He was wounded in battle and cast into the chaos. In his weakened state, he was unable to fight the whirlwind. His soul was ravaged, stripped bare."

"I know him, but he has no memory of me. Will he recover?"

"In time he will improve." Ehyeh paused and looked away, not meeting my eyes. There was a fleeting hint of sadness on her face, and Abigail wondered if there was more she wasn't telling her.

"Does everyone come through the whirlwind?" Abigail asked. "There aren't enough souls here, given the millions of people who'd ever lived."

"No, few souls do. When a soul is released by death, it begins a new lifetime. This cycle continues till the soul evolves beyond the need to live again, to learn new lessons. Souls that are truly evil are drawn to Gehenna.

"Evil can enshroud pure souls and drag them down to Gehenna. The Evil One and its demons draw their strength from these trapped souls.

"A few souls are held by an object in the land of the living. The object is always something of significance to the person. It acts as an anchor stopping the cycle of rebirth. There they remain until the object that holds them is destroyed."

"This is what happened to me isn't it?"

"Yes, your intuition is correct. You are held by an object in the land of the living because I need you there."

Abigail had rebelled against her father's control. He had limited her choices and kept her from pursing her dreams. Now she was bound to another path not of her choosing, but she could not refuse Ehyeh.

Abigail sat quietly for a few minutes absorbing all she'd been told. Ehyeh stared into the flame while she waited. Abigail came to the question she'd wanted to ask.

"Ehyeh, I had a dream, or perhaps a vision, and in it, I returned to the land of the living. I saw a young man whom I didn't know, but sensed a strong attraction to. He was tall and handsome. The experience was very real, but lasted only a few seconds, and then it vanished. What happened to me? Did I cross over the chaos and return to the living? Was I a ghost?"

Ehyeh took her hand and, as when Michael touched her, energy flowed into Abigail like warm, soothing water coursing into her.

"Abigail, you are one of the few who can cross between the living and the dead.

"The object that binds you also enables you to move between realms. It sings the note of your soul in the other realm, allowing you to change your note to match that of the living. It takes enormous energy to change your note. You crossed over by yourself for a few seconds, and with help, you can cross over for several minutes. The bond between the two of you will grow stronger over time, drawing you together."

Abigail now understood this was why she'd been exhausted after her experience with the man in his workshop.

"He summoned you, called you to him using the object."

Ehyeh was right. She'd sensed his calling, and had

been unable to resist his summons. Abigail trusted him, and though we'd never met, she felt as though she knew him.

Ehyeh released Abigail's hand and leaned back on her cushions. "Do you remember him holding something?"

"He held something in his hands, something small. I couldn't see what it was."

"It is a photograph of you taken by your parents after you died. If the man or anyone destroys it, you will vanish and begin a new lifetime, so you must implore him keep it safe. We need your help in our battle with the Evil One. The power of the Evil One has grown rapidly, much faster than we expected."

Mother's voice carried her concern. Figures on the tapestry behind Ehyeh changed again, faces of different animals lined up looking directly at me.

"Our spies in Gehenna and among the living have told us of a scheme by the Evil One to destroy all human life on Earth. We do not know the exact nature of the plan or when the Evil One intends to act, but the plan has been in motion for over a hundred years. The Evil One is a consummate tactician, patient, and cunning. Its moves are subtle, almost invisible. Its forces wait in the shadows, building their numbers, and aligning themselves."

"What is the purpose of this plan?"

"It is only the presence of true humans in the land of the living that prevents the Evil One from escaping Gehenna. The Evil One intends to destroy all human life, and rule forever in the land of the living."

A shudder ran through Abigail, followed by a raging anger that any being would conceive of such a plan.

"Like the picture that binds you, the Evil One is held by an object, a chalice. The man you met must find the chalice in the land of the living, and destroy it. Then the Evil

One will be trapped in Gehenna. Without the Evil One's presence, the Lilim will become dormant once again, unaware of who they are. While the man searches, you must challenge the queen to divert her attention until the man can succeed."

How was I supposed to challenge the queen, Lord Eymerich, or other members of the court? Abigail's talk with Mother made her more confident, more at ease in the spirit realm. She had a growing sense of her powers, but she didn't believe herself capable of confronting the queen.

Abigail looked down, clenching her hands in her lap. "You tell me that I'm an ancient soul, a strong soul, but I don't feel like one. I'm a girl swept up in events and circumstance I can barely comprehend."

"Your face tells me that the quest frightens you, that you're unsure of your courage and skills. You are a young lioness, untested in the hunt against a larger foe. The lioness is the mightiest hunter, and your strength runs much deeper than you know. You must believe in your strength of will, your skill, your courage, and your cunning. Like the lioness, these are your true weapons. They are far mightier than any sword you might wield."

Mother reached through the fire and placed her fingertips on the flaming stone pyramid between them. "Let me show you the courage of a great warrior who has come before. Touch the stone with me."

Fearing the fire, Abigail hesitated. Mother nodded, reassuring her. She reached into the flames, feeling nothing, she touched the cool smooth stone, and her reality shifted again.

Astarte, the Warrior Goddess

"The way of the warrior is resolute acceptance of death."
– Miyamoto Musashi

When Abigail touched the flaming pyramid stone, Ehyeh and the clearing in the forest disappeared, her vision wavered, and she found herself looking down on a stone temple in a barren desert. This was neither Gehenna nor Arcadia. It had the sharp hardness of the land of the living, but Abigail had no idea of the time or place.

The temple was open to the dark, moonless sky. Its broad altar supported a massive statue of a black-winged demon with the head of a bull straddling a raging fire. Braziers were set about the temple, and the fire on the altar filled it with flickering light. A short pedestal held a bronze chalice in front of the fire. Abigail heard the sound of ocean waves crashing nearby.

A priest dressed in a hooded crimson robe waved his arms in unison as the frenzied worshipers chanted, "Moloch, Moloch, Moloch!" A flute and drum played in the background. Soldiers in black battle dress, hands on swords at the ready, guarded the altar. On either side of the statue, hooded men dressed in black loincloths held children wearing coarse gray tunics. The children stood mute, unmoving, and expressionless, oblivious to the shouts of the worshipers.

Raising his arms, the crimson figure motioned for silence. The chanting subsided, and only the crackling fire beneath the statue could be heard.

"Moloch, mighty god of the underworld, we come to worship you, to receive your blessing. Take this sacrifice from our hands to honor you. Feast on our offerings and grow stronger." He surveyed the faces of the crowd who looked on with anticipation.

The priest took a small boy, held him in front of himself, and stroked his hair lovingly. Transfixed, the boy appeared oblivious to his impending fate.

"Sacrifice, sacrifice, sacrifice!" screamed the crowd. The drum beat rose in volume and pace. Smoke swirled about the legs of the massive idol. Sparks rose to join the black sky above.

The priest raised the child above his head, turned to face the fire, and threw him into the inferno. Cheers momentarily drowned out the screams of the writhing child. A low roar came from the statue as its wings rose and spread across the altar. Agitation rose to a fever pitch as the worshipers saw the statue move. Knowing his sacrifice had been accepted, the priest rejoiced and faced the idol with his arms outstretched.

"Moloch, Moloch, Moloch!" chanted the crowd ever louder. The priest raised a small girl above his head, preparing to repeat the same ghastly ritual. As she awoke from her trance, the young girl's screams resounded in the temple, exciting the crowd even more. The priest threw her into the flames, and the mob again shouted their approval, enticing Moloch's wings to extend further.

A tall woman with flowing auburn hair appeared at the entrance to the temple. She was dressed in a white tunic and loose blue pants, with leather armor on her chest and arms. She held a gleaming sword in one hand and a small round shield in the other. A gold band on her head reflected the flickering light.

She sized up the frenzied worshipers and then, taking a breath that appeared to fill her with strength, charged into the crowd clearing a path with her sword. The chanting turned to screams as she progressed toward the altar, leaving a trail of dismembered and bleeding worshipers in her wake.

The crowd backed away, forming a circle around the woman and chanting, "Kill her, kill her!" On the priest's signal, the guards charged her en masse. With two broad sweeps of her sword, she slew the first two guards. She deflected a blow while she parried with another guard. The sound of metal clanging against metal resounded throughout the temple. Flying sparks accompanied every blow. The woman moved at incredible speed, attacking faster than the guards could defend. In a short moment, two more guards lay dying, their blood draining onto the temple floor. The last remaining guard charged with sword held high, yelling a deep battle cry. She spun full circle in a blur with her hair flowing. Her sword met the man's throat, severing his head and sending it rolling toward the altar. His torso collapsed at her feet.

The worshipers began to close about her. With several thrusts of her sword, she cleared a path and leaped onto the altar confronting the priest. The men in loincloths fled, leaving their stupefied charges where they stood.

"We have another sacrifice for the lord of the underworld," cried the priest, raising his arm toward the idol. Slashing with her sword, the woman advanced on the priest. Horror showed on his face as he stumbled backwards to avoid her thrusts. Intent on the priest, the warrior paused in front of the statue when a mighty lightning bolt shot from its mouth and struck her, sending her flying off the altar. She lay sprawled on the temple floor, stunned. Silence, broken by the crackling fires, filled the temple as the crowd drew back, waiting to see if the warrior was dead. She stirred, clutching her sword and shield. Rising slowly, she eyed the hostile worshipers, who then charged at her. She took a broad stance facing them.

She swung her sword, disemboweling two worshipers and forcing the crowd to retreat. In a single leap that no mere human could perform, she bounded onto the altar, once more facing the priest. With a fierce cry that echoed throughout the temple, she ran directly at the priest. Her sudden attack surprised him, and he staggered backwards to the edge of the altar. As she sprinted toward the statue, a second lightning bolt shot toward her. She dove into a somersault, avoiding the bolt which struck the altar and caused the stone to explode, killing several more people. Rolling upright, she struck the bronze chalice a powerful blow with her sword and sent it flying from the temple, arching into the darkness beyond.

A deafening, painful roar came from the statue, drowning out the shouts of the crowd, silencing them as they looked on in horror as the demon statue became inert. Its wings drooped to its sides. The woman advanced on the cowering priest and, with a swift arc of her sword, sent his head rolling into the middle of the crowd. They wailed at the sight of the priest's head lying in the dirt, then fled in panic, screaming and trampling those that could not run.

The woman paused to observe the carnage that lay before the altar. The crackling fire was the only sound. She moved to face the idol, gazing up at it. As she held her sword high with both hands, her body began to glow, illuminating the temple. She swung her sword, slicing through the leg of the statue. Lightning sprang from where her sword struck, accompanied by a loud crack of thunder. Its leg crumbled, and the statue wavered momentarily; then with a mournful roar, it collapsed into the fire, sending a shower of sparks into the black night. The woman sank to one knee with her head bowed, her hands resting on the hilt of her sword. Awakened from their trances, the children gathered around the exhausted warrior.

The scene vanished, and Abigail again faced Ehyeh.

She was shaken, stunned by the vision she'd witnessed. Seeing children being burned alive was horrific. The female warrior's actions were brutal and savage, but she had saved the remaining children and destroyed the demonic idol. She was the bravest, most fearsome warrior Abigail could have ever imagined.

"Who was that woman, the warrior?"

"Her name is Astarte; she is Arcadia's daughter and its greatest warrior. She channels the power of Arcadia through her being and her sword. The battle I showed you happened long ago. It is one of many battles that Astarte and the Evil One have waged for thousands of years."

"Her bravery, strength and speed were incredible. Abigail had not thought a woman capable of such feats." She paused reflecting on the vision. "Those people, why were they sacrificing the children?" Such horror was beyond her.

"The people you saw in the temple were Lilim. They serve the Evil One and exist without compassion or empathy. When the Evil One's presence is felt, they awaken, becoming aware of their true nature. The Lilim are gathering as we speak in great swarms, ready to do the bidding of the demon of demons."

Ehyeh rested her hands on her knees. Her eyes pierced Abigail's soul, and her words chilled Abigail to the bone.

"Abigail, the way of the warrior is not always that of the sword. Sometimes the most damaging blow comes from the unexpected strike. The lightest touch, if unseen, can topple the fiercest opponent. Even the mighty Astarte cannot land a blow against the Evil One if she attacks head on. She would be cast into the void and shattered, ripped apart like Ranger. Stealth is your mightiest sword, and cunning is your strongest shield.

"You, and the man you are bound to, must strike when the Evil One is diverted. You must hunt like the lioness, hidden in the grass waiting patiently for your moment. Your prey must not see you till you are already upon it. The death blow must be dealt before the Evil One is aware of your presence. If it suspects you at all, you will be defeated, and the children of Eve will perish."

Ehyeh's face was cold and intent. Abigail had no doubt of the outcome if she failed. Ehyeh knew Abigail would do anything for her. Her allegiance to Ehyeh went to the core of her being. Abigail would undertake this quest, but at this moment, the task seemed impossible.

"The chalice you saw in the vision is the key. It is linked to the soul of the Evil One, and allows it to cross over to the land of the living. The chalice calls the Lilim and awakens them. You must destroy the chalice."

"Ehyeh, I will do anything you ask of me. I would throw myself into the void if it would help, but I don't know where to begin. The chalice is somewhere in the land of the living. How can I destroy it?"

"You cannot, but the man can. He is bound to you, albeit lightly now. You must strengthen the bond so as to become one with him. You and he must act in unison between the living and the spirit realms."

"How? I've only seen him for a few seconds. I'm not sure what I did to cause the meeting or how to cross over again."

"The souls of Arcadia will help you to maintain a bridge to the living. It won't last for long, but longer than you can do by yourself. When the bond is sealed, he will sense you and you him. You will share thoughts and feelings, sometimes vividly, other times as a mild intuition, like clouds drifting together and then apart.

"You must touch him to seal the bond. He is a good man, but lacks the confidence to begin. You must appeal to his heart, to his inner goodness. He will need your will, strength and courage."

Nodding her understanding, Abigail knew what she had to do. She also knew she was not the same woman who had entered this mysterious forest minutes earlier.

"You should leave now, my daughter; the souls of Arcadia have assembled."

"Aren't you coming back to Arcadia?"

"No, this is where I am. I've always been here and always will be, but I will be with you wherever you are."

"May I come see you again?"

"We shall meet many more times."

A veil lifted, and Abigail knew this was her destiny. Ehyeh had set this path before her, and there was no going back, but for the first time in Abigail's memory, it was a path of her choosing. The vision of Astarte had given Abigail confidence that she could aspire to be like Astarte, strong and fearless. She had indeed been sleeping, resting on a remote farm, shielded from the world, waiting for this quest to begin.

Abigail envisioned herself standing in an empty desert as a massive army of demons bore down on her. Only she could halt their charge. The consequences of not doing so were too terrible to contemplate.

Stepping into the dark forest, Abigail was transported back to the bright hilltop in Arcadia.

A Meeting in the Woods

"Truly the universe is full of ghosts, not sheeted churchyard spectres, but the inextinguishable elements of individual life, which having once been, can never die, though they blend and change, and change again forever."
– H. Rider Haggard

Abigail stood once more outside of Ehyeh's hut on the hilltop in Arcadia. Thinking about the man she was about to meet, she prayed Ehyeh was right and he would help. Abigail sensed a kinship, a budding intimacy with him, possibly the beginnings of the bond Ehyeh spoke of. The chalice was beyond her reach. Only the man could find and destroy it. If she failed to convince him, the Evil One would triumph.

On the top of the hill, people crowded in from every direction, more people than she'd seen on her walk up. All the souls of Arcadia had come to help her cross over. Michael raised his arms and looked over the assembled souls. A low rhythmic chanting rose softly from the crowd and gradually grew louder.

"Stand in front of me. I will help guide the energy toward you. Think of the man you saw before. Visualize him in your mind's eye. Think of nothing but him, and the bridge to the land of the living will appear," instructed Michael.

Michael stood behind her and raised his gleaming white wings and a warm, soothing energy flow into her, channeled by his angelic wings. Arcadia's energy was bright, pristine, and along with it came sensations from every soul in Arcadia. Abigail perceived a hint of their personalities, and glimpses of their life experiences. It was more than a gift of strength; it was an intimate communion, a mixing of souls. They believed in her as they did in Astarte. The energy from the crowds in the castle town was a muddy, fetid stream by comparison.

Abigail visualized the man's face and his kind eyes. Her thoughts reached out to him like tendrils drawing them closer. A round oval of light formed in front of her. As before, a gray swirling mist filled the oval and then cleared, revealing the man she'd seen briefly before, now standing in a dark forest with two dogs at his feet. He held the object that anchored her soul. The same compulsion to enter the circle overcame her. Abigail stepped into the circle and felt a strong chill as her body crossed between realms.

A cool night breeze touched her face, and she saw her breath on the wind. She smelled the forest and air filled her lungs once more. The scent of the moist earth reminded Abigail of playing in the woods ever so long ago. Everything told her she was back among the living.

Abigail stepped softly, feeling the soft forest floor under her feet. Her dress blew in the breeze. The man looked up at the sound of Abigail's footsteps crackling in the dry leaves. He looked curious, then shocked, and finally afraid.

"Abigail?" His voice wavered as he stepped backwards.

"Good evening, sir. I need your help," Abigail said softly so as not to add to his surprise.

She stopped beside him and realized that she stood over her own grave, and alongside those of her mother and father. Seeing her own grave did not move her. The person buried there was a distant memory, an echo of who she was now. But her heart ached for her dear mother, for the memory of their time together, for the love she'd shown her, for the price she'd paid, and as Abigail now understood, for the sanctuary she had given her. Abigail turned to the man, remembering that her time was short.

"Please don't be afraid. Take my hand so you can know that I am real, that I am no mere specter."

"How can you possibly be here? You died over a hundred and thirty years ago. This is your grave, for Christ's sake." The man remained transfixed, frozen, looking like he might flee at any moment.

Then the two dogs that had been at his feet rose and came to Abigail, wagging their tails and sniffing. She scratched one behind his ears, and he thumped his paw rapidly on the ground. After another sniff, they walked away. The man's face relaxed.

"You are real, at least Abe and Louie think you are," he said. "How can you possibly be here? Are you a ghost?"

"I suppose to you I am. I exist in a spirit realm, in a place called Arcadia, and I have crossed over to speak with you. Please touch my hand, see that I am real."

Abigail extended her hand again. The man inched closer. He lightly stroked her hand and, realizing Abigail had substance, gripped it fully. She felt the watery flow of energy exchange between them. Unlike the mild exchange with the souls of Arcadia, this one yielded a strong, intimate view of him. He had a kind nature and a deep well of goodness, but doubts lurked beneath his easygoing exterior. He accepted failure too easily. Abigail felt his feelings for his wife whom he loved very much. His eyes went wide, showing fascination mixed with fright as he sensed Abigail within him. He gasped slightly, and his body shook. He pulled away, but Abigail held fast.

"You have the advantage of me." she said. "You know my name, but I do not know yours."

"It's David, David Austin." A slight but relaxed smile flashed across his face. Abigail released his hand, and he stared at it, gaping at the sensations he'd experienced.

"I need to speak with you," Abigail said.

"Sure. But tell me, what just happened? A minute ago I was ready to run screaming back to the car. Now it's like you're an old friend."

"It is the bond. When we touched, we shared each other's feelings and memories. It's a joining of sorts. You've become a little bit of me, and I a bit of you. You can't be afraid of yourself, can you?"

"I guess not." He didn't look convinced, but neither was he afraid.

"Where is this place, David?"

"I'm not surprised you don't recognize it. It's all grown over. It's your family's farm, or at least where it was. The house and everything are gone. The forest has taken over."

Abigail looked about, but there was nothing of her home left to see. "What year is this?"

"It's the year 2007, a hundred and thirty years since, since—since you died." David looked pained. "You don't mind me mentioning your death do you?"

"No, it does not concern me. That young girl died a long time ago. I'm someone different now." Abigail felt a pang of nostalgia. "Sorry, I hadn't thought that all I knew would disappear. My father was fond of quoting Ecclesiastes, 'All is vanity. One generation passeth away, and another generation cometh, but the earth goes on forever.'" He had been prophetic on this point if nothing else.

"I have a sense that your father was a religious man, but not a very happy one. I don't know why I know this, but I do."

"When our souls bonded, we shared thoughts, memories, and emotions. You felt the exchange between us."

"I did. I think I did. Maybe? It's as though I've lived your life. I remember your house. It was right over there, wasn't it? And your room with the books, Dickens, I think." David stared at Abigail as the extent of their bond became clear.

"This dress you're wearing. It's the one you wore in the photograph. You were going to wear it to a dance. Am I right?"

"Yes. It was a benefit to raise money for the GAR hall. I was very excited to go. Mother knew how much I loved this dress. I suppose that's why she buried me in it."

"Well, the GAR hall is still there. Looks a bit rundown now. I drove by it today."

"And David, I also know you in the same way. I have memories of your childhood, of you playing a game called football, of your work as a carpenter, and of your wife, Sarah." Abigail also had memories she avoided. The memories a husband has of his wife. She pushed those memories aside lest they should embarrass her further.

"I feel like I'm standing naked in front you, but I guess it's fair. I remember things about you I probably shouldn't." David glanced up.

She returned David's slightly embarrassed smile.

"Abigail, what is it like on the other side? I've never believed in anything after death. I think I need to change that opinion."

"You should." Abigail enjoyed David's casual manner. "The place where I awoke is called Gehenna. It is a terrible place filled with lost souls and demons, ruled by an evil queen named Lilith. The other place, where I came from today, is called Arcadia. It is the opposite of Gehenna, a wonderful place filled with beautiful souls."

"Why did you wake up in—Gehenna, was it? I don't sense you're a bad person, just the opposite, in fact."

"I was sent there for a purpose, a very important purpose. A purpose we share, and that neither of us can do alone." David's brow furrowed. "You have something, a small card—you were looking at it when I arrived."

"I do. It's a picture of you taken after you'd died. I found it in a flea market, and it led me to your father's Bible and a letter that I think was written by your mother. See, this is the picture."

David held the photo out for her to see. Abigail recognized herself, dead, posed between her grieving mother and stoic father. Her body looked like a husk, not really her at all. But seeing her mother's grief etched on her face made Abigail's heart ache for her all the more. She grieved for the bleak days that followed for her mother, and the lonely death she must have experienced.

"This picture has trapped me, anchored my soul in Gehenna, which is where I must be for now."

The grim memory of Gehenna settled on her once more.

"David, you must take care of this picture. If it is destroyed, my soul will be released."

"Released from Gehenna, that sounds like a good thing. Why do you need to stay there?"

She looked back at David in the fading light and hoped he would believe what she was about to tell him. "I think you know why I've come. You learned it when we touched didn't you?"

"Maybe. Something is wrong. There is a truly evil person, someone who kills children." David looked at her, horrified, as her memories rose in his mind. "That's terrible," he said. "You think this person is going to do something bad, something horrible, and you want my help in stopping him, or is it them?" His eyes went wide and his jaw dropped. Abigail saw that he understood the enormity of the evil they faced. He experienced the same fear and uncertainty she had when Ehyeh told her of the quest.

"Yes, David, it is all true. You know it is because you have my memories. I have little time left. I need to return to Arcadia in a few moments. There is a great evil coming, and I need your help to defeat it. The forces of evil from the spirit realm, aided by some among the living, are plotting to destroy all human life. Their plan is underway, and coming to fruition soon. You and I must stop them. The fate of the world relies on you and me."

David eyes darted about. Abigail sensed him starting to pull away. She imagined that seeing a ghost at night who asked him to save the world was a lot to take in.

"David, I know what I am telling you is fantastic, overwhelming to comprehend, but you know I'm telling you the truth. You've seen it through my eyes."

"The fate of the world rests with me?" There was panic in his voice. She gripped his hand tighter so that he wouldn't pull away. "Why do you think I can help you? I'm just a dumb jock who flunked out of college, I make kitchen cabinets. I'm no fighter. I can't defeat the master of all evil."

"I need you to find something, an ancient bronze chalice. It holds the soul of the Evil One. Search the memories that came from me. You can see it in the vision of Astarte. You must find it and destroy it."

"Okay, so no problem, easy-peasy. Where is this chalice?" David said with a half-smile and rolling his eyes.

"I don't know. It is hidden. It was last seen five

thousand years ago in a temple dedicated to Moloch near Jerusalem."

David backed away, looking about the clearing as though seeking a place to flee. "What? Let me get this straight. Here I am, standing in the woods at dusk, taking to a teenage girl who died over a hundred years ago, who is asking me to put my life on hold, fly off to the Middle East, and find a bronze cup that you can't even tell me where it is, so that I can defeat the evil master of the universe. Have I got this right? What's next, werewolves and hobbits?" His voice cracked between gasps of air.

Abigail had no idea what werewolves and hobbits were, but it was clear that she'd asked for more than he was ready to give. Abigail stood beside him and took both his hands, looking into his eyes. "David, I came back from the dead to find you because you are the only person who can fulfill this quest. It is a monumental task, and one that is not without danger, but one I know you can do. The fate of the world rests with us."

David backed away.

"Abigail, it's a lot to ask, it's too much to ask, way too much." He waved a hand in the air. "I'm no soldier. I wouldn't know where to begin. I'm a small town guy. I've hardly ever been out of New England, never mind leaving the country." He paused and looked at the ground. "And it's not a good time. I have a wife, a business to run that's starting to take off. I can't throw it all away just because you ask."

Abigail felt the bridge start to weaken. "David, my time is nearly over." Her view of David standing in the woods wavered.

"I'm pleading with you, David. Find the chalice, destroy it. Please help me."

With those last words, the bridge to the land of the living vanished, and Abigail stood once more on the broad lawn in front of Ehyeh's hut. Michael's wings rustled as they folded onto his back.

As Ehyeh said, touching David had sealed their bond. Abigail felt a tether, an unbreakable gossamer thread, spanning the realms of the living and the dead. She was exhausted. She turned to Michael. "He's scared. I'm not sure he will help us."

"He has the will to succeed. There are others who will help him. Together they will find the chalice." said Michael. The scent of the nearby kiskana tree filled the air. The souls of Arcadia walked away in silence.

Ehyeh sat alone in the clearing under the stars. She stared into the flames rising from the stone pyramid, deep in thought.

Astarte, I am sorry I caused your death by tearing you away from your peaceful rest in the land of the living. The Evil One has moved quickly, and we could not wait. I am sorry I kept you from learning your true nature. If you had, the Evil One would have discovered you, and all would be lost. I am sorry I must hide Ranger's true identity. I feel your longing for him.

You have sacrificed much over the millennia. Before the game is over, I must ask you for the greatest sacrifice of all.

First Steps

"Sometimes, reaching out and taking someone's hand is the beginning of a journey. At other times, it is allowing another to take yours."
- Vera Nazarian

The house was dark when David pulled into the driveway. He sat transfixed in the silent car. He'd been on autopilot during the drive home, lost in a jumble of conflicting thoughts, trying—and failing—to make sense of the night's experiences. If a cop had stopped him, he would have been arrested, locked up as some raving, delusional lunatic, unable to form a coherent thought.

Part of him refused to believe that the girl in the photograph had appeared out of the darkness, held his hand, spoken with him, and then vanished, leaving him alone in the forest beside her grave. David felt like a character in a Stephen King novel.

For years, beginning with the nuns in Catholic confirmation class, David's view of religion and spiritual matters had been on a steady decline to the point where he was sure that death was the end of the line. His grandmother had been fond of quoting Rabelais, "I go to seek the great perhaps." That summed up his outlook. He didn't believe, but was willing to be surprised.

Abigail existed somewhere, in some other dimension, time, or place, and, from what she implied, he could expect to see her again. She had told David he could summon her. The thought itself, summoning the dead, scared him. Sarah would freak out if he materialized Abigail in their living room.

What terrified him most of all was what she'd asked him to undertake—a worldwide trek to find and destroy an ancient chalice that held the soul of the devil. Satan would be royally pissed if David destroyed his chalice. No, there was no way he could get his head around this idea. Doing what Abigail asked was beyond him. He didn't believe he was strong enough, smart enough, or brave enough.

Louie licked his ear, interrupting David's swirling thoughts. Holding the tattered box that contained the Johnson family Bible, David waited outside while the boys took their time going about their business. Once in the house, David put the photograph in the Bible alongside the letter, and placed the whole business in the hall closet under the pile of winter hats and gloves.

David vowed not to think about Abigail. Ever since he'd stumbled across her picture, his life was slowly being consumed by her. Now she pulled him all the way in, taking David farther than he was ready to go. He had to get her out of his mind, out of his life. David decided to take the Bible and the picture to Burt at the Kennebec Historical Society on his next free day. Burt would love to add them to his dead person picture collection. Let Burt save the world; he had a life to live. David belted down a double shot of Maker's Mark whiskey and went to bed.

Thanks to the bourbon and, undoubtedly, exhaustion from the most remarkable experience of his life, David slept through the night and only awoke when Sarah stepped out of the shower.

"Hey, you're awake. So, how was your ghost hunting? Did you get it out of your system?"

David sat up in bed. Sarah was a beautiful woman, perfectly proportioned, and seeing her wet from the shower filled him with desire.

"Well, I don't want to hear 'I told you so,' but it was a bust, a dead end. The woman in the nursing home had nothing for me. She barely knew her own name. Why don't you come over here and I'll tell you about it."

Sarah stood beside the bed, wet, naked, and beautiful. She noticed the lustful effect she was having on David, and got back into bed. After a blissful interlude, and after the glow faded, Sarah asked, "So all you learned was the name of the girl in the picture, but nothing else about her?"

"That's right. The family had lived in China. She died at nineteen of scarlet fever, but that's all I could find out. The old lady in the nursing home, Ethel Nadeau, never heard of the family and couldn't tell me anything more. I think I upset her by asking her questions, so I only stayed a minute." David lied. He was embarrassed at being caught searching for Abigail's grave, and he couldn't tell Sarah about meeting Abigail because her request scared the peanuts out of him.

"Well, sorry you didn't learn more, but maybe now you can get rid of that sad photograph. It gives me the creeps when I see it." Sarah twirled David's hair in her fingers.

"I'm going to give it to this guy at the Kennebec Historical Society. He's got a whole collection of dead people pictures. Maybe you'd like to see them?" David lied again, despite it all; he had no intention of letting go of the picture, he couldn't

"Yah, right." Sarah hit him with her pillow. "One's enough, thank you. I'm sure I wouldn't sleep for a week if I saw a whole collection of creepy, dead people." She hopped out of bed to finish drying her hair.

'I've got a ten o'clock lecture on Mesopotamian deities. I need to read through my notes once more before class. It's the first time I'm giving this lecture."

Sarah peered at David from the bathroom, hair dryer in hand. "You know, I've got that sabbatical coming up and I thought of doing research on the subject. Might mean some travel if I can get a grant."

"I'm sure I'll be too busy to go."

"You'd be bored out of your skull anyway. I'll be crawling around dusty museums for days, not much fun."

Sarah was right. The work of an ancient history professor bored David to tears, but it fascinated her.

A month passed since David's encounter with Abigail. He'd devoted fourteen hours a day to finishing the McCaskeys' kitchen. Work was a much needed diversion, something to focus on other than his meeting in the woods. He tried not to think about Abigail. Every time she surfaced, he concentrated on his work and drove her from his consciousness. The struggle began to pay off. David thought about her less every day and had begun to believe that she would not return. He planned on delivering the Johnsons' Bible and its contents to Burt, and then the entire supernatural mess would be out of his life, but there was always a reason he couldn't find the time.

David's attention to his work had another benefit. The McCaskeys were very pleased and suggested having a friend from a magazine do a story on their renovations, and that meant great PR for him. A number of other inquiries about new kitchens came as well. Business was looking up, but that was about to change.

The semester had come to an end, and Sarah had time off before committing to a sabbatical project. It hadn't occurred to David what that meant. It meant OCD spring cleaning, emptying the hall closet, and organizing the jumble of winter hats and gloves.

When he came home, Sarah sat at the dining room table, with the Bible open and reading the letter. The shit is going to hit the fan now, he thought standing beside her.

Sarah didn't look up from the letter. "I'm really pissed. You told me you'd gotten rid of the dead girl's picture. What's with this Bible? And this letter? You've got some explaining to do."

"You found it, huh? I've been heads down with work and hadn't had time to take everything back to Bert."

"I can't get over the contents of this letter. I've been reading it over and over for an hour." Sarah looked up. "I need the whole story this time, the truth, from the top." She glanced back to the contents on the table. "I want to hear everything, every tiny detail, lots of details, and no more B.S. Okay?"

David sat down. "Okay, but you're not going to believe it. I didn't tell you the truth, because I'd trouble believing it myself. I'm still not sure I want to."

"Wait a minute. I think this story needs a couple of drinks." Sarah's new hobby was craft cocktails. She went to the kitchen and returned shortly with two sidecars in martini glasses. She sat on the couch with her legs tucked beneath her and her cocktail in hand. "Okay, buster, let's hear it. All of it."

Over the next hour, and with the help of an additional sidecar, David told Sarah about the entire remarkable day, beginning with the stops in Biddeford and Augusta, about Burt's help, about Carol in China, the stunning visit with Ethel, and the climactic meeting with Abigail. As he related the events to Sarah, David realized that he hadn't erased Abigail from his mind. She was still there, now stronger with the retelling. Sarah, for her part, didn't say a word, no reaction whatsoever, just thoughtful attention.

When he finished, David drank the last sip of his cocktail and waited.

"Wow. That's quite a story. I halfway believe you. The fact that the Nadeau family held onto this Bible all that time is fascinating, spooky really, waiting for someone—you, apparently—to come ask for it. And I don't know what to think about you talking to a dead girl in the forest. It's too fantastic to believe. If it was anyone else, I would say it's time for a padded room and antipsychotic drugs."

Sarah looked at David, and he wondered if she contemplated getting him a reservation at the funny farm and a prescription.

"Save the world? Really?" she asked. "That's so out there. Did you meet Rod Serling too? Are you sure you didn't dream this?"

"Sarah, I held Abigail's hand. It was warm and firm, just as real as yours. I can still feel her to this day. I gotta tell you, the whole business scares the crap out of me. I can't believe I'm mixed up in a galactic supernatural power play. I've tried to ignore this since it happened, hoping it would just go away, but it won't, and I don't know what to do." There was a hint of desperation in his voice.

Sarah gave him a long look. "I know. It was a very real experience for you. It's upsetting. I'm not sure what to do either, or how to help you." Sarah rubbed the back of her neck for a while and thought. "This letter gets me. I've read it over and over again. The odd thing is, I really feel like it's addressed to me. It mentions the state and the road I grew up on, which makes no sense at all." Sarah's voice trailed off.

"I knew you grew up in Missouri, but the name of the road?

"Yes, right here it says, *'in Missouri and played on Mount Olive.'* Well, our house was on Mount Olive Road. How's that for a coincidence? When I read it, my first thought was that someone was trying to get my attention, and the hairs on David's neck stood up."

"God, how much weirder can this get? What about the rest of the letter? It doesn't make much sense to me." he said.

"You're right. Something weird was going on with whoever wrote the letter. It's not coherent, not a letter you would ever write to anyone. It's a collection of thoughts strung together. Look at this part." Sarah pointed with her finger.

"'I fear the story of Moloch from Leviticus,'" She read. "Moloch is mentioned in Leviticus in the Bible. The story of Moloch is drawn from Baal, a Samarian demon from the Mesopotamian_religions. Moloch was a particularly nasty guy, known for child sacrifice. The Canaanites worshiped him, and built a temple with a giant statue of him in the desert of Canaan. He was always depicted with the head of a horned bull. The temple was destroyed when the early Hebrew tribes converted to monotheism, due primarily to the influence of the Zoroastrians.

"Then there is this last mention of the Amorites. The history of the Amorites was first recorded on cuneiform tablets in 2400 BC. Hammurabi, the Amorite king of Babylon, wrote the first set of recorded law known, the Code of Hammurabi."

David loved listening to Sarah when she was in her full professor mode, connecting the inferences in the letter to historical facts.

"The Samarian gods were eventually supplanted by Zoroastrian monotheism. Many of the ancient Hebrew and Christian Bible stories were borrowed from the Zoroastrians. The story of Adam and Eve in the Garden of Eden was originally a Zoroastrian creation story. The name Eden came from the Samarian word Erida, the name of a region between the Tigris and the Euphrates rivers in Mesopotamia in what is now Iraq. It was known for lush vegetation and kiskana trees, which some researchers think is the tree of knowledge mentioned in Genesis. And, if you also consider this area was the Fertile Crescent, where the basis of agrarian society began, then this region is really the birthplace of our modern civilization, a hotbed of religions and culture."

Sarah had been on a tear and caught herself. She smiled. "Sorry, I've got a head full of this stuff from preparing my lectures."

"I'll have to come and sit through some of your lectures, interesting stuff."

"What do you think of this passage?" David pointed to the letter and read, "*I think of her walking in the fields just over the hill, out of sight but still present. I know in my heart that Abigail still lives.*'"

"Don't know," said Sarah pausing to think.

"Out of sight but still present," David said. "I'll tell you what I think. Whoever wrote this wanted to say that Abigail is still alive, in some other form and in some other place, close but not seen." David already knew this to be true, but he needed Sarah to believe as well.

Sarah went quiet, staring at the letter. "You're scaring me again. The scholar in me says this is all nonsense, mishegas, but then a small voice in the back of his head tells me there is something to this."

Abe scratched at the back door. David welcomed the opportunity to take the boys out and clear his head. When he came back, Sarah stared at the wall lost in thought. He sat next to her and held her hand.

"What do you want to do?" he asked.

Sarah shifted her position, moving her feet to the floor.

"Hey, didn't you say you could summon her,

summon Abigail. Let's do that. If this is real, then let's see the proof." Sarah slapped David on the knee.

"She did say that I could. Are you sure you're up for this?" He was shocked by Sarah's sudden willingness to dive into the deep end of the spooky pool.

"If this is real then I want to know now. If not, I'm taking the whole mess to Burt myself in the morning."

Sarah wasn't much for letting things sit. If something piqued her intellect, she was a bulldog, not resting till she had her answers.

"Okay, let me get the photograph." David retrieved the photo from the inside cover of the Bible.

"How you do it? Do we have to light some candles or something?" Sarah smirked.

He smiled at Sarah. "I'm new at this summoning the dead thing, okay? Let me think for a minute. All I know is when she appeared before, I was holding the photograph, stroking it, and thinking of her. Then, there she was walking toward me."

"Okay, big guy, let's see how good you are at conjuring."

"Alright, here goes." David took the photograph and sat beside her on the couch. Holding it as he had before, David ran his finger along the top and thought of Abigail. He imagined her face, her touch, her life as a minute ticked by. The world grew still and quiet again. Abe and Louie circled and lay on the floor. Sarah shivered as a chill passed through her.

A figure walked out of the darkened kitchen and stood in front of them. Sarah crushed David's hand. It was Abigail in her white dress. Sarah's eyes darted between Abigail and the photograph. Nobody spoke.

Abigail extended her hand to David with a smile. He took it and the familiar warm energy flow up his arm, filling him with her strength and experiences, and reinforcing the psychic intimacy between them.

The touch lasted only an instant, but David sensed that she was different now. She was more confident, no longer a simple country girl. Abigail had grown, and seemed older than before. "Abigail, this is Sarah, my wife. She wanted to meet you."

Sealing the Bond

"Together we shared a bond not even death would violate."
– Dee Remy

Panya and Abigail returned to Gehenna as they'd left, with the sentinels showing the way. Abigail paused when the castle's dark, foreboding structure emerged from the swirling gray mists. She dreaded returning, both because of what awaited her, and for what she feared most—being unprepared, unsure of how to react, being too easily tricked, too easily the victim of cunning and deceit.

"Are you scared returning to Gehenna?" she asked Panya, hoping to commiserate.

"No, Panya not afraid. Panya has been in the castle for a long time. The people in the court only look to the queen, and how they can become like her. They never look down to the lowly page."

Abigail smiled. "So you're unseen even when you're not bending time; being insignificant makes you invisible as well." Panya giggled, enjoying his ability to fool the mighty within Gehenna.

Abigail looked up once more at the partially visible castle. "Panya, I wish I could be like you, disguised by my insignificance, but I can't. I must join the fray of those trying to get close to the queen. This will not be an easy thing to do."

"Ehyeh thinks you are strong, very strong, so Panya does too." Panya smiled at her and squeezed her hand.

Abigail appreciated his reassurance though it seemed a small comfort. She took hold of his shoulder, cloaking herself in Panya's invisibility, and continued towards the black edifice ahead.

They entered the castle town and wove their way through the crowd of residents frozen in time. Jacob Farrington stood outside of Philberta's house where she'd seen him before.

"Can you wait for me? I need to speak to that man dressed as a soldier."

"Panya can wait." Abigail released her grip, time resumed, and the crowd returned to motion. Panya waited beside the wall.

She went to Jacob. "Jacob, it's me. Abigail." Jacob stared straight ahead. He was still locked in the emptiness from being ravaged in the chaos between realms. Abigail desperately wanted to reach him, to uncover whatever, if anything remained.

When Abigail bonded with David, her consciousness mingled with his. She wondered if such a thing was possible with Jacob. Could she recover what remained within him? She took his hand and let her energy begin to flow into him. With David, she'd immediately experienced his thoughts and memories. Jacob was an empty shell devoid of thoughts and memories. She let him see her memories of their childhood together. She showed him her remembrance of him marching past Mr. Small's store on his way to the muster in Portland. Abigail's memories filled the void within him. His soul absorbed them like water in a dry sponge.

Within Jacob she sensed remnants of who he was like faded images and distant echoes. Abigail pulled at these, trying to bring them into focus. She strained to hear the echoes. These images and echoes resonated within her, bringing to life ancient memories that had lain dormant within her. She saw them standing together on a stone plaza looking out on a lush garden and a city beyond. The city was called Byblos. Jacob was not his name. It was Tammuz. They were lovers. Abigail sensed warmth and tenderness from him, for him. She also felt an impending loss. Events were pulling them apart. She didn't know why or when, only that their duty commanded them to take separate paths.

There were other dim visions of them in other places and times. They were faded beyond recognition, but each hinted at a long history together. Abigail tried to bring more into focus, but she could not. Abigail sensed they'd shared many lifetimes together, but only shadows remained.

She let go of Jacob's hand. He turned and looked directly at her. For the first time, his eyes were not empty.

"What is your name?" he asked in a whisper.

"It's Abigail."

"No it's not. You have a different name, an older name. A name that is lost to me, but I know I once called you beloved."

"Your name is Tammuz. And in some distant past, I also called you beloved." The name came naturally to her lips.

"Yes, I am Tammuz. I've known you since the world was young, but so much is lost, so much has been sacrificed. I would grieve, but I know not what was lost. I can only ache at the void that exists." He placed a hand on her shoulder.

"Thank you for restoring some part of me. I was drifting in a void, empty, without thought, without words. It was like death, and you have restored a sliver of my life. I pray that Ehyeh will restore us both completely."

"Do you know Ehyeh?" Abigail asked.

"I know her through you, through your memories, and I sense I've seen her before. I know our loss came in service to her. That we gave up all we had, willingly, because she asked."

He was right. All that was precious between them had not been taken. They had given it freely, a sacrifice to a greater cause. What had they been called to do that required such an offering?

"Tammuz, I have to go. I need to return to the castle before I am missed."

"I know. This is not our time, but I pray that our time will come again, that we may find what has been lost." Tammuz turned and walked away.

In attempting to restore Jacob, Abigail found remnants of her lost lifetimes, of a lover, and for the first time she saw an immense void within herself. She could only guess at the enormity of what she'd sacrificed.

"Come, Panya. We need to return me to the castle." Panya nodded, his face mirroring the loss Abigail felt.

Panya left her locked in her room as though she'd never left. The metal clank of the bolt signaled the success of their excursion, not the imprisonment she'd experienced before. And though she'd not tried, Abigail believed the lock could be easily overcome using her growing ability as a maker.

Abigail rested in her mother's chair. Her head spun from the four realities she'd experienced: Maine, Gehenna, Arcadia, and Ehyeh's forest clearing. What was real? Were they all different illusions or different realities? Did it matter? Maybe not. Perhaps each experience was only another scene in one gigantic play.

Ehyeh came foremost in her thoughts. Abigail knew that she no longer stood alone. Their touch had sealed David and her together. Ehyeh had told her the bond would grow stronger. He was never out of her presence. If she listened, she could almost hear his thoughts like someone speaking in the next room, a murmur with only a few words understood. Abigail wondered if David also heard her thoughts. How much closer would the bond bring them?

As she thought about the answers to these questions, the stillness she'd experienced when she crossed over to the realm of the living before engulfed her anew. She was being summoned again, taken over by the irresistible pull. The oval of light appeared in front of her, filled with clearing mist which revealed a room. Steeling her nerve, Abigail stepped though the circle and was struck by the sudden chill marking the transit between realms. She entered the land of the living once more.

Abigail was in a dark room, maybe a kitchen, but its contents were unfamiliar. Light came from the next room. David must be there. He was the only person who could summon her. She'd just seen him a short time ago when they'd met beside her grave, but as Philberta had told her; time was not constant across realms. She had no idea how much time had passed for David. It might have been a day, a month, or years.

Abigail entered the other room and saw David sitting on a couch holding hands with a woman. She looked shocked, frightened as Abigail approached. Abigail reached out to David, anxious to touch him again, to renew their bond. When he took her hand the link between them surge once more. His thoughts and feelings flooded her like a wave. Seeing David's life with his wife made the longing for Jacob, the man she'd once known as Tammuz, rise within her.

David released her hand which brought Abigail back to the moment. "Abigail, this is Sarah, my wife. She wanted to meet you."

"Pleased to meet you, Sarah. I have but a moment

here. All that I told David is true. I need David's help to defeat the Evil One. I cannot do it without him. All life on Earth is threatened."

Before Sarah could speak, the dog she'd seen in the woods came and sat beside her. Abigail reached down and scratched his ear as she'd done before, and like before, he thumped his rear paw on the floor, making her smile. The bridge started to fade. In the last instant, Abigail looked at Sarah. "Help me." She had no idea if Sarah heard her.

The bridge dissolved, and Abigail stood once more in the castle room drained of energy. She was glad to have met David's wife, and, while the bond didn't extend to her, Abigail knew through her bond with David that he relied on her determination and intellect. David didn't believe he was capable of succeeding on his own. She'd said nothing during their brief meeting, but after she'd scratched the dog's ear, Abigail noticed a hint of a smile on Sarah's face. She hoped that seeing her, knowing she was real, had been enough.

Crossing over unaided left her drained, weary beyond measure. She dragged herself slowly to the balcony to look out on the town and replenish her strength. The presence of the crowds drew Abigail like a starving person to food. *What an odd sensation – to draw energy from the wandering souls in the town below, feeding on them like a parasite.* Not that the souls below seemed to notice. From her vantage point, they swirled like a current in a river.

As before, energy flowed to her, this time a torrent, reminding Abigail of the spring snow melt in Maine cascading down the river beside Weeks' Mill. She savored the sensation as her body rippled with new energy, filling her, renewing her strength. Abigail's hands tingled. She touched her fingers together and pulled them apart, drawing a line of sparkling light between them. Abigail was becoming comfortable in her new form, her emerging abilities, and with them, a growing confidence. She was becoming the mistress of her fate. She liked it.

Distant Lands

"I see a distant land: it shines so clear.
Sometimes it seems so far, sometimes so near.
Come, join together, take the dusty road." –John Rutter

David awoke to the sound of a man's voice over a tinny loudspeaker. "Allahu Akbar. Ash-hadu al-la-ilaha illa llah." The long melodious call spread across old Jerusalem, echoing as though being answered by a distant voice. He thought about the flight from Boston, and the two crying babies who took turns disturbing his brief bouts of sleep. David hoped their parents were as tired as he was.

A month ago, He'd summoned Abigail from the dead. Her appearance, and the fact that Louie, their dog, had remembered her, convinced Sarah that his meeting in the woods was no hallucination. And now here he was, lying in bed with the bright Mediterranean sun filling the room.

His eyes said it was daytime, but his body told him it was bedtime. He felt like crap. This must be jet lag her thought. The cool, pine-scented breezes of the Maine woods were gone, replaced by the smell of dust and heat. Everything he saw and heard had a harsh, unfamiliar edge. He'd entered a friendless territory. Not knowing the language, the customs, or even how to read the street signs raised an unexpected level of anxiety. David took a deep breath as though readying to jump into an unknown sea.

Sarah stood on the balcony looking out over the city. He joined her, wrapping his arms around her waist from behind, and kissing her neck. Her skin was salty and her scent familiar, comforting. The buildings and walls of the old city were a few blocks away. The sandstone walls looked worn from centuries of use, filled with holes and weeds growing out of crevasses. They cast long shadows in the late afternoon sun. A line of pine trees stood before the ancient city walls, appearing out of place, too new and too green. Summer heat radiated from the buildings, and the parched air assaulted his skin. David's eyes squinted from the reflected sunlight, reminding him he'd forgotten his sunglasses. From unseen streets, he heard the traffic sounds, and, in the far distance, high-rise buildings wavered in the late day heat. The ancient city, surrounded by the modern world, appeared defiant against the encroachment.

Sarah pointed to a large golden dome. "Did you hear the muezzin calling the azan? It's the Muslim call to prayer. His song calls the faithful to prayer five times a day. And see over there, in the distance? That's the Dome of the Rock. Muslims believe that is where the Prophet Mohammed ascended into heaven astride the winged horse given to him by the Angel Gabriel. Inside is the Foundation Rock that the Jews believe was where Abraham prepared to sacrifice Isaac."

Sarah placed her hands over his and squeezed tighter.

"And you remember *Raiders of the Lost Ark*?"

"Yah, should I have brought my Stetson and bullwhip?"

"I hope we won't need them," Sarah said laughing. "Underneath the Foundation Rock are caverns known as the Well of Souls. The Jews believe that King Solomon kept the Ark of the Covenant hidden in those caves. An Islamic legend says you can hear the voices of the dead whispering in the caves as they wait for Judgment Day. They've been sealed for centuries. No one living today has ever been in those caves.

"It knocks me over. This is the crossroads of the world. Roman soldiers walked on these streets. Sultans and crusaders fought here. This place is like some spiritual gravity well drawing all the world's religions into conflict. Depending on whose interpretation you believe, the Battle of Armageddon will happen to the south of here in the valley of Jehoshaphat, where God will come down from heaven and cast Satan into Gehenna."

Where had he heard the name Gehenna before?

Sarah was excited. The scholar in her and the opportunity for firsthand study had her pumped. David had a fleeting moment of panic as Jerusalem appeared hostile, like something sinister was hidden there. Sarah's mention of Armageddon didn't help matters.

"Is everything okay? You looked kind'a strange," Sarah inquired, touching his face.

"I'm good. It's so different from anything I've ever seen. My brain is going a mile a minute trying to take it all in." David kept his fears to himself for the time being.

"We've got to get you out of town more, though I have to admit, this is a big change from Portland, Maine."

"So when is our appointment?"

"It's at ten with the director of the Rockefeller Archeological Museum, Robin Kanarek. I emailed her my research proposal before we left. They have an example of a chalice from that age, and they can help us with the Temple of Moloch."

"I have a vague memory of the chalice from Abigail. It was from a long time ago and not very clear. Do you suppose you would ever recognize it?" David asked.

"Good question. We have no idea where it is now. I doubt that it is displayed in a museum, waiting for us to come check it out like some library book. If it is as important as Abigail says it is, I suspect it's hidden and heavily guarded."

Sarah's casual statement unnerved David once more. He immediately imagined burly men in black body armor holding assault weapons, standing in front of a stainless steel vault with laser beams sweeping the floor. *That's way too James Bond*, he thought. He forced the image from his mind, laughing at himself.

It had been easy to suppress the sense of lurking danger when they were planning their trip. Now the danger in Jerusalem seemed closer, no longer abstract but a real possibility. Home moved another thousand miles away.

At sundown, Sarah and David walked to old Jerusalem through the Zion Gate. The rounded sandstone archway was worn and darkened from two thousand years of hands touching it. An eight-pointed star mosaic decorated the walkway in front. The last of the daytime's heat radiated from the high stone wall as they passed through the gate leading to the Jewish quarter. Only the electrical wires strung between buildings reminded them that this was still the 21st century.

They ate falafel sandwiches from a market stall and continued to walk the old city till fatigue and sensory overload got the better of them. They returned to the hotel and collapsed.

They rose at four in the morning wide awake and sat on their balcony watching the sun rise over Jerusalem. David sipped unsatisfying coffee made with the small coffeemaker in the room, and listened to the city as it awoke.

Sarah and David arrived at the museum ridiculously early, fresh faced and ready to begin their search. Sarah waved at the guard inside. He touched his watch and pointed to a sign written in Hebrew. His meaning was clear, they'd have to wait, so they sat on a bench under a solitary tree and waited for an hour and a half. At ten, the guard opened the doors and waved them in.

"I'm Dr. Austin. I have an appointment with Director Kanarek," Sarah said. The guard was unmoved by the excitement in her voice.

"Yes, she called and said she is going to be thirty minutes late. She suggested you tour the Bronze Age exhibits while you wait."

The guard handed them clip-on badges. "These are scholar passes. They will get you into the archives as well as all exhibits. Please wear them at all times. Shalom." He went back to reading his paper. Sarah and David walked briskly down the main corridor.

"Let's do as Kanarek suggested, and see what Bronze Age artifacts look like. I have only the vaguest idea of what we're looking for," said Sarah following the signs.

The Bronze Age exhibits were at first disappointing, barely filling one smallish room, but David was riveted by the first item he saw: a bronze bowl in its own display case in the center of the room, dramatically lit from above. The bowl was about six inches tall and eight inches wide with handles on each side. Simple line drawings of antelopes decorated its surface. The bowl dated from 3500 BCE. The bowl was unimpressive, crude even.

"We're looking for something like this." he looked at Sarah. The memories he had from Abigail were not clear, but he sensed he'd know the chalice when he saw it.

"Really? It's not the key to saving the world I might have expected? I thought it would have some jewels on it or something," she replied.

"But at least we have an idea of what we're looking for. I've always thought of a chalice as a kind of big goblet thing like what I saw at Mass. This is just a bowl."

"It's the size and the handles that classify it as a chalice, and the fact that it was ceremonial, not for everyday usage." Sarah's analytical nature reassured him. She always sounded like she knew what she was talking about, although he sometimes wondered if it was only that her BS was better than his.

David turned to look at a display case against the wall. "Sarah, what is this relief about? It looks kind of racy. The sign says ancient female demon, possibly Lilith. Ceramic, Early Bronze Age, possibly Neolithic."

"Well, it is very old, probably six to eight thousand years old. When it says Neolithic, that's what we scientific types call a SWAG, a scientific wild-ass guess." Sarah smiled, knowing it was the kind of joke David appreciated.

"See how she has exaggerated labia and breasts, and she has feet like a bird and horns on her head. She is definitely a female demon. The owls on either side of her were thought to be harbingers of evil. These effigies were meant to be sexually enticing to attract you male types. It's a good guess that this is an early representation of Lilith. She is considered the queen of the underworld, the ruler of all other demons."

"Sarah, I know I'm getting all supernatural on you again, but I think Abigail mentioned Lilith when we spoke."

"What did she say?"

"The memories are kind of a muddle, but she said that Lilith was the queen of Gehenna, the place where she was trapped."

Sarah raised an eyebrow. Her face turned serious as she looked back at the figure. "We should keep an eye out for this girl. I bet we're going to see more of her before this is over," she said with a hint of foreboding. David shared her feelings. Seeing the statue brought them a step closer to the unseen danger David sensed.

"Ah, I see you've found our Lilith. A very nice early

example," said a loud voice from behind. They pivoted to see an older woman walking briskly toward them, wearing spandex bike shorts and a bright yellow jersey with Hebrew letters across the chest. Her bicycle shoes clicked on the floor, echoing in the empty corridor. She looked like she was in her fifties with the physique of a thirty-year-old.

"You must be Dr. Austin, and your husband, I assume. Nice to meet you. I'm Dr. Kanarek, but please call me Robin. Everyone here in the archaeology community is so stuffy and proper all the time. I so miss the informality of the US." Robin shook hands with Sarah but didn't offer her hand to David.

"Please excuse me for being late. I'm training for a triathlon, and my bike route was blocked by a settler protest this morning. It's too blasted hot to train later in the day."

"Yes, I'm Dr. Austin and, yes, this is my husband, David. And please call me Sarah."

Robin smiled. "Let's go to my office, and we'll see what help we can be."

In Robin's office, her secretary served them small cups of black, sweet coffee. There were stacks of books and papers everywhere, and Robin's desk had only enough free space for her laptop. The room smelled of dust and old papers. The director still in her biking clothes and needing a shower, fit the surroundings perfectly.

"So, you've come all the way from Maine. Beautiful state. I spent some summers there at a girl's camp near Litchfield. I'm originally from New Jersey, a tenured professor of archeology at Rutgers. In 1981, I immigrated to Israel after a messy divorce. I was looking for a change when I saw a posting for the museum directorship, and, well, here I am."

"I thought I heard a touch of an accent, but I couldn't

place it," said Sarah.

"Yes, you can take the girl out of New Jersey but you can't take—you know the rest. So, you're here on sabbatical and you're interested in Moloch."

"Yes, as you know, my research title is "*The Cross Cultural Connections between Demon Mythology of the Amorites and Early Hebrew Cultures.* I am tracing the spread of demon mythology beginning with the Amorites, through its adoption by the early Hebrew cultures, and eventually on to its inclusion in Western culture. Moloch is woven into Western literature, Milton's *Paradise Lost* for example, or even a contemporary example like *Howl* by Alan Ginsburg. In many ways, Moloch is a pseudonym for Satan."

"An interesting research topic. You're brave to take on such a subject. Most academics would avoid it, as it can easily border on the occult, become sensationalized, and thus lose academic credibility. My advice is to not let the crazy people get wind of this, or you'll find yourself on the cover of the *Enquirer* in the supermarket checkout aisle. That wouldn't be good for your career."

"I take your point," said Sarah. "I hadn't considered such an outcome, and I'm sure your caution is warranted."

"I've a graduate student assigned to help you in your research; his name is Shlomo Halberstam. He's a brilliant researcher, one of the best I've ever known, but he comes with a lot of baggage, so let me explain."

Robin leaded forward resting her elbows on her desk.

"Shlomo is a man trapped between two worlds and is not comfortable in either. He is a Hasidic Jew, a direct descendant of the famous Rebbe, Shlomo Halberstam, his namesake. Halberstam was the founder of Bobover Hasidism, one of the more extreme sects. Men in this sect spend their lives strictly devoted to Torah study, and rarely venture outside of their community, never with goyim."

"Excuse me, goyim?" asked Sarah.

"Sorry, it's a Yiddish word which means any non-Jew. To the Bobovers, it can also include any non-orthodox Jews as well. The term implies a certain condescension." Robin smiled, perhaps to excuse having used the term in the presence of two goyim from Maine.

"Anyway, I'm not sure how it happened, but Shlomo read *Siddhartha* by Hesse and become obsessed with Hesse and Jung."

"I'm familiar with Hesse. I read *Siddhartha* when I was in high school."

"Shlomo's interest in Herman Hesse's writings led him to the works of Carl Jung. His concepts connect the spiritual and mythological archetypes across cultural boundaries. An archetype is Jung's term for a culturally recurring symbol, image, or theme.

"Anyway, his interest led him to an increasingly secular area of study. This, combined with his interest in German philosophers, led to a break with the Bobovers. Shlomo left the community to pursue a PhD in Archeology. I say a break, but it's actually much more serious. He's been shunned by his community, cast out if you will, excommunicated as the Christians say."

"He gave up everything, didn't he?" asked Sarah.

"Yes, he is a man alone, wandering in the wilderness between worlds."

Dr. Kanarek leaned forward. "I've told you all I know about Shlomo. I've known him for a year and he remains an enigma, the most private person I've ever known. At some level I feel sorry for him. He's in his fifties and has lost everything—his community, his family, his life in most respects. And he can be one arrogant, condescending SOB."

Robin went to the door and beckoned with her hand.

A tall, thin, almost gaunt man entered and stood just inside the door, looking as though he wanted an easy escape route. He had a long, angular face and a sparse beard with gray streaks at the edges. Curls from under a black velvet skull cap hung along the side of his face. He looked unhealthy, with pale skin which David attributed to years of study in a sunless room. Under his black vest, thin knotted strings hung down. His white cotton shirt was buttoned at the neck. His eyes shifted quickly between Sarah and David.

"Shlomo, this is Dr. Austin from the US. The researcher I mentioned to you."

Shlomo shook hands with David. "Shalom, Dr. Austin."

"Nice to meet you. I'm David Austin. This is Dr. Austin, my wife." David pointed with his free hand to Sarah.

Shlomo dropped David's hand and folded his arms behind his back. His eyes darted to Sarah and then focused on the director who wore a hint of a smile. Robin appeared to have set him up for this patriarchal faux pas. David surmised there was some tension between Dr. Kanarek and her student.

"Dr. Austin." Shlomo nodded his head.

"Shlomo, Dr. Austin will be here for several days. I gave you her proposal regarding demon mythology and cultural connections with Moloch. This topic should be right up your alley."

"Yes, Dr. Kanarek. I have been gathering materials for several days and have laid out some exhibits in the archives. We can begin if Dr. Austin is ready."

Poor Shlomo looked like a thirteen-year-old boy who'd gotten detention in middle school, and had to spend it with a girl. Sarah tried not to smirk.

"Excellent. Dr. Austin, I'll leave you in Mr. Halberstam's capable hands," said Dr. Kanarek.

"Dr. Austin, before we begin, a question for you if I might ask? I've read the research proposal you sent to Dr. Kanarek, and I'm curious. Why did you not state that your real interest is Moloch's chalice?" Shlomo's tone was matter of fact, as though asking about a trivial thing.

David's and Sarah's hearts jointly skipped a beat, panicked that their big secret, the quest to save the world, had been discovered. *Were we really that obvious?* Sarah wondered. Dr. Kanarek smiled at Shlomo and looked to Sarah, who shifted uncomfortably in her seat. Robin seemed to enjoy Shlomo's earlier discomfort. Now she enjoyed Sarah's unease from Shlomo's insightful question.

Dr. Kanarek rose from her chair, signaling the end of the meeting. "Let me know if you need anything else. I need to shower and change into more respectable attire. This isn't the Jersey Shore, after all."

The Pilgrim

"If I am not for myself, then who will be for me? And when I am for myself, then what am 'I?' And if not now, when?" – Hillel the Elder

They followed Shlomo to an unmarked door at the rear of the museum. Shlomo swiped his badge, and a rush of cool air struck them as they entered. The vast room was refreshingly dry like a fall day in Maine. The lights flickered on automatically as they passed rows of gray metal shelves littered with ceramic fragments, boxes, and bound documents.

Shlomo stopped at two big work tables with a sign hanging from the ceiling, *Halberstam.* One table was Shlomo's desk with his computer and orderly stacks of manila folders. A half-eaten sandwich in white paper lay beside his computer. David was glad to know that Shlomo had to eat like everyone else. Books and papers were spread out on the other table.

"So why do you think I have an interest in Moloch's chalice?" Sarah asked, raising her voice and leaning in, not the least bit intimidated by Shlomo's seniority.

Shlomo looked startled by Sarah's tone. For the first time, he met her eye and spoke to her directly. "As I said, I read your research proposal. It is an interesting, unusual thesis, and one that has a personal attraction to me. I am a student of religious themes and images that span cultures. What Carl Jung calls archetypes."

"Yes, Director Kanarek told me of your interest in Jung. I'm not that familiar with his works, but it sounds like an interesting synthesis, Jung's Archetypes and Jewish mysticism." Sarah's hostility began to fade, and she settled into her academic demeanor.

"The Torah and Kabbalah are rife with hidden symbols." Shlomo's voice went up a notch, betraying his interest though he remained outwardly stoical.

Shlomo leaned in ever so slightly but continued to avoid eye contact. "In Kabbalah, the hidden meanings are implied by the number of times a subject is mentioned or implied. So, when I read your research proposal, I noticed you mentioned the chalice three times. If something is mentioned once, it has no particular significance, twice, it is important, and if it is mentioned three times, it is the author's true interest.

"Thus, my supposition is that the chalice is your goal, the true purpose for your trip to Jerusalem. Your reaction to my assertion validated my belief. I don't know why you're interested in it, but I expect the reason will reveal itself."

Shlomo glanced briefly at Sarah, who confirmed his analysis by the mild surprise on her face. When Shlomo had been introduced as a graduate research assistant, Sarah had expected a fresh-faced, naive, academic gofer, someone who would sift through the stacks chasing down obscure references. Shlomo was something entirely different.

Sarah stared at Shlomo in silence, flipping a pencil between her fingers. She put the pencil down, placing it horizontally between her and Shlomo as though it were some type of dividing line.

"That is an insightful inference, Mr. Halberstam. Do you mind if I call you Shlomo? We Americans always gravitate to the familiar." Sarah continued to talk down to Shlomo. She was particularly sensitive to condescension from male colleagues. For Shlomo's part, he appeared entirely unaffected by Sarah's antipathy.

For reason he didn't understand, David liked Shlomo. If he'd gotten off a flying saucer from Mars, Shlomo could not have been more different than David, but in an odd way, he reminded him of men from Maine. Not the city types you meet around Portland, but the guys who live up past Bangor, the men who spend their lives farming or lumbering. They are their own men, unaffected by the homogenization of mass market culture. They form their own opinions, keep their own counsel, and care little for your opinion, even less if you offer it without being asked. David found him interesting. This was no shallow pond sitting in front of David; his waters ran deep. David wondered if he would ever know or understand him.

"Thank you for asking. I am happy for you to address me in whatever fashion is comfortable for you. If you don't mind, for my part, I prefer to continue with a more formal salutation—Dr. Austin."

Sarah nodded. She and Shlomo both appeared comfortable with the emerging pecking order.

"Let's jump right into the research, shall we?" Sarah reached for her notebooks and laptop, creating a small flurry of activity.

"Yes," replied Shlomo, acknowledging Sarah's interest in moving on. "In your research statement, if I may paraphrase, you are interested in tracing the demon mythology beginning with the Bronze Age Assyrians and progressing through early Hebrew cultures and onto modern Western civilizations. Moloch is the specific focus of your research.

"Yes, that's correct. Moloch is a common thread that spans from 3500 BCE to the current day. By tracking his history, we can understand his cultural influences."

"Given your specific interest in a bronze chalice, I think you should tell me how this chalice figures in your research?"

"I am interested in how artifacts may have enabled

the dissemination and propagation of the Moloch mythos."

"That is an unusual concept. And why a chalice from the temple of Moloch? I have not seen it noted in the literature, nor in excavation inventories. Do you have a primary source confirming its existence?"

Sarah tensed, and leaned back in her chair. She could hardly tell Shlomo that her primary source had died over a hundred years ago and had recently materialized in their living room.

"I'm sorry. I found an obscure reference to the chalice in an historical account, but I don't have the citation with me at the moment."

Shlomo's eyes darted to Sarah's face, pausing like he was about to drill Sarah on the point. He seemed content to let Sarah's falsehood pass.

"Dr. Austin, I am a student of early Assyrian writing. It is both a personal interest of mine and the topic of my PhD thesis. The museum has the largest collection of Assyrian tablet fragments in the Middle East."

Sarah leaned in with her hands on the table.

"I searched for Moloch and various pseudonyms such as Baal, and for the words for temple and chalice, within common periods beginning with the early Bronze Age. There were several references to Moloch and temple from that period but no references to any type of chalice. So I broadened the search criteria to look for other types of containers. That proved interesting." Shlomo moved the first paper to face Sarah, and she bent low over the desk to study the pictures.

"These seven fragments are of the same age, composition, and shape, which increase the likelihood that they may have come from a single piece of writing. The first fragment says, 'In them we — set a tabernacle for Moloch —

offerings.' The blanks between the phrases are either lost or not correlated yet, but what is interesting is the use of the word 'tabernacle,' or at least that is how I translated it. It's a word that means temporary residence of the god. This may be what you are looking for."

"What do you think it means by 'Moloch's offering?'"

"Well, some fragments are missing, but we can make a reasonable assumption since this is in reference to Moloch. Moloch's temple was known for child sacrifice. This container may have had something to do with those sacrifices."

"That sounds gruesome. How long did that go on?" Sarah imagined such a scene and quickly drove the horrible image from her mind.

"I'm not sure. There is little known about the practices, but the temple did stand for a long time." Shlomo pointed to another page. "I found some additional fragments that may interest you. There is a moderate likelihood that these other fragments might also belong to the same piece of writing." He passed the second page to Sarah with more images of clay tablet pieces.

"Please, you'll have to translate again. My ancient Assyrian is not so good." Sarah's voice held a hint of sarcasm that Shlomo didn't seem to notice.

"Oh yes, my apologies. I read Assyrian text as one would read the newspaper. The first is the name of an Assyrian warrior goddess, Astarte. Very little is known about her. She shows up in occasional passages, always associated with some major event or battle. The second symbol is the word for destroyed."

Sarah pulled back from the table, still holding the paper. "What inference might you draw from these?"

"The Assyrians were polytheistic with over twenty-four hundred deities. The majority were minor gods. Astarte is special. She shows up consistently during moments of great conflict. Whenever there is a pivotal event, Astarte is there. She is what the Israeli Army calls a commando, a special warrior for the most difficult battles."

Shlomo leaned back. "You asked what I might infer, Dr. Austin. Because it is likely that these fragments came from the same tablet, the writing indicates that the temple of Moloch was destroyed by Astarte, a warrior goddess. The temple was destroyed in the mid-Bronze Age, probably during one of the internecine conflicts which were common in that period."

"It is very interesting that you made the inference and found a reference to Moloch's tabernacle. That is not a semantic connection I would have made. It does appear to confirm that there was an artifact which held the spirit or soul of Moloch." Sarah looked to Shlomo for confirmation. Shlomo had become the teacher, and Sarah was now his willing student.

"Yes. It is highly likely that there was a container, a chalice or tabernacle associated with Moloch's temple." Shlomo tapped his finger on the picture of the fragments.

"Now, the question before us is how do we track this artifact? Does it still exist? How would we identify it?" asked Sarah.

Shlomo became animated. He'd picked up the scent. David suspected that once he had it, he wouldn't let it go.

"There is little remaining intact from the late Bronze Age. However, Moloch's temple and anything in it would have been considered *umreyn*, unclean, and thus avoided by the early Hebrews. As in any unclean place, a devout Jew would have to perform a cleansing ritual upon returning home. Indeed, the site of Moloch's temple was a place where garbage was burned for several centuries. Given this, it is possible that any artifacts may have remained untouched for centuries."

"Interesting. Sounds like a long shot, but if I understand you, there may be some contemporary references to artifacts from that location."

Shlomo turned his laptop to face them. "So, I have the archeological report here. The apartment complex was built in 1971 during a period of rapid development after the Six-Day War. The archeological team excavated for six months prior to beginning construction. The site inventory lists very little, mostly broken pottery, as you might expect. There were remnants of a structure found, some columns and a foundation. There were inscriptions which verified the structure as Moloch's temple. The next part of the report details the four feet of burned vegetation covering the site."

"That's it? Nothing else? No other references to anything from Moloch's temple?" Sarah's voice held a touch of desperation. She looked deflated. There was nothing to go on, no artifacts from the site that we could track down. David could see by her expression that they were at a dead end. Maybe they were going home empty-handed.

"No, Dr. Austin, nothing. It is a very old site, and it was destroyed during a period of upheaval when many tribes and cultures were fighting over Jerusalem. This land has changed hands many times. It is clear from the site report that most of the temple's blocks were reused in other structures. Everything else was carried away. Metal of any kind was valuable, and artifacts may have been melted down. There appears to be nothing left."

David and Sarah were dejected, stymied on their first day. David's anxiety rose. He was driven to find the chalice but now he had no idea where to look or what to do next. He clenched his fists as he struggled to keep his emotions in check.

"Okay, Shlomo," Sarah said. Let's call it quits for the day. We need to regroup and think about what our next steps are. It seems like we've hit a brick wall."

"I agree, Dr. Austin. You may need to revise your thesis if there is no evidence confirming the existence of a chalice. It was an original thesis, an un-trodden path, if you will. I am sorry to see it end."

"Thank you Shlomo. I'm sorry too. Perhaps we should meet again tomorrow to wrap things up. Same time?"

Shlomo nodded, stood, and folded his hands behind him. "At ten tomorrow morning. Shalom, Dr. Austin, Mr. Austin." Shlomo's bony face showed no hint of disappointment.

Sarah and David walked silently back toward the hotel. The streets and shops in the old city were filled with tourists and merchants beckoning them to their stalls. They were oblivious to the cacophony, feeling despondent, lost in their thoughts.

"What are you thinking about, David?" Sarah asked as we entered the hotel lobby.

"I was thinking about Abigail, and how I didn't want to disappoint her. I don't know how, Sarah, but we've got to find the chalice."

"I know, I know, I wish I could see how. I don't know where to look. We've got no leads, no clues. I don't think the chalice was melted down, because Abigail believes it is still intact. It could be buried in the ground somewhere for all we know. I'd be lying if I didn't tell you that I don't think we're going to find it anytime soon. We were naive coming over here and thinking that in a hop, skip, and a jump, we'd find the chalice and be back home in time for the fall semester. What was I thinking, coming here so ill prepared?"

Sarah's pessimism was contagious. David's mind began to race through ever more desperate possibilities. Maybe he could go to other museums in the Middle East, searching for all the Bronze Age bowls. Sarah could go home and send money so he could keep looking. It all sounded impractical. He'd probably be taken hostage by some nutcase jihadist group and held for ransom. Sarah's pessimism was well founded. They needed a break, and soon.

At the hotel, they both showered, and Sarah took a nap. David sat beside her on the bed, wrapped in a towel, enjoying being clean and cool, but too keyed up to nap. He closed his eyes and thought of Abigail. The familiar stillness came over him, and David sensed Abigail was near at hand. *I'm worried that I would not be able to find the chalice. I'm worried that I'll fail at this task as I've failed at so many others in my life. I've grown used to failure, accepting it too easily, mostly because I am the only one it hurt. Now the stakes are much higher. Abigail, you're counting on me. The fate of the world might be in the balance.*

David heard Abigail's voice in his head as though she were speaking to him from a long corridor. *I'm worried that you've not made progress, but I'm more worried about your resolve. I know you doubt your ability to succeed. This is a hard fight that will take courage and sacrifice. You were chosen by Ehyeh because she believes you have the will to succeed. I believe you have the strength within you.* David felt Abigail's touch. *David, find the chalice and destroy it!*

"David, David, wake up." Sarah shook his shoulder.

"You fell asleep sitting up. It's getting late and I'm hungry. Let's get dressed and go to dinner," said Sarah as she started to pull her clothes on.

"Was I asleep? I had the strangest dream. I dreamt I was talking to Abigail." Sarah had gone to the bathroom to fix her hair and didn't hear David for which he was grateful. He wasn't in the mood to explain something new to Sarah. It wasn't a dream. He hadn't been asleep. He'd been talking with Abigail, *thinking with Abigail* was more liked it. What was strange was that He hadn't summoned her. And who was this Ehyeh that she spoke of?

They went to dinner at a family-run restaurant recommended by the hotel's night clerk. Sarah and David passed their meal making small talk, mostly speculation about how Abe and Louie were making out with the friends we'd left them with. Neither of them wanted to talk about the day's events, and the looming dead end they faced. On the walk back, Sarah stopped to purchase scarves as presents for friends back home. She was buying souvenirs, a sure sign she thought the search was over.

At the hotel, David asked for the room key and told the clerk how much they'd liked the restaurant.

"I'm glad. It is my uncle's restaurant. I will tell him you enjoyed it the next time I see him. And, oh yes, Dr. Austin, there is a message for you," the clerk added.

Sarah read it and grabbed David's arm. Her face brightened with enthusiasm despite her bleary eyes.

"David. It's from Shlomo. He says, 'There is another temple, artifacts listed. Will discuss in the morning.'"

The Trailhead

"I have been and still am a seeker, but I have ceased to question stars and books; I have begun to listen to the teaching my blood whispers to me." – Hermann Hesse

Shlomo unlocked the museum entrance at 9:30. The annoyed guard stood by the door. Flashing their badges did little to placate him, but he waved them through anyway.

"Shalom, Dr. Austin, Mr. Austin," said Shlomo. He wore the same clothes as yesterday. Sarah imagined his closet full of identical shirts and pants.

"Your message was both exciting and cryptic. What did you find?" Sarah' voice carried her excitement overcoming her professional reserve.

"I've collected some exhibits from my research last night. There are some intriguing connections, but the inferences that link them are thin. You will need to judge for yourself their relevance, since I'm still hypothesizing the true nature of your search."

The three proceeded briskly into the archives. Shlomo walked beside David, his hands folded behind his back with Sarah following behind. *Old habits are hard to kick*, David thought.

Shlomo took up his position beside his worktable. "After you left yesterday, I thought about your search. Dr. Austin, you strike me as an orderly and thoughtful person. I don't believe you'd come all the way to Jerusalem on a whim. You have some proof of the existence of Moloch's chalice which you have chosen not to share with me, but which, nonetheless, has convinced you. So I'll take it as a given that such a chalice exists. Where was it found, who took it, and where it is now are the pertinent questions."

Sarah eyed the carefully-arranged books and papers and then looked up at Shlomo, "Thank you for believing that David and I are not a pair of crackpots off on some bizarre search for lost occult souvenirs. I ask that you take it on faith that we have absolute proof of the chalice's existence. I can't tell you more at this time; maybe later, just not right now."

"Dr. Austin, faith is belief in the absence of proof. For the moment, I am agreeable to continue under this assumption."

Sarah shot David a *Thank God* glance.

Shlomo continued, "I believe my beginning assumption that Moloch's temple was *umreyn*, unclean, is correct. The early Hebrews and even the various invaders would have avoided the site. It is likely that any artifacts would have remained until excavated in the present day. Modern archeology methods are quite thorough, and significant artifacts would have been catalogued. So what does that leave us?"

He studied their faces. "That leaves us the nineteenth century, a period of time when European travel became common, but before the establishment of modern scientific methods."

"Why that period?" Sarah looked inquisitive.

"It was a period when wealthy Europeans came looking for souvenirs in the name of archeology," replied Shlomo without a hint of sarcasm. "After a little digging, I found the records of Johann Heinrich Westphal, a German tourist who traveled to Jerusalem in 1818. He apparently had some capacities."

Shlomo pointed to a book laid out on the table. "The map shown was drawn by Westphal, and is considered the first accurate map of old Jerusalem. And he kept a journal which was eventually published by the Detacher Palästina-

Verein, the German Society for the Exploration of Palestine, founded in 1877."

The couple from Maine listened closely, engrossed, as Shlomo peeled back the layers of antiquity as though he were reading today's paper.

Shlomo picked up the same dusty book and opened it to a marked page. "These are his notes. He spent a week at the temple of Moloch outside Jerusalem. He found a long list of items, all listed here, including several bronze bowls. All the artifacts were packed up and sent back to Germany. I've tried to search the Deutsch Museum in Munich where all artifacts from the now defunct society reside. It is impossible to identify which specific bronze bowls came from Moloch's temple. The early recordkeeping was too poor."

"Are we at a dead end again?" Sarah's voice betrayed the emotional whiplash she and David were feeling.

"Maybe yes, maybe no." Shlomo paused. For the first time, David thought that Shlomo was playing with them. "In Herr Westphal's notes, he mentions a trip to Ugarit on the Syrian coast to visit Baal's temple."

"Why do you think this temple is related to Moloch?" David asked. Sarah's face showed annoyance for his treading on her turf, but David's anxiety had got the better of him. He had to know that they weren't at a dead end.

"That's a good question. There has always been some confusion in early archeology between Baal and Moloch. The temple in Ugarit was founded by the Phoenicians. Herr Westphal was not a student of ancient Middle Eastern languages. He would have relied on local translators. These people, in turn, were simply translating the verbal folklore from the local populace."

"I see, then. It was all hearsay, folktales at best," noted Sarah.

"Yes, that's correct. Most significant is his description of the temple as a place of child sacrifice, Moloch's hallmark. I believe this was the first temple of Moloch established by Phoenician traders a century before the second temple was built closer to Jerusalem, after the first was destroyed. What I cannot connect are the fragments I showed you the other day to the first temple. I do not know if Astarte destroyed the first temple. There is no evidence."

"It would be nice to know how Astarte figures into the Moloch historical timeline, if at all," Sarah observed.

"Yes, I agree. The more we understand, the more we can make connections to other sources, and thus validate our—I mean your—theory, Dr. Austin. Now let me show you the most interesting item I found in the Jerusalem notes."

Shlomo laid open a different book and pointed to an entry. Sarah detected a hint of a smile on his face.

"'*Große Bronze Kessel, verziert, mit dem Symbol eines Stieres aus Ugarit,*'" Shlomo apparently read German flawlessly. Sarah wondered if he could translate as well.

"Shlomo, since neither David nor I read German, and evidently you do, would you mind translating?"

"Oh, yes, pardon. I learned German so I could read Hesse and Jung in the original language. It says, 'Large bronze cauldron, ornate, with symbol of a bull from Ugarit.'" Shlomo paused, gauging their expressions. "I think this is the artifact you're looking for. It is from a temple that we can logically infer was Moloch's original temple built by Phoenicians. It is ornamental, which implies it was used in a ceremonial setting, and it is decorated with the head of a bull, which is an icon for Moloch."

"It could be," said Sarah in a hushed tone. Her intellect struggled to contain her emotions.

Shlomo nodded. "As I said earlier, the connections are thin, but there are many of them. This artifact was never correctly documented as being from Moloch's temple, and it was carried away by this German tourist almost two hundred years ago, so it was hidden and remains hidden to this day. It's a very interesting situation." Shlomo stood back and clasped his hands behind his back.

"Neither I, nor any other researchers, would have identified the Phoenician temple as Moloch's temple. There was simply no evidence. Your focus on the chalice provides the connection via Westphal's notes." Shlomo flipped the book closed. "I am now more curious about your original source." Shlomo's voice sounded urgent, one of the few times he'd betrayed any emotion at all.

"We are not prepared to disclose that information as yet." Sarah was emphatic. David nodded in confirmation. They'd only spent a few days with Shlomo and knew little about him and, if possible, even less about his motivation. Until the couple from Maine learned more, he would have to remain in the dark.

"Shlomo, I am the one who began this search. I have the connection to the person who set us on this quest. We've only just met you, and you've been helpful beyond measure. Without you we'd be on our way home, already defeated, but, quite frankly, I, we, need to know you better before we can bring you into our full confidence. The stakes are phenomenally high, higher than you could imagine. We cannot risk failure." David surprised himself with his resolute declaration. He'd tapped a well of strength he'd begun to feel after meeting Abigail in the forest.

Shlomo stood inert for a few moments looking David in the eye. David forced himself to maintain eye contact. David could only guess at Shlomo's thoughts. The fate of their quest hung on what he decided at this moment. Could he, would he cross the schism between their worlds?

Shlomo's voice broke the tense silence. "I understand. This search for Moloch's chalice has great meaning for you both. I can see the unspoken desperation and possible fear in your faces. May we drop the charade of an academic paper as your motivation? I think we'll make more progress if we at least admit to each other that the chalice is the goal. We can leave aside your motivations for the moment." Sarah resumed breathing. Shlomo leaned in pressing for a reply.

Sarah looked at David and shrugged her shoulders. "He's already figured it out. What do we have to lose?"

"Yes, we agree. The chalice is our goal," David said.

He stepped toward Shlomo, getting in his personal space, close enough that Shlomo raised an eyebrow. "I should tell you that we mean to destroy it as soon as we find it. Do you have a problem with that? If you do, you'd better tell us now." David didn't speak in anger, but with absolute resolve, more resolve than he'd felt about anything in his life.

Shlomo studied David's face for a long moment, his eyes drilling into him. Before beginning this journey, David would have shrunk from Shlomo's gaze. Now David had the guts to face him down, maybe because of the importance of the quest, but more because of Abigail, her force of will bolstering him to see this through, to succeed.

"No, it won't be a problem. Once we find it, you may do with it as you like. I suspect the quest will bring its own rewards." Shlomo's voice resumed its constrained, inscrutable monotone.

"Shlomo," said Sarah, breaking the tension. "You said, 'once we find it.' Do you intend to continue to help us search?" Sarah now rose to her feet without breaking her focus on Shlomo.

"Yes I am, if you will have me, Mr. Austin, Dr. Austin." Shlomo replied with not a breath of hesitation.

Elizabeth

Hell hath no limits, nor is circumscribed
In one self-place, for where we are is hell
—Christopher Marlowe

August 1614

"Guard, guard, attend me!" The Countess Elizabeth Bathory shouted through the small slit in the wall. Her voice was thin and raspy; a voice used to command, now tinged with desperation.

The day was warm, and the scent of putrid, humid air filled the small room. For four years, the countess had been imprisoned, walled up within two rooms in Csejte Castle in northern Hungary. The guard remained at his station. He'd grown accustomed to the countess' ranting, although he thought her tirades were growing shorter and quieter.

"I demand to see Jó and Ficko Semtész, my servants. They are faithful to me. They will free me from this horrid place. Bring them to me at once. I command it." Her desolate eyes watched the guard in desperate hope that he would obey her command. She gasped for air between outbursts.

The guard remained in place with his eyes fixed on a small window set high in the wall, wishing he were somewhere else. He'd been present five years ago when the countess's accomplices, Jó and Ficko Semtész, were tortured and burned at the stake. Their testimony against the countess ensured her conviction. Only her status as nobility spared her from a similar execution. The other soldiers in the barracks said that the Countess Bathory was a witch and had personally killed over six hundred women and girls. They told stories about her bathing in the blood of her victims. His fellow soldiers did not envy the guard his duty.

The countess was quiet for the next hour. She typically screamed through the small opening for hours at a time. The guard was grateful for the silence.

"Summon István Magyar, the Lutheran minister. I would speak with him. He has unjustly confined me to these rooms. I had nothing to do with the fate of those peasant girls. It was Jó and Fricko who murdered them." Elizabeth's voice trailed off into a whisper.

The guard heard the same protests of innocence daily. His orders were strict, coming directly from His Highness, King Matthias. A servant brought food once a day. No one was to speak with the countess at any time. It would mean his life if he violated the king's orders.

The guard had expected his prisoner to demand a mirror, although she hadn't asked for one in several weeks. Mirrors of any kind were forbidden. Elizabeth Bathory was obsessed with her appearance previously spending hours in front of a mirror scrutinizing her face, primping, examining every line and wrinkle. Her castle had been lined with mirrors. She was denounced by the respected minister, István Magyari, at the court in Vienna. During her trial, her accomplices testified that the countess believed that bathing in the blood of virgins would maintain her beauty. Her demands for her "restorative treatments" had become more frequent as she aged. It was the demand for almost daily blood baths that led to the countess's trial and eventual confinement.

The guard caught glimpses of her face when she screamed her diatribes through the opening where food was passed. It was the face of a wizened, gray-haired old woman. Most of her teeth had fallen out and her face was shrunken, taking on a skeletal look. Her eyes appeared cloudy, and he doubted she could see much in the near darkness of her confinement.

Today the countess was unusually quiet with only a few outbursts, not the hours of demands and screaming he was used to. He heard her labored breathing and occasional sobbing. In the last few days, she'd developed a hacking cough which left her gasping at the end of each episode. He would have reported on her condition, but his commander said that no reports were required. His duty was merely to restrict access to the countess.

In the afternoon, the countess was completely still except for the occasional bout of subdued coughing. For the next three days, the Countess Elizabeth Bathory failed to appear to receive her daily meal. On the fourth day, his commanding officer arrived with three workmen and broke down the wall to the countess's rooms. She was dead on her cot, naked, her legs splayed, her arms contorted on her chest, and her desiccated skin stretched over her bones. Her face was frozen in a sardonic smile as though she'd welcomed her fate. It appeared that the corruption within her soul had eaten its way to the surface.

The guard trembled. Fearing for his soul, he made the sign of the cross. The corpse before him resembled a demon from hell.

The Salon

"When you are a child, there is joy. There is laughter. And most of all, there is trust. Trust in your fellows. When you are an adult...then comes suspicion, hatred, and fear." – Peter David

Abigail rested, grateful for the temporary sanctuary afforded by her cell in the castle. For a few moments, nothing new, mysterious, or threatening challenged her. Her rest was brief. She heard the familiar sound of boots approaching and rose facing the door, preparing herself for Lord Eymerich. She was ready for him. Her chair and table dissolved. Lord Eymerich stood between her and the queen. She was determined to conquer him, but she knew she must appear meek, unthreatening so as to lull Eymerich. She would be like Panya, a threat to no one. Abigail resolved not to be tricked into revealing her powers until she'd learned more and was ready to act.

The door opened and Lord Eymerich swaggered in. Seeing him again, his nature came into sharp focus; he was a pure sadist. Lord Eymerich enjoyed inflicting pain. He fed on the misery of others. Pain and torment were his sustenance. The more vulnerable Abigail appeared, the greater his enjoyment.

Following Lord Eymerich was a tall, thin woman wearing a long, full, red satin dress cinched at the waist with a belt of onyx, and with a broad lace collar covering her shoulders. A string of pearls held a gold pendant. Her face was thin with sharp, high cheek bones. She had cold blue eyes and black hair with elaborate braids woven with gold and pearls. A small, red velvet hat adorned her head. Abigail thought she was beautiful, but in Gehenna, her beauty was a mask, leaving Abigail ill at ease with what might lay behind the woman's facade.

"I trust you've had time to further contemplate your situation, and are ready to resume your tutelage?" Lord Eymerich said in a commanding tone.

"I am," Abigail replied, looking aside and making an effort to appear humbled by her prior experience.

"There's a good girl." Lord Eymerich smiled. "Let me introduce another member of the court. This is the Countess Elizabeth Bathory, originally from what you might know as the Hungarian Empire."

"Countess." Abigail bowed slightly, pretending to smile.

"I attended your presentation to the queen, an impressive display. I'm pleased to meet you in person. I have such affection for young girls, and I'm sure we can be close friends." Her voice was warm and pleasing, at first reminding Abigail of her grandmother, a thought she quickly dismissed.

"Yes, yes, Countess, there will be plenty of time for your games later. Now we must bring Mistress Abigail to our salon so that she can meet the rest of our close circle, and continue her education in the ways of the court." Lord Eymerich gestured to the door.

"Yes, My Lord. As you say, let's complete the task at hand," said the countess. She reached over and stroked Abigail's neck and shoulder lightly with her fingertip and sending a cold ripple of pain down her arm. The countess saw Abigail wince, appearing to take pleasure in her pain. The countess' malevolence ran as deep as Eymerich's, but Abigail suspected she was more devious and cunning, and likely more dangerous.

"Follow me," Lord Eymerich commanded as he turned, leaving the room in a brisk walk with his now familiar boots resounding on the floor. The countess followed with Abigail coming along behind. The countess scurried along, lifting up her skirts as she tried to match Eymerich's stride.. The last doorway entered onto a long, broad corridor lined with doors set in the gray stone wall along each side. The doorways and the vaulted ceilings were made of intricately carved stone. A frieze depicting demons bordered the ceiling. Each door was massive, made of dark red wood with coarse iron nails and black strap hinges, and each bore an inscription in various languages carved in the stone lintel over the door.

The entourage progressed to the far end and through a broad set of double doors onto a large room with a high vaulted ceiling. A wall of windows with leaded glass windows lined one side, and an arched doorway led to an expansive deck looking out on the town below. The room was richly appointed with heavy, dark furniture. Several large tapestries hung on the walls, one depicting a procession of young girls, heads bowed, entering a castle on a high hill. It was mysterious and ominous at the same time. Abigail understood the vulnerability of the young girls and, after her introduction to the countess, she thought that was probably the point. Another tapestry depicted priests torturing bound victims with fire and red, glowing irons.

Along the other side of the room was a raised dais with two elaborately carved dark wooden chairs. Four smaller chairs were arranged on each side. All heads turned as they entered, and the room grew silent. Lord Eymerich and the countess walked swiftly through the crowd and each took a chair on the dais. After they were seated, four men sat in the chairs beside Eymerich and four women beside the countess. Abigail stopped a few feet from the dais, uncertain of where to go or stand.

The room was crowded with people gathered in small groups. The people were dressed in fine clothing, some Elizabethan, some contemporary to Abigail's time, and others she didn't recognize. Abigail was drawn to the spectacle of it all. In the midst of all this danger and perdition, a smile came across her face. Here she was, the much sought after visitor. She'd once happily imagined this scene. Now she wondered if she would momentarily be torn to shreds.

Abigail looked about. Each person had something about them that was not quite human: a smile that stretched too far with too many teeth, eyes that were offset, a cloven hoof poking out from beneath a skirt, an angelic face with a serpent's tongue. *Were these human souls with demonic traits or demons in a human disguise?*

As if on que, a swarm of people formed a broad half circle around her, whispering, snickering, and pointing. Tension rode in Abigail's neck. She clenched her fists and struggled to appear calm. The power within her caused her fingertips to tingle. An urge to attack came over her, which she immediately suppressed. She had to appear meek and unthreatening; no more glowing from within. She was surrounded by demons and had to avoid any provocation.

A tall man stepped forward and stood beside Eymerich. He wore a black military uniform with tall black boots, jodhpurs, and a red arm band with a white circle and some type of symbol in the center. The man leaned in as Eymerich whispered in his ear. He stood up, nodded, and stepped off the dais approaching Abigail. The room became quiet.

"Fraulein Abigail, allow me introduce myself. I am SS Lieutenant Colonel Rudolf Hoss, formerly of the Third Reich." He stood erect and clicked his boot heels together. Abigail's eyes focused on the skull and crossbones on his hat. His demeanor and unfamiliar appearance left her at a loss for what to say. Before she could react, he grabbed Abigail's face by the chin and twisted her head back and forth examining her like some animal in a market. Along with his painful grip came a vision of him presiding over the murders of thousands of people. Abigail saw in his thoughts the pride the man had in his horrific actions. The man's heart was as black as night and his touch cold. Abigail had never known that such perversion existed.

"You look like you come from pure stock," he said in an imperious tone.

In a thoughtless flash of anger, Abigail grabbed his hand, and a bolt of energy shot into his arm causing him to stagger. Rage washed over his face. He stepped back, rubbing his arm and glancing at Lord Eymerich.

"Pleased to meet you too, Colonel." Abigail instantly realized her mistake. She'd been provoked yet again. Her anger this time was directed at herself. Lord Eymerich scrutinized her. The people behind Abigail drew back. The colonel took up position standing to the right of the dais, an upturned lip revealing his satisfaction.

Eymerich stood, clapped his hands, and spread his arms as though embracing the audience. "Mistress Abigail, welcome to our salon. This is where we spend our time with our friends. It is an illustrious gathering." Lord Eymerich motioned with his hand at the ring of people. "You will find this a unique collection of people from various ages. Each person here has distinguished themselves in their lifetime. Each has a unique history, and each has unique talents that qualify them as members of our elite society. We are the nobility of Queen Lilith's court."

The members of the salon clapped lightly, along with whispers and snickers. The crowd moved slowly closer, just an arm's length way. They touched her one at a time, and with each touch came a chill, a stab of pain, and a hint of the evil contained within the person. Abigail felt trapped and exposed by their closeness. She stood ridged, controlling herself, refusing to display any hint of the torment she experienced, not wanting to yield any satisfaction to her harassers. Lord Eymerich smiled like a young boy torturing an animal. Abigail's vulnerability showed through cracks in her brave facade. He leaned forward, eyeing her, seeming to savor the moment.

This excruciating receiving line continued until the last person stood before Abigail, a hulking beast of a man, well over six feet, broad-chested, with a cold piercing stare.

"Nice to finally meet you, Miss Abigail. You cost me a lot, more than I was willing to pay," said the man in a low voice.

"Have we met before?" she asked.

"My name is Frank Robinson. And no, we ain't met. You was already dead the day I came to kill you."

A chill ran through her. The evil of Gehenna had reached for her when she was alive. Her hiding place among the living had been discovered. Frank took a step closer and looked directly down on her. He grabbed Abigail's arm, and she sensed him searching her thoughts. She grabbed his hand and shot a bolt of energy through him. He winced and let go. Frank paused and then formed a crooked smile. "I'm sure we ain't done with each other," he said and walked away. Abigail relaxed for a moment until she noticed Lord Eymerich's gaze.

"Elizabeth, don't you think we should have more appropriate attire for our young charge? This dress she's wearing is more suitable for a maid, not a member of the court." The crowd stepped back as though on command when Lord Eymerich changed the subject.

"You're quite right M'Lord," said the countess. This childish frock is not at all appropriate."

The countess motioned to the first of her ladies in

waiting. "Rachael, stand so that Abigail may observe your dress."

Rachael approached Abigail. She was tall and muscular with a harsh angular face. Her fingers were unusually long, and her nails looked almost like claws. Her dress was full length and made from red velvet with an intricate bodice covered with embroidery and jewels. Her hair was done in elaborate braids woven with gold. A small red hat fit her head snugly.

"Abigail, my dear, all my ladies wear dresses similar to Rachael's. Get rid of that childish smock and make a dress like Rachael's for yourself."

Could I make such an elaborate dress? Could I change my own appearance? Should I? If I had such abilities, should I hide them from Eymerich? Abigail's heart raced, fueled by indecision. Her eyes flicked from Lord Eymerich to the countess. Eymerich looked serious, seeming to contemplate what Abigail's next move would be. The countess smiled as she saw the panic on Abigail face.

Abigail's choice was not whether to make a new dress or not but to strike a balance between being strong enough not to be destroyed and no so strong as to be an immediate threat to Eymerich or the countess. She circled Rachael observing every detail of the clothing, the fabric, the cut of the bodice, even the delicate beading. She began to imagine her own dress, slightly more elaborate, with finer cloth. She stopped after one circle. The image was clear, she knew what to make. Abigail raised her arms over her head, clasped her hands, and willed the new dress into existence.

A demon shrieked and the crowd murmured.

The Challenge

"The greater the obstacle, the more glory in overcoming it." – Molière

Abigail opened her eyes. She faced the countess looking down on her from the stage. Abigail couldn't tell if she was pleased or enraged. Abigail curtsied and took a step back. She paused and looked at her gown. It was every bit as elaborate as the countess'.

The countess clapped her hands. "It is time for a dance." She returned to her seat and motioned for Abigail to stand to her right.

Rachael and the three other ladies formed a circle with their arms curved upwards toward the center and one foot pointed backwards. Every face in the crowded salon looked on with almost uncontained excitement. Lord Eymerich signaled with his hand, and gentle harp music and a quiet drum began to play from the back of the hall. The countess leaned in, watching gleefully as the four ladies began a slow dance. They moved gracefully in time to the music, moving in a circle, gliding in and out, spinning with arms held aloft. Each woman wore a broad, sardonic smile.

The tempo increased and the music became strident. The movements of the four dancers grew faster. They clenched their fists and made mock attacks on one another. The drums became louder and the music discordant. Rachael and the other ladies began to transform before her eyes. Their faces became elongated, large fangs appeared, and their skin changed to gray scales. Their feet become cloven hoofs at the end of legs covered with coarse hair. A ballet of devils performed in front of her.

The on looking crowd became frenzied and also transformed, mimicking the dancer's appearance, demons dressed in regal clothing. A putrid odor filled the room. The dancers picked up black iron tridents. They swung the tridents over their heads and struck the floor in rhythm to the drum beat. Each strike caused sparks to fly. Each strike elicited a screech from the crowd.

The dancers began to strike each other with their weapons. Every thrust that found its mark caused a great roar from its victim and shouts of glee from the crowd. Their movements became a frenzied blur of motion in time with the deafening, grating, music. The frantic mass of demons undulated in time with the discordant sound. Abigail covered her ears, closed her eyes, but nothing blocked out the revel of the demons.

The room hushed. All returned to normal, or at least the appearance of normal. The four women looked as before, young women in fine dress. The people in the crowd were once again courtiers in their finery. Lord Eymerich and the countess stood and looking down from the dais. Abigail turned to face them, and Rachael and her companions stepped behind and pressed her toward the dais.

"Abigail, I shall make you one of my ladies in waiting, and you too shall learn our dance." With those words, one of young woman shrieked and collapsed on the floor, writhing and moaning. Rachael bent forward toward Abigail's ear and hissed, twisting her head side to side, her eyes filled with an all-consuming fury. The other women raged in silence, resembling wild beasts. Abigail was frozen, thinking only of the countess's intention for her future.

Guards took the woman on the floor by the arms and dragged her from the salon. Her cries disappeared in the hallway beyond. The countess and her ladies were indifferent to her plight.

"Lady Abigail, please take your seat beside me." The countess pointed to the empty chair. Abigail froze. The idea of sitting beside these women, of becoming one of them, frightened her. *How had they become so fearsome? Was this to become her fate?*

She sat as instructed. Rachael and the other two women glared at her. Their faces changed again, becoming thin and pointed, almost bird-like. All three moved their heads in quick, jerky motions. Rachael hissed softly at Abigail and flexed her fingers as if preparing to strangle her. These women who were once human, now appeared demonic.

Abigail sat for several minutes with a white-knuckled grip on the arms of the chair. Rachael's face reverted to a human appearance. The countess was engaged with Lord Eymerich. With everyone's attention elsewhere, Abigail's tension subsided and she relaxed her grip. She imagined herself as an invisible observer, unseen by the threats surrounding her. Abigail knew it was an illusion on her part, but it allowed her to think about the rapid series of events. When she'd grabbed the colonel's arm, she'd seen a vision of his past life. Abigail shuddered at his past deeds and the blackness within him. The ability to see into his soul was a surprise, an ability not mentioned by Philberta or Ehyeh.

Abigail noticed Rachael looking away. She touched her arm lightly with her finger and Rachael's terror flooding into her. Rachael was consumed with terror. There were vestiges of humanity, but her transformation into a demon was complete.

Abigail pressed harder, trying to see what had brought her to this state. She'd been hanged at the age of sixteen for killing her abusive, drunken father. Abigail experienced the pain and torment of the woman's life. She felt the terror of the father's final attack. He intended to kill her. Rachael had struck him on the head with an iron bar and continued hitting him till his head was a bloody pulp.

Her time in prison awaiting her execution was more horrible than her life with her father. Her death had been a relief from a life of suffering.

Rachael was not a strong-willed person, and while much of her substance had survived the chaos between realms, she had been unprepared for the countess' torture and had eventually been transformed both physically and mentally into the half-demon, half -human creature that sat beside Abigail. When the countess was done, nothing of Rachael remained. Abigail had a moment's pity for Rachael. She had been abused her whole life, and her death was unjust. She had been cast into a pit of demons and been changed into one herself. Pity was tempered by the knowledge that the countess was no doubt planning a similar fate for her.

Abigail sat, quietly suppressing her emotions. The countess reached over and began stroking Abigail's head. Each caress sent a painful chill racing through her. She grimaced with each stroke, which seemed to please the countess. Abigail suppressed the flow of energy from her, fearing that it would reveal to the countess her true nature.

"Countess, what has become of the woman who collapsed on the floor?"

"She has been taken down to the lower levels where she will remain." She rested her hands on her lap.

"What is below? Are there other rooms like this one?"

The countess smiled. "Dear child, so many questions. You may learn things you might not care to know."

"Yes, Countess, you are correct, of course." She stroked Abigail's cheek with her fingernail. The countess' nail creased her skin almost cutting it.

"You have much to learn. Lord Eymerich has asked me to assist in your education. We shall retire to chambers shortly to begin." She withdrew her hand and looked away.

Abigail remained still, with her head lower, appearing docile. Now was not her time to act. She looked around uneasily as the business of the salon resumed its normal course. Various people walked up and spoke with either Lord Eymerich or Countess Elizabeth. Their talk was about nothing in particular, seemingly just gossip and the events of the court. No one paid any attention to Abigail, now that she was part of the countess's entourage, with the exception of Rachael. She continued her malevolent gaze, her breath seething with anger, barely able to control her rage. Abigail had successfully infiltrated the queen's court. Her position was tenuous. She could be dislodged or attacked by some unknown force at any moment, but she had a moment to collect her thoughts.

Then a distant trumpet played three rising notes, and the salon became instantly silent. The three notes were repeated four times. Lord Eymerich jumped to his feet, raising a fist in the air.

"Curse that witch. The queen summons us for the vision time. She is doing this too often." He shook his fist as the herald repeated. The salon crowd murmured their agreement. Lord Eymerich walked briskly toward the entrance as people parted before him like boats in the water.

"Come, Lady Abigail, ladies, let us do as our queen commands." The countess stood up and began to follow Eymerich. Rachael grabbed Abigail's wrist and dug her nails into her.

"I will see you in the countess's *chambre de sang* before the next vision time comes to pass." She spoke with a hissing sound, and her eyes filled with venom.

If she could have, she would have dismembered Abigail on the spot. Rachael dropped Abigail's arm and shoved her in the direction of the countess, who was now halfway across the room. Abigail stumbled on the hem of her gown and then hurried to catch up with the countess. She wondered if she needed to take Rachael's threat seriously. *What was the chambre de sang?* Panya had spoken of the vision time, now she would witness it firsthand.

The Man in the Tower

"Every man has his secret sorrows which the world knows not; and often times we call a man cold when he is only sad."
– Henry Wadsworth Longfellow

Sarah and David waited for Shlomo under a broad tree in Harva Square watching people hustling on their way to work. They were planning to travel to Ugarit on the Syrian coast by bus to Damascus before making their way by car.

The minarets of the Sidna Omar Mosque cast long shadows in the early morning sun across Hurva square. The air was still cool, but the sun warmed the beige paving stones hinting at the midday heat to come.

"I thought about Shlomo on the walk over here. I don't understand why he agreed to come with us to Syria," said David.

"I wondered the same thing the moment he asked to come," replied Sarah. "It was too quick. He didn't ask any questions. And what about his thesis work? Is he putting that on hold while he looks for obscure clues with us?" Sarah wondered about Shlomo's motives as she watched the people scurrying through the square on their way to work.

"He's been incredibly helpful so far, and certainly knows the local territory. Let's go with him to Ugarit, and then we can decide where we go from there," David added.

"I agree, but I don't trust him. We'll take this a step at a time." Sarah took David's hand. He wasn't sure if she was reassuring him or herself, or both. "He's holding out on us. Why I don't know. Let's keep him at arm's length till we know more about him."

Since arriving in Jerusalem, David had repressed a mild state of panic. The city was alien, far removed from the quiet, verdant confines of Maine. Now his panic eased, possibly because Abigail felt closer. His connection with her at first was like seeing her through a fog, only vague outlines visible. The more he thought of her, the stronger her image, her memories, and her strength came into focus. David became invigorated as though waking from a deeply restful sleep. The path ahead was uncertain and dangerous, but now he saw it as a challenge to be overcome, a peak to be scaled, not as an insurmountable threat.

"Shalom, Dr. Austin, Mr. Austin—or should I say good morning?" Shlomo's deep voice brought David's thoughts back to Hurva Square.

It took them a second to recognize him. He was dressed in khakis with a dark blue knit shirt. He'd shaved his beard. His ringlet curls were gone, as was the fringe of strings hanging from under his shirt. A Yankees hat replaced his yarmulke. Sarah had mistaken him for a ubiquitous New York tourist.

"Shlomo, what happened to you?" David stood and looked him up and down. "You've changed a lot since yesterday afternoon." For an instant, a hint of a smile betrayed Shlomo's thoughts, but his stone-faced facade snapped back into place.

"I thought it best to adopt a less conspicuous mode of dress, since we will be traveling to a Muslim country."

"Shlomo, if you don't mind my asking, this is a bit radical for you, isn't it?" Sarah sounded concerned. "I mean, you've been in traditional orthodox dress your entire life. This is a big change. Are you okay with this?"

"I appreciate your concern, doctor. It is something I've considered for a while, envisioning the change before I was shunned. I've known for years that the Bobover culture held little meaning for me. I kept up pretenses for the sake of the community, and for my wife and children. I was the

Grand Rebbe, a person of great importance and responsibility, a position I didn't take lightly. There came a time when the pull to a different life became too great. The charade could no longer be maintained, and this precipitated my shunning." Shlomo paused. He seemed relieved to be telling them his story.

"I've maintained the traditional dress out of habit, and simply because I owned no other clothes. We are traveling to Syria, and I worried that my Hasidic dress would be a distraction, drawing unwanted attention, or possibly causing trouble. So last night I observed a few American tourists and bought some clothes like theirs."

"And your beard and curls?" Sarah motioned to the side of her face with her finger.

"Ah, yes, that was difficult. I went to my usual barber but he refused me. He is a pious man and shaving a man's beard and pe'ot, the curls in front of the ears, is forbidden. I didn't feel safe going to a Palestinian barber, so, after some searching, I found an Armenian barber. He was quite surprised, but the color of my money was correct, and so, here I am as you see me."

"Well, Shlomo, I'd say your disguise is perfect. I thought you were a New York City tourist when I saw you. I didn't recognize you till you spoke," Sarah said.

"Yes, me too," added David standing and pulling his suitcase closer. "Shall we buy our bus tickets for Damascus?"

"I've already made arrangements. I mean, if you don't have objections, I can explain as we walk." Shlomo pointed to the street beside the synagogue.

"A car is waiting at the Ha-Shalshelet gate on Guy Street. My luggage is already there." Shlomo walked ahead with his hands folded behind; not everything had changed.

"I thought we'd take the bus," said Sarah. "David and I discussed our finances last night. We're good for another few weeks, but then we'll be out of money, and one or both of us will have to go home unless we resort to hitchhiking and camping out."

Still looking straight ahead and not breaking his pace, Shlomo said, "A Gulfstream jet is standing by at Ben Gurion airport. After a brief stop for an immigration stamp in Cyprus, we'll land in Damascus before noon. I've arranged for a Land Rover and driver to meet us at the airport."

Sarah and David froze in their tracks. Shlomo kept walking. "Shlomo, stop!" Sarah shouted. David stuttered, not knowing what to say. Shlomo walked back to where they stood. Finally, Sarah managed to get a few words out.

"Shlomo, what have you done? We can't possibly pay for a private jet."

"I'm sorry. I can see I should have consulted you first."

"Can you afford this? Because we certainly cannot." Sarah was excited and not in a good way.

"Why, yes, I can. I may have been shunned by my Bobover community, but I still have access to all its financial resources, which are considerable, I might add. When I was made Grand Rebbe, I was made the sole executor of the Bobover financial corporation. The Bobover have been both shrewd and frugal for centuries. Their financial assets are in the neighborhood of twenty-one billion dollars, if I have my currency conversion correct. I can assure you that finances will not be an obstacle." As surprising as Shlomo's announcement was, the deadpan manner in which he made it was almost comical.

The hair on David's neck stood up. His instinct was to grab Sarah and put some distance between them and

Shlomo.

"Do you mean to tell me that you have retained control over the entire Bobover fortune?" Sarah asked, continuing to look bewildered.

"Yes I have." Shlomo's voice held a note of satisfaction. His revenge, and possibly a last laugh, had been retaining the Bobover purse strings. In David's days as a jock, he would have said Shlomo had the Bobovers by the short hairs.

"Aren't they kind of upset about that?" David asked.

"They are very upset from what I've heard, but it's their own doing. You see, the Bobovers are very hierarchical with all things leading to and coming from the Grand Rebbe. The Rebbe has absolute control because he is, after all, anointed by God. So when I was made Grand Rebbe, I was assigned one hundred percent control over the fortune. There were a few loopholes which I managed to close before the extent of my heresy became known, and I saw the end was inevitable.

"After I was formally shunned, a group of goyish lawyers came to see me, asking that I relinquish my rights. I refused. They came back three times demanding that I relinquish control. Each time I refused. Finally, they came and asked, quite contritely, I might add, what I wanted. I told them I needed only a small stipend. I live modestly and my needs are few. However, I told them that if I ever need money I would contact them, and I expected that my requests would be promptly satisfied—otherwise I would re-exert my control. Aside than that, they were free to manage the fortune as they saw fit, provided they made no wholesale transfer of assets. I have Price Waterhouse in Zurich audit them continuously.

Shlomo started walking again, continuing to talk. "For three years, I have asked for nothing beyond my stipend as I pursued my studies, but yesterday I called the goyish lawyer. He arranged our transportation and any financing we might need. They are happy to oblige since it keeps me away, and they know I will not deprive them of their gelt."

"Well, it sounds like a workable arrangement," Sarah said in a small voice, raising her eyebrows.

David did not sense any malevolence from him. Indeed, his instinct was to trust him, even though his brain told him he had no reason to. The alarms subsided. He glanced at Sarah and nodded in Shlomo's direction. She nodded in return with a look that said she wasn't pleased.

Just then, Shlomo slowed his pace to a near crawl and then stopped without saying a word. Sarah and David almost collided with him. They both expected Shlomo to say something. When he didn't, David looked a few yards ahead and saw a small woman in a long skirt with her hair wrapped in a scarf pushing a baby carriage, with a small boy holding onto one hand and shopping bags in the other. Her eyes fixed on Shlomo, momentary puzzled, followed by a shocked expression. She immediately looked away, crossed the street, and stood facing the wall. The small boy looked at Shlomo, but the woman turned his face to the wall. Shlomo stared at their backs. People hurried past navigating around him. The mother and children remained fixed. Shlomo resumed walking faster than before as though this diminutive woman frightened him in some way. He offered no word of explanation.

David looked at Sarah. Her puzzled expression matched his exactly. Neither of them knew what had just happened or what to do next. David's first thought was to walk up to him and say something like, "Hey, what was that all about? Old girlfriend?" Sarah suspected as much and shook her head at him, putting her finger to her lips. They'd known Shlomo for a few days, but knew nothing about him personally. Shlomo resided in an intellectual fortress, alone with his thoughts and having little need for other people. His privacy was paramount.

They followed silently and arrived at a giant black Suburban SUV, the kind you see following the VIP's limo. The driver quickly put their bags in the back and opened the doors for them. Sarah had the feeling they was being hurried along. A serious looking man sat in the front seat with an assault rifle. The glass in the windows was shaded and unusually thick. Bulletproof?

"Shlomo, whose car is this?" she asked. The silent tension of the walk dissipated.

"It's the Bobover Grand Rebbe's. The new one. He always travels in an armored SUV with a bodyguard. Jerusalem can be a dangerous place." Shlomo tapped the driver on the shoulder, and they sped off.

The SUV made it to the airport in record time, and was waved through the checkpoint guarding the private terminals. They came to an abrupt halt beside a gleaming private jet, all white with a thin blue line along the side and bearing United States registration numbers. The uniformed crew was visible at the controls. A young woman in a very modest, full-length skirt and her hair covered by a scarf stood by the stairs.

"Shalom Mr. Halberstam, We're fueled and ready to depart, Damascus by way of Cyprus at your convenience."

Sarah and David hustled up the stairs, as the driver loaded their luggage into an aft compartment. The attendant pressed a button, the steps retracted, and the cabin door closed with a soft mechanical hum. She spoke into the intercom, "Ready," then turned to us.

"Please take your seats and buckle in. The takeoff can

be quite steep." She took a jump seat beside the cabin door. Sarah and David sat facing each other in large, plush, white leather chairs decorated with gold piping. Burl wood trim lined the sides of the cabin, and a soft gray carpet covered the floor. Sarah sat wide-eyed at the lavishness of travel for the rich and famous. David hoped he didn't look like the hayseed he felt like.

In a matter of minutes, the jet rocketed upwards to thirty-eight thousand feet and almost immediately began its decent into Cyprus, more of a ballistic trajectory than a flight. The jet landed in Cyprus and taxied to a parking spot. The engines remained running while an official looking vehicle pulled up. The attendant asked for their passports. Shlomo handed her a US passport as well.

"Shlomo, you are a US citizen? I assumed you're Israeli." David asked.

"Dual citizenship, US and Israeli. My mother is an American, from Williamsburg in Brooklyn. She was betrothed to my father when she was seven years old and they were married when she turned 16 in Israel. The Bobovers have considerable political influence, and the US diplomatic passport was a courtesy from your State Department because the Bobovers maintain what amounts to a consular office in Brooklyn. My duties as the Grand Rebbe took me to Europe and the States regularly." Shlomo was a never ending source of amazement.

The attendant returned, closed the cabin door, told the pilot they were ready, and returned their passports.

"You have Cyprus immigration stamps dated today. There will be no issues clearing immigration in Damascus," she said. "Please buckle up again, we are departing immediately." They party had been on the ground barely ten minutes from the time the tires touched. David felt like they'd been initiated into some secret society where the normal rules of life didn't apply. When the jet leveled off, Sarah surprised David and maybe Shlomo too, by leaning forward and asking Shlomo the question that had been hanging in the air.

"Shlomo, who was that woman you saw on the street?" Her voice was soft with a motherly tone. David's eyes darted to Shlomo to hear his answer.

Shlomo looked mildly surprised that Sarah had asked.

"That was Huldah, my wife, and my children." Shlomo paused, and his words gathered tension as though we'd trespassed on a private space.

"At first she didn't recognize me without my beard and pe'ot. I shocked her quite badly, I'm afraid. I've not spoken with her or my children in the two years since I was shunned. I've never held my daughter. She was born after the shunning. The shunning commands that she must not look upon my face. That is why she crossed the street and turned her back on me, cursed my name three times and spit upon the ground."

"How awful for you," said Sarah looking aghast. She had no use for fundamentalist religions, which made witnessing the silent drama on a Jerusalem side street all the more painful because it had been made by man, not the work of God.

"Like my fathers before me, my marriage was arranged by my father. We were married when I was thirty one and she was sixteen. I'd met Huldah on the day we were betrothed and for a second time on our wedding day. She was a dutiful wife, fulfilling the commandments of the Torah. There was no love between us, as you would understand, merely two people performing their duties as commanded following five thousand years of tradition."

Shlomo's eyes darted across their faces to gauge their reaction.

"After I was shunned, I sent a letter to the new Grand Rebbe asking for a *get*, a religious divorce. Only the husband can initiate such a request. The essential text of the *get* is quite short: 'You are hereby permitted to all men,' meaning the woman is no longer married. Huldah is a righteous woman from an old, prestigious family. My shame is her shame. She is tainted and no other man will have her. Her family in the US will not take her back."

Shlomo took a deep breath as though releasing the pain that came with the words. "My children's future within the Bobovers will be difficult as well. My son will not be invited to the Yeshiva. My daughter will not have a proper dowry for a good marriage. During the high holidays, Huldah will stand at the back of the woman's balcony alone, not in the front as was her place of honor before. No one will invite her to Shabbat, the Sabbath evening meal. I am dead to her. She will not accept money or anything from me. She will live alone on anonymous charity for the rest of her life, clinging to the fringe of Bobover society."

The more Shlomo revealed, the more his tale seemed fantastic, believable only if you didn't examine the details too closely. David didn't think Shlomo's intentions were malicious because, for the first time, he saw real emotion on his face. Shlomo grieved at the pain he caused his wife and the loss of his children. A shunning would have destroyed any other man of his background, leaving him a wandering wraith. Shlomo was liberated, free to pursue his search for knowledge, but at a terrible cost—the sacrifice of his wife and children upon his alter of intellectual pursuit.

Vision Time

"Its preparations are concealed, not published. Its mistakes are buried, not headlined. Its dissenters are silenced, not praised. No expenditure is questioned, no rumor is printed, no secret is revealed."
– John F. Kennedy

Lord Eymerich's entourage walked briskly and silently down the long corridor, and entered the great hall with the owl statue. His entourage filed into the first of seven galleries overlooking the chamber. He and the countess stood poised at the railing with their attendants on either side. Abigail stood to the countess's left with the other ladies in waiting. Seeing them, they were anything but ladies, they were a pack of frenzied animals, and being in the owl chamber increased their agitation. Only the countess's presence restrained them. Rachael hovered close behind Abigail causing her to turn constantly for fear an attack.

The main floor with the owl statue and throne, where Abigail had first met the queen, was empty. Above her hundreds, maybe thousands of other beings filled in the galleries. The guards closed the massive black doors with a resounding thud, sealing the chamber like a tomb. Four flaming cauldrons on the dais lit the statue with a flickering light and illuminated the hundreds of faces peering down from the galleries.

The chamber became deadly silent when the queen appeared at the top of the stairs. As when Abigail first saw her, she glided down the stairs as though on a mechanical conveyance. The six children followed. The queen centered herself on the dais flanked by the children. The same small boy stood beside her, clutching her gown. Abigail thought at first he clung to her for reassurance as any small child might, but his face betrayed him. He gazed up at the people in the galleries with a satisfied look. He had no need of protection by the queen. There was neither fear nor self-doubt in his face.

She raised her arms preparing to address the audience. Her gown's white shimmering fabric reflected the flames from the cauldrons making her whole body appear on fire.

"My lords and ladies of the court." The queen's strong yet feminine voice echoed throughout the vast chamber. "The fulfillment of our great plan is at hand. Soon we will be freed from the imprisonment of Gehenna. Our power will be such that none can stand against us in this realm or among the living."

A fierce, inhuman screech erupted from the assembled beings, sending a chill through me. Abigail stepped back, looking wildly from side to side. Her vision wavered momentarily as though looking through heat rising from a flame. The illusion of the royal court vanished revealing the chamber and its occupants for what they were.

The owl chamber was a vast cavernous pit. The ornate galleries were rocky ledges. The flames from the cauldrons rose to the ceiling, and a putrid, sulfurous stench filled the air. The owl statue became a great beast with the head of a horned bull, its eyes glowing. The soldiers lining the hall were transformed into devils, their lances into glowing tridents. The floor was covered with black faces, eyes wide in terror, mouths agape, rising and sinking as though in an oily tar.

Beside Abigail, the countess's face was transformed to that of a dog with huge fangs, a broad bony body covered in dark scales, and gnarly claws. Her legs were furry with cloven hoofs. Lord Eymerich was a gigantic ogre with gray skin, a tail, and an erect phallus. Every being in the gallery was changed in some way, demons all, and all horrible and grotesque. Only the queen in her glimmering white dress and her children remained the same.

The screeching stopped, and the scene of Hades reverted to the courtly illusion. But Abigail had seen everything as it truly was. The nature of where she was and the challenges she faced became deadly clear.

"Now attend, my children, the summons is at hand." The queen turned and faced the front of the dais. A small dot of light appeared in front of her, and, at the same time, the wings of the owl statue opened and spread across the dais arching over the queen. Lord Eymerich, the countess, and all the members of the salon were frozen as though in a trance. Abigail experienced a strong pull from the queen as she began to draw energy from the demons within the galleries in order to open a bridge just as Abigail had used the souls in Arcadia. This time the strength was not a gift. The queen wrenched all the power she needed from the crowd. Her actions tore at the very fiber of those that looked upon her. The countess's face reflected the agony of having the life force brutally torn from her. Abigail now understood Lord Eymerich's rage when the call went out to attend the vision time.

The small dot grew into a large circle of sparkling light before the queen. The swirling mist within the circle cleared, revealing an older, white-haired man standing on a platform in a dark forest, and beside him on a pedestal was the chalice, a simple bowl with handles on each side. The queen and the boy stepped through the portal to the other realm. The man bowed as the queen approached.

"Falcon, our faithful servant, tell us of your visit with General Kim."

"Yes, my queen, your prince in the far east, the Condor, visited General Kim at his home in North Korea. Aamon supplied a jewel which channeled the power of the

Lilim. He touched the General's wife with it and drove her to madness, leaving her writhing on the floor in front of the General. The Condor told the General that the same fate awaited him and his children if he wavered once more. It was a most convincing demonstration."

"Well done. We are pleased." The queen smiled and stroked the head of the small boy beside her.

"Thank you, my queen. Also, I understand from the general that the problems with the Central

Committee members have been resolved."

"Yes, Falcon, they have all been killed in separate incidents. No one will perceive any connection between their deaths. There is no one now who stands in the way of our plan."

"Excellent, Your Majesty." Falcon's voice brimmed with excitement.

"Tell us of the preparations for the great plan."

"We have secured the influenza virus from a body frozen in northern Finland since 1918. Dr. Ashe has begun work on the recombinant sequencing to combine the airborne characteristics of the influenza virus with the hemorrhagic characteristics of Ebola. The Lilim are immune to this virus, as we lack the receptor it uses to attack the cells. The engineered virus is airborne and highly contagious. We project seventy percent contamination of global populations within three months, and ninety percent within six months."

"Excellent, Falcon, you have done well." The queen's body pulsed with light. "When will you be ready?"

"The virus will be tested on a group of political prisoners within the next week, and production will be complete within three weeks."

The queen approached the man and stroked his jaw

with the back of her hand. He closed his eyes and gasped. The flow of energy from the queen illuminated his body lighting him like a lantern in the darkness, his face reflecting his ecstasy."

"You have done well, Falcon. You are our faithful servant. Soon you will rule the world for centuries by our right hand when we are freed from our bondage in Gehenna."

The queen withdrew her touch, and Falcon dropped to his knees, clutching his left arm, his face grimacing in pain, and gasping for breath.

"We shall talk again soon." The queen smiled at his pain. She stepped backwards, and the circle of light disappeared. A quiet, collective moan rose from the galleries as the vision time ended. Everyone around Abigail appeared shrunken, drained, blanched of color by the ordeal of the queen's vision time. The queen ascended the stairs, but stopped halfway up and looked at the tiered balconies above her as though she was searching for a particular person. She glanced at her companion, the small boy, and continued up the stairs disappearing through a door. The children followed.

Abigail remained with her back against the wall. The shape of the queen's plan came into view. She knew what influenza was. It killed many people in Maine every winter. She'd not heard of Ebola but guessed it was deadly. Abigail believed the mysterious man called Falcon when he said it would kill almost every human within six months. Ehyeh's warning became frighteningly real as the mechanics of the plan were revealed. The plan was marching apace with nothing other than David and her to stop it. Abigail's head was spinning with fear, panic, and anger. Her anger led to strength, and with it came resolve. She would stop the queen. She just didn't know how.

Once the queen left, the guards opened the great doors, and the galleries began to empty. The members of the salon, headed by Lord Eymerich, silently proceeded back to the salon. Panya stood at attention by the door from the labyrinth to the corridor leading to the salon. He looked straight ahead as they passed with no hint of recognition. Abigail hoped he would follow her to the salon.

The entourage trudged silently, slowly through the corridor. Lord Eymerich and his followers looked straight ahead with fixed eyes as though sleepwalking to some unseen destination. Abigail had been immune. Her strength remained intact, and, unlike everyone else in the chamber, she had not changed form. She'd stayed in her red dress.

As she walked, Abigail heard David's thoughts, distant at first, as though he were standing across a crowded room, making it hard to pick out his voice. Then his voice moved toward her and became clearer, stronger. The distance continued to close till there was no longer any distance between them. David was within her, seeing her memories, feeling her emotions, and hearing her thoughts. For the first time, she saw his shame, both at his past failings and his expected failure to find the chalice now. His lack of confidence ran deep. He was a man riddled with doubts which he hid from those around him by his humor and easygoing manner.

David flipped through Abigail's memories of the vision time as one would turn the pages of a photo album. He saw the man called Falcon talking to the queen in the forest, and the chalice on a pedestal set before the owl statue. He saw the queen's chamber filled with demons. David focused on the image of Lilith. Abigail felt him being drawn to the queen, attracted to her beauty. He imagined himself standing beside her. Abigail reacted immediately to the impending danger. The very image of Queen Lilith was enough to seduce him. She shouted at him, *David, do not think of her, she is evil, she will corrupt your will. David, remember your quest. The chalice stands beside the owl in the dark forest, destroy it. Find Falcon, he will lead you to it. David, the queen's plan is to release a plague, a virus that will kill every human on Earth. They will be ready within a few weeks.*

Abigail didn't know if he heard her or not. David had disappeared from her thoughts. She hoped he realized the danger the queen posed. She'd seen the queen's enormous powers over the living. Abigail feared what effect Lilith might have on David.

Falcon

"Surely some revelation is at hand;
Surely the Second Coming is at hand." –W.B.Yeats

Three black Suburban SUVs idled in the parking lot surrounded by dark Idaho forest, their parking lights on, and exhaust vapor rising in the cool night air. Four men, wearing night vision goggles and with assault weapons at the ready, guarded the perimeter. Two men in khaki pants and dark shirts waited beside the middle SUV.

"I don't like the idea of Falcon wandering around these forests at night. It's a security breach waiting to happen." He stared into the darkness wishing he had night goggles as well.

"Ben, the last guy who insisted on accompanying Falcon on his walks is now looking for small time counterfeiters in Philly; not a great career move. It took you a while to get assigned to Falcon. I suggest you keep your mouth shut," advised the team leader.

"What's he do out there in the dark? I can't see shit."

"You read the briefing papers. You know what the Babylon Woods are. In a few weeks, most of the cabinet members, the Joint Chiefs, and CEOs from the Fortune 100 will be getting drunk, playing summer camp, and singing in front of that big owl statue for five days. They've done this every year for the last thirty, a secret gathering of the world's most wealthy and powerful men acting like a bunch of twelve-year-olds. They used to run around half naked, but now they've had to let a few women in, so the boys keep their clothes on."

"Sounds silly to me," said Ben.

"Falcon likes to walk around here at night, says it helps him relax," added the team leader, hoping to make the activities seem less ridiculous.

"I still don't like it. He's a target out there alone."

"I wouldn't worry. This is twenty square miles of the most secure wilderness in the country. Even the mosquitos get a security check." The man smiled at his own joke. "Few people even know this place exists. Army rangers patrol the perimeter. There's satellite recon and infrared scans by drones. If a bear takes a shit out there, we'll know it."

The team leader looked at his watch and spoke into the mike on his wrist. "Team status check."

"Car one ready, car two ready, car three ready, perimeter team in place, com team online, air two holding five minutes out," came the replies in rapid fire succession. Good. Everyone was on their toes. This was the best detail in the Secret Service, and he meant to keep it that way.

"Anyway, Ben, you're new on the team. It takes a lot to get promoted to this assignment, you've got a good record, don't fuck it up. Falcon likes to do things his way with no questions asked. There are the Service's protocols and then there are Falcon's. We follow Falcon's."

Ben nodded. He didn't like it. The people he was charged with protecting didn't always know what was good for them, but the team leader was right, he was the new guy, and it wasn't time to rock the boat, not yet.

"I've got movement on the path, looks like Falcon," said the voice in Ben's earpiece. The perimeter team member saw Falcon in his goggles, the heat radiating from his body silhouetted against the cool forest. Ben opened the passenger door, illuminating the end of the forest path.

Falcon emerged walking slowly, staring at the ground, and rubbing his left arm. Immediately the team leader was alerted. Falcon was in his late sixties with a known heart condition.

"Sir, are you alright? Do you need medevac?" He raised his wrist to his mouth to issue the alert for medevac but was halted by Falcon's steely glare.

"I'm fine, goddamn it. Let's get back to the ranch." Falcon climbed into the SUV's back seat and stared straight ahead. The team leader closed the door. He knew better than to suggest that Falcon put on his seat belt. Again, Falcon's protocols — not the Service's — applied.

"Falcon on board, saddle up, returning to Cerberus. Check in."

"Perimeter team secure, car one ready, car two ready, car three ready, com team — Cerberus alerted — twenty-five minutes out, air two taking lead," crackled the voices in his ear.

"Acknowledged, let's roll."

The three SUVs sped down the forest road with blue lights flashing, past the guardhouse, and onto the state highway en route to Falcon's home, the Cerberus ranch. Two thousand feet above the Blackhawk helicopter scanned the road ahead of the convoy.

The Tripwire

"Some Cupid kills with arrows, some with traps."
– William Shakespeare

The Bobover jet landed at Damascus International Airport and taxied to the private terminal area where a black Land Rover and driver were waiting. The flight attendant again handled the formalities with the immigration officials. Sarah noticed that Shlomo's passport had two US hundred dollar bills tucked inside, apparently standard procedure.

In no time, they were speeding away from the airport on a modern four-lane road which quickly became two lanes, and then one single bad lane. All traces of Damascus disappeared in the distance, replaced by featureless desert. Shlomo sat in the front seat, speaking occasionally to the driver in Arabic, with Sarah and David in back looking like wide-eyed tourists.

"Shlomo, how long till we get there?" David asked, disoriented by the rapid-fire events of the day, he needed something to focus on.

"The driver thinks it's a two-hour drive if we don't have delays."

"What do you expect we'll find there?"

Shlomo turned in his seat to face the rear seat. "I expect we'll find nothing," he replied in his customary deadpan tone.

"Nothing?" exclaimed Sarah. "Then why are we going there?"

"Nothing is unusual; we are going there to confirm that there is nothing there." Shlomo paused, meeting their eyes. He had a flair for the dramatic, possibly a holdover from his years as the Grand Rebbe.

"The history of the Phoenician traders is important in understanding how their culture spread though the region. All Phoenician sites are well-documented. Ugarit has extensive, well-documented ruins, but there are no records of any Moloch temple, no site surveys, no excavations, no listing of artifacts. As the celebrated English detective Sherlock Holmes said, this is the curious incident of the dog in the night-time."

"Okay, I'll bite. What about the dog in the night?" David asked.

"The curiosity is that the dog didn't bark in the night even though the house was being robbed." Shlomo showed a hint of a smirk. "Sometimes absence is the most interesting clue." Shlomo looked at the driver and then back at Sarah and David.

"There is a hole in the archeological record concerning Ugarit. Someone has gone to great lengths to wipe the record clean of references to Moloch. There are no other published accounts, not even references to any temples in other research. This was no easy task. It was only by inference that we discovered Ugarit's relationship to Moloch. I think we need to find out who has suppressed these records and why."

Sarah raised her eyebrows at David and her head tilted. He shared her feelings. The enormity of their task loomed large like an enormous mountain peak emerging from the mist. Whoever we were dealing with had substantial resources as evidenced by their ability to alter the historical record.

As they continued on in silence, the rutted dirt road turned into no road at all. The driver navigated toward a set of GPS coordinates, following the rolling landscape as best he could. The Land Rover strained, its wheels spinning on the uneven terrain. David began to feel woozy. As they cleared a rise, the party saw the ocean and heard the waves crashing on the beach. The driver pointed to a hill and said something in Arabic.

"He says that's where the ruins are," translated Shlomo without looking back. "The ruins of the ancient city of Ugarit are eight kilometers to the north. This temple was positioned away from the population at that time,"

On top of the hill was a pile of low rubble, hardly one block on top of another. From what they could see, it was a wasted effort to travel here. On an adjacent hill, was a Bedouin tent with an old man sitting under an awning. The driver drove up the hill and parked in front of the rubble. They all got out and surveyed the desolate scene. A gust of wind blew sand into their faces as if warning them away. Two desert jackals appeared on a far hill and watched them. Sarah imagined them as guardians of what had transpired here ages ago.

David's first thought was that they'd come a long way for nothing. The site was large, at least a hundred feet in each direction. A few columns lay broken on the ground, as did a few whole square blocks and many broken ones. At first glance, there was nothing to identify the ruins as having anything to do with Moloch.

"I'm going to have a look around," said Sarah, grabbing her hat and camera from the Land Rover.

"Okay. Shlomo, what do you think?" David asked, hoping for another revelation to erase his disappointment. He wasn't sure what he'd been expecting, but this wasn't it. He had a hard time seeing where this might lead them.

"The site is of poor quality. It is hard to discern the layout of the original structure. There are no remaining reliefs or inscriptions." Shlomo's voice trailed off without further comment. The driver leaned against the Land Rover smoking. David watched Sarah scampering among the stones that littered the hillside.

The Bedouin who'd been sitting beside his tent walked up the hill and spoke in Arabic to the driver, who then pointed to Shlomo. The old Bedouin was dressed in long black robes and a black turban, both dusty and frayed. His wrinkled and weathered face was covered with the white stubble of a week-old beard. He was thin and short, not even coming up to Shlomo's shoulder. Shlomo and the old man spoke for a minute.

"The old man wants to know if we're lost, if we're looking for the beach. I told him that we were interested in Moloch's temple. He said he knows nothing about this site. That no one ever comes here."

Just then Sarah rejoined us. "Shlomo, I found a block that has a partial bull's head carving. Let me show you."

The three searchers walked down the hill with the old man trailing along. We climbed over some rubble to a large cracked stone. Sarah had turned over a stone fragment with a stylized relief carving of a bull's head on a man's shoulders. The old man looked at the carving and then back at us.

"This is it. It's small, easily overlooked but unmistakable. This was Moloch's temple." Sarah was quite proud of her find.

Shlomo nodded. "I think we should get back in the car and leave."

"Leave?" said Sarah, "we've only just arrived. There is clear evidence that this was a temple to Baal or Moloch. I think we should survey the entire site. There may be other artifacts. Some possible clues."

"No, we need to leave now. I will explain on the way back to Damascus. It may not be safe here." Shlomo's voice was quiet but firm.

The old man spoke to Shlomo again in Arabic. Shlomo listened, nodded, and walked back up the hill. Sarah and I followed along, leaving the old man standing beside the bull's head relief. At the Land Rover, Shlomo watched the old man return to his tent.

"Shlomo, what's wrong? Why do you think we're in danger? There's no one here except that old coot. He doesn't look very threatening."

"The fact that he is here at all is concerning. What is he doing here? He is not grazing animals. He has nothing in his tent other than a skin of water, a low chair, and a wooden box. This is not a traditional encampment. He has no obvious purpose here other than to watch the temple, to watch for us. I fear we've set off an alarm. Let's get in the car. I want to see something."

Shlomo spoke to the driver. "I've ask him to stop over the next ridge. I want to see what the old Bedouin does when we're out of sight."

The driver stopped as directed. "Come with me but stay low," said Shlomo, taking some binoculars with him. They walked back to the crest of the rise and crawled to the edge. Shlomo looked through the binoculars. "Yes, it is as I feared. Take a look." Shlomo handed David the binoculars. He saw the old man talking on a large handheld phone. David passed the binoculars to Sarah.

"Do you see it? He has a satellite phone. He has alerted someone to our presence. What is it that you Americans say? The cat is out of the bag," Shlomo said.

Children of Lilith

"The world is full of massive things in motion. Little creatures get hurt." – Robert Fanney

Philippe Lambert stood at the lectern set on the conference table at la Société pour la Préservation de Antiquités Assyriennes—the Society for the Preservation of Assyrian Antiquities—in Paris. He was impeccably dressed in his bespoke linen suit and shirt from the Left Bank tailor, Arnys, the same tailor patronized by President Mitterand. Lambert liked the association. His hair was well oiled, shiny, and black. He had a trim toothbrush mustache. A bright pink Hermès tie completed his look. The small lectern suited his diminutive stature. He believed it made him look taller, which bolstered his ego. His height of five feet two had always been a sore point with Philippe. He had been bullied as a child and never given his due respect as an adult.

Tall windows filled the conference room with light. The high ceilings, paneled walls, and provincial antique furniture gave the room a palatial feel which Lambert believed reflected his destiny. The invited patrons, mostly old ladies and pensioners, listened casually as they picked at their pastries. They came once a month to his lectures on Middle Eastern history. Lambert knew nothing of history, but his secretary did. Annette St. Pierre, a PhD ABD (All But Dissertation) in early Middle Eastern history from the Sorbonne. She prepared his lectures including phonetic spellings of all academic words. Annette liked her job. It paid her twice the salary of a tenured professor for performing light office duties and trivial research. The arrangement worked for all concerned, Lambert maintained the Société's facade as a philanthropic organization, and Annette had her revenge by living well on all those people who'd refused to hire her because of her failure to complete her dissertation on time.

Lambert had been speaking for ten minutes when Annette knocked on the conference room door.

"Excuse me, Monsieur Lambert." She spoke in an apologetic tone, knowing that Lambert did not like being disturbed, but she had been given emphatic instructions regarding this situation.

"Yes, Mademoiselle St. Pierre, What is it?" The lecture had been going well and Lambert became annoyed at losing his momentum.

"There is a call for you on line 9. I have it on hold in your office."

Lambert's face went blank for an instant; then, regaining his composure, he smiled at his audience. "Mesdames et Messieurs, please excuse me. This is a call from one of our representatives in the Middle East with news about the rescue of an important artifact. I will be back shortly. Annette, will you see that everyone has fresh coffee and pastries?"

"Yes, Monsieur Lambert," replied Annette. The small crowd stirred in their seats at the prospect.

Lambert walked briskly down the hall. He enjoyed playing the expert, but distained the old codgers who turned up once a month. *The old farts only come because we stuff their gullets with pastries,* he mused.

He turned his attention to the call. An alarm had been raised. Line 9 was exclusively for satellite phones used by various operatives throughout the Middle East on watch for anyone tracing the location of Moloch artifacts. He closed the heavy padded doors to his office, ensuring he would not be overheard. Like the conference room, his office had floor-to-ceiling glass windows and gilded wooden paneling. A door opened onto a balcony overlooking a quiet residential street three stories below.

Lambert sat at his massive oak desk, unlocked the bottom drawer, and removed a small wooden box and leather binder. He held the box in both hands, feeling its smooth texture with his fingers. The box held his ring, the most precious object in the world to him. He ran his fingers over the mystical symbols inlayed in gold on the cover:

The same symbols were engraved on the ring, set on either side of a skull, reminding Lambert that he would serve the goddess unto death.

Lambert had been recruited to head the Société three years ago. As part of the position, he was required to join what he'd was told was a fraternal society, the Sons of Lilith. He'd agreed because the pay was incredible, and refusing was not an option. He'd joined eleven other initiates at the Babylon Woods in Idaho at a nighttime ceremony deep in the forest. The initiates had come from around the globe, and all had been given code names of birds. His was Raven. They stood in a line before a massive owl statue on a broad stage. The light from flaming cauldrons flickered against the polished ebony statue. A small pedestal held a crude bronze bowl in front of the statue. A man known only as Falcon wearing a black robe and a mask in the likeness of his namesake addressed them, educating them about the goddess Lilith, Adam's first wife before Eve, and how her children inhabited the same world as the children of Eve.

Lambert had thought the ceremony was melodramatic, silly, like something meant to scare children at summer camp. But then Falcon took the bronze bowl, raised it before the statue, and spoke words he could not understand. The forest became still. He ceased to hear the flames crackling in the cauldrons. A chill swept through the forest. The wings of the owl statue opened and arched across the stage. A circle of light appeared filled with swirling mists which cleared revealing the goddess. She was beautiful, tall and stately, with black hair and piercing eyes. She stepped onto the stage accompanied by a child clutching her gown. She was luminescent, lighting the clearing in the forest. Lambert reveled in the power emanating from her, an invisible force pulsating against and through him.

"I am Queen Lilith. I have walked this earth for thousands of years. I am Adam's first wife. I lived with him in the land called Eden. Adam refused me as an equal, and I refused to submit unto him. Before the time of Eve, I left Adam in Eden and founded my own dynasty with Samael. Our children have lived side by side with the children of Eve for centuries." Lilith moved to the edge of the stage and extended her arms.

"You are the Lilim, my children. We have searched for you that we might bring you home to your true family. Search your hearts, you know that you've always walked alone, separate, uneasy with the children of Eve. You knew you didn't belong. You were lost wandering the wilderness searching for your home, for where you belonged. Welcome home, my beloved children."

Tears ran down Lambert's face. It was true. He'd always been a man apart, ill at ease, and uncomfortable with people. He was not respected by men, and shunned by women. His small stature had always set him apart, but this feeling ran deeper, a sensation that he was different from those around him, almost a different species. Now he understood. He'd come home, and the beautiful woman before him was the mother of all those like him.

Falcon beckoned Lambert to kneel before Lilith. She touched him, filling him with her magnificence, anointing him. Her power flowed into him, transforming him, wiping away his past, his self-doubts, filling him with power, and consecrating him to her service. Lambert could think of no more joyous task then serving her. The goddess touched the other eleven initiates in turn. When she was done, he remembered she looked tired. She spread her arms in a benediction to the initiates, and then she and the child faded away like smoke dissolving in the wind. His head cleared. He was imbrued with a new purpose. The owl statue resumed its original position, inert once more.

Falcon took Lilith's place on the stage.

"You are no longer initiates. You are the princes of Lilith. You will rule with us when our plan comes to fruition."

Falcon handed each prince a small wooden box containing an identical ring. He then described the grand plan for the return of the goddess, and told them they were the twelve chosen to rule the world with her when she returned.

Lambert wore the ring late at night, believing he could feel the presence of the goddess, and wondering if she heard his prayers. The goddess would soon return to rule the world, and he, her faithful servant unto death, would be the prince of all Europe.

He took a breath and picked up line 9. "Location and report," said Lambert sharply in Arabic, his Lebanese accent still discernable.

The unsteady voice on the phone hesitated between sentences. "Ugarit. Three people arrived an hour ago, two men and one woman. One man and the woman were American; the other man may have been Israeli. They arrived in a Land Rover with Damascus registrations

MDC345. They had a driver who stood by the car smoking the entire time."

"Yes, continue," Lambert said impatiently, wanting to know why he'd been alerted.

"I approached them, asking if I could help with directions as I was told to do."

"Yes, yes, very good, you followed directions perfectly. Continue." Lambert lowered his voice remembering the simple, uneducated Bedouin he was speaking with.

"They asked about the site, asked if this was Moloch's temple, if there was a nearby museum. I said the site was unknown, of no importance. They examined the stones for some time and noticed a bull's head carved on one. They seemed very excited."

The voice paused again, and then continued, "When anyone asks about Moloch or the temple, my instructions are to send them to the Syrian Archeology Foundation at 89 Mabarah Street in Damascus. They wrote down the address and left a few minutes ago."

"You have done well and followed procedure to the letter. There will be ten extra pounds in this month's payment," said Lambert with an inner smile. Ten Syrian pounds was a small fortune to this man and his family, but a pittance to Lambert. He hung up the phone.

These people were not sightseers on holiday looking for a beach. They were specifically searching for Moloch's temple and artifacts. They were knowledgeable, noticing the bull symbols confirmed that. He needed to alert Falcon.

Lambert switched on his computer behind his desk. He disliked computers, preferring handwritten letters, but letters did not provide the anonymity of the Deep Web with its layers of servers, encryption, and message forwarding that routed data around the world, guaranteeing secure, untraceable communications. The young man with a crew cut who had installed the computer last year had told him the system was originally developed by the US Navy and employed military level encryption. He wondered how his superiors had access to such technologies, but he knew better than to ask any questions. When he was recruited, it was implied that his predecessor's job performance had not been satisfactory, with a further implication that such failure had dire consequences.

Lambert carefully typed. *Three visitors to the Ugarit site ten minutes ago. Two Americans, one man and one woman, with a third man, possibly an Israeli, and specifically looking for Moloch artifacts. They are en route to the Damascus location. The normal diversion plan will be employed. If not successful, we will escalate to the hostile diversion plan. Will await your orders on possible termination of subjects.*

Lambert read over his message. He didn't send messages often and wanted to get the wording correct. He pressed "send," knowing it would take several minutes to arrive. Where it went he didn't know, but he knew that Falcon would respond shortly. He dialed the Damascus number. A woman's voice on the other end answered, "Syrian Archeology Foundation."

"Mr. Titi Villus please."

"Oh, yes. One moment please," came the response after a short pause.

"This is Mr. Titi Villus." The voice was deep and masculine. Lambert had recruited the speaker, Tali Alay, a Turk, to run the diversion site. He spoke passable Arabic, but his Turkish origins were betrayed with every word. He looked more like a longshoreman than an archeologist, and dressing him in respectable clothes did little to hide his true nature, that of a clever thug. Like Lambert, he was a man practiced at theft by subterfuge, a con artist. Unlike Lambert, he was also a killer, a skill mastered when a few of his con jobs had not gone as planned.

"Raven here. Three subjects on the way to your location, an American man and woman, a third man possibly Israeli. Open the archives and prepare for their arrival."

"Understood. When are they expected?"

"They left Ugarit 30 minutes ago, so expect them at your location within three hours. Report back when the subjects have been diverted," replied Lambert.

"Mr. Titi Villus will be waiting," said Alay.

"Report back to me once they have left your location."

"Yes, sir, immediately." Alay hung up and went to look for his coat and tie.

Philippe Lambert stood, smoothing the wrinkles in his linen suit. He longed for the day when the goddess, his queen, would return. He longed for her touch, and the power and glory it imparted. He would reign for centuries by her side basking in her glory.

Lambert walked back to the conference room where his audience awaited. Pearls before swine, he snickered to himself. He couldn't remember what he had been talking about, and he hoped his doting, crumb-covered audience couldn't either.

Hide and Seek

"Nothing good comes from hiding in the shadows." – David A.
Broughton

On the road back to Damascus, Shlomo turned to face Sarah
and David in the back seat.

"The old Bedouin man said we should go to the
Syrian Archeology Foundation in Damascus if we wanted to
know more about the temple ruins."

"What do you expect we'll find there?" David asked.

"I expect to find nothing, resoundingly nothing,"
replied Shlomo without a hint of concern.

"Nothing? Again? More subterfuge? Don't these
archeological groups keep good records? Preserve things?"
David couldn't help sounding exasperated.

"That site has been sterilized. Purposely cleaned of
anything relating to Moloch. It is only through Sarah's
curiosity, luck, and their carelessness that we were able to
find a clue."

"So you expect that the next location is some kind of
fake designed to throw off any inquiries." Sarah chimed in.

"Correct. Whoever these people are, I'm convinced
they have the chalice you seek. They're well financed and
organized, the extent of which we can only guess at."

"So that old man is a sentinel, and the place he's
sending us is either a sham or a trap," David said. Shlomo
nodded.

Shlomo took a breath. "Well, let's speculate, as much
as I dislike it. These people have gone to considerable time
and effort to alter historical documents removing references

to Moloch's temple and the chalice. They're intent, fanatical even, on remaining hidden."

"Yes, I agree," said Sarah. "I'm impressed, and a bit scared, by the effort they've expended to remain hidden. They are clearly obsessed with secrecy."

"Indeed." replied Shlomo. "Secrecy is their hallmark. Given that, I would surmise that a well-choreographed dead end designed to stymie any academic research awaits us. They want to terminate any lines of inquiry."

David realized that they were in trouble again, that the cold trail they were following was about to ice over completely.

"Sarah, Shlomo, I think we all agree that the chalice is so well hidden that is unlikely we'll ever find it through normal means. The pile of stones we just left was our only lead, and we only found it because of you, Shlomo. Now we're headed to what we believe is a carefully arranged dog and pony show meant to send us home empty-handed."

"Are you suggesting that we should pack it in?" asked Sarah sounding incredulous.

"No, not at all. My point is that we can't find the chalice by looking for it directly. It is too well hidden. But we can look for the people who have hidden it, and hope—I know it's a long shot—that if we find them, we'll find the chalice."

Sarah and Shlomo were silent for several moments, and David expected one of Sarah's loving dope slaps.

"I think you're correct, Mr. Austin. It is our only logical choice. After the Syrian Archeology Foundation, we'll have no leads, no path to the chalice."

Sarah smiled slightly and twirled her fingers in David's hair.

David watched the barren landscape rush by in silence for a few minutes, wondering who they were up against. He feared their opponents were more organized, better funded, and, without a doubt, more ruthless than they were. Their only hope was to go unnoticed, to allow the dragon to continue sleeping, certain its treasure was safe.

The trouble was they'd already given the dragon a poke. They'd alerted the old man, who had contacted his employers. The mouse needed to return to the undergrowth, and the dragon to its slumber.

"Shlomo, I think it is best if these people don't know we're looking for them. As you said, they seem to have buckets of money, and a lot of people working for them. They could do us some serious harm if they thought we were a real threat."

"Yes, I'm sure their resources are considerable, and while we don't know their intent, we should assume that they are hostile."

"David, what do you have in mind?" Sarah leaned in.

"Until we came across the Bedouin, we were off their radar. Now we're a blip. They will want to resolve this blip, to believe that it has gone away."

"Yes, you're right. They need to believe that any perceived violation of their security has been resolved," said Sarah turning in her seat to face David directly.

"Exactly," David replied, pleased that Sarah had gotten his point.

"What do you suggest we do, Mr. Austin?"

"Shlomo, you said that you were expecting a well-organized dead end as a way of throwing people off the trail."

"Yes, I'd be surprised if we found anything else."

"Then let's play along. We should go there and leave discouraged. Tell them that we're giving up. That we're going back to Jerusalem. Let them think that their quarterback fake-out has worked. Let's drop off their radar."

Shlomo raised an eyebrow. "Quarterback fake-out?"

"Sorry—American football—it means fooling the other team."

Shlomo nodded. Sarah squeezed David's hand. "Okay, so we go in, we listen to them tell us that there is nothing known about the site, put on our long faces, and leave?" she asked.

"Exactly, but I think I should go in alone," said Shlomo.

"Why?" David sounded put off that his plan had changed.

"The early Hebrew warriors would always hide their true numbers from their enemies by marching single file. We don't need to let these people know any more than we have to. If they ask about you two, I will tell them that you were tourists along for the ride, sharing the cost of the car, and that you've since left for Crete."

'Okay, good point," said Sarah nodding at David to emphasize the wisdom of Shlomo's plan.

"I will play that part of a PhD student from Brooklyn, which should be easy since it is mostly true."

"What are we going to do after we've played our part in their charade? What's our next step?" asked Sarah. David admitted to himself that it was a good question. He had no idea how to uncover a powerful, ruthless, global, super-secret organization.

"That, I'm not sure of," said Shlomo. He looked worried, which made David worry even more. "Normally, I would say, follow the money. It would lead us to whoever is financing the organization, but in this case I'd suspect the money trail is well hidden, too many shell corporations and secret bank accounts. It might take years to piece it together. No, our only hope is that they have made some mistake that we can take advantage of. The bull icon fragment at Ugarit was such a mistake. Without more such luck, you and Mr. Austin may indeed be going home."

Shlomo was right. For the second time in two weeks, they were up against it. Unless they got lucky, they'd have nowhere to go, no clues, no bread-crumbs to follow. Shlomo had saved the day before by finding Moloch's original temple, and then only because he was brilliant, and whoever had tried to hide its location had been sloppy, stupid, or both.

The threesome remained silent contemplating their odds of success. Houses and streets replaced the barren landscape. They'd be back in Damascus shortly. David's thoughts returned to his first meeting with Abigail, standing in the twilight forest with her white dress flowing in the breeze, the same white dress from the photograph. The photograph was etched on his brain. He remembered every detail. He saw it perfectly.

David began to drift off. The constant noise of the Land Rover faded, and he began to hear Abigail's thoughts. He'd heard her thoughts once before in Jerusalem, softly, like someone talking at a distance, faint and incomplete. Then it was hard to tell if what he heard was an illusion or real. Now there was no distance between them. The SUV disappeared and David found he was sharing Abigail's body, seeing through her eyes and hearing through her ears. Their thoughts, their inner narrative, became a single voice.

Abigail was in a vast, dark, cavernous chamber lined with eight balconies filled with demons of every conceivable horrific form. The sounds of the demons screeching and writhing filled the air.

Abigail was alert, scanning those around her, wary of an attack at any second. David felt her tension rising and also tremendous energy welling up within her, a power he would never have guessed she possessed, and that he wasn't sure Abigail was aware of herself. She was ready for battle, poised for the first attack. She possessed an innate knowledge, an instinct for fighting. If attacked she would react instantly. She was surrounded by hundreds, possibly thousands of demons, and would likely not succeed against such odds, but David sensed no doubt, no hesitation within her. She stood bravely in what David could only imagine was hell itself.

The demons, oblivious to Abigail, were fixated on a woman standing on a stage lit by four flaming cauldrons. The light from the flames flickered across the faces of the ghoulish audience. The woman was tall, stately, with black hair adorned by a golden crown of flames. Her alabaster skin appeared radiant in the dark chamber. The woman stood before a massive owl statue which appeared to move in the shadowy light.

David didn't know who she was, but she was beautiful, enticing. The more David looked at her, the stronger his attraction to her became. She reached out to him, drawing him closer. David longed to go to her, to stand in her presence.

Then David heard Abigail shouting inside his head, *David, do not look upon her, she is evil, she will corrupt your will, remember your quest.* Abigail broke his fixation on the woman.

David heard the terror underlying Abigail's thoughts. She'd been shaken by what she'd seen. *David, the queen's plan is to release a plague, a virus that will kill every human on*

Earth. They will be ready within a few weeks.

"David, wake up. Are you okay? David!" It was Sarah's voice. She stood outside the open door of the Land Rover shaking David's shoulder. "Honey, is something wrong? You were mumbling about something, but I couldn't make out what you were saying."

David rubbed his eyes, brushed back his hair, and then focused on Sarah. "Shit, that scared the pants off me."

"What scared you?" she asked.

"I think I was just inside Abigail's head. She's in a dark cavern somewhere filled with demons with a beautiful woman in standing in the center wearing a crown of flames."

Shlomo stood behind Sarah, his wide eyes riveted on David. He had some explaining to do.

The Warrior

"The real voyage of discovery consists not in seeking new landscapes, but in having new eyes." – Marcel Proust

Abigail followed the members of Eymerich's entourage as they silently shuffled into the salon, looking shrunken and dazed. The queen had drained them. All appeared washed out, drained of color, and weakened almost to the point of losing their human appearance.

Abigail sidestepped along the wall, trying to blend in and hoping for time to digest what she'd witnessed. Her strength remained intact, her dress still vivid red and hair auburn. The facade of the queen's court had momentarily vanished, revealing the true nature of Gehenna. She'd seen her cross over and learned the enormity of the queen's plan. Ehyeh had told her of the scheme, but to hear the details and how close it was to fulfillment filled Abigail with terror.

Lord Eymerich rose from his throne and stood unsteadily, looking like he might collapse. His blustering bravado had vanished, and he spoke in a thin voice. "Let us retire to chambers to renew ourselves and pray that the wretched queen does not summon us again anytime soon."

The salon inhabitants dragged themselves into the corridor. The countess rose, motioned to Abigail, and whispered, "Attend us." The other ladies in waiting followed, forming a small procession. In the corridor, each salon member entered a different door. The German colonel in the black uniform who had manhandled her earlier entered a door with black iron letters over it: "Arbeit Macht Frei." "Contra Naturam" was carved over the countess's door. Abigail didn't understand either phrase, but she guessed they were remnants of their occupants' prior lives.

The countess led them into a large dark room with an iron candelabra hanging from the ceiling, lighting the center of the room and leaving the edges in shadows. An immense golden bathtub stood gleaming in the center. Its sides were decorated in a relief of young girls dancing, and large ball-and-claw feet supported it. The head of the bathtub curved upwards and was topped with a tall Teutonic eagle, its wings outstretched, holding a scepter in one talon and a heraldic shield in the other. Along the edges of the room, Abigail saw figures lying against the wall barely visible in the gloom. They stirred as we entered, and she heard the sounds of chains clanking on the stone floor.

The ladies in waiting reverted to their demonic forms. And while they remained female, wearing the same elaborate dresses, their cloven hoofs showed beneath their skirts and clattered on the floor. They looked almost comical, like horrid circus animals prancing about in royal gowns.

The countess trudged to the side of the bathtub and disrobed with the help of her attending demons. She had changed. Her face was wizened, wrinkled, and her eyes and cheeks sunken. She had the skeletal body of an old woman. Her parchment skin was covered in sores and drawn taught over her ribs and pendulous, shrunken breasts. Her thin, stringy hair barely covered her scalp. The countess stepped into the tub and reclined with her eyes closed, resembling a long dead corpse in its coffin.

The demons dragged several figures from the shadows, pulling them by chains attached to iron collars around their throats. They were women, younger than her, naked and covered with filth. They cowered at the sight of the countess. The demons yanked the chains, cruelly jerking their heads, pulling them closer to the golden tub.

Two demons grabbed a young girl and bent her over the bathtub. She was young, barely thirteen or fourteen, just beginning her transformation into womanhood. Grime and dirt covered her alabaster skin, and her golden hair hung limp on her shoulders. The third demon approached the countess bearing a knife on a red satin pillow. Its long curved blade and jeweled handle glistened in the candlelight. The countess took the knife and, with one swift stroke, sliced open the girl's throat. Her gurgling screams echoed in the chamber as a torrent of blood flowed from her wound showering the countess. When she was drained and limp, looking like death itself, the young woman was cast to the ground. Abigail stepped backwards, repulsed by the ceremony, till her back pressed against the wall. The same horrific process was repeated with eight other women, all young, all barely through puberty.

The countess began to rejuvenate as Abigail watched. Her skin became supple, her flesh restored. Her hair returned to fullness, and her breasts became round and full. She stretched as though awaking from a long sleep. A demon took a golden cup and poured blood over her arms and legs as the countess luxuriated in its effects.

Her horrific bath transfixed Abigail. She'd never witnessed such horror. The nature of where she was and the dangers she faced became starkly real. She was in the *chambre de sang*, the countess's blood chamber where she renewed herself by bathing in blood. The young women lay in a heap upon the floor, some moaning, others barely stirring. The souls of these young women were trapped, doomed to forever participate in this grisly ritual.

The countess, now partially revived, turned to Abagail. "Take the knife, Lady Abigail, that you may participate in our rejuvenation." The countess smiled, seeming to enjoy the anguish that showed on Abigail's face. She handed her the knife as the two demons positioned another victim beside the bathtub pulling back her head exposing her throat.

The knife, still dripping in blood, rested on Abigail's open palm with the terror of its victims radiating from it. The knife's accumulated evil crept up her arm like ice. She could not perform such acts merely to hide her identity. The thought filled her with rage and revulsion. Abigail had to stop this ceremony and prevent its reoccurrence. There was but one choice, destroy the countess.

The countess was not yet fully restored, and Abigail hoped, was still in a weakened state. Energy rose within Abigail as she readied herself. Abigail grasped the knife, feeling its cold weight in her hand. She stood beside the next victim. The young woman looked at Abigail, her face contorted in horror, and struggling against the grip of her captors. Abigail hesitated. Once she attacked, it would be a fight till one of them was destroyed, but there was no time to plan—the countess was gaining strength by the second.

Abigail moved as if to slice into the young woman. She stiffened, expecting to feel the knife cutting through her throat. At the last instant, Abigail pivoted and plunged the knife deep into the countess's chest. She arched her back and screamed at the ceiling. Her eyes fixed on Abigail as rage exploded within her. The demons dropped their captive, staggered backwards, screeching and clawing wildly, but confused, uncertain of what to do.

The countess swung her arm, striking Abigail across her face, breaking her grip, and knocking her to the floor. The countess leapt from the tub dripping with blood, her vigor more restored than Abigail had realized. The countess grabbed the knife and pulled it from her chest, screaming as she did so. As Abigail watched, the countess reverted to her demonic form. Her head became that of a wolf with red eyes and sharp fangs. Her long and sinuous arms ended in great hands tipped with pointed nails, her body covered in dark scales, and her legs covered with black fur ending in hoofs. She roared, twisting her head from side to side as she moved toward Abigail.

Abigail struggled from the floor and stepped backwards looking wildly for some place to run. There was only the golden bathtub, and the three demons prevented her from moving to the other side. She had no choice but to stand and fight. As Abigail raised her arm to defend herself, she saw that she held a sword. *Where had it come from?* This was the second time in Gehenna that she'd unwittingly made an object. The gleaming sword became an extension of her arm. Abigail swung it back and forth with broad sweeping slashes, feeling it singing in her hand as her energy flowed through it. Abigail's courage rebounded.

The monster stopped her advance, as surprised by the sword as Abigail was. The demon countess became silent and lowered her stance. She took a step back and circled Abigail, trying to gain position by forcing her against the bathtub. Without waiting for her, Abigail charged, holding the sword in both hands, and thrust at her body. She screeched and jumped backwards, barely avoiding Abigail's sword.

She grasped the knife she held by the hilt and, with a blur of her arm, threw it at Abigail. Instinctively, Abigail struck the knife with her sword in mid-air. Sparks flew as the knife tumbled into the darkness and clattered against the wall. The countess raised her head, looking for the knife. Unable to see it, she screeched and became even more outraged.

Out of the corner of her eye, Abigail saw the demon she knew as Rachael charge and leap into the air. The countess saw her too. She readied herself to attack when Rachael landed on her. Time slowed. A surge of energy flowed within Abigail. Her sword glowed and, in a blur, she spun and caught Rachael in mid-air, slicing her body in half. The blade sizzled as it cut, leaving a putrid smoke trail. The demon's body fell to the floor twitching.

Her spin had left Abigail facing the countess. She stopped, rearing back, and staring at Rachael lying dismembered on the floor. Abigail sprinted at the countess again, but her reactions were too quick and the countess jumped over Abigail, twisting in mid-air and raking her back and shoulder. Pain coursed through her and she cried out. The countess landed behind Abigail and lashed out with her claws. Abigail leaped ahead of her reach, rolled on the floor, and jumped to her feet. The countess ran and leaped at Abigail again with her talons ready to rip into her.

Abigail dropped to one knee and swung her sword in a broad arch, slicing deeply into the countess. The countess fell to the floor and skidded for several feet as her screeching echoed throughout the chamber. Before she could recover, Abigail jumped, landing with her legs straddling the demon. She plunged her sword through the countess' body and into the stone beneath. She screamed and writhed, impaled by the sword. Her arms and legs flailed wildly, but the sword held fast. She grabbed Abigail's legs, sinking her claws deeply into her. Searing pain shot through Abigail.

Gripping the sword with both hands, Abigail used it to pull the energy from her, the same energy the countess had just drawn from the young women during her blood bath. The more Abigail drew the energy, the faster it flowed as her ability to resist weakened. Her hate-filled gaze fixed on Abigail as the countess realized the fate awaiting her.

"Who are you that you can defeat me? You are no mere child." Her voice began to weaken. "I curse you and spit at you from the depths. I—I will drag…"

Her voice faded to nothing. Her flailing slowed. She released her grip on Abigail's legs and whimpered quietly. Abigail focused all her will on drawing the last bit of energy from the demon. What had been a torrent became a trickle.

She stopped moving altogether. Her body became a translucent outline in the darkness. The countess could no longer maintain her form. With one last pull, Abigail drew the last bit of energy from her, and her wretched body dissolved in a wisp of gray mist. Abigail felt her soul fall into the chaos surrounding Gehenna. The Countess Bathory's soul was condemned to drift forever, fragmented in the violent turbulence between realms, a true living death for eternity.

Abigail pulled the sword from the stone floor. Along with the energy she'd drained from the countess came her memories. The countess had performed this same blood bath ritual when she lived in a stone castle on a hill in Hungary. She'd sent her soldiers out at night to capture young women and take them to her dungeon, where the countess tortured them for months. She bathed in the still warm blood of her victims, believing the ritual would restore her youth. This horror continued for years until she was discovered and arrested. Because of her royal stature, she was never tried, but was condemned to live out her days in a sealed room with only a small door through which food was passed. She had died in madness.

The countess's *chambre de sang* was a ghastly reenactment of her life. The young women had unwittingly shared in her illusion, condemned to relive the horror of their own deaths over and over, condemned to exist without hope, condemned to satisfy the countess's vanity and blood lust. In Gehenna, belief creates reality from illusion.

In the now silent chamber, Abigail sat cross-legged with sword in hand reflecting on her victory. The energy had risen in her like a tempest and then, just as quickly, receded, leaving her calm once more. The countess in her demonic form had been quick and brutal, but Abigail's speed and power had been more than a match for her. Her body seemed larger, her arms stronger, and her reflexes faster. The sword that had appeared in her hand was no inert blade. It was part of her, an extension of her hand, just as Abigail's hand was an extension of her arm. Her energy flowed through it, was focused and directed by it. Abigail was no longer prey, she was becoming a predator.

The golden bathtub containing the young women's blood was the last evil artifact of an evil reign. Abigail pointed her sword at it. A bolt of lightning shot from the sword with a deafening crack, lighting the room as bright as day. The bathtub dissolved. Abigail looked at the sword in her hand absorbing what she'd done. In the last few moments, she'd sent a demonic soul into the chaos, destroying the artifact that was the focus of her power — all this within the devil's own castle. Abigail hadn't known she was capable of such deeds.

Rachael's body vanished. The other two demons lay inert on the floor, appearing dead, seemingly incapable of moving without the countess. The young women's head wounds had disappeared when the countess vanished. They sank to their knees and bowed their heads.

A young woman stepped from the shadows. She was tall, big-boned with broad shoulders. Her hair was cut like a man's, and her face, while kind, was plain, mannish. She wore a brown shirt, a short, gray homespun dress, and a pair of ragged boots. "Mistress, are you a warrior, a goddess, or both? You are dressed as a warrior, but you have the strength of a goddess. You have destroyed the countess, something no one would have thought possible."

At first, Abigail didn't understand what she meant until she looked down. Abigail no longer wore the red dress. She was dressed in dark blue, loose-fitting trousers with a white, full, calf-length skirt over them. She had a tight, richly embroidered tunic that fastened at the shoulder. Her chest was covered with leather armor inlaid with gold. She had similar armor on her forearms. A woven gold belt cinched Abigail's waist. Her hair was pulled back in a tight braid woven with gold cord, and a gold band with a single red jewel surrounded her head. She didn't understand her appearance but the mysterious had become commonplace.

"Please stand, all of you." Abigail's years as a Quaker had taught her that pride was a sin, and this display of honor made her uncomfortable.

The women rose, naked and filthy, still wearing iron collars with chains. Abigail saw her own face reflected in theirs. Her heart ached at the misery they'd endured. Abigail passed her sword over the crowd, dissolving their restraints. She released the remaining woman still chained to the wall. All the women gathered under the candelabra filling the chamber, surely numbering more than a hundred. Abigail raised her hands over them, and using her ability as a maker, she clothed each in a new clean dress, cleansing and restoring them as best she could.

The woman who had spoken before looked at herself and the others. They embraced one other with sobs of relief and tears rolling down their cheeks.

"Goddess, my name is Ilona Harszy. You've saved me and the others from endless torment at the hands of the countess and her demons."

"I'm not a goddess." Abigail replied sharply, embarrassed at the thought. "I'm only a farm girl not unlike yourselves."

"This cannot be, you must surely be a goddess. No one else could have defeated the countess. Long ago, we were all taken from our families, and tortured and killed by the countess. We have relived those events for what feels like centuries. Because of my size, my parents sought to disguise me as a man, but the countess's guard discovered me when I went to the village. That was my misfortune, and my fate was sealed in her dungeon." Ilona's voice was low and hoarse. She looked over her shoulder and beckoned the women lurking in the shadows to come forward.

"After each ritual, our wounds healed, and we were chained to the wall awaiting the countess's return to renew herself once more. I do not know why, but God abandoned us, leaving us condemned to an eternity in this hell. None of us committed such sins that we deserved this punishment. We had given up hope of ever being freed from this cycle of torment, but you have saved us."

"None of you deserved any punishment. You have committed no sin. You were trapped here by the countess's pervasive evil."

The faces in the crowd looked dejected. "So we are doomed to remain here for eternity? Is there no escape?" asked Ilona.

"Don't give up hope. You are innocent, and Gehenna will not hold you forever. I will find a way to free you, but for the moment you must remain here," Abigail said.

"Goddess, until this moment we were bereft with nothing but blackness and pain before us. You have given us hope. We trust that you will rescue us from this place of torment." Ilona continued, "Goddess, I beseech you. Please tell us your name."

To dispel their notion that she was a goddess, Abigail restored her white dress and let the sword vanish wanting them to see her as a peasant girl like themselves, as Abigail of China, Maine.

"I told you. I am not a goddess. My name is Abigail. Like you, I grew up on a farm, and while I wasn't murdered, I died young. We are kindred spirits, lost together in this wretched land, but you are no longer alone." She stepped to Ilona and embraced her. Ilona rested her head on Abigail and sobbed, pouring out centuries of pain in her tears. The young women drew close. Abigail shared the joy within them, knowing that hope had returned. In that moment, the grace of Arcadia filled the room.

They all stood in silence, embracing each other in a circle of intertwined arms for a long time, when Abigail noticed the familiar silence surrounding her. David had summoned her. This wasn't the best time, but she had no choice. The compulsion was building, and in a few moments Abigail would be drawn through to the land of the living.

Abigail stepped away and faced the women. "My sisters, I need your help. I've no time to explain now, but I am being called by a man in the realm of the living. I need you to stand behind me and to allow me to draw upon your energy."

"Yes, Goddess — Abigail," said Ilona. She motioned for the women to form a semicircle behind her. Abigail felt a well of energy forming, not the same as in Arcadia, but much purer than the energy she'd drawn from the town. The Arcadian energy had been like a mountain stream, clear and pure. The energy from the town was impure like water from a fetid swamp. The energy she drew from the countess's captives was pure and vibrant, more than enough to form the bridge.

The point of light materialized in front of Abigail and expanded to a circle. The mist cleared, and she saw David on the other side. She stepped through, feeling the familiar chill as her body changed to the vibrations of the living.

The Charade

"Things come apart so easily when they have been held together with lies." — Dorothy Allison

Tali Alay set about cleaning the office in preparation for his visitors. He removed the overflowing ashtrays and threw out the tabloid newspapers and men's magazines, none of which were appropriate to the academic charade he was preparing. He opened the conference room where the archives were kept which smelled of disuse and old papers. The long table had a thin layer of dust as did everything in Damascus. Tali opened the window and wiped the table and bookshelves. He had no idea what the archives contained and no interest in learning. Raven had shown him the room when he'd taken the job six years ago and told him to stay out. If anyone came asking about archaeological sites, he was to show them the room but offer no assistance or help of any kind.

Tali Alay had grown up on the streets of Ankara, Turkey, living by his wits since the age of nine. He'd quickly learned that he could make people trust him with his easygoing manner and quick smile. His life as a con artist began with hustling tourists, and later in life he'd made a career by selling fake antiquities to wealthy but naive collectors.

Tali liked the job. He considered it his retirement plan. He was well paid for doing nothing. He came in late, took a long lunch, and left early. His assistant, Mrs. Attai, opened and closed the office, answered the phone which rang once a week at best, and brought him coffee and his paper when he arrived at eleven.

In the washroom, Tali completed his transformation into Titi Villus, the director of the Syrian Archaeological Society. He shaved his three-day-old beard, combed his hair straight back using a cream that made it shine, and dressed in a clean shirt, a tie with Oxford University stripes, and a blue jacket. Tali knew that fulfilling the mark's expectations was half the con. When the visitors arrived, they would find a well-dressed professor who would send them away under a facade of authority.

Tali—now Titi Villus—had been waiting at his desk for several hours when the door buzzer rang and the voice on the intercom said in Arabic, "Mr. Tovrov to see Mr. Villus." He waved at Mrs. Attai, signaling her to buzz the visitor in. A tall, thin man wearing American clothes appeared at the top of the stairs. His eyes darted around the office appearing to take in everything.

"I'm Titi Villus, the director of the Syrian Archaeological Society. How may I help you, Mr. Tovrov?"

"My name is Shlomo Tovrov. I am a researcher from Brooklyn, New York. I visited the ruins at Ugarit today, and an old man there suggested I should come here if I wanted to learn more. I've not heard of your organization before. Does the society publish a journal? Do you sponsor research? Are you affiliated with any institutions?"

"You are a man of many questions, Mr. Tovrov. Our institute has limited funding, and has not sponsored any research in a number of years. We maintain an archive of materials open to all scholars like yourself. What university did you say you were with?"

"I am an adjunct professor at NYU. I'm researching a book on demonic legends in early Babylon with a focus on Moloch. I understand that the ruins at Ugarit were a temple to Moloch."

"I see, Mr. Tovrov. As to the site at Ugarit, unfortunately almost nothing is known. The site has long ago been picked clean of any identifying artifacts and there is almost no mention of it in our documents. I'm afraid it remains a mystery lost to the ages."

"I see. Mr. Villus, might I spend some time with your archives today?"

"Why yes, of course. This is why we are here. You may have access during our normal business hours. I'm afraid I can't allow you to stay later. We do have our policies. Did you say you were from the States? I can't quite place your accent."

"I studied Arabic in Jerusalem."

"That must be the accent I heard. Are you traveling alone? Are there others in your party?"

"No, I'm alone, a solitary scholar. I traveled with some tourists to Ugarit to share the cost of the car, but they were more interested in the beaches than the ruins. They've gone to the airport. I think they said they were going on to Crete."

Tali nodded without comment, unsure if this man was trying to con the con man. "Let me show you the Archives." He gestured toward the library. "I'm afraid you have only one hour till we close for the day. I hope that will be enough."

"It will have to be." said Shlomo. Villus, that's an unusual name. Where are you from?"

"I'm Turkish, but I've lived in Syria for many years. Please sign our register and note your local address, if you don't mind." Tali pointed to a book on the table.

Shlomo signed his name and the name of the Damascus Hilton.

"I see your last visitor was four years ago. You've not had much interest in your materials."

"Yes. Eh—ours is a unique collection that only appeals to certain historical specialties," said Tali. The lack of names in the guest book was a mistake he would correct tomorrow. "I'll leave you to your studies Mr. Tovrov."

"Mr. Villus, a question for you. Do your archives cover only northern Samaria, or do they also contain Babylonia as well?" Shlomo waited for a response.

Tali had no idea. His silence changed from awkward to nervous as the seconds ticked by. "Both subjects are covered in varying detail." He flashed a grin. "I'll leave you to it." Tali turned on his heels and ducked into his office.

Tali waited at his desk. He desperately wanted a smoke, and for this visitor to leave. There was something not right about the professor from America. At five minutes to four, the visitor emerged from the library.

"Thank you, Mr. Villus, for letting me into your archives."

"You're quite welcome, Mr. Tovrov. Did you find what you were looking for?"

"Yes," said Shlomo pausing to see Mr. Villus's expression. Tali's right eye twitched, and his stomach had turned when he thought that the charade had failed

Shlomo continued "There is no mention of anything to do with Moloch and Ugarit in your archive." Shlomo expected a dead end and he'd found it.

Tali visibly relaxed, pleased that drastic actions were not needed, and the snoopy researcher was leaving empty-handed.

"I'm sorry we couldn't have been more help."

"Yes, me too. Thank you." Shlomo put on his Yankees cap and moved to the stairs where he stopped.

"Mr. Villus, one final question if you don't mind?"

"Certainly."

"Where did you get that ring? It has an unusual symbol, the triangle with the zig-zag line within."

Tali's face dropped. His right hand instinctively touched the ring on his left. Pausing longer than he should have, he said, "This ring, it was a gift to my father by a business associate many years ago. My father later gave it to me. I'm afraid I know nothing more about it. I wear it for sentimental reasons. If you will excuse me, I need to lock up now."

Shlomo nodded and stepped quickly down the stairs. Tali bolted down the stairs as soon as the visitor left the building. On the street, his visitor's head was visible above the crowd, walking away. Tali waved at a boy, a barefoot street urchin, and handed him a coin. "Follow that tall man with the American hat. Find out where he goes, then report back to me, and there'll be another coin for you." The boy gave Tali a thumbs up and darted through the crowd after the tall American.

Tali had made a mistake, a simple but possibly a grave mistake. He'd forgotten to take off the ring that Raven had given him. It was meant only to be worn to identify him to other organization members. Raven had given him strict orders not to wear it otherwise. Raven had been very clear that mistakes regarding the existence of the organization were not tolerated, as his predecessor had learned.

Tali would have to clean up this mess before Raven found out.

Intimate Thoughts

"I wonder if this is how people always get close: They heal each other's wounds; they repair the broken skin."— Lauren Oliver

David had seen the chalice through Abigail's eyes. It was on a platform, possibly on a stage, in dark woods. It was unimpressive, more like a brass pot, as big as a good sized mixing bowl with handles on either side, and a bull's head with horns embossed on the front. His heart raced. The chalice was out there somewhere, but he was no closer to knowing where. The good news was that he'd know it if he saw it again.

The new mystery was the man called Falcon. Who could he be and where were these woods? Knowing that the chalice was in a forest didn't really narrow their search much. Falcon was dressed in summer clothes, suggesting he was in the Northern Hemisphere, and he spoke English like an American, but he wasn't from Maine, probably not New England, or the South. David had a single piece of a jigsaw puzzle, and all the other pieces were still in the box. He needed to assemble more of the puzzle to know where this piece fit.

That last thought he'd gleamed from Abigail was that the queen's plan involved some kind of plague. The stark terror of the plan took his breath away. Everyone he knew — friends, relatives, even children, all human life would die. Knowing was a curse. He didn't want to burden Sarah with the knowledge, but didn't think he could keep it from her.

And where was this psychic connection with Abigail going? It was already more intimate than he felt comfortable with. Things he barely admitted to himself were laid open to her. And yet the experience was invigorating. The deeper the connection, the stronger and more confident he became.

It was a drug that scared him, but one he couldn't resist.

Their hotel was above a row of stores on a back street in Damascus. Shlomo referred to it as a workingman's hotel, which was not what Sarah was used to. Even David thought the room was dumpy, and his standards were pretty low. The paint was old, the bed lumpy, and the bathroom not so clean. Shlomo had chosen it because it was in an out-of-the-way neighborhood and they would avoid attracting attention. But he'd failed to consider that pulling up in a fifty-thousand-dollar black Range Rover with a driver would cause a curious crowd gathered as they unloaded. They might as well have hung out a sign.

"So what else can you tell me about your experience with Abigail?" asked Sarah, "Has this kind of thing happened before and you didn't tell me?"

"I think I told you the highlights. It was like watching a movie with a sporadic commentary. If Abigail didn't understand something, then I didn't either. I told you what the chalice looks like. I saw it, it's real, and a man called Falcon had it in a dark forest. He wore a bird mask.

"She heard them talking about combining influenza and Ebola in a lab somewhere in North Korea. The work isn't complete yet, but it seems to be on schedule."

"Oh my God! If they manage to make a contagious airborne version of Ebola, it could kill millions, maybe billions of people." Sarah's voice trailed off. "When we started all this, even when Abigail came to us, part of me never quite believed this was really happening. Now it's like a tidal wave rushing at us."

David knew what she meant. There's knowing about something, and then there's believing it in your gut. "That's it—the whole thing. And no, in case you were wondering, this thought sharing with Abigail hadn't happened before. This was new, really new, all the way around. In Jerusalem, when you were taking a nap, I heard Abigail talking to me, but I thought it was a dream and didn't think anything of it."

"I don't know, David. This is all strange stuff. I'm worried, worried about how far this may go. Would you lose control? You'll have to be on guard. You zoned out in the car with your eyes wide open. It was creepy." Sarah rubbed David's hand.

"I have no control, at least not yet. It's not like when I summoned her before. The only thing I can tell you, and I don't know why I know this, but she's closer. Don't ask me what that means because I don't know. That's just how it feels."

Sarah fixed on David with an 'Oh, my God!' look. "Okay sweetie, we'll roll with it." She ruffled his hair.

Sarah went to the bathroom, and cleaned the sink and toilet with a towel before closing the door. "Shlomo will be back from checking out the Archaeological Society soon. We'll see what, if anything, he's found out." Sarah's voice echoed from the bathroom. "He's going to ask about Abigail. He won't let it lie. He's a bulldog. What do you think we should do?"

"That's a real good question." David paused, wondering about Shlomo. "Do you think it was a good idea to let him go to the Whatchamacallit Society by himself? What if he's off meeting with the bad guys?"

Sarah came out from the bathroom. "This place is disgusting. It's like sleeping in the men's room at a bus station." She wiped her hands. "Well, he could be, but I doubt it. There have been several times he could have thrown us off the trail and he hasn't. I'm not sure what his motivations are, but he's not the opposition.

"So, I think it's time that we lay it all out for him, and

ask him to return the favor," she continued. From what you told me about the plans for a pandemic, the stakes are enormous. We need to be sure about Shlomo. There is more going on here than what he's told us. We can't afford secrets."

"I don't know. The guy is such a mystery. I can't get a read on him, but something is going on under that stone face." David replied.

"What do you want to do?" Sarah sat on the bed beside him.

"We need him. He's wicked smart. He knows the history of Moloch better than anyone. And the fact that he has more money than God is a big help." David agreed. "Let's have a talk, tell him that he needs to come clean with us, and if he does, then we'll invite Abigail for a chat."

"You make it sound like you're having her over for a beer, not summoning the dead." Sarah chuckled. They were both adjusting to living in the Twilight Zone.

David smiled, but Sarah's joking comment highlighted the fact that his relationship with Abigail had changed. Whatever forces separating David from Abigail had grown weaker, the boundary thinner and more porous. David worried that the separation between them might dissolve altogether, that there would be a cosmic rift between the real world and wherever it was that Abigail existed. David was walking on the edge of a precipice.

Secret Societies

"In all chaos there is a cosmos, in all disorder a secret order."
– Carl Jung

Sarah and David fell asleep on the lumpy bed despite the heat, the smells, and the street noise. It wasn't so much a nap as a crash. The excitement and the pace of the last few days had caught up with both of them, well beyond their limits for absorbing the new and bizarre.

David awoke with a start when Shlomo pounded on the door. He'd been deeply asleep, and sat up quickly, disoriented till he remembered where he was. His heart resumed its normal pace.

"Sarah, David, open the door." Shlomo shouted in a whisper.

Sarah was still asleep, wrapped up in a blanket despite the late afternoon heat. David shook her shoulder and opened the door. Shlomo stepped in quickly, locking the door behind him. He barely noticed that Sarah and David were still half asleep.

"How was your visit?" David asked.

"It was all I expected – and more. The office was sparse, but with an academic look and feel. I met the director, a Mr. Titi Villus. He claims to be a Turk who has lived in Syria for many years. He dressed the part, even wore an Oxford tie, but he seemed devoid of any knowledge of history or archeology. He didn't know the difference between Samaria and Babylon." Shlomo spoke rapidly – David would have thought him excited if he had been anyone else.

"Did I wake you?" He paused looking at their blurry faces.

"Well yes, but please continue. We want to hear what you found." David said as he smoothed his hair.

"Yes, well, he left me alone in their archive. It was clear that no one had been there for years. The materials were trivial, old, covered with dust, outdated, nothing of any authority. I found a brief mention of the Ugarit site describing it as temple to a minor god built by the Phoenicians. The records indicated that the site had been excavated in the early 1900s, but nothing other than broken amphorae was found."

"So as you expected, a purposeful dead end staged to lead us astray. So are we at a dead end? We've nowhere else to look, no clues," David said, expressing some disappointment.

"No, not so," replied Shlomo, displaying a rare smile on his Mount Rushmore face. "We have a clue. It's not much, more of a hint, but I believe it gives us a definite direction. And David, as you pointed out with surprising insight earlier, it points us to those hiding the chalice, not the chalice itself."

"Shlomo, what is it?" Sarah blurted out displaying her anxiety.

"Mr. Villus wore a ring with a distinctive symbol on the crest. When I asked him about it, he instinctively covered it with his hand. It clearly had some special significance for him. He related some halfhearted story about the ring's origin. I believe the symbol is a rune, an archaic pagan Norse symbol. I need to research it to verify my suspicion and divine its meaning."

"What did it look like?" David asked.

"A triangle with two lightning bolts in it, like stylized S's. If I'm correct, the organization we're searching for is older and more sinister than I'd first thought."

"Where do you think it leads us?" Sarah asked.

"To Germany in 1919."

David mind struggled to remember the history of post-World War I Germany, but before he could form a question, Sarah jumped in. "Shlomo, you're not suggesting ..."

Shlomo nodded. "I may be. Let me check my facts before we speculate further."

"Sarah, what are you two talking about?"

"The Nazi party organized in 1919," she said. "If Shlomo is correct, our search for the chalice is connected to the most evil regime in modern history. I'm beginning to see what Abigail meant."

Shlomo sat up like Abe and Louie seeing a squirrel. "Ah yes, this Abigail person. I'm glad you brought up her name again. Is there someone else joining our quest? Who is this Abigail?"

David glanced at Sarah and she nodded. "Go ahead, tell him. It's time to put our cards on the table. He deserves to know."

David opened his shirt and took out the transparent case where he kept Abigail's picture hanging around his neck and handed it to Shlomo.

"This is Abigail. She died in 1872 at the age of nineteen in China, Maine. She's asked us to find and destroy Moloch's chalice so she can defeat the Evil One in the spirit realm."

For the first time in their short history together, Shlomo looked shocked. His eyes darted from the photograph to Sarah and David's faces. He saw that they were serious and then looked back at Abigail, lovingly positioned post-mortem between her grieving parents. He repeated this cycle several times. His belief rose and fell as he sorted through the possibilities—they were crazy, they were making it up, they were telling the truth, or someone had deluded them. Shlomo's iron logic short-circuited.

Shlomo's face resumed its stoic facade, but his voice betrayed his angst. "You're not serious. Surely, you have more evidence than this picture."

David asked Shlomo to sit, and told him the tale of how they'd found the picture, his search to learn Abigail's identity, Ethel Nadeau's revelations, and the graveside meeting. Shlomo sat motionless with his fingertips pressed together and stared at the floor.

"I didn't believe him either, but David made her appear in our living room," Sarah interjected. "She's definitely real."

"She was the one who told you to look for Moloch's chalice, specifically Moloch? You didn't add that detail yourselves?" Shlomo asked emphatically, as though the entire discussion hung on this one point.

"No, we've added nothing. Abigail told us to find Moloch's chalice and destroy it. I'd never heard of Moloch until then." David said.

"I'd heard of Moloch, but only in passing. His legend has no particular meaning for me," added Sarah.

After another pensive moment, Shlomo sat upright, and handed David the photograph. He crossed his arms. "I'd like to meet this Abigail." It was a challenge, not a request; his disbelief hung in the air.

"Okay. But Shlomo, you need to understand I've only done this once. I don't know if it will work again."

"I understand," said Shlomo. He sat back waiting like a sphinx.

David closed his eyes and listened for Abigail. His connection to her drifted in and out like some kind of psychic tide. She was not so close that he could hear her thoughts, but he had a sensation that she was happy and at rest. David hoped she was up for another visit.

"David, are you okay now? Do you need more rest after the episode in the car?" asked Sarah touching his arm.

"No, I'm good." David gave her a wink. "I think Abigail has a little free time now."

Sarah smiled, but he saw her concern. She moved to stand in the corner opposite the bed and facing the door to the bathroom. David took Abigail's photograph and sat on the edge of the bed. As before, he focused on the picture and stroked the edge. His sense of her had grown, his knowledge was more intimate. Whatever boundary separated them had weakened. she was a mere arm's length away.

The now-familiar sensation of stillness returned, an uncanny feeling that everything had slowed and stopped. The noise from the street quieted, and despite the Damascus heat, a coolness wash over him like an outside door opening in the winter. A new and different Abigail stepped out of the darkened bathroom and stood beside the bed.

Gone was the nineteen-year-old schoolgirl. The person standing in front of David was a mature woman, taller and more muscular than he remembered. Her face shone with determination. She was dressed as an ancient warrior in leather armor and a white skirt over blue trousers. She wore a simple gold crown with a single red jewel. Her hair was braided with gold cord.

David stood and took her hand. Her energy coursed into him. His body jerked slightly from the sudden rush. Previously, the energy had was tenuous, flowing cautiously like a first time lover exploring another's body. This time her energy came without any hesitancy, flowing with assurance.

David's body felt illuminated.

He caught his breath. "Abigail, this is Shlomo. He's been a great help to us. I wanted him to meet you."

Abigail took a single toward Shlomo, and he flung himself the prostrate on the floor with his arm out straight.

"Goddess, I'm not worthy," said Shlomo, his voice quivering. Sarah and David were stunned, staring wide-eyed at Shlomo.

Illusions

"I have called on the Goddess and found her within myself."
– Marion Zimmer Bradley

The shimmering circle of light appeared and the swirling gray mist cleared, revealing a door into a lighted room. Abigail stepped through as the cold boundary between realms washed over her. Her feet stepped on hard reality once more. The air smelled of heat and dust.

Abigail's long full skirts and bodice were gone. She was again dressed as a warrior in long loose pants and leather armor. As before, she had no recollection of willing this change, but now the clothing was natural, familiar.

David and Sarah looked pleased to see her, but surprised by her appearance. A third man seated in a chair sat erect, gripping the chair's arms. His eyes raced around the room as though searching for the source of the illusion, and then fixed on Abigail.

David stepped forward and delicately took her hand. Bright clear energy flowed between them. He inhaled sharply as the energy illuminated him, renewing and strengthening their bond.

"Abigail, this is Shlomo. He's been a great help to us. I wanted him to meet you."

Abigail stepped forward to take his hand so as to learn who he was, when the man unexpectedly threw himself prostrate on the floor. Sarah and David stared wide-eyed, as perplexed by the display as she was.

"Goddess, I'm not worthy," he said. His whole body shook as though terrified.

Goddess. Why did everyone calling me goddess? It's true,

I've grown stronger, possibly one of the strongest souls in Gehenna, but a goddess? No, not me. I'm not a goddess, I'm just Abigail.

Abigail knelt beside him and placed her hands on his back. Her energy flowed into him, revealing his life like the pages of a book.

His soul was eons old with the weight and solidity that came from many lifetimes. He'd been born into a great family of rabbis. His rabbinical training began when he was five. At thirteen, he was inducted into a secret brotherhood, the Tzadikim Nistarim. At twenty, he was the leader, the Baal Shem. He had dedicated his life to uncovering and destroying the Lilim, sacrificed everything—his friends, the love of his wife and children, all personal desires—in pursuit of this goal. Abigail's heart ached at the sacrifices this man had placed on the altar of righteousness. His grief burned within him, fueling his unwavering devotion to his task.

Abigail could not bear the thought of this great soul being prostrate before her.

"Please stand. You are a righteous man and have no cause to bow before me."

She placed her fingertips on his shoulder, and raised him to his feet, lifting him like a feather. She looked into his eyes, and saw him in Arcadia's gardens speaking with Ehyeh. He was her messenger as much as she was.

"Goddess, you cannot know how I've longed to see you, how I've lived for this moment. I have prayed for your return. You've always appeared at the crucial moments throughout the ages when Samael was afoot in the land. You've come to save us again."

"The end of your search is near at hand," Abigail said. "Please, help David. You share the same goal. The chalice is the key. Destroy it and the Evil One, the one you call Samael, will be forever trapped in Gehenna. Then the Brotherhood's centuries of struggle will be over, and your quest complete."

His face became serene. "Yes, we will destroy the chalice. We will not fail you," Shlomo whispered as though praying and bowed his head. Sarah and David glanced at each other. She took David's hand. Their wide eyes remained fixed on him.

Shlomo was part of Ehyeh's plan, a plan whose scope and dimensions Abigail had yet to fully understand. David and Sarah, among others, were actors in this plan, each with a part to play. They were all being swept along in the cascading events, racing ever faster toward an unseen destination. Together, they had the power to make small changes bending the currents toward their goal.

The bridge began to weaken, causing Abigail's vision to ripple as though looking through water. The crisp, sweet reality of the land of the living drifted away. She stepped backwards, acknowledging Gehenna's grip. She wanted to spend more time with David. He was filled with doubts, filled with thoughts of fleeing back to the safety of his life in Maine. David was still the linchpin. This cosmic struggle Ehyeh had set in motion might still fail. Evil would win if David faltered.

Band of Sisters

"For there is no friend like a sister, in calm or stormy weather"
– Christina Rossetti

The bridge disappeared, and Abigail stood once more in the countess's chamber facing Ilona and the other bewildered women. The crisp reality of the living was replaced once again by the illusionary spirit realm. Her long, floor-length dress was restored, and all hint of the warrior vanished.

Abigail sensed the growing weight of expectations. *Shlomo also called me "goddess. Why?"* David lurked in her thoughts, constantly there, and always in need of encouragement. Now she was back in Gehenna with a hundred expectant faces looking at her, waiting for her to show them the way home.

"Mistress, what happened? Where did you go? Who were those people?" Ilona fired off questions as the other women drew closer hanging on Abigail's answers.

"What you saw, my sisters, was the land of the living, but in a different time—many hundreds of years have passed since you died." Hundreds of quizzical looks stared back at me.

"It's hard to explain. We are in a spirit realm. It's an ethereal world where nothing you see or touch is truly real." Abigail held her palm face up and made an apple. She tossed it to Ilona who grabbed it out of the air. A low murmur spread, rising and falling like a wave around the room.

"I am still learning about Gehenna, its mysteries and its perils." Abigail scanned he faces fixed on her. "For the moment, we are safe. The countess will never return." A collective sigh of relief rose from the women. Abigail kept to herself that the countess was one of hundreds of demons within the castle. She knew the women's safety was tenuous at best. Eymerich might bolt into the chamber at any moment and a new reign of terror would begin.

"There is a boundary, a great chaotic void between the living and the spirit realms. I can, with your help, cross over for brief periods. Those people you saw are helping me defeat the queen."

"You are truly a goddess. None other than the queen herself can cross over, and she has all of Gehenna to help her." Ilona averted her eyes as though unworthy of looking at Abigail.

A group of women dropped to their knees and began to pray, "*Salve Regina Abigail, mater misericordiae. Vita, dulcedo, et spes nostra, salve.*" Others backed to the wall, but most just stood, waiting with mixed apprehension.

The Quaker in Abigail could not abide this glorification. She stopped the praying and made the women stand. She took Ilona by the hands and looked round at the other women.

"Dear Ilona, my sister, I am not a goddess. I have abilities, yes, but I am not all powerful. I fear the void between realms. I fear the queen. I can be easily hurt or destroyed."

Ilona and the other women relaxed as Abigail now appeared to be one of them.

"I must return to Lord Eymerich's salon. Like the countess, I suspect he has secrets that I need to learn about." she said to Ilona.

Just then, the door to the salon opened and Panya stepped in. Abigail went to him.

"What is it, Panya?"

"Jacquis has brought newly arrived souls. Lord Eymerich has hid them in the labyrinth beneath the castle. You should come. You need to find where they are hidden and rescue them, just as you did with the countess's women."

That was Eymerich's secret and, Abigail suspected, the secret of all who rule in Gehenna. They feed off souls they have trapped. Panya was right. If she intended to challenge Eymerich, she needed to take away his source of strength. "I will. You go back to the salon and watch. I need to speak to the girls."

Panya left, closing the door behind him, and Abigail returned to Ilona's side.

"Who were you speaking with, mistress?" Ilona looked puzzled.

"That was Panya, the page. He said that Lord Eymerich went into the labyrinth."

"I didn't see anyone," said Ilona.

A Revelation

Abigail had dissolved in front of Shlomo a moment ago. He reached for the arm of the chair, steadied himself, and sat, his arms folded across his chest. "Ahhhhhhh!" A loud wrenching cry erupted from Shlomo as he bent over his knees. Sarah jerked and grabbed David's hand as he pushed back on the bed, pressing against the wall. *Jesus, the man is coming apart!* Shlomo rocked with his eyes closed and his lips moving for several minutes.

Sarah and David looked on silently, unsure whether they should approach the man. His body shook as though an inner tectonic force was tearing his granite facade apart. Then, just as quickly, Shlomo sat up, took a deep breath with his eyes closed, and calmly rested his hands on his lap. The facade held. He glanced at his bewildered comrades, then looked straight ahead, and spoke in a measured tone.

"I've clung to my mission my whole life, clung like a man holding on to a cliff face by sheer force of will, unable to climb higher, afraid of losing my grip and falling to my death. It wasn't for myself that I've struggled. I've carried the weight of my brothers who came before me, and the weight of all those who have suffered because of the Lilim. If my resolve had faltered, if I'd lost my grip, I would have betrayed their sacrifices.

"But now, now I've seen the goddess as foretold. She is the herald of the battle to come between the children of Eve and the children of Lilith. When she touched me, I felt her strength, her goodness. I still feel her even now. Her power is resonating within me like the note of a bell with perfect pitch. My faith, my vigil, my sacrifices, my fight against the Lilim are righteous. I am no longer clinging to the cliff. I'm standing on firm ground, and my path forward is clear. You cannot imagine the relief, to know that the task that I've dedicated my life to—that I've sacrificed all for—is true. I may live to see the defeat of the Lilim."

Sarah leaned in. "I don't understand. I never asked about your beliefs. You're such an intensely private person, but I thought that you'd sacrificed your religion for your intellectual pursuits."

"We've all come to this endeavor with secrets, Dr. Austin."

Shlomo looked at David with a sideways glance. "I've just met yours."

"David, you were sent by the goddess, and you are joined with her. You hear her thoughts. That's a powerful secret. I surmised from the moment that Director Kanerek told me that you were interested in Moloch's chalice that something was afoot. Moloch is well known but his chalice is a complete mystery."

Shlomo took a deep breath and relaxed a little more.

"My search for the Lilim produced little results. I was stymied. It was your interest in Moloch's chalice that was the key to unlocking a new line of inquiry. I found the references to Moloch's tabernacle based on your interest in the chalice. As we've seen, an attempt has been made to erase all trace of it from the historical record. So when you came looking for it, I had to find out why." For the first time, Shlomo's voice was collegial, not superior.

Shlomo breathed deeply, and resumed speaking in a steady, measured voice. "I understand why you and Dr. Austin were secretive. I, like you, have not told you all there is. What I'm going to tell you is known by only a small handful of men, smaller than the number of men required for a minyan, the ten men required for Jewish services."

Shlomo paused as though gathering his will to form the words. "I am a member of a secret brotherhood, the *Tzadikim Nistarim*, which means the Concealed Righteous. Our order was founded by Moses around 1100 BCE. The exact date is unknown, but it was sometime before King Solomon built the first temple in Jerusalem. Moses was the first to have the title Baal Shem, Master of the Name in English, 'the Name' being the name of God. There have been many who have held this title throughout history. Some Baal Shem you would know of and find surprising, others are completely anonymous. Our brotherhood has existed through the centuries for one purpose and one alone. To search out the Lilim and destroy them."

"If you don't mind telling us, who is the current leader, the Baal Shem?" David asked, thinking he already knew the answer.

"Your instinct is correct, David. I am Baal Shem."

"Holy Shit," David said quietly.

"You can say that again," added Sarah. "So this shunning is all some type of ruse, isn't it? You know something. Something has caused you to stage this elaborate subterfuge. What is it you know? And why such an act?"

"You are perceptive, Dr. Austin," Shlomo continued. "I sent you and Mr. Austin home after the first meeting so I could confer with the other members of the Brotherhood. We needed to adjust to the revelation you presented."

"So all that you've told us before was a lie? How can we believe you now?" Sarah hated being deceived.

"Yes. Please forgive me. I needed to know if you were who you presented yourselves as, or if you were Lilim attempting to infiltrate the Brotherhood."

"And your wife, the shunning, was that also stage acting?" Sarah looked as incredulous as she sounded.

"Yes and no. The shunning was a ruse, a public and a very painful charade. To my Bobover community, I am shunned. My wife and children are outcasts. That is all true. It was the only way for me to remove myself from the public eye. I have, as your Hollywood dramas might say, gone underground. I needed to become anonymous to continue my search for the Lilim."

"I thought your story about retaining control of the Bobover fortune sounded fishy," said Sarah. "An organization as old and wealthy as the Bobovers would never be so lax with financial oversight."

"The Bobovers are a legitimate religious sect, but one that was founded as a cover for the Brotherhood. Hiding in a semi-monastic community has its advantages."

"So who the hell are these Lilim?" David asked, unable to contain himself.

"Yes, let me explain." Shlomo paused gathering his thoughts. "Eve was not Adam's first wife. His first wife was Lilith, created by God as his companion. Lilith saw herself as Adam's partner, his equal. Adam in his pride demanded that Lilith submit to him, commanding that she lie beneath him in a submissive pose. She refused, so Lilith left Eden and traveled to the shores of the sea where she met Samael. You know Samael as the devil, the presence of evil on Earth.

"Lilith lay with him and spawned a race of children, half-human, half-demon, the Lilim. They've lived among men ever since, invisible, passing for human but not truly human. Usually, the Lilim do not know their origin or nature. They live their lives on the fringes of society, alone and apart, never fitting in. Many become criminals or worse. Some awaken spontaneously to the understanding of who they are. Others are awakened by other Lilim. When the

Lilim become aware of who they are, they seek each other out. They gather like a storm of locusts, building on each other's strength, and drawing more Lilim to themselves. Each time a gathering builds, the fate of the world is in jeopardy. Evil rises out of the shadows, and its presence is felt on Earth.

"Dr. Austin, what you and Mr. Austin don't know is that the Lilim worship Moloch. He is their patron saint, if you will. I've been studying Moloch, hoping to find a way of uncovering and ultimately destroying the Lilim. I've been stymied for years; no direct linkages exist. I've pursued Jung's archetypal symbols as a potential path, and while this allowed me to better understand the Lilim, it brought me no closer to finding them, to defeating them. I'd hit a brick wall, as you would say."

"So that is why you so easily dropped everything to join us," David said.

"Moloch's chalice was the first new clue I've had in two decades. I had to find out what you knew." Shlomo's face was relaxed as though decades of tension had vanished.

"Is this what you've seen? Have you seen signs of gathering? Are the Lilim awakening?" Sarah asked in a low tone, as if she already knew the answer she was afraid to hear.

Shlomo nodded. "Yes, correct again, Dr. Austin. Our brotherhood has seen signs, hints, rumors that the Lilim are gathering. The signs are unmistakable for those who look—small wars driven by ethnic and religious conflict, sudden outbreaks of disease where there was none before, industrial and toxic pollution that poison whole ecosystems, small conflicts that without cause escalate into major wars. These are all signs of the Lilim. World War I began when a small group of Serbian nationalists assassinated a minor duke. That conflict escalated, aided by the Lilim, into a world war.

Its Treaty of Versailles laid the ground work for the rise of the Nazi Party by imposing harsh reparations on Germany. All these events were guided by the Lilim.

"As we discussed earlier, the last time a gathering occurred was in Munich in 1918. This gave rise to the Nazi party. The Nuremburg rallies were gatherings of Lilim which served to awaken thousands more Lilim, who formed the core of the Nazi party. The chalice was the catalyst for these events. The Lilim were able to enlist millions of non-Lilim, the children of Eve, in a war whose ultimate purpose was their own eventual destruction. What the Nazis referred to as the non-Aryan races."

Sarah and David were spellbound. David had to remember to breathe as Shlomo spoke.

"What did the Brotherhood do to stop the Lilim?" asked Sarah.

"You need to understand that the Brotherhood moves in secret. Our touch is that of a feather, our voice a whisper. Our members work alone, always standing in the wings, never on stage. We look for the precise moment when the course of history can be altered by the unseen hand, or the word spoken in a quiet moment." Shlomo closed his eyes for a moment and continued.

"The Brotherhood infiltrated the Nazi high command. We placed a lieutenant in charge of managing Hitler's schedule and appointments. Hitler was under the direct control of Lilith, and the psychic strain was slowly driving him mad, ruining his health. As he became more unstable, our agent was able, on rare occasions when they were alone, to plant ideas or suggestions."

"Like what?" Sarah asked.

"Two subtle suggestions—that England was not a threat and that Russia was."

"What difference did that make?"

"It made all the difference. Since Hitler didn't see England as a threat, it was free to be the staging area for the Allied invasion while vast quantities of German men and supplies were destroyed in the Russian winter campaign. Hitler never learned the lessons of Napoleon's march into Russia. Without these fatal mistakes, England would have been invaded, and the Nazis would have consolidated their power and gone on to create an atomic bomb, possibly ahead of the US. They could have conquered Russia at their leisure, and most likely destroyed all the American cities on the Eastern Seaboard."

"I knew Germany had worked on a nuclear program, but I didn't think they'd come close to a workable bomb," said Sarah.

"They were much closer than is generally known. It was only because of the secret work of the Brotherhood that Germany did not succeed."

"How did you prevent the Nazis from building a nuclear bomb?" David was hanging on his every word. Shlomo's tale was one fantastic revelation after another.

"The head of the Nazi nuclear weapons project was a brilliant physicist named Werner Heisenberg. You may have heard of the Heisenberg Uncertainty Principle? He was actually quite close to completing the theoretical work for an atomic bomb. The Brotherhood managed to place an assistant in close contact with Heisenberg. The assistant introduced a minor mistake, a subtle change into Heisenberg's underlying calculations. The effect was profound. It caused Heisenberg to calculate that he needed a sphere of weapons grade plutonium four feet in diameter, far more plutonium than the Nazis were capable of producing. In actuality, a sphere the size of a golf ball is sufficient. Eventually Heisenberg found the error, but by then the war was over."

"Oh my God!" said Sarah. "If the Nazis had consolidated power and had time to perfect a bomb, they could easily have won the war, and the Lilim would rule the world today."

Shlomo nodded. David shuddered. His view of World War II was the popular American vision of the powerhouse of democracy saving the world. In Shlomo's version, it was a comment whispered in a madman's ear and a tiny error introduced into a vast calculation that changed all of human history.

"Do the Lilim know about your brotherhood?" asked Sarah.

"Yes, sadly they know us all too well. The Lilim, once awakened, are consumed with hatred for the children of Eve. As history has shown with the Nazis, they had no compulsion about killing millions. If the Nazis suspected a member of the Brotherhood lived in a city or village, they would kill everyone."

"Everyone?" Sarah asked with a pained expression.

"Yes." Shlomo spoke with an intensity David had not heard before. He saw Shlomo clench his fists turning his fingers white.

This explanation of history chilled the Austins to their core. David assumed when they'd begun their quest that it was dangerous, but he had no idea, no conception of the enemy they were up against. Shlomo peeled back one layer of evil after another, each one more horrific, more invincible than the last. The mountain they were scaling was, in reality, a volcano, and the ground beneath their feet might dissolve in to lava at any moment.

David gripped Sarah's hand as the threat to them became clear. Sarah was everything to him. David feared they might never return to Maine. They might never have children. He might never again sit on a stool in the diner drinking coffee with the guys and telling lies about fishing. They might never swim in Lake Cobbossee with their dogs, Abe and Louie, again. For the first time in his life, David feared dying.

Sarah moved closer to him on the edge of the bed and covered his hand with hers. "Are you okay, David? You look like you're going to zone out on me again."

"I'm fine. I don't think I quite understood who we were up against, set me back a bit. That's all." He forced a smile for her.

"I know what you mean. I kind of wished I hadn't started cleaning out the hall closet and never found the Johnson family Bible. We might be kayaking on the Kennebec right now." Sarah gave his hand one more reassuring squeeze and got back to business.

"Shlomo, you said you thought you'd recognized a symbol on the ring worn by the man at the fake institute. What do you think it is?" Sarah asked.

"The Nazis used many Nordic symbols called runes. The SS symbol was the most famous. I believe the symbol on Mr. Villus's ring is the same, one of many used by the Nazis in Lilim ceremonies as part of the initiation into the SS, the heart and soul of the Nazi party.

"We need to go to Germany, to Wewelsburg castle in the upper Rhineland. The Brotherhood has had the castle under surveillance for years. We've known it was a hive of Lilim activity, but had no reason to act. The castle was the Nazis' spiritual home, the center of Nazi mysticism. I hope we can recover the trail of the chalice at the castle."

"When do you want to leave?" Sarah asked.

"Tonight. We can fly to Paderborn, the airport closest

to the castle. I will arrange for a car to meet us. We should be at the castle by early afternoon tomorrow."

Shlomo took a satellite phone from his bag and stood by the window so the phone could acquire its satellite link. David lay back on the bed with his feet on the floor, taking in Shlomo's revelations. A hundred years ago, the Nadeau family had prepared for his arrival, which David thought gave him seniority on this adventure, but Shlomo's brotherhood had been in search of the Lilim for three millennia. He'd been trumped.

Without warning the window beside Shlomo exploded, showering the room with glass. Shlomo fell to the floor. Bullets tore through the room, ripping holes in the walls and shattering the lights. David grabbed Sarah and rolled off the bed onto the floor, pinning her between the bed and the wall and shielding her with his body. After a momentary pause, a second volley of bullets raked the room, filling the air with plaster dust from many small explosions as the bullets shattered the walls. The firing stopped. The sound, still echoing in his ears, was broken by tires squealing in the street below.

The pillows where Sarah and David had been sitting seconds ago were riddled with holes. David heard unintelligible shouts growing louder in the street, and distant sirens coming closer. He was shaking from head to foot. David tried to speak but the dust caught in his throat. Finally he managed, "Are you okay, Sarah? Are you hurt?" No answer. She wasn't moving. Her face was covered in plaster dust.

David looked over the top of the bed. Dim light from the street illuminated the room. The swirling dust settled, revealing Shlomo lying on the floor with blood pooling around his head.

Friends and Enemies

"In order to know your enemy, you must become your enemy."
– Chris Bradford

There was no way of hiding the fact that Abigail had sent the countess into the void. Her path to the queen's inner circle led through Lord Eymerich. Abigail had to claim the countess's position, which meant confronting Eymerich. She could not allow him time to react. Time was her enemy, and hesitation would lead to defeat.

Abigail changed her dress to match the countess's, complete with hat and shoes. Ilona's resolute face dissolved into bewilderment at Abigail's sudden transformation.

"Please watch over the women. I'm returning to Eymerich's salon to confront him. Hopefully, I will return shortly." Ilona nodded, trusting more than understanding.

"We will await your return," she said, and took a step back to stand with the crowd.

Abigail left the chamber and hurried down the hallways to the salon with her feet catching the heavy petticoats. She paused in front of the doors to gather her wits, when Jacquis entered the hallway walking briskly. He was looking down, lost in thought. Abigail clenched her fists as he approached. He looked up and halted, then hesitantly approached, stopping a few steps away as though afraid to come closer.

"Mademoiselle Abigail – or should I call you Lady Abigail?" He bowed. Abigail couldn't tell if he was mocking her or not.

"You may call me Lady Abigail."

"Why are you dressed as the countess? Is she in her

chamber?" Jacquis looked back down the corridor.

Abigail placed her hands on her hips and raised her chin. "I have sent the countess into the void. I will be taking her place at court."

Jacquis' face went blank. His eyes fixed on her, he spoke slowly. "I see you have learned the ways of the queen's court, advancement by assassination." He bowed slightly. Abigail could not tell if he was mocking her or acknowledging her position.

"You are correct, sir, I have learned how to make my way in this forsaken land." She spoke to him as to a servant, as to one who had displeased her. Abigail wanted to scratch his eyes out.

He paused again, clasped his hands behind his back, and took on the fatherly tone he'd affected when they'd first met. "Indeed, you are not the frightened young girl I found and brought to the castle. If I didn't know better, I'd have thought you'd grown. You appear bigger to me, taller maybe. You are certainly stronger, more confident, and—to have dispatched the countess, a remarkable feat. One I wouldn't have thought possible." Jacquis' voice betrayed a great weariness within him.

"Yes, I'm not the naive young woman you led like a lamb to the slaughter. I understand the nature of Gehenna now." Jacquis had whisked her off to the castle with no warning, knowing the terrors she would face, and he'd done so with a Judas smile.

"You've learned the ways of the court, its nature—at least partly." He glanced sideways meeting her eye. "But not completely, I think? I hope you truly understand the sea you are swimming in, the dangers that lurk beneath the surface."

"Is this another of your half-truths? Another

deception?" Abigail asked in a growl. His continual half-truths, his riddles infuriated her.

"In Gehenna, it is not easy to tell one's enemies from one's friends, nor are either constant. A friend may not stay a friend, nor is an enemy always an opponent."

"Do you pretend to be my friend? Would a friend have cast an unsuspecting person into a pit of vipers?" Abigail shouted and stepped forward with one fist raised at him.

Jacquis stepped back and held up his hands to stop her advance. "What I'm saying is that in this evil land of shadows, we see darkly as through clouded waters. You think of me as an enemy, as one who cast you into the pit. I did as you say, but I did so to keep you from a far worse fate."

"Worse than Eymerich or the countess? Why would—"

"You could not have avoided them!" Jacquis shouted and then lowered his voice. "Eymerich is too powerful, second only to the queen herself. I timed your visit such that the queen saw you first. She tested you and saw your latent powers. It was no accident she picked Lord Eymerich to train you. The queen suspects Eymerich of treachery. She wanted you beside him, hoping you'd divert him. And you have, you've destroyed the countess, his greatest ally. Lord Eymerich is worried, possibly even afraid. He doesn't know the extent of your powers. Nor do I, nor does anyone else, I might add."

Jacquis' words rang true. Abigail had no idea who was friend or foe. She faced layers of intrigue, plots within plots. Each time she pulled back the curtain, the scene and the actors changed. *Was Jacquis a friend?*

"I assume then the queen is pleased?" Abigail asked

sarcastically.

"I am not privy to the queen's thoughts. She's preoccupied these days and is rarely seen other than at vision times. But if I were to guess, I would say she is content to know that Lord Eymerich is engaged with you, and not with intrigues against her." Jacquis regained his composure, looking like the fatherly figure she'd met when she appeared in Gehenna, although now she knew he had more secrets to tell.

"Jacquis, I know that you bring new arrivals to Lord Eymerich, who takes them to the labyrinth. What is he planning?"

Jacquis raised an eyebrow, took in a deep breath and smiled. "Ah, you have spies. I have underestimated how fast you've learned. Eymerich is right to fear you." Jacquis looked away, considering his next words. "Do you know why souls find their way to Gehenna?" he asked. Abigail shook her head slowly.

"I'll tell you. Some souls are pure evil, as black as the darkest night. Eymerich and the countess are two such souls. They are the embodiment of evil beyond redemption or mercy. Others are here because of misfortune such as the young women killed by the countess. Her blackness enshrouds their souls and drags them down. You, however, are a bit of a mystery. I'm not sure why you are here."

Jacquis paced in small steps. "As for myself, I'm here because of my own sins. An inquisitor killed my family, everyone I knew and loved, and finally tortured and killed me. My sin was to allow his blackness into my soul. I became consumed with the desire for revenge. I forsook all mercy and forgiveness, all I held holy. This need for revenge churns within me still. It has chained me to Gehenna."

Jacquis stood still as a look of deep sorrow washed across his face. He stepped back and bowed slightly.

"Mademoiselle Abigail, Please forgive me. I was untruthful with you. I did not act with kindness and mercy. For that, I am sorry, another of my many sins, and I beg your forgiveness. There may come a time when I may redeem myself in your eyes, but for now, my demons will not allow me to stray from my path."

Abigail felt like Jacquis' confessor, as though he expected her to grant him forgiveness. The contents of Jacquis' soul were written on his face. He had lost his faith, forsaken grace. Their comforts were lost to him. For Jacquis, there was no hope of redemption. All that remained was a consuming hatred fueled by the fire of revenge. Jacquis stood with his head bowed. Abigail imagined him contemplating his sins. She looked on him with a mixture of anger and pity. Abigail could not decide whether to strike him, comfort him, or both.

She pushed the door open and walked smartly to the center of the crowded salon. Jacquis followed her in and stood discreetly at the back of the room. The courtiers, startled by her sudden appearance, pushed each other out of her way, clearing a path, murmuring and hissing as she passed. Abigail stopped in front of the dais directly facing Lord Eymerich as the salon became silent. Lord Eymerich turned see what the commotion was. He looked puzzled when he saw her standing before him, but then his face grew cold.

"Why are you dressed as the countess. Where is she?" His words hung in the air as a threat, not a question.

"I have destroyed her and flung her withered soul into the chaos between realms. She will drift forever in the maelstrom," Abigail shouted so all could hear her. She drew herself up, hands on hips, displaying as much authority as she could muster and hoping desperately that her display was convincing.

Lord Eymerich rose from his chair, clenching his fists as rage spread across his face. Bedlam broke out in the chamber as human shouts mixed with demonic screams. The crowd drew closer forming a ring and pushing Abigail toward the dais. She smelled the warm, sulfurous breath on her neck and cold fingers raking her arms and back. The courtiers waited for Lord Eymerich's rage to explode and signal her destruction.

Eymerich paced the dais studying Abigail, perplexed, as though he didn't recognize her, perhaps wondering if she was a doppelganger sent to trick him. The salon members' heads swiveled in unison, following his movements. He paused. A hush spread over the crowd as they awaited his next action.

Slowly the anger left his face, and he stood at ease with legs apart and hands folded in front. Lord Eymerich looked past Abigail and nodded as his upturned lip formed a smile. Abigail heard the sound of boots on the stone floor behind her, and large gloved hands grabbed her shoulders.

Abigail reacted instantly, swinging her arms up and around to break the painful grip. She pivoted and saw a surprised Colonel Hoss. Before he could react, Abigail grabbed his arm and shot a bolt of energy through him. His jaw dropped, his throat made a gurgling sound, and his eyes rolled back in his head. She twisted his arm, forcing him face down on the floor as his hat with the skull and crossbones emblem rolled away. All the while, Abigail drained energy from him, leaving him unconscious.

The colonel lay splayed on the floor, appearing lifeless. The circle widened as everyone stumbled backwards. The sound of screeching filled the chamber as a few members began to revert to their demonic forms. Her attack on Colonel Hoss had unnerved them. A few courtiers transformed entirely into demons and hung from the walls by their claws. The people closest to Abigail retained their human bodies and courtly dress, but their faces elongated into canine shapes with bared fangs. They made low throaty growls and shuffled back and forth, unsure of her next action. Faces in the chamber showed a mixture of hatred, uncertainty, and fear.

Lord Eymerich looked grim, steely eyed, but no longer supremely confident. He held out his arms and yelled, "Rip her to shreds!"

Instantly, gnarly black hands with claws grabbed her by the throat, others dug into her side, and more grabbed at her arms and legs. Abigail struck the first demons and thrust them away with surges of energy. After each fell, two or three more took its place. Demons leaped through the air and landed on her shoulders, other crawled on the floor to grab her feet. Abigail was engulfed in a mass of slithering fur and scales.

She fell to the floor as razor-sharp claws dug into her flesh. An aching coldness spread over her, and thoughts of hate and violence emanating from her attackers filled her mind. Abigail could not pull away. There were too many of them, and their grips were too tight. Desperation began to set in. She'd only seconds to fight back. Abigail summoned all her will to fight them off, but they were too quick and too pervasive. She could fight two or three, possibly a dozen, but not fifty or sixty. Abigail tried to make the sword she'd used to defeat the countess, but the demons' frantic actions prevented her from focusing.

Abigail caught Lord Eymerich's eye through the swarming mass. He looked on expectantly as he saw her faltering. She'd been outwitted again. He knew Abigail could vanquish any single demon or more, but couldn't handle a swarm. A single cut was nothing, but hundreds of cuts overwhelmed her.

Abigail's energy ebbed away. Each bite, each claw mark drained her a little more. The frenzied attack prevented her from reaching out to the women in the countess's chamber for strength. The hate and malice emanating from her attackers began to consume Abigail. She strained, weakening, losing her ability to resist like a person drowning in putrid water. Abigail gasped for strength as a drowning person would gasp for air. There was none to be found. Abigail began to slip beneath the chaos.

Her last fading image was of Eymerich standing with his hands on his hips. His satisfaction appeared complete as a grin spread across his distorted face. The last thing Abigail heard was his throaty laughter as it faded to silence.

Rescue

"For someone who needs refuge, a key is provided." – Anna Keesey

Sarah coughed, moaned, and reached for the back of her head. "What happened?"

"Are you okay? Hurt anywhere?" David saw no blood. He pulled her upright looking for any injury. His heart pounded. "Someone shot at us. I don't know if they're gone or not. Stay low."

"I think I hit my head," she said feeling for a bump.

"Sorry, hon, I threw us to the floor when the shooting started."

Sarah stared at the bullet-tattered pillows, tears streaming down her face making lines in the dust. David kissed her on her forehead, and then crawled through the broken glass to where Shlomo lay. He rolled him over and saw that a bullet had grazed the side of his head. David felt his carotid artery. He was alive, but bleeding like crazy.

David got a towel from the bathroom, wiped away the blood and dust from Shlomo's head, and pressed on the wound. Sarah looked at David as he cradled Shlomo's head in his lap. Sarah's face was a muddy mess of plaster and tears. David's mind raced through unworkable possibilities of what to do next. The sirens grew louder. In minutes the room would be crawling with police asking him questions in a language David didn't understand.

Shlomo stirred, moaned, and reached for his head.

"What—what happened?" he asked, struggling for consciousness.

"Lie still, you've been shot, you're bleeding."

Shlomo focused on David for a second as his comprehension returned. He raised himself up slightly, and his eyes surveyed the room. Then he lay back and placed his hand over the towel on his head.

"David, the satellite phone; get it, hurry."

David scanned the room looking for the phone. The floor was littered with glass, splintered wood, and plaster. A green glow shone from under the bed. It was the phone, he grabbed it and shook off the dust.

"Okay, got it, now what?"

"You'll need to go outside for a signal. Then dial star, star, four, seven, eight, two, pound. When you connect, there will be no reply, but someone will be listening. Say 'Gideon has fallen,' and give the address of the hotel. Then..." Shlomo lost consciousness again.

"Sarah, stay with him." She nodded. David crawled into the hall. Two Arab men shouted at him as he ran down the stairs. A turbulent mob from the street had filled the lobby. The desk clerk pointed, and the focus of the crowd turned to David with everyone shouting and waving their arms.

There was no way he was going to make it through the lobby to the street beyond. He had to try for the roof. David turned to run up the stairs when he realized he had no idea where they were. His mind had literally been elsewhere when they arrived. David saw hotel business cards on the front desk and began pushing through the crowd. A short, fat man with a head like a basketball and wearing a sweat-stained wife-beater T-shirt grabbed David's shoulders. He yelled at David in Arabic, his spit hitting his face. David had no idea what he was saying, but he intended to hang onto him.

There was no time for diplomacy. David smashed his

forehead into his captor's nose. The man shrieked and grabbed his bleeding nose. David kneed him in the groin and shoved him. His bulk took down five other people like a bowling ball clearing the way to the front desk. David grabbed a business card with the hotel address and bolted up the stairs.

The two men he'd pushed before were still in the hall talking, and resumed shouting as David ran up the staircase. He slammed his shoulder into one of them, knocking him aside. *Why does everyone in this country shout all the time?* On the top floor at the end of the hall, an iron ladder led to a trap door in the ceiling. David climbed the ladder and pushed, and with a second strong push the door opened revealing a starry sky. *Thank God.*

David heard the sirens stop in the street. He only had a few minutes until the police swarmed the building. The satellite phone display showed a spinning circle and displayed "Acquiring Signal." *Come on, come on.* The icon continued to spin. David turned hoping that facing another direction might help. "Ready."

He frantically dialed **4782#. After three long rings he heard a distinctive click and silence. Was it working? David wished someone would have said, *Good evening, how may I help you.* I managed to get out, "Gideon has fallen, 18723 Bashier Street, Damascus." There was no response, only silence.

"Gideon has fallen, 18723 Bashier Street, Damascus." he repeated.

A male voice replied, "Message acknowledged, response initiated," followed by a *click.* The phone buzzed and went dead.

Whatever Shlomo had wanted, David had accomplished. Voices from the hallway got louder. Someone shouted. David turned and saw a policeman pointing a gun at him. David held up his hands and dropped to his knees. David didn't know what he said, but surrender seemed in order. Three more policemen appeared. The first policeman pushed David to the ground, grinding his face into the dust on the roof. He handcuffed David and pulled him to his feet, and yelled something unintelligible inches from David's face. His breath smelled foul.

"I'm an American citizen. I want to see a US representative." The policeman's face morphed from perplexed to concerned as he realized the situation was above his pay grade. His buddies were playing with the satellite phone, annoyed that they couldn't turn it on.

Confusion ensued as they discussed what to do. One policeman had the foresight to call someone on his radio, and after a short delay, he received curt instructions. David guessed they were going to the police station so things could be sorted out.

The three policemen spoke in excited phrases, pointing at his handcuffs and the ladder. They figured out that they could re-cuff him once David climbed down. They descended to the lobby, which had been cleared of the hysterical mob. A sea of flashing blue lights filled the street and an ambulance was parked in front. Shlomo had been bandaged and strapped to a gurney. Sarah sat on a chair covered in plaster dust with two policewomen in head scarves standing over her. Her face had been wiped clean. She brightened when David entered, but her eyes were red and glassy. She was doing her best to avoid falling to pieces.

Shlomo raised his head to look at David. He saw him mouth the words, *Did you call?* David nodded. A policeman pushed Shlomo's head down, and he slumped on the gurney.

An older policeman with lots of insignia on his uniform barked orders to a covey of police flunkies hovering about. He walked up to David with David's passport and compared his face to the passport.

"You're Mr. David Austin? What is your business in Syria?" he asked in English with a strong but intelligible accent. These weren't the Kennebunkport cops. This man could cause them serious harm if they didn't straighten out this mess quickly. A vision of being strapped to an iron grate with electrodes attached to David's jewels flashed through his mind.

"My wife is a college professor. We're here doing research. Well, she's doing research; I'm along for the ride."

He nodded. Apparently David's story jived with what Sarah had already told him. He flicked his wrist at Shlomo.

"And this man?"

"We met him at the Rockefeller Archeological Museum in Jerusalem. He's assisting my wife." He grunted, annoyed that David hadn't offered a different story.

"So," his voice was loud and accusatory, "why were you hiding on the roof using a spy phone." He was inches away from David's face, his breath smelled like bad cigars.

"I wasn't hiding. I tried to call the US Embassy for help. It's a satellite phone. I had to stand in the open to get a signal."

He snapped his fingers at a man holding the phone who immediately handed it to him. "We have been unable to turn this on. Turn it on now and show me the number you dialed." He snapped his fingers again, pointing at David's handcuffs. A policeman jumped and removed the cuffs.

David tried the phone, but no matter what he did it wouldn't turn on.

"I don't know what's wrong. It was working. Your

men must have broken it." David looked at him. "It's a very expensive phone." David thought the captain was going to explode. He grabbed the phone and tossed it back to the startled policeman.

"You will be detained while we investigate." The captain, or whatever he was, looked extremely annoyed with the whole situation. There had been a violent attack in his district on his watch, and he had no good answers for his superiors. He turned to his men and barked a series of orders, likely interspersed with a few profanities. They began leading Sarah and David out of the lobby toward a police van and wheeling Shlomo to the ambulance.

As they got to the door, a petite older woman entered the lobby and blocked the exit. She wore a conservative gray suit with a mid-calf-length skirt, square black-framed glasses, no makeup, and gray hair in a neat bun. Her eyes darted about assessing the situation. Two large men in dark suits, each with a single earpiece, flanked her. She looked like a Schnauzer between two Great Danes.

She beckoned the captain with her finger and presented her credentials. All activity stopped while he examined her documents. The captain looked down at her, red-faced as though he were about to explode. She spoke quietly in Arabic, and pointed to a space behind the counter out of earshot. For several minutes, she spoke and he listened. At first, he stood defiantly with his arms folded, but as she continued speaking, his stance relaxed, and he began nodding. The conversation ended with him offering a quick salute. Whatever she had said, she was now in charge. She handed him two envelopes, one thick, one thin, and a manila folder.

The captain spoke to several officers, and after a succession of nods, they left the lobby, except for two officers who seemed to be waiting for the woman.

She went directly to Shlomo. "Are you all right? We have a doctor waiting at the airport. Immediate evacuation is underway."

"Yes, I believe I'm fine, a possible concussion." She nodded to one of the men who spoke silently into the microphone attached to his shirt cuff. She turned to Sarah and David.

"My name is Vindex, Miss Vindex. Dr. and Mr. Austin, please come with me. We have transportation waiting. We will gather your belongings. You must hurry. It is not safe here." She wasn't entertaining questions. Two men wearing black coveralls and carrying black cases walked swiftly through the lobby and up the stairs.

The street had been cleared by the police. A large, dark-blue panel van pulled up outside with the engine running. A door on the side opened, revealing a lighted interior, a combination armory and medical unit. There were seats along one side and a place for a gurney on the other. Overhead cases held dangerous looking assault rifles. The woman, their apparent deliverer, entered and sat beside Sarah. Two men loaded Shlomo's gurney, and a medic examined him, checking his eyes with a penlight.

"Go," Miss Vindex commanded. The police who had come to arrest us now provided an escort as the van sped down the narrow street.

"Are you the person I called?" David asked.

"Yes. We've been shadowing Mr. Halberstam since your second meeting at the museum."

"Do you work with Shlomo? Are you part of his Brotherhood?"

"Some questions must, of necessity, go unanswered. Let's say that we provide specialized concierge services, and leave it at that." She checked her watch.

"We've had you under surveillance since your arrival in Syria. In the event of emergencies such as tonight, we have prearranged evacuation plans. Your hotel room will be cleansed of all fingerprints and DNA traces. Your names will be removed from the hotel records. There was a hidden video camera in the lobby, and we have secured the tape."

"How did you get around the police?" Sarah asked.

"Bribes, Dr. Austin. The Middle East is a culture of bribery. I gave the police superintendent the numerical ID and password for a foreign bank account containing fifty thousand Euros. Higher up officials have come to expect their 'remunerations' in offshore accounts, as it avoids any domestic complications. I gave him a separate envelope containing Syrian currency to pay off his subordinates, and lastly, I gave him names and forensic evidence for a cell of Sunni separatists on whom he can blame the attack. He will look like a hero to his superiors. He might possibly earn a promotion."

"I'm glad you came. At first, I didn't think anyone was on the line because I heard no response, but they said something the second time."

"You failed to end your message with the correct key phrase, a procedure we use to detect unauthorized requests, so we sent a kill code to the phone. The buzz you heard was the phone's memory chips being destroyed. However, we knew Mr. Halberstam was at this address, so we treated the request as legitimate anyway." The woman checked her watch. "We will be at the airport in six minutes."

She turned her attention to Shlomo. "Mr. Halberstam, Are you feeling better? Do you still wish immediate evacuation?"

"Yes. I'll see the doctor for ten minutes. Please have the pilot file a flight plan for Crete, and then under the alternate registration from Crete to Paderborn in Germany."

The woman nodded and spoke to a man wearing a headset in the front passenger seat.

David turned to Sarah and picked a few pieces of plaster out of her hair. "Quite a day, huh?"

Sarah nodded, struggling unsuccessfully to hold back tears. "Lecturing to three hundred half-awake freshman at eight a.m. sounds pretty good to me right now." She patted his leg. "How you doing?"

"I'm fine—well, no I'm not. I'm really pissed off. Someone tried to kill us, to kill you." David smacked his fist into his hand. It was the first time in his life he'd felt truly violent, a rage that blocked out any other thoughts. He wanted kill whoever had shot at them.

"It must have been Shlomo's visit to the fake institute that triggered the attack. I'm surprised. It sounded like Shlomo played his part of the dejected researcher perfectly. Why would they risk drawing attention to themselves by trying to kill us so publicly? It seems wrong from everything we've surmised." Sarah's analytical brain was working again.

"I don't know. Maybe they're not as organized or as smart as we've assumed. Or they make mistakes like everyone else."

"I never thought I would find such comfort in the word 'evacuation.' I'm glad we're getting out of here. I'll be happy when we're in the air again," Sarah said.

David shared Sarah's relief that we were fleeing. The speeding van provided more safety with each mile. Part of him wanted to continue running away, to turn back the clock to before he'd found Abigail's picture. Another part of him wanted to get a gun and hunt down their attackers. David settled on the fact that neither option would happen. They were fleeing Damascus, thankfully, but then flying to

Paderborn and the Nazi castle. They were escaping one dangerous situation, one that had almost killed them, and charging headlong into another.

Running Out of Time

"The future is uncertain, but the end is always near."
– Jim Morrison

The display in the jet's cabin indicated Mach 0.85 at forty thousand feet. In two hours they would touch down at the Paderborn airport in northern Germany. Shlomo was asleep on the couch under a blanket, a white bandage covering the spot where the bullet had grazed his skull. Exhaustion and the sedatives ensured his rest.

The plane departed for Cyprus, and shortly after takeoff the pilot announced their expected change of flight plan and veered northwest toward Germany. David had never been shot at before. He found the experience exhausting and their rescue bewildering. He was far out of his comfort zone, feeling adrift with no control over his fate. David's eyes drooped and he succumbed to sleep.

A hand touched David shoulder. "Hey, you awake? I thought you'd be dead to the world for a few more hours," said Sarah.

"Would you mind phrasing that in a different way?" David replied.

"Oops, sorry," said Sarah with a sheepish grin. "Bad choice of words."

"Do you think Shlomo is going to be functioning when we land?"

"I hope so. The doctor wanted him to rest in bed for two weeks. Said he had a concussion. Shlomo said he'd take it easy for a few days but bed rest was out. What's the name of that castle we're looking for?"

"Wewelsburg. It's in the northern Rhineland, an area

called Westphalia, a short drive from Paderborn. The pilot said we'd be landing a 10 a.m. Shlomo wants to be there before noon."

"I don't know. By the looks of him, I think we should get a hotel room and rest for a day. I thought Damascus was going to be easy. Now we're going to the castle—Nazi SS central. God knows what we're going to run into."

Sarah raised her eyebrows, and nodded. "Yeah, I know. Our cover's blown. They'll be expecting us."

"You think?" David said sarcastically. He got two water bottles from the galley and handed one to Sarah.

"Thanks," she said. They sat side by side in the captain's chairs for a long time without talking. David had the sensation of flying into battle. Hurtling toward an enemy he could neither recognize nor understand. David worried that anyone they saw, perhaps the person standing next to him, might be the enemy waiting to kill them at the next opportune moment.

The sound of the jet began to fade, and David heard Abigail's thoughts coming closer, clearer. Each time their thoughts overlapped, she was stronger and more confident. She was looking out on a group of people. It wasn't a friendly crowd. Every face was leering at her. She was in great danger from these people.

Then Abigail went quiet. David's connection remained, but her thoughts were gone, a conspicuous silence. He saw her in his mind's eye but she was distant like a person fading in a rising fog, a form but no visible details.

David heard the sound of the jet returning, and saw Sarah kneeling in front of him, her hands on his arms. "How's Abigail?" she asked in a surprisingly normal tone. "I guessed you were doing your thing with her. You went catatonic again like in the car ride back to Damascus."

"I'm glad it didn't freak you out. Pass me my water." David needed a moment to think about how to tell her the bad news. "She's good. Stronger than before. She just fought a battle and defeated someone called the countess. I didn't get a clear picture, but it was fierce."

"Geez, I wish I could see what you do. From the little you tell me, it sounds like there is an epic battle waging on the other side." Sarah gave her husband a squeeze.

"Sarah, I told you about the Lilim planning to release a plague. What I learned is that it's going to happen within a week or two. We're almost out of time."

"Jesus, Mary, and Joseph." Sarah's face went blank.

Sterilization

"Never interrupt your enemy when he is making a mistake."
– Napoleon

Philippe Lambert read the wire services news reports for the Middle East daily, scanning for anything suspicious. He happened upon a report from Damascus about three American researchers being attacked. The coincidence worried him. Three researchers had been at Moloch's Temple on the coast and were last reported on their way to the Syrian Archeology Foundation offices in Damascus where that fool Turk, Alay, was supposed to follow procedure and send them away.

Lambert touched the intercom, "Mademoiselle St. Pierre, Please get me Mr. Villus at the Syrian Archeology Foundation in Damascus." His intuition told him that something had gone horribly wrong.

The intercom crackled, "Monsieur Lambert, Mr. Villius is on line one."

"This is Raven, regarding your report from yesterday's visit. Did you follow procedure?"

There was a sight pause. "I'm waiting." The tension rose in Lambert's voice.

"Yes, yes I did. I did as the procedures dictated. A single man, tall, dressed as an American but with an Israeli accent came to the office. He said he was from Brooklyn, New York, but had been raised in Jerusalem. He was interested in Moloch's temple. He spent an hour in the archives then he left. He said he'd found nothing."

"That's it? You did nothing else?" Lambert pressed.

"No Raven, nothing."

"How do you explain the attempted killing of three Americans last night in Damascus?"

"The papers said it was an Al Qaeda group. The police have been rounding up people today. I'm sure it's just a coincidence."

"What were their names?"

"The American who came to the office called himself Shlomo Tovrov, but his real name was Halverson. Alay spoke quickly as though haste would put Raven's mind at ease.

Imbecile, thought Lambert. "And how did you find out his name?" The pause on the phone told Lambert all he needed.

"The American told me."

"The American told you that his real name was Halverson?" Another pause as Alay's credibility crumbled.

"No, I knew he lied about his name, so I had him followed to his hotel."

"So you broke procedure. What else did you do?" There was no mistaking the anger in Lambert's voice; all pretenses were gone.

"Nothing, I swear. I asked at the desk about their names. I had to bribe the manager. That is nothing unusual for Damascus."

"What were the names of the other two?"

"A Dr. Sarah Austin and a David Austin."

"Fine, thank you for your report. Please remain at your desk till I call again. I will need to speak with you further today. Understood?"

"Yes, Raven. I'll wait for your call."

Alay was lying. He'd made a mistake and had tried to

cover it up by killing the Americans. His failed attempt had been stupid, brutish. If investigated, it would put a spotlight on the Foundation, and possibly even the Société. Questions would be asked. This was unacceptable.

The situation would have to be sanitized, but first he had to report to Falcon.

Lambert turned on his secure computer and pecked away with two fingers, composing a full report including the names of the Americans and his recommendation for sanitizing the location. Lambert was terrified of making even the smallest mistake. Falcon disliked mistakes of any kind, and reacted swiftly to bad news. Lambert pressed *send* and the electronic message passed through a dozen servers around the globe until it stopped at Falcon's ranch in Idaho.

The computer screen in the vice president's communications center flashed red, indicating a priority message. The sergeant on duty printed the message and walked to Vice President Connolly's study. A wall of glass faced the Portneuf River with the Bannock Range in the distance. Fly fishing gear stood in the corner. The vice president was working at his desk.

"Priority message, sir." The sergeant handed over his message and waited at attention in case there was a reply. He enjoyed the scenic view, a welcome relief from the dark confines of the communications bunker.

The vice president read the message. He paused, lost in thought, staring out the window at the mountains.

"Thank you, Sergeant; that will be all." It was a breach, Falcon thought, a minor one, one that would not have worried him in the past—but they were only days away from the event. The event they had been waiting centuries to unfold. There had been many attempts in the past, but it was only recently, within the last ten years, that a real possibility for victory over the children of Eve had presented itself.

No, no breach was trivial now. The Damascus site would need to be sterilized. The organization needed to be alerted, the Americans found and eliminated—nothing could be left to chance. The vice president rolled his chair to his secure computer, turning his back on the bucolic scene outside. He sent a world-wide alert to all Lilim organization sites describing the breach along with the names of the three Americans. If the Americans popped up at any other sites, it should be reported immediately. He then sent a message to Raven confirming sterilization.

Falcon returned to his desk, resuming his work and thinking that it would be a fine afternoon for fly fishing.

At 1700 hours Damascus time, a private jet inbound from Avignon touched down at the Damascus airport, and three men, all trim and muscular with military crew cuts, stepped off and boarded a waiting SUV. They were dressed in casual sportswear and each carried a large black duffle bag. They went directly to the Syrian Archeology Foundation at 89 Mabarah Street.

Upon entering, one man went to Mrs. Attai's desk. He told her that the office was closing effective immediately, and her services were no longer need. He handed her an envelope containing a half year's pay as severance. Mrs. Attai, bewildered, stared at the young man who spoke in Arabic with a French accent. As a way of emphasizing *immediately*, he handed over her coat. She put it on and flew down the stairs before the stranger could change his mind about the money.

The other two men went to Mr. Alay's office and closed the door. One man grabbed Alay and placed a hand over his mouth while the other man injected him with a dose of phenobarbital. In seconds, Alay was slumped in his chair. The men searched the office for Alay's ring with the Norse symbol that had been his downfall. They found it in his pants pocket along with the keys to his apartment. The search of the office turned up nothing else related to the organization. They carried Alay by the arms to the SUV and put him in the back, after binding his hands and feet with duct tape.

The leader waved at a waiting moving van. They had orders to empty the entire contents of the office. All books and papers were to be burned and the furniture sold. They'd been paid double time to complete the work that night. Within one hour, all that remained of the Syrian Archeology Foundation was dust on the floor.

After a search of Alay's apartment, the men drove a semi-conscious Mr. Alay two hours into the dessert. They dug a shallow grave and, with one bullet to the back of the head, ended Mr. Alay's time on earth. He had come to the same fate as his predecessor. Before filling in the grave, one man put on a disposable hazmat suit, gloves and goggles. He then poured a greenish liquid on the body, a genetically-engineered bacterium with a ravenous appetite for human flesh and bone.

Within twenty-four hours, Mr. Alay's remains would be liquid goo seeping into the ground.

By one in the morning, the men were on the return flight to Avignon. Lambert reported to Falcon that the sterilization of the Damascus site was complete.

The Prize

"The ones who win usually don't need the prize."
– Jake Colsen

The upside-down room came into focus, and searing pain coursed down Abigail's arms and legs. She tried to call out but heard no sound. She was naked, hung upside-down on the wall of the salon. Iron straps were wrapped around her arms and legs and drawn tight. Abigail could barely move. She was drained, weak, teetering on the edge of the void.

"Ah, I see you've awoken. Good. You don't know the pleasure it gives me to have a new trophy displayed on my wall." Abigail turned her head and saw Lord Eymerich looking up at her. He stood there in his crimson cardinal's robes and hat, dressed as he had been in the fourteenth century when he was the Inquisitor General of the crown of Aragon.

Abigail wanted to leap at him and tear at his throat, but she was helpless. The more she resisted, the stronger the pull on the straps that bound her. Abigail tried to scream, but no sound came.

"You are such a foolish child, disappointing really. I had thought that you would be a more entertaining adversary, but you've proved too easy, too headstrong. You knew nothing of Gehenna, and yet you charged headlong into situations where you understood nothing that awaited you. You believed your victory over the hapless countess meant that you were ready to challenge me." Eymerich laughed the same screeching laugh Abigail had heard before losing consciousness. Again, her mouth moved but no words came.

"No, my dear Abigail, you cannot speak. Those straps

that bind you to the wall are not simple iron. I created them and gave them a purpose. They will keep you drained of energy, weakened to the point where you can barely holding your form. This is one on the many things you've failed to understand. In the land of the living, things are either alive or not. In Gehenna, there is no such distinction. The straps that bind you are imbued with my will, what you might think of as a consciousness." He held up his hand, and the straps obeyed by raising Abigail in the air and slamming her against the wall.

"You will remain there because it pleases me. We shall have other sport with you from time to time. It will be some time before I grow weary of this diversion." As she watched, Eymerich morphed from human to the demon form Abigail had seen during the queen's vision time. Her eyes followed him as he strode out of the empty salon, the talons on his feet scraping on the stone floor. A lingering putrid smell remained behind.

Abigail struggled to remain awake, but the icy cold of the iron restraints paralyzed her. When she tried to form a vision of Ehyeh to draw energy from, the straps snapped taut, dark energy shot through her arms and legs, convulsing her in searing pain. Abigail thought of the women she'd left in the countess's chamber, and again, the vile energy racked her body. Only when she thought of Lord Eymerich did the pain subside.

A new terror filled her. She was being trained, programmed. Abigail remembered how Rachael had been corrupted, transformed into a demon by the countess's torments. Lord Eymerich had begun her conversion. Pain racked her body again. She resisted and the pain increased. If she allowed an obedient thought, the pain subsided. If she thought about denying Eymerich, the pain reached new intensity till there was nothing but pain—no thoughts, no experience of any kind, just exquisite agony. Time lost its meaning. Her existence continued in waves of pain crashing like giant waves from an angry sea. Blackness engulfed her once more.

Sons of Perdition

"For there is no friend like a sister, in calm or stormy weather."
– Christina Rossetti

At 10 a.m., the jet dropped through the low clouds and immediately touched down at Paderborn Lippstadt Airport. At the corporate terminal, a man in a dark suit holding an umbrella waited in the drizzle beside a silver Mercedes SUV. The cabin door opened, and a gust of cold, damp air swept in. The customs inspector entered. He gave them a routine glance, scanned their passports with a handheld device, and left without speaking—a bored man putting in his time till he could draw his pension.

The stewardess handed them two large umbrellas. "Thank you and have a pleasant journey," she said, as though their next stop were a tropical beach with fruity drinks. The rain and dark clouds better reflected Sarah and David's mood.

The dark-suited man handed Shlomo the keys and a large envelope, and placed their bags in the SUV.

"Okay, we're set. We have five thousand Euros, some background information on the castle, a hotel reservation for the next week, and the SUV's GPS is programmed with the Wewelsburg Castle's address," said Shlomo.

"Mr. Austin, you'd better drive. I'm not sure the pain medicine has worn off yet." Shlomo handed David the keys. He pressed the start button, and the Mercedes came to life like Bavarian clockwork. David touched the green arrow on the GPS, a woman's voice with a detectable French accent said, "Proceed five hundred meters to terminal exit, then right on to airport loop road." The display indicated twenty-five Km.

Several turns later, they were on Route 44 to Wewelsburg. David drove in the right hand lane as Porsches and BMWs whizzed by at speeds well above the limit on the Maine Turnpike. Shlomo read though the documents and then looked out the passenger's window at the wet, gray scenery.

"Shlomo, there is something I didn't get a chance to tell you before. Getting shot at interrupted my train of thought. Abigail heard Lilith talking to the man called Falcon. They're planning on starting a plague, one that infects humans but not the Lilim. She didn't know exactly when but thought it was soon, within two weeks." His words came quickly, reflecting his anxiety. They were in a race and were losing ground.

"It's as I feared, the crisis is at hand. The Lilim are gathering and the goddess has appeared. The forces of good and evil are aligning themselves. We don't have a minute to lose." Shlomo's monotone voice was in stark contrast to the urgency implied in his words.

"Okay you two, what's our plan? Do we have a plan?"

"Excellent question, David," said Sarah. "I think our plan is to hope that we'll find our next clue."

"Shlomo, any thoughts?" Sarah asked.

"I hate to admit it, but Dr. Austin you're right. We're here because of an educated guess. I know that the Lilim were the core of the SS within the Nazi party. The Wewelsburg Castle was their mystical home. Moloch's chalice is the artifact that connects Lilith with her children, so it stands to reason that it was here at one time. Clearly, it's been moved. We need to find something that indicates where it went."

"What are our chances?" Sarah asked.

"Slim, very slim, I'm afraid. These documents are the synopsis of the recent history of the castle. As the American Army approached, the SS removed everything from the castle and sent a convoy to Bavaria in hopes of staging a last stand in the mountains. They tried to blow up the castle but lacked sufficient explosives, so they set it on fire. The castle was rebuilt, and is now a museum and youth hostel."

"Sounds like the Lilim have cleansed this site as well. It's not promising," said Sarah.

"Our quest that began with you happening upon the photograph has been a litany of vague clues and impossibly lucky happenstance. Too lucky and too improbable, I think. Whatever hand of fortune has guided us so far, I pray it continues," Shlomo said.

"Amen to that," added Sarah.

They sat in silence during the short highway drive. Every so often, a car would whiz by at high speed. The muscles in David's neck were taut, pulling his head back against the headrest. His hands sweated on the steering wheel. David had been numb since their escape from Damascus. He wiped his clammy hands on his pants, then rolled his head in circles and took a deep breath. Something was wrong, waves of intense pain spreading in his arms and legs. Abigail flashed in his vision.

"Shlomo, grab the wheel," David gasped. His back arched. David clutched at his chest, and his legs pulled up. He tried to scream but nothing happened. David's body convulsed in agony. Shlomo pulled to the side and got his foot on the brake, just as David passed out.

David awoke lying on the back seat with his head in Sarah's lap, and Shlomo standing beside the open door peering down at David.

"What happened? Abigail again?" Sarah asked in a

concerned, maternal tone.

"It's Abigail. She's in terrible, blinding pain." The memory of the pain persisted like a nightmare. David trembled at the thought of it returning.

"Mr. Austin, you must try to control your bond with Abigail. You cannot leave your mind open; use your will to block the connection. If Abigail is somehow compromised, not only will you experience her suffering, but there is a possibility those aligned against us might learn of our efforts through you."

"Do you really think so?" asked Sarah.

"I do not know. What I do know is that we are dealing with phenomena beyond our understanding, and we must allow for any possibility. Mr. Austin's bond with Abigail is our greatest advantage, but it could quickly become our greatest liability." Shlomo always had encouraging words when things were tough.

"You know, I can't control this connection to Abigail. It just happens." David was annoyed, both at his apparent helplessness and at Shlomo's suggestion that he should be able to control himself.

"Shlomo, if you're up to it, I think you should drive." David said as he rose up on the seat, feeling like himself once more.

Sarah looked troubled but didn't speak. They resumed the short remaining drive to the castle. David glanced at Sarah in the rearview mirror. She was deep in thought. If she shared his tension, she hid it well. He wondered when the next cascade of agony might fall on him.

"Turn left on to Burgwell Strasse. Your destination is five hundred meters on the right," directed the female voice from the dash.

"There it is," David said. The rain had stopped, but a heavy mist remained with clouds hovering above the treetops. Wewelsburg Castle stood on a hill looming out of the fog. It was several stories tall, appearing quite broad, with a round turret on the left-hand side. It was made of beige brick with a dark roof, and had a number of small windows covered in iron bars. The castle looked joyless, austere, as though the evil that had risen from here to sweep across Europe and Russia still lingered, still echoed in the present.

"The notes about the castle said that Jews were used as slave labor during its extensive renovations. Five hundred of them died and are thought to be buried somewhere on the grounds," said Shlomo softly. "I should say Kaddish, the prayer for the dead." His voice trailed off as he looked out the window.

Shlomo pulled into the deserted parking lot. A sign, *Jugenherberge*, pointed to the left, and *Kreismuseum* pointed to the right. The threesome followed the path into a V-shaped courtyard with the turret at the union of the two arms of the castle. A wooden door made from timbers set on a diagonal was marked with another sign, *Eingang*. *Entrance* was spelled in smaller letters below.

They entered a room paneled in dark wood with heraldic plaques bordering the ceiling. A woman seated at a desk at the far end stood as we came in. She was short and stocky, wearing a gray-green suit with darker green piping, a skirt that came to mid-calf, and blonde hair pulled into a tight bun.

"*Guten Tag.*"

"Hello," David replied.

"Ah, you've come to tour our museum, yes?" She forced a smile.

"Yes. We're tourists from America."

"Ah, Yes, *gut, gut*. We get so few tourists on a day like today." She waved her hand in the air. "Yes, *gefällig sein* — oh pardon, my English not *gut*. Please, sign our guest book, and then we can have the tour, so *bitte*." She motioned to a ledger on the table.

David signed in as Mr. and Mrs. Johnson, Kennebunk, Maine, USA, and Mr. John Smith, Brooklyn, New York. She looked at the register and smiled.

"Yes, *gut*. My name is Frau Schmitt. We can begin the tour, yes? This way, *bitte*."

They entered a long corridor with an arched ceiling. The ceiling lights produced alternating sections of light and dark. The air smelled slightly damp and musty. Frau Schmitt's shoes squeaked on the stone floor.

"We are entering the central hallway of the main building. The castle was built in 1609 by the Prince-Bishop of Paderborn. His name was Fürstbischof Dietrich von Fürstenberg. The castle has been destroyed and rebuilt several times over the centuries."

She led them to a room with glass display cases filled with historical drawings of the castle in various states of decay or renovation, likenesses of past noble residents, and heavily corroded artifacts from various excavations. Frau Schmitt droned on about the Thirty Years' War, the Swedish occupation, the Seven Years' War, and the castle's partial restoration as a youth hostel in the 1920s.

They gravitated to the last display case which contained pictures of SS officers. Frau Schmitt took note of their interest. "In 1934 SS-leader Heinrich Himmler signed a hundred-mark, hundred-year lease, and the castle was converted to a school for SS officers, although it was never used as such. It did serve as the spiritual focus of the SS, with many marriages and ceremonies in the hall of the twelve pillars, what Herr Himmler called the Supreme Leader's Hall."

"David, Shlomo, look at this." Sarah's attention was riveted on a picture of a large golden bowl. It was decorated with symbolic faces and figures, some figures holding dead and bleeding people. "Ah, yes, that is the Chiemsee Cauldron. It was made in Munich for use in SS ceremonies. Herr Himmler kept it in a secret safe in the crypt under the room of the twelve pillars. When the SS fled the castle ahead of the American Army, they took all their artifacts, papers, flags, and the cauldron with them. The Chiemsee Cauldron is named after the lake in Bavaria where it was rediscovered in 2001. It is now in a vault in Switzerland. There are many legal claims concerning its ownership."

"David, is this it?" Sarah whispered. Frau Schmitt overheard and stepped closer, clearly interested in his answer.

"To what are you referring, Herr Johnson?" Frau Schmitt asked with an inquisitive stare.

"Oh, nothing. I have a certain interest in World War Two relics. This is one I've not seen before."

Frau Schmitt stared intently and then nodded. "So, we continue the tour, yes? We go to the room of the twelve pillars."

Their guide walked quickly to a pair of large wooden doors at the end of the hall set in a pointed archway reminiscent of a church. The doors were made of the same diagonal planks as the castle entrance. Frau Schmitt pulled on the large iron handle and held the door for them. "This is the room of the twelve pillars, obviously referring to the pillars supporting the ceiling."

The vaulted ceiling was two stories tall. In the center

of the vaulted ceiling, barely visible in the low light, was a swastika. In between the columns were downward sloping shafts with windows. The walls appeared to be several feet thick.

Shlomo stared at the floor. "Frau Schmitt, what do you call this design on the floor?"

"Ah, yes. That is the black sun. It's an ancient Nordic symbol. It was added by Herr Himmler. He used many Nordic symbols and runes. The SS symbols on their uniform are Nordic runes."

The design on the floor was a black circle with twelve zigzag lines similar to the arms of a swastika radiating outward. They examined the design on the floor, and the swastika set in the symbolic heaven above. David imagined the chalice placed in the center of the black sun and the Lilim dressed in their black SS uniforms communing with Lilith. The vision chilled him. He stood within the beating heart of the greatest evil of the last century. Sarah was frozen to the spot.

"Below us is the crypt, also built by Herr Himmler. It was thought to be intended as a tomb for Herr Himmler and senior SS officers, but, as we know, it was never used as such."

"And you said that there was a safe there where the cauldron was kept?" asked Shlomo.

"That is correct. It was emptied by the retreating soldiers and has long since been removed."

"Can we see the photographs once more?" asked Shlomo.

"Yes, *bitte*." Frau Schmitt pointed to the door.

In the display room Shlomo bent over the cases and studied the photographs of the SS. There were a number of weddings, groups of officers, and ceremonies with banners and Nazi heraldry. He moved quickly from photo to photo.

"Frau Schmitt, there is a man standing in the back of many of these photographs. He's dressed in black but without insignia. Do you know who he is?" Frau Schmitt followed Shlomo's finger from photo to photo.

"I'm not sure who he is. I suspect he was a member of the castle staff. There was a permanent staff for the castle's operation."

"Do you have any records from that time?"

"No, nothing. The castle was partially demolished and burned by the SS soldiers. These photographs have come from various other sources."

"I see, thank you." Shlomo turned his back to Frau Schmitt and motioned to the door with his eyes. "Thank you for the tour, but I think we're out of time for today. We must be in Frankfort tonight, and it's a long drive."

"Oh, yes. *Bitte schon.* I'm glad you came to see our castle."

Outside, the rain had picked up and they were dripping by the time they got back to the SUV.

"We've been shown our second well-staged dead-end," said Shlomo. "I suspect that the good *frau* is on the phone right now, alerting her superiors to our presence. After our reception in Damascus, I'm afraid we can expect another attack."

"Do you think your ruse about driving to Frankfort will work?" David asked.

"Not for long. It could give us a day at most, but that might be enough."

"What are you thinking? That unidentified man in the photos?" asked Sarah.

"Yes. Germans are accountants at heart. They are

meticulous record keepers and never throw away anything. I'm guessing that that man was the local director of the castle working for Himmler. It's the only reason why he could place himself in all those photographs."

"Good catch, Shlomo. I never would have noticed him or made the connection." Sarah raised an eyebrow at me.

"So how do we find out who he was, and if there are any records remaining," David asked.

"Excellent question. We can try the local library; maybe get the name of some local historians, or possibly the town hall. We need to move quickly. The Lilim will be on our trail soon, and we may hit another tripwire in our search."

"Tripwire?"

"There may be more than one person in Wewelsburg who would alert the Lilim to our presence, as did the old man at the ruins in Syria."

"In the past, I would have thought you were paranoid, but not anymore. We can't tell friend from foe." David said.

"We have no friends. From this point forward, we should assume everyone is Lilim." Shlomo continued, "Speed is our only ally. We must find out what happened to the chalice and stay ahead of our pursuers."

"David, what about the cauldron? You're sure that's not the chalice we're looking for?" Sarah asked, her voice carrying a hint of hope.

"Yes, I'm sure. I saw it when I had the vision with Abigail. It's smaller, more rustic, primitive really. It looks like a squat bowl with two handles. It would fit within the cauldron."

"I wonder if the cauldron was a container made to hold the chalice. It might have had a lid that wasn't found," Shlomo added.

"Makes sense to me. The chalice is the supreme artifact for the Lilim. It is Lilith's connection to her children. I can easily imagine the Nazis making a golden case for it and taking it out of the safe with great ceremony. The Nazis were big on ceremonies, look at the Nuremberg rallies. They were way over the top," said Sarah.

"I agree," said Shlomo. "Now we need to find out where it went. The Lilim would never throw the chalice in a lake. It was sent someplace that the Lilim would consider safe. Away from the war, maybe, probably out of Germany. With the chaos of the invading armies, it would be too easy for it to be stolen or destroyed."

"Okay, we've got a few hours left. Let's find the local library and hope our luck holds out," David suggested.

Shlomo nodded. David was happy to be leaving the castle. It gave him the willies.

"Mr. Austin, Frau Schmitt is watching us from the castle window," said Shlomo

Soldiers of Lilith

"What God abandoned, these defended, and saved the sum of things for pay." - A.E. Housman

Frau Schmitt rushed to the window with a pair of binoculars. She could only make out a partial license plate as the SUV drove off. She dialed Raven on her secure Blackberry.

"*Oui*," said Mademoiselle St. Pierre.

"Schmitt calling."

"One moment please." She buzzed Monsieur Lambert on the intercom.

"Yes, Mademoiselle."

"Monsieur Lambert, a woman named Schmitt on the special line, line nine."

"Thank you, Mademoiselle. You may take an extra hour at lunch today." Lambert wanted her out of the office while he focused on the crisis.

Lambert picked up the phone and pressed line nine. "Raven, report please."

"They just left here, the two Americans and the Israeli described in your email. The Israeli has a bandage on his head. They are driving a silver Mercedes SUV, German registration, last four numbers are three, eight, one, one. They signed the register as Dr. and Mr. Johnson, and a Mr. John Smith.

"Those names are obvious fakes. Is there CCTV footage?"

"Yes, Herr Raven."

"Good, transmit it right away."

"They said they were going to Frankfort."

"Did they say why?"

"No, Herr Raven. They were quite interested in the photographs of the SS officers and asked about a man in several of the photographs. I told them nothing of him."

"Do you know who it is?" Lambert raised his voice.

"No, Herr Raven. These photographs are simply a few that came from the town archive. They show various SS officers in weddings and other ceremonies. We checked all the SS officers shown. They are all dead, killed in the war."

"Then who was the man they were looking at?"

"I don't know, Herr Raven. I will take the photographs to Herr Brewer in town. He is the local historian. He may know."

"Fine, do so quickly and call me when you know." Lambert hung up the phone. Damn it, that fool in Damascus had somehow pointed these Americans to the castle. They were looking for something, tracing the path of the Lilim across the globe. He had to stop them before they made the next leap. If not, their next stop could be Idaho.

Lambert's computer alerted him that Frau Schmitt had posted the video footage. He reviewed the footage and saw the American tourists along with a tall, gaunt man. The couple looked typical right down to their sneakers; only Americans wore sneakers to a museum. The tall man was an enigma, clearly not an American but otherwise no hint of his origin.

Lambert called a compatriot at Interpol.

"Van Houten."

"This is Raven. There has been a second level security breach in Wewelsburg. I have a video clip I'm sending you. The man and woman may be Sarah and David Austin accompanied by a Shlomo Halberstam. They visited our site in Damascus. I need you to run a facial recognition on the video to verify their identities. I need confirmation on who these people are. How long will it take?"

"I can begin as soon as you send it. If the video is of good quality, well-lit, and in focus, it could take only a few hours. Otherwise, it might take days. And you need to understand that, at best, the success rate is less than fifty percent. I will check those names through immigration as well."

"Fine. Call me immediately if anything turns up."

"Understood."

"Also, I need to find a silver Mercedes SUV, German registration, last four digits are three, eight, one, one."

"I can run a search on the registration and find the owner of the SUV, but it may not be helpful. It's likely a rental or leased by a corporation."

"Issue an alert for the SUV. If spotted, have the local police report its location but do not approach. Make up some pretext for the alert. Again, call immediately if the SUV is located. This has the highest priority. Understood?"

"Yes, Raven. I understand. I will take some facial images from the video and send faxes to local hotels with a message that the people are wanted for questioning. Do you know where they might be?"

"Excellent. Yes, they left Wewelsburg Castle and may be driving to Frankfort."

"I will fax their photos to all hotels in both cities and along major highways. If they stop any place, we should know."

"Fine. Contact me immediately as soon as you know anything."

"Yes, Raven. Immediately." Van Houten hung up.

Lambert sat back in his chair and took a long deep breath. With the help of a few well-placed Lilim within Interpol, the entire EU police force was engaged in locating the threat to his queen. He would do anything to protect the queen. Even now, he felt a deep knot in his chest, knowing that there were people who were a threat to her. His heart pounded at the thought of it.

Lambert dialed the chateau outside Avignon that housed the Sicarii, a group known as the dagger men. The dagger men's numbers had risen and fallen with the fortunes of the Lilim over the centuries. They began by fomenting a revolt between the Jews and the Romans and reached their pinnacle in the guise of the Waffen-SS.

"Chateau de Guardien, *bonjour.*" The female voice sounded perky. The Chateau de Guardien was a winery set in remote hills to the west of Avignon. It maintained a small production to keep up the public façade, but its true purpose was as barracks and training for the Sicarii.

"*Bonjour.* Monsieur Muller, *s'il vous plait.*"

"One moment please."

"Muller."

"Raven here. There has been a second-level breach in security. Two Americans and an Israeli who have knowledge of our operations visited the Wewelsburg Castle a few hours ago. An Interpol alert has been issued. I need four sanitation teams, one for Wewelsburg, one for Frankfort, and two for highway patrols in between."

"I understand. We're ready. I can deploy the teams within the hour."

"Good. Contact Van Houten for pictures and details on their SUV."

"What is the disposition of the subjects?"

"Sanitize according to procedure if possible but terminate at all costs."

"Understood. Is that all?

"Yes, keep me informed." Lambert hung up.

Lambert pulled his chair over to the computer and began painstakingly typing his report. It was bad news, and, after the problem in Damascus, he worried that the Americans showing up in Wewelsburg would be seen as a failure on his part. Failure was never tolerated. Mindful of his predecessor's history, he feared a sanitation team might be dispatched for him as well. He completed his report, describing the events and the actions he'd taken. Lambert hoped Falcon would be satisfied. He went to the balcony overlooking the street and lit a cigarette as he listened to the traffic noise in the distance. It was a cool day in June, unusually wet. The light mist was refreshing, but his mild panic remained. As long as his queen was threatened, Lambert would not rest.

Deliverance

"And so, she turned her back on the abyss for another day."
– Megan Kennedy

"Lady Abigail, are you all right? What are you doing up there?" The voice came like a faint cry in the storm that engulfed her. Abigail opened her eyes and saw two little girls in white dresses holding hands. They looked up at her, puzzled.

"Where are your clothes?" the second little girl asked. Abigail tried to speak, but the straps pulled ever tighter and she relapsed into torment encased in a freezing blackness.

Abigail awoke expecting pain. Agony echoed in her thoughts. Its absence left a void. She had to force herself to remember who she was, where she was. Abigail looked up at the ceiling moving by and felt her body bouncing rhythmically. She saw Ilona's strong chin and face. Ilona carried Abigail in her arms.

Abigail didn't know how, but she'd been rescued. She was safe. She let herself go, and sleep embraced her.

Abigail awoke again, and her arms and legs moved against something soft and warm. She was in a bed, covered in a blanket with her head on a pillow. She smelled lavender. Dozens of young faces smiled back at her. "Lady Abigail, how are you?" Ilona was wiping her brow with a cool cloth, reminding Abigail of her Mother nursing her when she had been taken ill. Abigail strength began to return as sweet, warm energy flowed into her from the circle of women. With each breath, energy streamed like a warm shower purging the evil that had polluted her.

Abigail pushed her head up on the pillow. "Ilona,

what happened? How did I get here?" Abigail looked around. She was in a large room made of dark timbers and wood. Oil lamps hung from the ceiling and walls.

"The twins, Constanta and Contessa, found you in Eymerich's hall. They told us, and we rushed back to rescue you. You were naked and hanging on the wall. You couldn't speak, your face was contorted, and your eyes rolled back in your head."

"How did you get me down? Where are we?" Abigail didn't recognize the room.

"It was hard. We pushed a table against the wall so we could reach you. I touched one of the straps that held you and horrible pain shot down my arm and knocked me to the floor. The straps pulled you higher and shook you like a rag doll."

"When I touched the strap, I saw that it was alive, a demon, and you were its captive" Ilona's face turned grim as she relived the moment.

The horror of the experience rushed back. Abigail recalled the horror drowning in a sea of evil, darkness, and pain, with only Eymerich as her savior. His demons had been wearing her down, replacing her essence with Eymerich's own.

"I needed a weapon, something that would kill the demons that held you, but there was nothing in sight." She looked to the twins and stroked Contessa's head. "Well it happens that the twins are makers, very good makers. They asked what I needed and I said a sword. They held hands and Constanta touched my arm. Then this sword appeared in my hand." She raised her arm and showed Abigail a gleaming silver sword. It had intricate etching along its blade, a simple hilt, leather grip, and a gold ball as a pommel.

"I've held this sword a long time ago in a place I only have vague memories of. This sword is a part of me. It feels like an old friend that I've known for many years. The memories are shrouded, but the emotions are strong. I don't remember where or when, but I've stood by your side with this sword in my hand before."

A memory fragment flashed in Abigail's thoughts. She saw them together, dressed as warriors, running across a vast plain at night with swords in hand. They were charging into battle, reveling at the conflict awaiting them.

"Yes—yes, like you, I don't remember where, but we have fought together, and—I think we shall again." Abigail took Ilona's hand in hers and let their memories mingle, filling gaps in their respective memories. They were charging toward a stone temple on a moonless night. They'd been searching for the temple for months. There was a great evil there that must be destroyed. Ilona's eyes went wide as their shared memories formed.

"With the sword in hand, I jumped back on the table and struck the strap that held your arm. A piercing shriek echoed in the room, and black liquid dripped from where I struck. My second blow severed the strap, the pieces fell to the floor and slithered away like a snake. I cut the remaining straps with the same effect. I caught you as you fell. Your body was ice cold, and your skin gray, almost translucent." Ilona pulled a stool close and sat down.

"We brought you here and stood vigil over you. We didn't know if you would recover, but slowly your color returned, and we knew you were healing."

"I don't recognize this place." Abigail gestured to the room. The blonde twins smiled and stepped closer.

"We made this. It's like the house we grew up in, but we had to make it larger to have room for everyone." One twin began the sentence and the other finished it as though a single person were speaking through two mouths. They were clearly pleased with themselves.

"I told them we needed to hide you, and this is what they made. This room is concealed behind a secret door in the countess's chamber." said Ilona.

Abigail sat up and swung her feet onto the floor. She was dressed in a white peasant dress similar to the twins. Contessa and Constanta smiled when Abigail noticed.

"Thank you, Contessa, Constanta, Ilona, and all of you for rescuing me. I would have eventually been lost, transformed into one of Eymerich's demons." Abigail had set out to rescue the countess's captives, and had herself been rescued.

Abigail now understood that damnation—transformation into a demonic servant—was worse than death, a fate that she had only narrowly escaped. Abigail had conceived of *making* as limited to the inanimate. Eymerich had demonstrated to her that anything could be imbued with consciousness. Abigail also realized she could create living objects that were an extension of her will. The sword that had appeared when she fought the countess was part of her. She and the sword had moved as one, fought as one, and controlled the flow of energy as one. Abigail needed to surprise him when they met again.

Herr Bauer's Daughter

"For there is nothing lost, that may be found, if sought."
– Edmund Spenser

"My notes say that the castle previously contained the Schutzstaffel Bibliothek, the Library of the SS. The closest existing library is Erzbischöfliche Akademische Bibliothek in Paderborn, the next town. It's an academic library and as good a place to start as any. Any remaining SS materials are likely housed there." Shlomo entered the address in the GPS which indicated a twenty-minute drive.

The Bibliothek looked more like a monastery with its austere German architecture; three stories tall done in gray brick with white trim and a black roof. We entered through a Gothic doorway with a crest above the door.

"Guten Tag, meinen Herren und Dame." The young woman behind the counter had neon pink hair in sharp contrast to her black suit jacket.

"Yes, good morning." David hoped she would switch to English.

"Ah, yes, you're Americans. How may I help you?" She sounded like she'd just walked out of a Bronx deli.

"We're researching the history of the Wewelsburg Castle and were hoping some of the records from the war might have made it to this library."

"I think so. Let me call Herr Gruber. He is the official in charge of the archives. One moment."

She spoke on the phone briefly and hung up. "Mr. Gruber will be right down. He doesn't get many requests, so I'm sure he will be most helpful."

"If you don't mind me asking, where did you learn your English?" David inquired.

"I did my undergraduate and graduate work at NYU. I lived in Brooklyn for seven years. Die hard Yankees fan. How 'bout that Rodriguez? He's having a good year."

"I'm a Red Sox fan, myself; don't pay much attention to the evil empire."

"Red Sox are a bunch of pussies," she retorted with a smile.

Before we could continue the New York–Boston rivalry banter, a short, elderly man marched through the Gothic stone archway at the end of the room.

"Good day, my name is Gruber. How may I assist you, *bitte?*" He peered at them over the tops of his glasses, his hands folded behind his back. David thought he might click his heels to attention.

Shlomo nodded for David to take the lead. "We're researching the Wewelsburg Castle during the final days of the war. We're hoping that your library may have some of the records from that period."

"Yes we have some. The records are quite limited. It was a chaotic time, you understand, and then there was the fire, so not much remains." Herr Gruber turned and walked toward the archway. "Come, *bitte.*"

They followed Herr Gruber to a polished, stainless steel elevator, and ascended to his domain on the third floor. The door slid open, revealing long rows of gray metal shelves with boxes and journals arranged in precise order.

Herr Gruber pointed to an oak table. "Sit, *bitte.*" He disappeared into the stacks and returned with a cardboard box and a large journal tied with a red ribbon.

"These were rescued during the fire which destroyed the castle. It is all that remains, I'm afraid."

He laid open the journal on the table. There seemed

still to be a faint hint of smoke rising from the pages. "This is the housekeeper's journal. It lists the cleaning schedule of the visitor's rooms, who stayed there, and who cleaned the rooms. There were many notable people from the Third Reich." Herr Gruber flipped several pages. "Ah, yes, here is Herr Himmler. His last visit was May of 1943."

Herr Gruber surveyed the three visitors. "So, what is it you would like to know?"

"We're trying to track down the location of any artifacts that the SS might have used at the castle, any antiques in particular. It's part of a study of stolen art works," said Sarah.

"Yes, yes, a terrible thing, all the looting. Terrible." The old man went to the cardboard box and pulled out a folder of photographs.

"Yes, these." He laid out four photographs of SS soldiers loading boxes on trucks. "To the best of our knowledge, the commandant emptied the castle of everything and took it to Bavaria."

"Yes, the Chiemsee Cauldron was found at the bottom of Lake Chiemsee in Bavaria in 2001," said Sarah.

Shlomo had bent over the table, studying the photographs in turn. "Herr Gruber, do you know when these were taken?"

Gruber turned them over. "No, I'm sorry, there is no notation. We surmised they were all at the end of the war."

"Look closely. In these three, it is clearly summer. The trees are covered in leaves, and the soldiers are wearing combat uniforms." Shlomo looked at Sarah and me.

"This one is during the fall. The leaves are down, but there is no snow. Also, the soldiers are in dress uniforms. There are two officers and what might be an honor guard with flags. These two soldiers are loading a single crate onto the truck." Herr Gruber looked closely, confirming Shlomo's observations. "Yes, I think you are correct, Herr?"

"Smith," replied Shlomo without looking up. "Any idea what this occasion was?"

"No, I'm sorry. We have nothing but the photographs, no other records describing them survived."

David sensed disappointment settling on the search party again; another dead end. Sarah studied the photo. Shlomo stood with a hand on his chin deep in thought. Herr Gruber looked at his watch like he was ready to go home to dinner.

"Herr Gruber, at the castle, we saw several photographs with a tall thin man in dark clothing but without insignia. He was in the background of many photographs. Who might that have been?"

"It was not the commandant you say, no SS insignia? Well, it must have been a member of the staff. There was a large staff from the town who managed the castle. It was run much like a hotel."

"Who was the manager?"

Herr Gruber looked through his box of papers and pulled out a single sheet. "This is the listing of all the civilian staff. The name at the top is Hans Bauer, *Hauptgeschaftsfuher*. The title translates to what you would call general manager." Gruber raised an eyebrow and continued. "Interesting. I know the family, but I never knew what Herr Bauer did during the war. Most people do not speak of that time. Herr Bauer died in the 1960s, but his daughter still lives in Wewelsburg. She must be in her eighties."

"Do you have her address?" Shlomo asked.

"Yes, I'm sure it's in the telephone directory. One moment, *bitte*." He left and returned a moment later with an address on a slip of paper.

"Herr Gruber, are these the only remaining records from the castle?"

"Yes, well this is all that I'm aware of. There may have been other records taken away to Bavaria, but I have no knowledge of such things. It was a desperate time, a time of great chaos."

Shlomo glanced at us, indicating that we should go. "Thank you, Mr. Gruber. You've been most helpful." Herr Gruber smiled slightly at Sarah and nodded.

Shlomo turned and moved quickly to the elevator, motioning to Sarah and David to follow. They walked briskly through the lobby, waving at the pink-haired girl who was on the phone. She waved back as they left.

Shlomo trotted to the car and punched the address into the GPS.

"You think this man Bauer's daughter might know something?" asked Sarah.

"I hope she does," answered Shlomo. He pointed out the windshield waving his finger. "David, please drive. We need to keep moving."

David pulled out, guided back to Wewelsburg by the GPS.

"Shlomo, you think there's something different about the other picture. Some type of ceremony?"

"I'm speculating again, something I loathe, but which I'm beginning to have more faith in. I am certain the chalice was here. The cauldron, as you guessed, is a case, a tabernacle for the chalice. I'm assuming that when the war was known to be lost, the Lilim would have made plans to move the chalice to a safe location."

"I agree." added Sarah.

"So, my speculation is that the fourth picture is the

chalice being moved. Hence the honor guards, the officers, and the dress uniforms," said Shlomo.

"It's lucky we found the few photographs that we did," added Sarah.

"No matter how hard the Lilim have tried, it is impossible to remove all evidence," said Shlomo, continuing to look out the window. "The question is, where did the chalice go?"

"We've not much to go on, nothing really. Abigail saw it in the woods in front of a giant owl statue, but that tidbit doesn't help. I'm sorry." Sarah's voice carried her annoyance, and David shared her frustration.

Shlomo looked over his shoulder at Sarah. "We have one last hope. Bauer's daughter. Maybe he kept some papers. He looked like..."

"Really? That's it? You have some wild guess that this man, whose identity we're not even sure of, might have kept some papers, and that his aged daughter didn't throw them out twenty years ago?" Sarah face was beet red. She stopped and looked away at the damp streets outside the rain-streaked window. "Sorry, sorry. I didn't mean to lash out at you like that."

"It's okay, honey, don't worry. We've been lucky so far, let's hope our luck holds out a little longer." I saw her face in the rear view mirror. She was on the verge of tears.

"Dr. Austin, I know this is hard. I share your feelings. Finding the Lilim is my life's work. I'm committed to tracking them down and foiling their plans. Yes, I'm grasping at straws because that is all I can see before us, but I will not let any clue, no matter how obscure or remote, go unexamined."

"You're correct of course. I'm sorry for losing it. Since Damascus, the stress has been gnawing at me." Sarah smiled back at Shlomo and patted him on the arm. "I'll be all right."

Shlomo offered a rare smile. It was true. They'd all been under terrific stress since being shot at. An unseen enemy pursued them leaving Sarah and David on edge, their nerves raw. With Shlomo it was hard to tell; his drive to find the Lilim suppressed all other emotions. They sat in silence for the rest of the drive. The hum of the wheels of the SUV on the wet roads provided a kind of comfort. David imagined himself driving in Maine, although outside the car nothing appeared familiar. Everything was foreign, possibly hostile.

"Your destination is one hundred meters on the right," the GPS directed.

Pre-war, three-story residential houses lined both sides of the street. Only the street number distinguished their destination from the others. The stucco around the wooden double doors had started to break away, and the window frames needed paint. They walked through a tunnel-like passage leading to an inner courtyard. On the far side were steel doors, modern replacements starkly out of place in the once elegant building. There was graffiti on the walls and bags of trash in the corner. A panel beside the door had a row of buttons with names. Shlomo found A. Bauer on the list of buttons beside the door.

"*Bitte, bitte.*" The voice was old and shaky.

"*Guten Tag, Frau Bauer. Mein Name ist Schmied. Wir sind an seinen Vater und seine Arbeit an der Wewelsburg interessiert,*" said Shlomo.

"*Bitte kommen in den dritten Stock,*" came the reply.

The door buzzed. "Come on, she's on the third floor." Shlomo bounded up the stairs two at a time with Sarah and David trying to keep up.

A trim, elderly woman answered the door. She wore a

simple blue dress, and her gray hair was braided in rows around the back of her head. *"Guten Tag. Sprechen sie Englisch?"*

"Yes, you heard my accent no doubt. My name is Halverson and these are my colleagues, Dr. Austin, and her husband, Mr. Austin. Thank you for seeing us."

"Come in, *bitte*, what can I tell you about my father?" She steadied herself with a hand on the wall as she teetered down the hallway. They followed her to a sitting room where she lowered herself into a chair by the window. The arms were frayed, discolored and the cushions molded to the shape of her small frame. A table beside the chair was covered in old photographs, prescription bottles, and a stack of books. We sat on the couch facing her. Her swollen ankles spoke of her failing heart.

"I understand your father was the general manager of Wewelsburg Castle during the war, when it was in use by the SS."

"Yes, this is so. My father managed the castle for six years, leaving only when the soldiers evacuated and set fire to the building. Father was a very important man in those days, well respected in the town. Men would tip their hats to him in the street. He took his orders directly from Herr Himmler himself. Father was a loyal National Socialist." A spark of pride came through in her voice but she caught herself. "Yes, but that time has passed. Those were not good days for Germany." She spoke as though the loss were still fresh.

"I assume he supervised all aspect of the castle's operations" Shlomo spoke softly.

"Yes, he was a very precise person, he supervised every detail, everything had to be just so."

She tapped her finger on three imaginary objects

indicating that everything must be in its place.

"I imagine he kept careful records."

"*Ja*, he had three men for the record keeping. Herr Himmler required the most meticulous reports on every aspect of the castle's operations. He once told Father that the castle was his most important legacy."

"I see. I'm sure he was most exacting. From all we've heard, he was an excellent manager." The elderly woman sat up a bit straighter in her chair, smiling and nodding to Shlomo.

"*Meine Frau*, did your father keep any records from his days at the castle?" Sarah and David both leaned in. She looked at Shlomo for a long pensive moment, then rubbed her hands together and looked out the window. Her face contorted, and she placed her fingers over her mouth as though holding in a sob. Finally, she looked back at Shlomo.

"After the war, our family lost almost everything. Our money was gone, and we had to sell many of our possessions. After Mother died, I cared for Father for many years. He was never the same after the castle burned, never well. His vitality was lost with the castle. Just before he died, he told me to not let anyone into his office. That I should protect his papers at all cost.

And I have, I have kept his papers all these years, but now I am an old woman. I am not well and I have no family. I'm afraid of what may become of his papers after I die. Father would be most angry if his papers were thrown out."

"So, there are still records then?" Sarah asked, looking ready to jump to her feet.

"Yes, his office is down the hall. Everything is as he left it. I used to go in and dust every week, but now it is too much for me." She tapped her chest. "Who did you say you were again? Have we met before?" Her face looked like that of a bewildered child.

"We are historical scholars. We're here to help you. We can arrange for his papers to be properly archived by Herr Gruber at the Bibliothek in Paderborn. I'm sure you would like to protect your father's legacy." Shlomo's voice was soft and encouraging. Frau Bauer smiled at the thought. She'd spent her life caring for her father. Preserving his legacy was her life's work.

"Yes, I would like that." Frau Bauer's eyes became watery. She appeared to lighten, to rise in her chair at the thought of her burden being lifted.

"If you would permit, we would like to conduct a preliminary survey of the contents today and then arrange for them to be preserved."

Frau Bauer rose slowly from her chair and beckoned them down the hall. The last door entered into a large room. Frau Bauer switched on the light hanging from the ceiling. An oak desk sat in the corner, its top neatly arranged as though Herr Bauer would return at any moment. A worn oriental rug covered the floor, and along the wall were nine tall oak filing cabinets. The room smelled of dust and old paper.

"These are all the records from Father's office at Wewelsburg Castle. He had them moved here when he heard that the SS were planning to abandon the castle."

Sarah looked like she was about to cry. Shlomo was wide eyed. David's heart raced as he wondered where we should begin.

Descent into the Abyss

"When you look into an abyss, the abyss also looks into you." –
Friedrich Nietzsche

Abigail rose from the bed. She was cleansed and renewed; stronger and, again, more learned in the mysteries of Gehenna. But believing that she had mastered the knowledge of Gehenna was a trap in itself, one that left her vulnerable.

Strength ruled in Gehenna, and the power of creation was without limit. Abigail had to find and wrest Eymerich's source of power from him. The next time she confronted him, the balance of power had to be in her favor.

"Ilona, I need your help on a dangerous task. One from which neither of us might return."

"Lady Abigail, my hand, my heart, my soul is pledged to you. I am forever by your side."

"We're going into the labyrinth under the castle to find the souls that Eymerich has hidden there. I suspect many dangers await us, and our return is uncertain. Eymerich stands between me and the queen, and I must defeat him." Abigail grasped Ilona's forearm.

"The queen? You cannot defeat her. She commands all of Gehenna. She draws her powers from every demon in the castle, the town, and whatever evils lurk in the labyrinth below." Ilona's face betrayed the uncertainty Abigail felt.

"You're right. She is seemingly all powerful. I do not know how to challenge the queen. If I had to today, I would fail. But I must find a way soon."

Ilona nodded. "I once asked my father what faith was. He wasn't sure. I don't know how you will defeat her, but I have faith that you will."

Abigail spirit rose with Ilona's confidence. "We need to hurry. Are you ready, my sister?"

"I'm ready," replied Ilona in her husky voice. She clutched the hilt of the sword stuck in her belt.

"We want to come too," said two small voices in unison. Abigail turned to face the expectant-looking twins, Contessa and Constanta.

"You want to follow us into the labyrinth?" she asked. "Why?"

"Because you need us," said Contessa. "Because we can help," continued Constanta, echoing Contessa's words.

"You are right. I do need you, very much. I need you to stay here and look after the other women. This great room you made is wonderful. It gives them a place to hide and be safe. I want you to look after them. Make them some food, see that they are comfortable. If you can do that for me, it would be a big help."

Their faces turned sad, and they looked at their feet. "Can you do this for me?" she asked.

"Yes," came their simultaneous replies. Abigail stroked their heads, and the twins looked up as their disappointment vanished.

"Thank you, I'm counting on you."

"We'll take good care of everyone," said Constanta. She took Contessa's hand and walked away to begin their duties, though Abigail couldn't imagine exactly what they might involve.

As Ilona and Abigail turned to go, a shrill voice called out, "I'm coming too, and don't try to stop me."

They turned back to the group. "Who said that? Show yourself." Ilona's command echoed in the vast room. A tall, slight woman pressed through the crowd and stood with her hands on her hips. Her straight black hair partially obscured her face. "I'm coming," she repeated softly. Her eyes met Abigail's and didn't waiver.

"Who are you and why do you want to enter the labyrinth? Do you understand the dangers that await you?" Abigail asked.

"My name is Violetta.

"Come closer." Abigail motioned with her hand as Violetta hesitated. She radiated defiance, a shield covering her fear.

"Again, why do you want to join us?" Abigail asked.

"You need me. I can see what is unseen and I can hear what is unheard." She raised her head and her hair fell back, revealing more of her face.

"Tell us of these things you claim to hear and see," Ilona challenged. Violetta shot a sideways glance at her and then met Abigail eyes once more.

"I hear you. I hear what's in your head." Her voice carried a deep, underlying anger.

"How do you know? By seeing my face?"

Violetta's face became steely and she stared at me. Abigail couldn't tell if she was going to answer her or lash out for asking the question.

"Yes. I've been cursed since childhood. I've always sensed what people were feeling." Her words came slowly as though they pained her. "At first, I made people uncomfortable. Then as I got older and could sense more, I made people angry. They called me a witch. The townspeople and children threw stones at me.

"When the countess's soldiers came in search of young girls, our neighbors sent them to take me." The anger echoed in her voice. "My parents didn't resist them, didn't try to hide me. My mother turned away when they took me."

Abigail experienced Violetta's betrayal as painfully as a knife slicing through her. The chamber stilled as her words settled.

"When I awoke here, I found my ability had progressed beyond mere sensing, to hearing. If I'm close enough, I can hear thoughts as though the words were spoken."

"Everybody?"

"Yes, everybody I've tried it with. I need to look at them, focus on them, and then it comes to me. It's like hearing one conversation in a room full of people talking." Violetta paused and looked at me. "You're thinking you need to get me in front of Lord Eymerich so I can hear what he's planning."

"Exactly. Your ability will be a great help. I can sense what people are feeling, some things about their past, but I have to touch them, and if I'm not careful, they feel what I'm thinking, so I've been hesitant about who I touch."

You will need to stay by my side and let me know what the courtiers in the salon are thinking, Abigail thought.

"Yes, I will if you desire it so. I've stopped listening to the countess and her demon ladies. Their thoughts are vile and hateful, painful to hear. I'm afraid to leave this room, I'm afraid of the voices I may hear, but, if you need me, I'll be steadfast beside you." Violetta voice didn't miss a beat, but it conveyed her anger and was tinged with uncertainty.

"There's more, I see things," Violetta said as though apologizing.

"And what is it you see?" Ilona asked, her tone changed to curiosity.

"I can see Lady Abigail's footprints. And where she has touched, it leaves a yellowish glow."

"Really?" Abigail was intrigued.

"Yes, I can see where you stepped when you came in, and I can see where you touched the bed with your hand. In fact, in the chamber, I can make out a faint glow in red where the countess was. I can still see the spot on the floor where you killed her. The glow fades, but it takes some time."

"Can you see where everyone has been?"

"'No, I've only seen this glow from you and the countess. No one else in this chamber leaves a mark."

"This may be our key to finding out where Eymerich and Jacquis go. You might be able to follow his footsteps through the labyrinth and the dungeons below," said Abigail. Violetta's face softened for an instant and then resumed her facade of defiance.

"All right," Abigail said. "You can join us, but I warn you. We may not return. The only thing I know about the labyrinth is that its terrors are beyond my imagination."

"I understand. I've heard the determination in your thoughts. I will follow you," Violetta said, brushing her hair back behind her ears.

"It is Ilona and I who will follow you," Abigail retorted, "since you can see where Eymerich has walked." A half-smile flashed across Violetta's face, and then her defiant expression returned.

Abigail led her small army through the chamber to the corridor where Violetta took the lead, pointing out invisible footprints. She stopped in front of a small, nondescript door.

"He went in there." Violetta stepped back and

pointed. The door radiated heat along with a putrid smell.

Kingdom of Pain

"The path to paradise begins in hell." – Dante Alighieri

Regnum Doloris was carved above the doors.

"What does that inscription mean?" asked Violetta.

"It's Latin. It means 'Kingdom of Pain," replied Ilona with an air of grim determination.

"Everyone ready?" Abigail asked. No one spoke. "Good, stay close. We mustn't become separated or we'll be lost, perhaps forever." Their eyes darted from face to face looking for courage. The time for bravado was over. The time for real bravery had begun.

They entered the small door which opened onto stairs leading down into a cave. The walls and floor were black and soft, sponge-like with putrid water dripping from the walls. Abigail felt a rhythmic pulsing under her feet. Light shone through a ragged opening ahead.

A naked old man, his head bowed, sat cross-legged beside the opening. A tattered gray cloth lay across his lap. His parchment-thin skin stretched over his bones, looking as though it would crack. His bald head reflected the torchlight. As we approached, Abigail saw writing on his skin. Words in different languages and scripts appeared and then faded away in a constantly changing display.

The old man looked up. His eyes seemed to have been gouged out and replaced with hot coals that glowed red in stark contrast to his bleached white skin.

"Who are you?" Abigail asked, mesmerized by the writing flashing across his face.

"I am Azra. I am the gatekeeper to the underworld."

He held up a small balance scale. "I judge all who enter. I weigh the hearts of the sinners who come before me and determine their fate for all eternity."

He sat up straight and looked at them. "Step forward that I may judge you."

Abigail took a single step forward and looked down into his red formless eyes. He held up his scale which remained balanced.

"You have no sin. Your soul is pure." The writing vanished from his skin. He looked away, raising a hand in front of his face as though pained by the sight of her.

"Why are you here?" he said in a loud, angry voice, resting the balance scale in his lap.

"We seek the innocents that Lord Eymerich has brought here. We have come to rescue them."

The old man stared at the floor. The mysterious writing reappeared, moving across his skin in a renewed frenzy. "Eymerich's sin is too great for my scale. He is beyond my judgment." He bent over with his head almost resting on the floor, as though his body had deflated. "What you seek is through this gate. I warn you. None besides Eymerich have ever returned."

They moved to the gateway. Everyone's eyes were fixated on the old man with a mixture of fascination and terror.

"Violetta, lead on, we must hurry."

"It's this way." She pointed to a stairway that curved downwards into darkness.

"Okay, hold hands," Abigail said as they entered the darkness. As we descended, the air became cold and fetid, foul, as though some creature had died at the bottom. They came to a long corridor. Unlike the fine stonework of the castle, this corridor was built with crude, ill-fitting stones. The floor was wet and sticky. The occasional torchlight glistened on the wet floor in between long stretches of darkness.

The passageway opened onto a cavern with an oily stream and a narrow stone bridge. Within the stream, Abigail saw faces moving in the current. They rose to the surface like so many bobbing apples, their faces masked in the black oily liquid. Emaciated demons lined the banks, jabbing iron spears at the faces to force them beneath the surface. Violetta gasped at the scene in the stream. She seemed more affected, perhaps because she could feel the agony of the trapped souls.

"Everyone, hold hands and look at your feet as we cross the bridge." They crossed single file, taking small, tentative steps. The demons, intent on their work, ignored their crossing.

Violetta continued to lead the way, following the tracks only she could see with Ilona close behind. The uneven slippery floor, the debris, and the darkness caused them to test every footstep, which made for slow going.

Large fissures lined the tunnel with flickering light and sulfurous smoke came from the openings. As they passed each fissure, the women heard distant screams and a dull roar coming from within.

"Is there someone in there?" asked Ilona in a whisper, her face horrified. They all moved to avoid the foul smoke.

"I think I heard my father's voice. He called my name," said Violetta, looking like she might crumble to the floor any second.

"Are you sure? I didn't hear anything."

"There it is again. He's here. He's in one of these pits." Violetta started toward one of the fissures. Abigail grabbed her hand and drew her back.

"It's not real. No one else heard anything. It's a trap. You can't trust anything you see or hear."

Abigail pulled the women together into a circle with her arms around them. "This is a horrible place filled with evil and suffering. I know that you're afraid. I'm afraid too. I don't know why those people are in those pits, or even if they are real or not. We can only trust ourselves. We need to stick together, to stay strong and complete our task." The women nodded. Violetta looked horrified. Her face grimaced with each scream, as though she shared the pain of the distant sufferers. Ilona looked stoic, and took comfort from gripping her sword.

"Eymerich has hidden his secret down here because he believes no one is brave enough to follow. We'll see many horrid things ahead, but if we stick together there is nothing that can hurt us. All right? Is everyone okay?" They were hanging on, but barely. Only their belief in Abigail prevented them from fleeing.

Ilona bent close to Abigail's ear. "I think someone is following us. I've seen movement, a shadowy form behind us."

"How can we be sure? There are many illusions here." Abigail replied. "Violetta, do you see anything?"

"No, nothing. Only the footprints we've been following."

Ilona whispered, "Let me try something." She pulled her sword, and ran back making broad sweeping arcs as she ran. "Show yourself or I'll cut you in two," she yelled.

As she approached the cavern entrance, a small weak voice cried out, "Stop, stop." A figure of a young woman became visible and disappeared several times. Ilona came up short and held her sword above her head ready to strike.

"Show yourself, and stay visible," Ilona commanded.

A lanky, thin girl winked into visibility, cowering at Ilona's size and sword.

"Who are you? Why are you following us" Abigail asked as she approached. She seemed to fade and then become fully visible once more.

"M-my n-name is W-Wendlandt. I-I-I followed you be-because I was a-afraid of staying behind in the chamber." She clutched her hands to her chest and backed against the cavern wall. Abigail motioned to Ilona to drop her sword. She stood in the shadows with her shoulders hunched, a thin waif of a girl, with pale, sallow, almost translucent skin, and long thin hair framing her face.

She looked as though she were going to fold in on herself, as though Abigail's words caused her pain.

Abigail knelt on one knee. "How is it you can be invisible?" She reached out to take her hand.

"Don't touch me." She yelled and her image flickered once more. "I hate it wh-when anyone t-t-touches me." Her eyes danced to meet Abigail's then looked away again. She curled into a ball on the floor.

"In-in my village, I-I was known as the-the mouse because I-I was-was always hiding. I've been afraid my whole life, a-a-afraid of people. Even when I went to the village with my mother, I would hide behind her.

"Wh-when I came here, I-I found I could stop people from touching me. When the countess's demons took people to bleed them, I-I could push them away. I say push, but I didn't touch them. It was as though they couldn't get close to me." Wendlandt seemed to relax and sat up against the wall.

"I didn't realize that when I thought I was pushing the demons away, I had also become invisible."

"Yes, you're right. She may be helpful," said Violetta. Abigail looked at her.

"Sorry. That's what you were thinking. To have a person who could be invisible would be helpful while we look for Eymerich's hiding place."

She looked embarrassed as Abigail glared at her. She had never worried about the privacy of her thoughts. "Violetta, I don't want you in my head. I know you can control when and from whom you read thoughts. Don't read my thoughts unless I ask you to."

"Yes, Lady Abigail." She looked away. In the meantime, Wendlandt had stood up and no longer looked like a beaten dog.

"We can't send you back, and yes, you may be helpful. Invisibility is a good trick. You need to come with us." Her face lightened and she stepped away from the wall.

"I-I c-c-can only be in-invisible when I'm frightened."

"I don't think that will be a problem in the labyrinth of Gehenna," said Ilona with a smirk.

The women chuckled, followed by a silent reflection on the truth of Ilona's remark.

Abigail stood and looked around. "All right, let's continue. Violetta?"

"The tracks lead that way," she pointed and began walking.

As they neared the far end, a loud rumbling noise erupted, the walls began to move, and fissures closed. Then the cavern became still. The silence was more foreboding than the screams they had heard before.

"H-how do w-we know the floor won't drop out fr-from under our f-feet?" asked Wendlandt, her face contorted. She appeared frozen to the floor.

Abigail tried to take her hand, but she moved away from her.

"Gehenna is the realm of illusion. Many things we'll see will play on our fears, but none of it is real." Ilona took her hand and pulled her forward. Wendlandt walked slowly as though being led to the gallows.

"Show us the way, Violetta." Abigail said firmly, so as to not let her own fear show. They entered the dark tunnel which opened onto a deep, narrow canyon filled with molten rock and rising plumes of fire. Threads of the fiery rock crept up the walls of the pit as though trying to escape. The fire would reach a certain height and then fall back on itself, splashing into the pit. Scattered throughout the canyon were small islands with blackened bodies lying on them. As they watched, human forms crawled out of the fire onto the rocky islands. When two or three bodies had gathered, a great arm of molten rock rose up and swept the blackened bodies back into the fire, and then disappeared beneath the magma. The flaming, molten rock appeared as alive as the demons that lined the river of drowning souls. The young women looked on in terrified amazement as the entire scene played out again on different islands.

"Lady Abigail." It was Violetta who broke their fixation. "He went this way." She pointed to a narrow path cut from the side of the canyon.

"Where is Wendlandt?" Abigail asked, fearing we'd lost her along the way.

"I'm h-h-here, Lady Abigail." Ilona flinched, and Wendlandt became visible beside me. "I'm s-s-sorry. The sight of the monsters s-s-scared me. I c-c-couldn't help h-hiding."

"Come, walk beside me," said Ilona, trying to sound reassuring.

They followed her single file, steadying themselves on the rough wall as they went. They passed another opening with smoke rising from it. Ilona continued on the path around the edge till she came to stone steps leading down, deeper into Hades. Cold air rushed at them as they groped their way down, one step at a time.

The stairs led to a hallway with rooms on either side. They heard screaming and ran to the first room, where Abigail saw an old woman in a tattered nun's habit. Five naked, emaciated children holding small iron tridents were stabbing at her as she frantically raced around the room. She shrieked in pain as one child after the other stabbed at her and found their mark. Violetta stood beside the archway, entranced by the woman's torment.

"Why doesn't she leave? There's nothing holding her." The expression on Violetta's face turned to horror. She turned away. "I can't look on this, the pain is too great."

"What is it?" Abigail asked, taking her hand.

"I heard her thoughts. That woman was the mother superior of an orphanage. She's responsible for the deaths of hundreds of children, all starved or beaten to death. She believed then, and thinks even now that she was doing God's will." Violetta's empathy caused her to experience the suffering of every tortured soul they'd happened upon.

Abigail raised her chin with her hand. "I suspect that the worst places in Gehenna are reserved for those that committed their crimes in the name of God." She nodded, somewhat comforted but still feeling more pain than the rest of them.

In another room, a man in an elaborate military uniform studied a map spread out on a table, frantically moving small soldier figurines around the map and barking orders to nonexistent aides. All the while, he stood on the bodies of mutilated soldiers who clawed at his legs, shredding his pants and leaving his legs bloodied.

Each room presented a different tableau of a person locked in endless misery reflecting their sins. Abigail motioned with her head for Ilona to continue. If these rooms represented the sins and punishment of individual people, it would take an eternity to examine each one. The search party continued, huddled as a group in the middle of the hallway.

What appeared to be a single hallway was actually many connected passages that went on at random. They would have been hopelessly lost if not for Ilona's ability to see Eymerich's footsteps.

They came to a natural cavern with irregular rocks on the walls and ceiling. Set in the wall at the far end was a pair of heavy wooden doors with wrought iron hinges and a lock. The doors were surrounded by carved stone like that of the castle. To one side, a stairway led down into the chamber. In front of the doors slept a gigantic three-headed dog with black and shiny fur. It leaped to its feet when they entered and stood as tall as three grown men. Each head snarled, flashing white fangs with drool flinging from its mouths.

The women froze, ready to flee if the creature attacked. Abigail motioned to the women to stay back while she stepped forward. The individual heads snapped frantically at the air, but the dog didn't move from its spot in front of the doors. Abigail moved from side to side, and it mirrored her actions, threatening her but not moving from its place as though bound by an invisible chain. They needed to find a way to distract the giant beast, as it also blocked the path forward.

"Ilona, did Eymerich go in there?"

"No, his footsteps go through the passage to the left. There are other footsteps, faint ones that lead down the stairs and enter the door. I think they were made a while ago."

This was not where Eymerich kept his secrets, but someone supremely powerful did. There was only one demon that had the power to maintain such a place Abigail thought. She had to get closer to the doors.

"Wendlandt, if I hold your hand, can you hide me as well as you?"

"I-I don't k-know."

"Let's try, take my hand. We'll take a step toward the beast and see if he reacts."

"I'm f-frightened. That beast will surely eat us."

"I know you're afraid. I am too. It is your fear that enables your invisibility." Abigail held out her hand again. "You and me together."

She reached, hesitated, and then took Abigail hand lightly.

Wendlandt's face went blank with fear, but she held Abigail's hand and followed, one terror-filled step after another.

"Abigail, it's working. You disappeared. I can't see either of you," said Ilona.

"Good, I hoped this would work. Make sure the dog keeps focused on you."

Wendlandt and Abigail moved to the side of the great three-headed dog. The other kept calling to it, and its three sets of eyes remained fixed on them. The closest head turned toward them, sniffing the air as though alerted to their presence, but then turned back. Wendlandt gripped her hand as though her life depended on it, her eyes squeezed shut.

They walked silently to the double door directly

behind the three-headed dog. Abigail touched the door lightly with her fingertips, and she heard a thousand small voices calling out. A tremendous surge of energy engulfed her. Unprepared, Abigail staggered and fell on her back. Wendlandt tumbled with her, and fortunately never released her grip. The beast turned at the sound, its three heads growling, and glared wildly in all directions. The pair remained still in the awkward positions they'd landed in.

"Beast, beast. Here look at me. I'm the one you want." Ilona waved her arms to draw the beast's attention.

The dog turned again to face Ilona. All three heads roared. It pawed at the floor with its massive claws scraping against the stone. Abigail recovered from the shock and, to her surprise, she was energized with new, perfectly pure energy, which further confirmed her suspicions about who was behind the doors. They rose slowly and made their way back to where Ilona stood. Abigail let go of Wendlandt's hand and Ilona jumped, startled to see them.

"What is it? What's behind the door?" asked Ilona. She looked at the door as though a monster might burst forth.

"I only glimpsed what is hidden there, but that was enough. It's Moloch's ghastly horde."

Abigail met Ilona's eyes and, without speaking. In that moment, she looked older, stronger, and very familiar. "The labyrinth holds more than one secret," she added.

"Let's hurry," Abigail said. "Wendlandt and I will draw the beast's attention so that you and Violetta can make a run for the passageway. Ilona nodded, Violetta looked unsure.

"Give me your hand, Wendlandt." Abigail reached toward her. She cringed as she grasped Abigail hand. They moved to the far side of the cavern beside the stairs. Abigail released her hand and she disappeared from sight.

"Beast! We're here. Look at us." Abigail waved her arms to draw its attention. Roars from all three heads echoed in the chamber. Its saliva flung in all directions as it leapt toward her. Abigail saw Ilona and Violetta sprint for the opening. Abigail reached back to take Wendlandt's hand to make their escape. She was gone. Abigail searched wildly, waving her arms in every direction.

"Wendlandt, where are you? Where did you go?" There was no answer and no time to find her. The beast was slow but almost upon her. Abigail spun to face it and, in the same instant, materialized a pike and jabbed at the middle head, halting its advance as the other two mouths bit at the air.

With one well timed thrust, Abigail caught the right head in the eye. The head shrieked, and the giant animal backed up. The impaled head pawed at the pike, trying to dislodge it. The middle head bit at the pike, which only enraged it more. Abigail seized the moment and ran for the opening. A giant head crashed into the opening as she cleared the opening. Abigail felt its hot breath on her neck and its saliva on her arms.

Ilona waited with her back against the passageway wall. She thrust her sword at the snarling mouth, cutting its jowl. Its roar deafened them, but it backed away, stymied by the small opening.

"What happened? Where's Wendlandt?" Ilona returned her sword to its scabbard.

"I don't know. I let go of her hand so the beast would see me and move away from the passageway. It worked, but then, when I reached for her she wasn't here. I had no choice but to attack the beast or be torn limb from limb."

"I'm h-here." They all turned, and Wendlandt became

visible, standing behind them and cringing against the wall.

"I barely escaped. Why did you leave me?" Abigail struggled to control her voice. The smell of the animal's breath lingered.

"I-I w-was a-afraid. I ran." Wendlandt could hardly speak. The sight of the giant three-headed dog lunging at them had been too much for her. Abigail hadn't considered how deep her fear was rooted.

"It's all right. We're all safe. Let's keep going shall we? Violetta, straight ahead?"

"The marks left by his footsteps are brighter. We're getting closer," said Violetta. She picked up the pace, appearing excited about closing in. They walked at a fast clip, almost a trot, until the passageway became low and narrow. The group slowed and walked bent over.

"Violetta, are the footprints still bright?"

"Yes, very bright. We must be close, but I can see nothing except the footprints. I keep bumping into the walls." She was right. The tunnel had become almost pitch black. She made two kerosene lanterns like they'd had in Maine, and handed one to Violetta, keeping one for herself.

"Let's keep moving. I don't like being in this confined space." Abigail commanded.

"Yes," replied Ilona. "If we're attacked we could be trapped."

The tunnel became lower and the women were forced to walk hunched over with their knees bent.

"There is some-something behind us. I-I heard a noise." Wendlandt became almost transparent as her fear increased. Abigail heard a sound like something being dragged on the ground. She held up the lantern and saw two small glowing red objects moving slowly from side to side.

Whatever it was, it was coming closer fast.

"Get ready to run," Abigail said. She made a sword and readied herself. The two glowing objects were close. Abigail held the lantern higher and the head of a giant snake came into view.

"Run!" she yelled. "Run!" Abigail pushed Wendlandt ahead of her, and the women ran with their heads down in the low tunnel. Behind them, Abigail could hear the hissing of the giant snake over the sound of their thundering feet. She looked over her shoulder and saw the snake a few yards behind, his forked tongue swiping the air.

"Faster, run faster!" Abigail yelled. The snake's tongue flick against her back.

In the next instant, they burst out of the tunnel into a large chamber. Abigail ran a few more yards and turned to face their pursuer. The snake's head almost filled the tunnel opening. It hissed twice and flicked its tongue but didn't leave the tunnel. Abigail looked at Ilona. She was poised with her sword, ready to fight, with Violetta and Wendlandt behind her. Abigail turned back to the tunnel and the snake was gone. For whatever reason, it did not leave the tunnel to pursue them.

The tension in Abigail's shoulders faded and she looked around. The cavern contained a dark, forlorn, formal garden laid out with walkways, fountains, and statuary. There was no color anywhere, all the trees and plantings were black or shades of gray, leafless, and dead.

Snares of the Heart

"A trap is only a trap if you don't know about it. If you know about it, it's a challenge." – China Miéville

The cavern was cold, permeated with the scent of decay. The garden spoke of sadness and death like a tomb, not a place of beauty and life. Ilona led the group to a small gray stone cottage with a tile roof. Black, dead vines covered one side. The light of a single candle shone through a leaded glass window.

"He went in there." Violetta pointed. "The marks are very bright. He was there a moment ago. He may still be there."

The quiet cottage might easily be a trap thought Abigail

"I'm going to take a look inside. Wait here till I know it's safe." They all nodded, and seemed relieved to wait outside. Abigail tried the door and it opened easily. Inside was one large room. A large bed with red velvet bed curtains stood against one wall. Beside it was a small altar with painted panels that swung open. Instead of the scenes of saints and angels, it had depictions of devils and demons forcing naked people into pits of fire. The cross on the altar hung upside down.

In the center of the room stood a large oak desk with a great empty bookshelf behind it. Laid open on the desk was a leather-bound ledger. On its pages were lists of names, the heresy each was accused of committing, and the sentence imposed. The last entry on each line was Lord Eymerich's signature. A bright red cassock hanging beside the bed confirmed her suspicion. This room was a re-creation of Eymerich's chambers when he was alive. This was his sanctum.

At the end of the room, a stone fireplace still had glowing embers. Resting on the hearth were iron pokers, and one had a circle with jagged lines, a copy of the symbol in the bookcase. Hanging from the ceiling were iron manacles attached to a rope and pulley.

There was no sign of Eymerich. The cottage was a dead end. If he'd come in, he wasn't here now. Abigail stepped outside.

"What did you find?" asked Ilona.

"The cottage is empty. It looks a re-creation of Eymerich's chamber when he lived."

"There are footsteps leading off in that direction." Violetta pointed to the far end of the cavern. Ilona looked puzzled, but even more so, she looked angry. She'd been on his trail and didn't like having her quarry elude her.

"W-what's n-next Miss A-Abagail? Are w-we going b-back?" Wendlandt asked, looking eager to leave. Violetta was fidgety, ready to begin her hunt again. Ilona appeared prepared to do battle with someone, anyone. Abigail looked about wondering what to do next. *What was the purpose of this cottage and garden?* There was a mystery here that Abigail had yet to discern. Eymerich's cottage radiated evil. The garden was a horrid parody. At that moment she wanted nothing more than to get her hands around Eymerich's throat.

"I don't know, but the key is this cottage. It has great significance for Eymerich. Maybe we can figure this out." Abigail had dragged these women down into the depths of Gehenna, exposed them to the horrors and dangers of the labyrinth. Worst of all, she still had no idea what Eymerich was planning.

As Abigail stared at the cottage, she heard a familiar voice in the distance. "Abigail, come here, please, I need you." Jacob's voice called her. She heard it as clear as when he'd walked her home from school. Abigail spun around, trying to locate his voice. "Abigail, it's me, Jacob. I'm waiting for you." The voice was pleading like he was injured or in danger.

"Did you hear that?" Abigail asked.

"Hear what?" asked Violetta.

"I heard Jacob Farrington calling me. He's here someplace."

"We heard nothing," said Ilona. She looked at the others and they all shook their heads.

Abigail looked at them in disbelief. How could they have not heard? Jacob's voice was clear and distinct. She had lost Jacob before; she couldn't lose him again. She had to find him.

"Wait here. I'll be right back." Abigail ran through the garden to where she'd heard Jacob's voice.

"Abigail, come back. Something's wrong. This isn't right," called Ilona.

"Abigail, my darling, please come quickly. I need you." His voice was stronger. Abigail was getting closer. Desperation rose in her throat. His voice came from a curved archway in the garden wall. Eymerich must have abducted Jacob and hidden him in the labyrinth. The thought of him at the mercy of Lord Eymerich was more than she could stand.

Abigail ran through the archway. A frigid blast swept through her. Abigail tried to turn around, but everything went black.

Abigail opened her eyes, steadied herself as her vision came back into focus. She stood beside a stately brick house looking downhill toward a lake. The day was sunny, and the air warm, slightly humid with the smell of dry hay. *It must be August.* Large puffy clouds lulled overhead, casting passing shadows which slid gracefully across the fields and onto the lake.

A man and two children walked up the road from the lake.

"Run to your mother, children." It was Jacob wearing a broad straw hat, his shirt damp from the heat. The boy, the spitting image of Jacob, and a little girl who resembled Abigail's mother ran to her.

The boy hugged her leg and the little girl raised her arms.

"Pick me up, Mommy."

Abigail lifted her and rested her on her hip. The little girl put her arms around Abigail and kissed her cheek. Jacob stood beside Abigail and stroked her head.

"We were down by the lake and they both said they wanted to see their mother."

Jacob kissed her on the lips. The taste of him and his scent soothed a deep, long ignored ache within her. Tears blurred her sight. She had two beautiful children and a loving husband. They lived on a beautiful farm.

"What's wrong, darling, you look sad."

"No, Jacob, everything is fine." She touched his face, making sure he was real. *Had I been dreaming, trapped in some horrible daytime dream?*

"Sit in the shade and watch the children. I'll bring us some lemonade. There is still some ice in the ice house." Abigail sat beneath the maple tree and watched Jacob disappear into the house. The sunlight filtered through the leaves, creating a mottled mosaic on the grass.

"Mommy, watch me, watch me," said David, holding

his hoop and stick.

"I'm watching."

The child rolled his hoop across the lawn trying unsuccessfully to keep it upright with his stick. Little Louisa toddled along behind trying to keep up, not sure what the game was. She quickly grew tired and came to sit on Abigail's lap. They watched together as David chased his hoop across the yard and back. Abigail drank in the moment. She squeezed Louisa, and her tiny hands hugged Abigail's arms in response.

Jacob returned with two lemonades with shaved ice on a tray. It was cold but without any taste. Jacob must not have used enough lemons. He sat beside her, holding her hand and sipping his drink. They watched little David play with boundless energy until their drinks were finished.

"I'm going to hitch up Moses to the wagon and take David and little Louisa to Small's Store. Do you want to come? We've got time before supper."

"I'd love that. I've not been to the store in a long time. I'll get my bonnet."

"All right, I'll take David with me. It's about time he learned to hitch up a wagon. He's becoming quite the little man." The boy beamed at his father.

"Be careful, keep him away from those big hooves of Moses. He's not used to small children." David ran to them with a cherubic smile. Abigail stroked his head. "David, go with your father." She ached seeing them walk hand in hand.

Abigail put Louisa down, and they walked into the house. In the front parlor, Mother's rocking chair and table were beside the fireplace. The steeple clock on the mantel struck two o'clock. Abigail's bonnet and Louisa's were on the pegs by the front door. She tied hers under her chin, then knelt and tied Louisa's. Abigail picked her up and looked in the mirror.

Louisa pointed at herself. "I look like you, Mommy." She hugged Abigail's neck and kissed her again, her tiny lips warm against her cheek. Abigail never thought she could be this happy. She had everything she'd ever wanted. Abigail carried Louisa outside and saw Jacob with little David sitting beside him coming up the drive in the wagon pulled by Moses. A soft, warm breeze carried the scent of the lavender and daylilies that lined the road. Abigail wanted nothing more than for this day to go on forever.

Jacob let David hold the reins. "Look, Mommy, I'm driving. I'm driving old Moses."

Abigail handed Louisa to Jacob, climbed onto the wagon and settled Louisa on her lap. They rode down the long sloping hill and onto the road to town. In a few minutes, they came to Weeks' Grist Mill where Isaac tended his garden. He waved as they drove by. Moses pulled them up the rocky road beside the surging river.

"I'm sure we'll see your teacher, Miss Crommett, today," said Jacob smiling and patting Abigail's leg.

Miss Crommett was not a fond memory. Why had Jacob mentioned her as if it were a meeting she looked forward to? Hadn't she and her sister moved away years ago? Louisa looked up at her.

"I love you, Mommy." She was such a perfect child, and Little David was a perfect little boy. Jacob was handsome and affectionate. It was a beautiful summer day. Everything was perfect, but one disquieting thought crept in. Everything was too perfect and, at the same time, not quite right. Isaac looked as she remembered him. He hadn't aged a day in all these years. The last time she'd seen him, it was spring and he was turning over his garden getting it ready for planting. He was doing the same thing today, but his garden should be fully grown by now. And why was the river running so full? It felt like August, which was usually dry. The river should have been a trickle.

Why wasn't she sure what month it was? What year it was? She didn't know her children's birthdays. Abigail didn't remember giving birth at all. She'd been doing something important, something she could only remember fragments of. She had a great task before her, a fight or a battle. A queen? The queen? She had to get to the queen and stop her. Stop her from what? What was it she was planning? It was killing, wasn't it, killing everyone?

Her children smiled at her, pulling her back to the vision of an idyllic life. Abigail had everything she could ever want. What woman could want for anything else? She hugged little Louisa and smelled her hair. Holding her satisfied a long unfulfilled need, a need she'd always suppressed. *Why had I denied myself such happiness?*

"Duty," said a voice within her. *Duty had always come before my desires. What was my duty?* The memories came slowly, unwillingly, as though being pulled from a hidden place. Abigail did have a duty to fulfill. A man, David in the land of the living waited for her, as did many others.

They all depended on me. Did I have to sacrifice every chance of happiness to fulfill my duty? Was struggle and combat my only path? Must I give up the love of my husband and children?

Abigail raised her hand to cover her mouth as the painful realization became clear. She trembled and tears came to her eyes. Nothing was real. She was within an illusion that touched her deepest, long suppressed desires, a cruel dream meant to waylay her.

"Jacob. Stop the wagon."

"Darling, what is it?" Jacob pulled on the reins. She

put Louisa on the seat beside her and stroked her head. This bucolic existence was everything she'd ever desired. Her heart ached at the beauty of it all. But Abigail knew she had a duty to perform, and this vision, this illusion was a trap.

"Louisa, you are such a beautiful little girl, the image of my mother. I wish I could stay with you."

She smiled, but it was no longer an angelic smile. Her smile stretched from ear to ear, showing more teeth than any child should have. Her innocent expression was replaced with a demonic glare.

"Mommy, don't you love me? I love you." Her voice was lower, almost a growl.

Abigail jumped from the wagon. This vision of a perfect life, one arranged to entice her into yet another waking slumber, was gone. The color drained from the trees. The sky turned gray. The air became chilled, and foul odors filled her nose.

"Enough of this charade!" Abigail shouted. The children stood up, and their skin transformed into black and gray scales. Their feet turned to hooves and their hands became elongated claws. They hissed at Abigail.

"So you've seen through my deception. I told that idiot Eymerich this wouldn't work." The image of Jacob wavered and morphed into Frank Robinson. The children, now half human, half demon, jumped from the wagon and disappeared into the woods. Then the wagon, the road, the woods, and everything disappeared, leaving only Frank towering over her in a gray mist.

"In life I was hired to kill you. You cost me a thousand dollars, not to mention getting me killed, all because you died before I could get to you."

"I was fooled at first but I saw through your clumsy theater. The illusion of perfection is no substitute for real life and true happiness."

"You hid your thoughts well when you touched me in the salon, but not perfectly. I saw your regrets about your mother, your loss and guilt about leaving her. I saw your hopes and dreams, your longing for a family of your own. You have vivid memories, and I thought they would make an effective net to snare you with while Lord Eymerich and I completed our plans." Frank's laugh filled her head once more, pounding like a hammer.

"I can't stab you or shoot you. I know better than to try and strangle you. But revenge is a dish best served cold, and dark."

Frank Robinson's image disappeared, leaving his voice filling the air, coming at her from all directions. She covered her ears but his voice penetrated her to the core.

"I shall think of you often—wandering, lost, cold, and bereft in the darkness. I must leave you now and assist Lord Eymerich. His plan for ruling Gehenna is almost complete, and I don't want to miss the show." A final laugh trailed off, leaving Abigail in complete silence. The gray mist closed in on her like a covering of ice. Abigail's energy drained away.

Abigail made a torch, but the light didn't penetrate the darkness. Her feet disappeared into the black, formless mist. She walked with her hand outstretched, holding the torch above. Abigail reached a wall. It was completely black. The torchlight revealed nothing, no stone nor brick, just a barrier.

She walked along, feeling the featureless wall as she went.

Abigail came to a point where the wall turned a corner, but was unable to tell if this was a doorway, another room, or a hallway. She went on for hours trying to make a mental map of where she was, but it was no use. Wherever she was, whatever the walls or barriers were made no sense. They followed no pattern, only walls randomly erected which seemed to move if Abigail retraced her steps. She tried making more torches and leaving them as markers, but after she moved a few feet away, they were swallowed up in the darkness. Abigail had no idea how far she'd gone or if she could ever find her way back to the entrance.

Abigail searched interminably, but to no avail. She saw nothing, and felt only random walls and passages. She screamed as her frustration boiled over. There was no echo. The sound was as muted as the light from her torch. Abigail's confidence about easily finding her way out waned. She was lost, really lost. Her powers as a maker didn't help. She had no idea if she'd traveled further into the maze or not. Abigail closed her eyes as the cold darkness embraced her.

A wave of fear swept through Abigail at the prospect of wandering forever in the dark labyrinth. She'd been foolish again ignoring Ilona's warning and rushing headlong into the trap that Eymerich and Frank had set for her.

Abigail's thoughts went to Ehyeh, sitting beside her flaming pyramid with the universe swirling above her. *Had I failed her? Had I failed David? Was I doomed to wander in the darkness forever?* Queen Lilith's evil plan was racing to its devastating conclusion. The earth and all that was good and wholesome would be destroyed, and it was her fault; a despair as dark as the surrounding blackness engulfed her.

"Abigail, snap out of it." It was David's thoughts reaching   out   to   her   across   the   great   void.

Dagger Men

"Desperation can make people do surprising things."
– Veronica Roth

Hours passed as Sarah, David, and Shlomo combed through Herr Bauer's files. Shlomo was the only one who could read German, so the digging went slowly. Anna had thankfully fallen asleep in her chair, leaving them undisturbed. Herr Bauer had been a meticulous organizer with everything in chronological order and cross-referenced by activity, subject, and person; a model German bureaucrat.

"I'm looking at September of 1943 for any documentation coinciding with the photograph we saw," Shlomo said. "This folder contains receipts for items shipped from the castle. This was before the Allied invasion in 1944, but the Nazis knew the invasion was imminent. The war on the eastern front was going badly, and the Americans were pushing up through Italy. Anyone could see that the war was already lost, only a long death-struggle lay ahead."

"Have you found anything?" Sarah asked.

"Maybe, maybe. There is a shipping order here for one crate. It's stamped with an SS authorization and countersigned by the SS commandant. Most of the shipping documents don't have these. The document says the crate contains relics."

"That could be anything," David remarked.

"True, but this was shipped to the Keroman Submarine Base at Lorient in France for U-boat U-576." Shlomo handed Sarah the shipping document. The paper had yellowed, and the ink was faded, but she could pick out the key words he'd mentioned. "Dr. Austin, does your phone have a signal here?"

"Yes, what do you want me to look up?"

"Google 'German navel archives U-576' and see if you get a hit."

Sarah typed away for a minute, then looked up, "It's searching. Okay, here it is. U-576 was lost off the coast of North Carolina." She looked at David and Shlomo. "Do you think the Nazis shipped the chalice to the US? The forest where Abigail saw it could be anywhere in the continental United States."

"If so this narrows our search, but not by much. It's a big country with a lot of forests. Where do we look?" David asked.

"I'm afraid Mr. Austin is right. We have nothing to go on other than a chance that the chalice was shipped clandestinely to North America in the fall of 1943. It could have been offloaded anywhere on the East Coast by parties unknown."

"Okay. Do you suggest that we charge back to the US and cruise the coastline looking for signs of Lilim?" David asked, somewhat sarcastically.

"Not in so many words, but yes," replied Shlomo. "We can do nothing but continue to trust the invisible hand that has guided us so far."

"Shlomo, that's a remarkable statement of faith. Do you really think some unseen force is helping us?" Sarah smiled.

"I would like to think so, maybe its luck, but we've been far too lucky. My faith has changed and morphed many times into new understandings. I'll trust my faith, such as it is, to guide us in this new direction for a while."

"All right, I'm in, what have we got to lose? Let's pack up and call the jet." David shot Sarah a reassuring smile.

Shlomo put the document folders away and slipped the shipping notice into his pocket. "I don't think Frau Bauer will miss one document."

They let themselves out, leaving Anna slumped in her chair, fast asleep with a book on her lap. Shlomo called the flight crew from the SUV and notified them of their next destination. He then called the Bibliothek and spoke to Herr Gruber about Anna's treasure. David imagined her relief at having her burden removed.

David recalled the Paderborn airport address in the GPS. The rain had let up, but the weather had tuned cooler. His shoes had gotten wet walking to the car and the cold radiated up his legs, the kind of cold you couldn't shake.

"David, turn up the heat, I'm freezing," said Sarah. Shlomo sat beside her, his arms hugging his chest. The weather didn't suit his Mediterranean sensibilities either.

David turned the knob till the display read 25, stared at it for a second, and then realized in was in Celsius. David craved something familiar, anything. He wanted to see a sign he understood. He wanted to go to a diner and order eggs over easy. He wanted to go kayaking on Moosehead Lake and listen to the male loon's love songs echoing across the lake. He longed for home.

They drove through a roundabout and pulled onto the main road to the airport. They had the highway to themselves. The GPS showed they'd be at the airport in twenty-five minutes. David looked forward to the sanctuary of the jet, a warm and comfortable cocoon. It would spirit them away from the danger he felt surrounding them.

"Shlomo, where did you tell the jet to take us?" Sarah asked

"New Jersey."

"Why there, of all places?"

"Teterboro Airport, it's out of the way, used exclusively for business travel. The customs and immigrations are attuned to business travelers. We can be on the road twenty minutes after we land."

"Good." Sarah said.

"Where are we going after we leave the airport?" asked David, sounding weary.

"I'm not sure," replied Shlomo reluctantly, almost as an apology. "I need to rest a bit on the plane. I hope to have an inspiration before we land."

"I think we're all beat. The down time will do us good. Maybe we can divert to Aruba for some R and R." Sarah chuckled.

"As much as I would like that myself, Dr. Austin, time is our enemy. We need to keep moving, even pick up the pace if possible."

Sarah groaned. "Sounds exhausting. I feel like we're in the Boston Marathon halfway up Heartbreak Hill, and you're telling us we have to sprint to the finish line."

"I'm not familiar with the terrain you speak of. I understand you're tired, as am I, but I sense we're close. We can't let up now." David saw Shlomo smile at Sarah in the rearview mirror.

"After Heartbreak Hill, I hope our course is flat and the finish line is around the corner," David said.

"Let's hope so," replied Sarah forcing a hopeful tone.

David looked in the mirror to catch Sarah's expression, but the van behind them had switched on its high beams with two additional lights on its roof illuminating the inside of the SUV. David squinted, and flipped the mirror down, and slowed, hoping the van would pass. He had trouble seeing the road as his eyes readjusted.

The van pulled out as if to pass but then pulled up next to the SUV. The lights on top of the van threatened to blind David.

"David, quick, get away from that van!" Shlomo shouted.

He stepped on the gas and accelerated past 160, nearly 100 mph. The van kept pace with them, the spotlight making it almost impossible for David to see.

"David, be careful!" Sarah screamed.

"Sarah, David, get down, they're—" The windows of the SUV exploded, showering David with glass. He threw himself across the center console and stabbed at the brake with his foot. David heard the sound of automatic rifle fire mixed with Sarah's screams. Small round holes appeared in the ceiling.

The world switched to slow motion. The SUV swerved wildly, crashing into the van and then into the guardrail. David felt himself spinning, suspended by his seat belt. Light from outside rotated through the SUV, followed by a violent crash, the screech of scraping metal, and the explosive sound of airbags. David was pressed against his seat with his head pinned to the headrest. Lights continued to glare. Another crash was followed by the groan of collapsing metal. David's weight pull against the seat belt again, and his arms flung from side to side. The SUV had crashed on its side and rolled over and over, bouncing as it went. The shoulder strap cut deeply into David's chest.

The SUV skidded to a stop on its side facing forward. There was a sudden silence. Something warm ran into David's left eye. He was surrounded by deflated airbags, engulfed in the scent of the explosive used to inflate them. A cold moist breeze came through the broken windshield, bringing him back to consciousness. The roof of the SUV was crushed. He was covered in nuggets of broken glass. David's seatbelt held him with his arms draped over the center console. As he began to focus, David saw the van backing up toward them.

"Sarah, Sarah, are you all right?" he heard a whimper from the back seat. David tried to turn to see her but a pain shot through his shoulder. David had trouble moving his left arm, his ankle hurt and was stuck on something, but everything else seemed to work.

"Shlomo, are you there?" Nothing.

David heard two men shouting in French and looked out through the broken windshield. Two silhouettes were walking toward them with rifles. He couldn't reach the seat belt release. Even if he could free himself, there was nothing he could do. It would take minutes to crawl out of the crushed SUV. David wasn't even sure he could stand.

They were trapped and would all be dead in a few seconds. *Why had I ever bought that stupid picture? What had I done to Sarah? I had failed Abigail. The Lilim plot would succeed and human life would be destroyed. My whole life was one failure after another.* Tears ran sideways across his face as David lay trapped and awaiting his fate.

He heard a sound, a loud horn, alternating high and low. The approaching men stopped and shouted in French. The siren came closer, and blue lights flashed on the wet road. The men in the road fired bursts from their automatic rifles. The muzzle flashes lit up the road. The siren stopped and was replaced by the sound of screeching tires. A volley of single shots rang out, and one of the silhouettes fell backwards with a thud. The remaining man continued to fire. The muzzle flash lit his face, a black mask with two eyes. He bent down to retrieve his comrade. Several more shots rang out and ricocheted off the road. The standing man fled to the van, leaving his compatriot where he lay. More shots broke the momentary silence, followed by the sound of the van speeding away.

"*Wer ist das? Sind Sie verletzt?*" a voice shouted from outside. A flashlight shone in David's eyes. He heard more high-low sirens in the distance. The world began to spin. "Help, help us," he pleaded as everything went black.

The Falcon in the Forest

"Failure, loss and defeat are just mile markers on the road to success."— Jeffrey Fry

Something beeped rhythmically. Bright lights stung David's eyes. Breathing was painful. It hurt to move his head. They'd been attacked. He remembered the SUV tumbling over and over. The beeping got faster. He remembered expecting to be shot by two men dressed in black when blue lights arrived. He wasn't dead, so where was he? He blinked and slowly adjusted to the light. He was in a bed, and there was an IV drip in his arm.

"Herr Austin, can you hear me?" A woman's face was inches away from his, smiling and smelling of cigarette smoke. She wore green scrubs.

"Yes, where am I?"

"You are in hospital, the Ostwestfalen-Lippe Hospital. You were in a terrible accident, but everything will be good, yes?"

"Where is my wife? Where's Sarah? Is she okay?"

"Yes, Frau Austin is here. She is in the next room. She was wounded but it's not serious. She is resting now. Not to worry." The nurse patted his arm.

"The doctor will have a look at you and then the police will speak with you, yes?" The nurse left the room and a minute later a short man in a white coat came in. The doctor explained in excellent English that David had a sprained ankle, two badly bruised ribs, a mild concussion, and a number of cuts and bruises. He said that the ribs would be painful but should heal in a month.

Sarah had a gunshot wound to her upper left arm which had fortunately missed the bone, arteries, and nerves.

She had similar cuts and bruises. She was sedated following surgery to remove the bullet, but would be awake in several hours and David could see her then. His anxiety faded, and the beeping from the heart monitor slowed, reflecting his relief that she was safe.

"What about the other man in the car, Shlomo. How is he?" The doctor's face turned grim.

"I'm sorry to tell you that your friend did not survive. He received multiple wounds, several of which were fatal." He stopped speaking as he gauged David's reaction. "I heard from the police that he most likely saved your wife's life by shielding her with his body."

Shlomo was dead. David stared at the ceiling as tears rolled down his cheeks. Shlomo was the noblest person he'd ever met. He'd dedicated his life, he'd sacrificed everything to battle the Lilim. Now he'd made another sacrifice, the final one. He'd given his life to save Sarah. David owed Shlomo a debt that he could never repay.

"Herr Inspector Schmitt would like a few words with you now. In these special situations, we cannot refuse a police request. I've asked him to be brief. Try not to become excited." He walked to the door, and a tall gaunt man wearing a wrinkled brown sport coat stepped into view. The doctor spoke a few words to him as he pointed at David. The tall man nodded.

"Mr. Austin. You've had a busy night. I'm glad you're still with us. My name is Schmitt, Inspector Schmitt with the North Rhine-Westphalia Police. I'd like to ask you a few questions if you're up to it."

"Okay, sure." David took a tissue and wiped his face, embarrassed by his tears in front of another man.

He put on half-frame reading glasses that perched on the end of his nose and opened a small, worn notebook, pen at the ready. If he'd had a flask of bourbon in his hip pocket, he could have been a character from a Raymond Chandler novel.

"I'm sorry about your friend. I can tell you that he saved your wife's life. The officers on the scene reported that your friend shielded your wife with his body. The wound your wife sustained on her arm came from a bullet that had passed through him before striking her." Tears streamed down David's face again, he stifled a sob. *Damn it.*

"Your friend was Israeli. You and your wife are Americans. What was your business in Germany?" He asked in a quiet but direct tone.

"My wife is a college professor doing research on Middle Eastern religions. We met Shlomo, Mr. Halverson, at the Rockefeller Archaeological Museum in Jerusalem. I was helping my wife track down an ancient Babylonian artifact, a chalice. We think it was used by the SS as part of the rituals at the Wewelsburg Castle."

Schmitt wrote busily in his small notepad. The retelling of past events all sounded so matter-of-fact, mundane, with none of the emotion and stress they'd experienced. It had seemed like months of struggle, but David had recapped it all in a few sentences. It didn't seem real

"I see. Do you know why Interpol posted an alert for your whereabouts?"

"Interpol? No. I have no idea. What did they want?" The beeping increased. Schmitt glanced at the monitor.

"That's what's unusual. The alert seeking your whereabouts did not list a reason. Not standard procedure." The inspector flipped through his notes. "But that is another matter," he said absentmindedly. "Who attacked you, and why?"

David paused, caught off guard by the suddenness of his question.

"I—I don't know. This black van pulled up beside us, shone a bright light on us and started shooting. That's all I know." The inspector's eyes drilled into him. David strained to maintain eye contact. David didn't want him to discover this was the second time that someone had tried to kill them. David was raised Catholic with an ingrained need to confess. Inside him was a twelve-year-old boy who wanted to tell all to this policeman.

The good inspector would never have believed his convoluted story about a dead girl in a photograph, or Moloch's chalice, or the end of civilization. He'd be locked up for months while the police plodded along, trying to sort out the crazy guy's story. By then it would be too late. No one would connect a global pandemic with a story told by a wild-eyed American in Germany.

"I see. No idea why a professional hit squad would ambush your party on a major thoroughfare? It seemed like a desperate attack. High risk, lots of exposure by what appears to be a very secret organization." His empathetic demeanor turned icy cold, stern.

"What do you mean, professional?"

"The body left behind had no identity papers, no tags on his clothing. His fingerprints are not on file, and most worrisome, he had a fully automatic assault rifle of unknown manufacture with no serial numbers. This was no casual robbery. The group that attacked you is well financed, highly organized, and unknown to the German police or Interpol.

"We recovered a document from Mr. Halverson's person; an SS document. It describes a shipment to France and consignment on a U-boat. Do you know about this document?"

"Yes." David explained the visit to the castle and finding Herr Bauer's daughter and records. This would keep the Inspector busy for a day checking out their story. It was also likely to alert the Lilim that he and Sarah were still alive, if they didn't already know.

Inspector Schmitt closed his notepad and returned his glasses to his inside coat pocket. As he leaned on the bed railing, David could see the stubble around the corners of his mouth that he'd missed while shaving. David felt his breath on his face.

"Mr. Austin, I know you're lying. You know who these people are. You know why you were attacked. You and your wife are the only lead we have to a new and dangerous criminal or possible terrorist group. I'm afraid you will both be detained until you decide to cooperate." He sounded like a judge handing down a sentence. Sarah and David would not be leaving any time soon. The inspector walked to the door and spoke with a uniformed policeman who took up a position outside the room.

Shifting in bed, David winced at the pain from his bruised ribs. He needed to see Sarah, to talk with her, to make sure she was all right. He needed to be there when she woke to tell her about Shlomo. Things had gone from bad to worse. Shlomo was dead, Sarah was wounded, and he was injured. Short of being dead, David could not imagine a worse situation. The Lilim were close to releasing the engineered plague, and they were confined, powerless to stop them. They were out of clues and fast running out of time.

He lay back on the bed, pressed the button that turned off the lights, and closed his eyes. David listened for Abigail's thoughts, hoping that the connection between them remained intact. She needed to know that they were in trouble. After a few minutes, he felt a weak response.

Abigail was lost, in complete darkness. She'd given up searching.

Abigail, snap out of it, David yelled silently. *I can feel the strength in you, and there is a vast pool of energy nearby. Reach for it. You can see it if I can.*

David felt the blackness creeping into her like freezing rain. She was slowly succumbing to despair. It clouded her mind.

Abigail, remember who you are. You're incredibly strong. Use your strength. You can beat this thing, shouted David across the boundary that separated them. She heard him. He sensed her energy stirring within her.

Search your mind, the pool of strength is there. Before David could hear her reply, someone shook his shoulder brusquely and his connection to Abigail abruptly vanished.

"Damn it, what do you want?" It was the nurse looking taken aback.

"Herr Austin, it's time to visit Frau Austin. She is asking for you." David sat up in bed, startled, and fully back to the here and now. An orderly the size of a linebacker stood beside the bed with a wheelchair.

"Herr Austin, we are going to put you in the chair, yes?" said the nurse.

"I'd rather walk if it's all the same to you."

"No. It is not permitted. It is the chair please."

Before David could debate the point, the orderly hoisted him up like a doll and plopped him in the chair while the nurse transferred the IV bag. Seconds later, they rounded the corner into the next room where Sarah sat up in bed. She looked as bad as David felt, with bruises on her face and her arm in a sling. The orderly parked him beside her and left.

David clasped her hand, and she burst into tears. The last 24 hours had taken a toll, and seeing David released a floodgate of emotions. Sarah was a strong woman, but circumstances sent her over the edge. David held her hand and rubbed her wrist.

"It's okay Sarah. It's all right. We're both alive and not seriously hurt." Her sobbing continued for a few minutes running its course.

He handed her a tissue. "I'm sure I look a fright," she said apologetically.

"Oh it's not so bad. Cuts and bruises everywhere, gunshot wound on your arm, red puffy eyes, and a hospital Johnny with peek-a-boo slits." He smiled. "All kind of alluring really."

"Right. Very attractive I'm sure." She touched her hair that was wrapped up in a cloth. She flashed a hint of a smile. "How's Shlomo doing? Is he on this floor too?" She saw his expression change. "What is it?"

"Sarah—Shlomo's dead. He was killed in the attack. He saved your life by shielding you."

"Oh, David." Sarah's face crumbled into tears again. She turned on her side and pulled her legs up, curling into a ball, and cried softly for some time. David sat quietly rubbing her shoulder and letting her burn through the grief.

"David, I think I'm done. I'm not sure I can go on with this. It's the second time we've almost been killed. They're going to keep coming at us till they succeed. The closer we get to them, the more brutal the attacks will become. I want to go home, to sleep in my own bed, to weed my garden. I want to see Abe and Louie." Sarah looked at David with red, puffy eyes.

"Maybe we should go home, have a rest, and regroup." Sarah smiled at him weakly. David knew he couldn't press her. She'd been through too much.

David leaned back from the edge of the bed and noticed that the uniformed policeman had stepped into the room. He'd been listening to their conversation. David wheeled over to him and pointed to the door. He didn't move. He pushed him and his face flashed with anger as he reached for his nightstick. David pointed to the hallway again.

"*Schnell.*" He'd seen enough World War II movies to know that *schnell* meant quickly. German Army officers were always yelling *schnell* at everyone.

The policeman stepped outside the room, but continued to block the door, looking very unhappy as only a German whose authority has been challenged can look. David backed up and shut the door in his face with great satisfaction.

"I think he was listening to us and heard you say this was the second attack."

"Why would he listen? Isn't he here to protect us?"

"No he's not. He's our jailer." David related the conversation with the police inspector, and his intention of keeping them till he determined the reason for the attack.

"This is horrible. We could be here months while they chase down leads. And knowing who we're up against, they won't find anything."

"I know. We're stuck here. We can't go home. We'll never find the chalice. The Lilim plan will succeed. I don't know how, but we've got to get out of Germany."

"David, maybe I'm being paranoid, but do you think they have the room bugged?"

David skipped a breath in a moment of panic. It was entirely likely. Interpol was involved, a special branch of the

Westphalia Police, and, no doubt, some unspecified counterterrorism units.

"Give me a second." David turned on the TV and flipped channels till he got to CNN International. If they were going to have noise it might as well be in English.

"I wish I had another one of Shlomo's sat-phones so I could call for help." David whispered to Sarah.

"I'm sure the police are not going to hand it over," Her voice was surprisingly relaxed, sounding more confident, more back in control.

David sat back in his wheelchair and watched the International CNN news which provided a bit of normalcy in the midst of the chaos swirling around them.

A reporter came on. "We're here in Idaho at Vice-President Connolly's secluded ranch speaking with the head of his Secret Service detail. Mr. Blakley, this must be an awesome responsibility, protecting the second most powerful man in the world. A man who is a heartbeat away from the presidency," said the TV host against a background of a lake and distant mountains.

"Yes it is. Protecting Falcon—that's his Secret Service code name—is a challenging assignment...."

David turned to Sarah as a shiver ran down his spine. Their eyes met. Her jaw dropped open. "It can't be. That's crazy," she said.

"I understand the vice president's annual gathering of the rich and powerful in the Babylon Forest is next week. This must be an especially busy time for you?" asked the reporter.

"I'm not at liberty to discuss the vice president's activities or his schedule."

"Yes, I'm sure. Can you confirm the rumors of a giant

owl statue and nighttime rituals?"

"The Babylon Forest conference is a chance for leaders of industry and various government officials to relax together and to let their hair down. Think of it as a summer camp for the over-fifty crowd. Mostly they eat, swim, play games, and discuss matters of mutual interest," replied the Secret Service agent, reciting his prepared talking points.

David turned the sound down. They looked at each other wide-eyed "This has to be it. It's as Abigail described. It all fits," David said.

"Where are my clothes? How do we get out of here?" Sarah's confidence had returned.

The Dark Demon

"I take pleasure in my transformations. I look quiet and consistent, but few know how many women there are in me." – Anaïs Nin

The darkness held Abigail in a frigid shroud that drained her vitality and would soon encase her entirely. She feared falling into the chaos between the realms if all her energy dissipated.

Then she heard David's thoughts like a lifeline thrown to her from a distant, unseen shore. She was not completely lost. His memories of Damascus and Germany rushed forth. He and Sarah had nearly been killed, and Shlomo was dead. Abigail shared David's pain from Shlomo's death. They were likely trapped for some time, and they'd lost the trail of Moloch's chalice.

David's bleak situation mirrored her own—trapped with no apparent way out or direction forward. Queen Lilith and the Lilim were on the verge of victory. Abigail desperately focused on David's thoughts, her solitary connection outside of the ice maze. The cold reacted like an enraged beast against David's thoughts, its icy claws digging deeper into her skin.

David's voice became clear and strong. The stakes were too high and the sacrifices too great to lose heart now. He was trapped, but he wasn't ready to give up. His words came at Abigail like a slap in the face breaking her out of her stupor. He sensed the energy from the women she'd rescued. That was the way out. She didn't need to be in the presence of the women to draw their energy. She could reach out to them with her thoughts. Immediately, their energy flowed to her.

As though taking in an enormous breath, she pulled

energy from the young women Abigail visualized in the distant chamber. It filled her as never before. Her body glowed white as the energy streamed in as from a hundred rivers. Her body seemed to have no limits. Her grasp was infinite.

David's thoughts vanished. The bond was still there, but he'd been drawn away. Abigail was alone in the darkness once again. She'd had enough of this prison, and extending her arms released a burst of pure white searing energy in all directions like a circle of lightning radiating outward. The walls of the maze dissolved as the energy struck like a giant wave washing away a sand castle. The darkness writhed as the white energy ate away at it. It rose up, shrieking like a beast being attacked by a thousand swords. The dark formless demon had grown into her with tendrils like the roots of a tree. This formless demon was a parasite feeding on her strength. The energy burned away the fibers that encased her, and sliced through the demon's dark, misty flesh wherever it touched. The demon retreated wailing like a dying animal with nowhere to hide. Abigail guided her energy to chase it down and engulf it. Its screams diminished as it disappeared into a distant corner. The echoes of its screams faded to silence.

She'd heard its thoughts. Like the demons that had bound her to the wall in Eymerich's salon, this demon was base and primitive. It fed on energy. It created terror in any being it encountered so as to better feast on its energy. It was a child of the labyrinth, another of its many manifestations. All that she'd seen—the souls locked in an endless re-creation of their sins, the black river with drowning souls, the vast pit of molten rock, even the black garden—were different forms of the many demons lurking in the labyrinth.

The walls and the darkness were gone. Abigail stood alone in a vast empty cavern. Her vision of the two peaks came to mind. The unseen woman on the distant peak was close. Abigail saw her auburn hair flowing in the wind, and a sword on her hip. She stood erect with her hands on her hips gazing into the valley before her. Her back was to Abigail and she couldn't see her visage. Abigail knew she would soon meet her face to face.

Abigail reached out to David with her thoughts. He was there, resting, trying to decide his next move. She enveloped him in energy, eased his fears, and erased his doubts. Her energy filled him with courage. She saw him lying in a bed with his body glowing at the edges. Then Abigail's vision of him disappeared. Something had broken his concentration again.

Abigail moved her hand down across her body and restored the white dress with the pink bow. Appearing once more as Abigail from China, Maine would hide her strength and preserve her advantage, making sure her enemies, especially Lord Eymerich, continued to underestimate the young woman from Maine.

Abigail counted on using his arrogance against him.

She was on the hunt, searching for Lord Eymerich. Abigail walked to the cavern entrance with her shoes resounding on the stone floor, and quickened her steps in anticipation of the battle to come.

Rescued, Again

"Women rescue men just as much as, if not more than, men rescue women." – Criss Jami

Where was Idaho—past Montana but before California? David wished he'd paid more attention during fifth grade geography. Potatoes, snow-topped mountains, and fly fishing came to mind. His bucolic image was darkened by the evil he expected to find there. They had to find their way there, not that he had any idea what to do when they did.

Dinner came—chicken, potatoes, and sauerkraut—a reminder that he was trapped in Germany. What would Jason Bourne do? He'd knock out the guard, steal his gun, dress as a doctor, wheel Sarah out of the hospital, and then hotwire a fast car in less time than a normal person would take to put groceries in the trunk. He knew he wasn't Jason Bourne, so he'd have to find another way, but whatever that was, it wasn't obvious.

His thoughts drifted back to Abigail again. He closed his eyes trying to hear her thoughts, and the bond became stronger like turning up the volume on a radio. She was free of the trap and had found her source of energy which coursed through her like an inner tempest.

She reached out to him. Her embrace filled him with a great wave of energy, and in an instant, his consciousness expanded and the universe rushed in. David gasped, shivered. He felt like he'd been blind his whole life and now saw a great vista for the first time. His doubts about himself, his courage, his ability to see this quest through to the end vanished. David experienced a new clarity of purpose, and a steely determination.

The nature of their fight crystallized. It was a battle

between all that was good and all that was evil. The conflict had gone on for eons, and now it was their time, Abigail's and his, to lead the charge. The Lilim and Falcon remained formidable enemies, but ones he now believed could be defeated. David didn't know what Abigail had done, but he liked it.

Someone shook his shoulder, and the current reality snapped back into place. David was once more solidly in his hospital bed, but now facing Miss Vindex, wearing the same trim gray suit she had worn in Damascus. A tall, barrel-chested man in a blue suit and tie and the police inspector stood by her side.

"Mr. Austin, are you well, can you travel?"

"Miss Vindex." David bolted up in bed. "God, am I happy to see you." Her face remained all business as she awaited answer.

"Yes, I believe so. But how..."

She held up her hand to stop him and turned to the police Inspector. He glowered, looking down at her with his arms folded across his chest. Miss Vindex spoke rapidly in German, and even though her head barely came to the men's shoulder, she was clearly in command. The tall man in the blue suit nodded on queue every time she turned to him. The inspector tried to speak, but she cut him off with a wave of her hand. The inspector's face looked like a boiled beet. The barrel-chested man took the inspector out to the hallway and spoke in a conciliatory tone. The Inspector nodded, and his shoulders slumped as he resigned himself to the loss of his prisoners.

The inspector spoke to the uniformed guard, and they left together.

Miss Vindex turned to David while the tall man in the blue suit waited outside like an obedient servant.

"Mr. Austin, I spoke to your doctor, and he tells me you and Dr. Austin are well enough to travel. We should leave immediately. The sooner you are out of Germany, the better. The man in the hall is Mr. Abernathy, special attaché to the US Ambassador." Her voice changed to a whisper. "In plain English, he's the CIA station chief in Berlin. They owe us some favors."

"What about Shlomo? We can't leave his body here." Miss Vindex's face contorted slightly before returning to her *I'm in command* demeanor.

"We've made arrangements for the repatriation of his remains." She looked away.

"What will become of him? He's been shunned by his community."

Miss Vindex turned back to me. "I will tell you this because you were compatriots and because Mr. Halverson confided in you his true identity. A great man has fallen, possibly the greatest leader the Brotherhood has ever had. He accomplished great strides in the quest to defeat the Lilim. He will be interned with the other past leaders of the Brotherhood. The Brotherhood will mourn his passing. His name will be spoken for the next century." She turned quickly and spoke to Mr. Blue Suit waiting in the hall. He nodded and walked away.

"Miss Vindex, how is it that you show up just when we need you?"

"Mr. Halverson alerted us to your itinerary, and we then positioned support elements in the event they were needed. Our team has monitored your movements since you arrived. I'm sorry to say the Lilim took us by surprise. The Lilim are usually very secretive with subtle, almost invisible actions. This attack was overt, public, and messy; a body was left behind. All of which indicates that they are desperate to eliminate you." She listened to her earpiece.

"The convoy is waiting at the entrance. Mr. Abernathy has provided a field team to escort us to the airport. We will return you and Dr. Austin to Maine."

"No," David said sharply, and swung his legs over the side of the bed "We're not going home. We're going to Idaho. That's where the chalice is."

Miss Vindex's eyes opened wide. "How can you know this? We had no communications from Mr. Halverson regarding the whereabouts of the chalice."

"The chalice is with a man called Falcon." David lowered his voice glancing at Abernathy in the hall. "You may know him as Vice President Connolly. He's Lilim and he is gathering other Lilim in an Idaho forest. They are preparing to release an engineered plague within the next few weeks. I know for a fact that the chalice is there. I've seen it."

She stared at David for a long moment. He wondered if she intended to sedate him or fulfill his request.

Her head tilted slightly. Her face softened and she spoke softly. "It's you isn't? You're the speaker. You speak with the goddess."

The speaker? Had David been expected by the Brotherhood, just as the Nadeau women had expected him, waiting a century for him to arrive? *Was I really at the center of all this?*

David hesitated, unsure of the title he was about to accepted. He nodded. "It is me. Shlomo never called me speaker, but I do speak with her. Even now, I hear her thoughts and she mine."

"I never suspected you. Mr. Halverson told us that the speaker had arrived, but he didn't say who it was. I thought it might possibly be your wife, Dr. Austin. But it's you. You're the speaker." She repeated the words as though trying to convince herself.

Then she continued, "We knew that the great epoch was at hand. The Lilim were stirring, gathering in large numbers, all the signs were there. The arrival of the speaker has been foretold as the harbinger of the great culmination, the great battle between the children of Eve and the children of Lilith. I'm not sure why Mr. Halverson kept your identity secret." Miss Vindex's face softened and her lips moved silently as she recited something to herself. Then, just as quickly, her face hardened and her voice grew stern again.

"Yes, Mr. Austin. I will make the arrangements immediately. You will have the complete support of the Brotherhood. You will find instructions on the plane for contacting us. Ask for whatever you need. Our resources are considerable." She motioned with her hand, almost as a salute. David's request had become a command.

Miss Vindex left the room and returned a few minutes later accompanied by a man in a black jump suit with an assault rifle over his shoulder pushing a wheelchair. A flustered nurse came and undid David's IV. Still wearing his hospital johnnie, he was wheeled into the corridor where Sarah waited in a matching wheelchair. When her gave her a thumbs up, she mouthed, *What's going on?*

"Don't worry. Miss Vindex has arranged to fly us to Idaho. I'll explain on the plane."

Miss Vindex touched her earpiece. "Okay, the elevators and corridors are clear. Let's go," she said signaling with her hand.

The guards pushed them at something between a fast walk and a slow run. The waiting elevator took them down to the eerily empty lobby. Three black SUVs idled outside. Two German police motorcycles, their riders in bright yellow uniforms, were positioned in front and two others in the rear. Two guards grabbed David by the shoulders and lifted him unceremoniously into the middle SUV. Sarah was similarly plopped into the seat beside him. Miss Vindex climbed into the shotgun seat and spoke into her microphone. "Ready?" and a second later, "Go." The doors slammed shut and the SUV accelerated.

A female guard in the third row seat handed Sarah new clothing and covered her with a blanket as she began to dress. She passed David underwear, khaki pants, a shirt, shoes and socks. There was no blanket for his modesty.

After they'd dressed, Miss Vindex turned from the front passenger seat. "It's fifteen minutes to the airport. The Gulfstream is fueled and waiting. We've put out a news story that all three of you were killed in the attack. This will give you cover for several days, but we should not expect the Lilim to be deceived for long. Your flight plan is filed for Tel Aviv as a further diversion. Once airborne, you will be rerouted to Idaho Falls, which is the closest airport to Vice President Connolly's compound."

She looked them over. "Dr. Austin, do you require any pain medication?"

"No, I'm under control. It hurts but nothing I can't stand." Miss Vindex nodded, seemingly pleased at Sarah's stoic attitude.

Sarah leaned over. "David, how did you arrange this? I thought for sure we were trapped in Germany for weeks if not months."

"It's Miss Vindex's doing. Believe me, I'm as surprised as you are."

"What about Shlomo's body?"

"Miss Vindex has made the arrangements. He's being buried, or interred I should say, with the other leaders of the Brotherhood. He's being well seen to." He gripped her hand.

"I can't believe he's dead, that he saved my life. If

anything, I should've saved his."

"Shlomo knew that we are the key to defeating the Lilim. He did what he had to in order to ensure that we'd continue. Our quest is part of a war that's gone on for centuries. It wasn't only the Nadeau women, Shlomo and the Brotherhood expected me too. Miss Vindex called me the speaker, the person who speaks to the goddess."

"Jesus, Mary and Joseph! Abigail is a goddess?" Sarah's voice trailed off.

David turned to face Sarah squarely. "Listen, I know you're tired, that you want to go home, but we've got to see this through no matter what. We can do this. We can destroy the chalice, defeat the Lilim, and save the world."

"Yes, I believe you can." Sarah touched his face. She looked at David in a way he hadn't seen before. "Who are you, soldier, and what have you done with my husband?"

Miss Vindex put her finger to the earpiece. She grabbed the microphone and barked, "Alt plan one, alt plan one."

The convoy accelerated, then swerved into an alley and screeched to a halt.

"Out, quickly," shouted Miss Vindex. The men in black had them by the arms yanking them out of the SUV and through a gray door as the convoy sped off.

"There is an accident on the access road to the airport. We suspected the Lilim might stage an ambush, so we've arranged an alternative exit route. The convoy will continue to the airport as a diversion." Miss Vindex led the way through a utility corridor to a freight elevator.

"A helicopter is waiting for us on the roof," said Miss Vindex, appearing completely composed as if this were an everyday occurrence. Sarah looked unnerved. David's heart thumped. Ten minutes ago they were resting in hospital beds, and now they were racing to escape another deadly ambush. Sarah moved closer to David as the floor numbers slowly tick off.

The door opened into a machine room filled with giant blowers and electrical panels. Miss Vindex led the party quickly upstairs leading to the roof. The guards' heavy boots rang on the metal steps. A gust of wind struck as they stepped onto the roof. David squinted, blinded for a few seconds by the sudden daylight. Minutes later, a large blue and white executive helicopter approached and touched down with its engines whining. The guards sprinted with Sarah and David in tow to the waiting door. In seconds, they were buckled in and rising rapidly. The helicopter pitched forward dramatically like a carnival ride as the aircraft picked up speed. Sarah held onto her seat with her one good hand, her eyes squeezed shut. She hated carnival rides.

Miss Vindex spoke into her headset, then to the pilot. He shook his head, and yelled, "*Nicht. Verbotten.*" The helicopter swerved away from the airport. Miss Vindex pulled a small pistol from her handbag, pointed at the pilot's head, and continued speaking in German. The pilot leaned away from the gun barrel with his eyes bulging and sweat forming on his brow. He scowled, nodded, and resumed his original course.

Miss Vindex turned to us. "I suspect the terminal area has been compromised as well, so I've arranged an unorthodox boarding procedure. The Gulfstream is waiting on the ramp at the end of the runway. I've requested the pilot to touch down beside the jet, and you will board there. The plot is not pleased, but I've assured him we will clear up any difficulties. Germans are never happy about breaches of protocol." She offered a half smile.

The airport came into view as they cleared a hill, and the helicopter descended toward a large circle surrounding an H painted on the tarmac. Then the pilot spoke rapidly into his headset and swerved toward the waiting jet, skimming across the runway feet off the ground. A commuter plane streaked overhead. Its engines screaming as it climbed for altitude after aborting its approach. The pilot shouted into his microphone. David guessed the control tower was not happy about their disrupting the flight pattern.

The helicopter reared backwards like a wild horse as they braked and touched down hard on the grass. Sarah and David jumped from the helicopter. His ribs screamed in protest. Sarah threw off her sling and winced as they ran to the waiting Gulfstream. David heard sirens, looked over his shoulder and saw blue lights approaching. The stewardess beckoned frantically as they bounded up the stairs. She pulled the door shut and the jet immediately began to roll. Before they reached their seats, the jet accelerated down the runway with its engines roaring. As they buckled in, the jet's nose lifted and the aircraft leaped from the runway.

David struggled to calm his breathing; each deep breath was like a knife in his injured ribs. Sarah sat upright, eyes shut, breathing deeply. They were safe, rocketing away from danger at five thousand feet per minute as the Gulfstream shot through the clouds.

Pain is Strength

"The only way out of the labyrinth of suffering is to forgive."
– John Green

Abigail walked to the entrance of the dead garden, her shoes echoing in the empty cavern. She'd done away with the countess's elaborate hair style. She'd always worn her hair up when she was a girl in Maine, as was the Quaker fashion. Now her auburn hair hung loose about her head and shoulders. Abigail liked how it bounced and swayed as she walked. It felt natural as if she'd always worn it down. It reflected her confidence. Abigail looked forward to meeting Eymerich again.

Ilona grabbed her arms, her face beaming. "Lady Abigail, we thought you lost. We tried to follow you, but the swirling mist became as hard and cold as ice. We waited for long time, and weren't sure what to do. Then, with a flash of lightning, the dark ice disappeared."

"I was lost, but a friend showed me the way." The women looked puzzled. "I'll explain when we have more time."

"You've changed your dress. You look like a young girl again," said Ilona.

"Yes. This was the dress I wore when I arrived. Pretty, don't you think?" She fanned out the skirt with her hands. "Not exactly a warrior's outfit, but sometimes a disguise is the best armor."

Ilona smiled. "I've heard that predators will make themselves look small to draw in their prey."

Abigail smiled back at her. She'd read her mind.

"There is a lot to explain, but our time is short. The

mist you saw was alive, a demon, another manifestation from the labyrinth. It has joined the countess in the void." Abigail placed her hand on Ilona's shoulder. "Come, let's look in the cottage. I think what we seek is hidden there."

They entered the cottage together. "Violetta, tell me what you see?"

Violetta walked around the room. She stopped at the fireplace to inspect the iron pokers. At the desk she flipped through the pages of the book. Then she turned and looked at the symbols lining the top of the bookshelf.

"There are footsteps around the room. Eymerich was here recently. The iron poker with a circle symbol similar to the one on the book shelf was touched by him. The last page of the book has three new names. It's the same handwriting as the rest, which I guess is Eymerich's. Beside each name is the notation, 'marked.' Then on the bookshelf, he touched two of the symbols. The one with the two S's side by side and the center one with the circle and jagged lines."

Violetta's face contorted in pain. She shook her head, placed her hands over her ears, and looked up at us. "I hear screams, echoes of screams. Someone was terribly hurt here. Recently." Her face reflected the pain of the prior events.

The bookshelf behind the desk drew Abigail's attention. Across the top were seven symbols painted on separate panels, none of which were familiar. The one in the center was a black circle with twelve jagged lines radiating outward. Abigail studied them but none made any sense.

She touched the circle with the jagged lines on the top frieze of the bookshelf. Nothing. She touched the symbol with the two S's side by side. It was loose. Abigail pushed hard and it slid backwards.

As it moved, the center symbol moved, protruding out. She pushed the circle with the jagged lines and it slid back into place. Then, with the sound of scraping wood, the bookshelf glided to the right revealing a stone archway and stairs leading down.

"Wh-wh-what's down th-there?" Wendlandt moved to peer down the stairs.

"What's down there is the key to Lord Eymerich's destruction." Abigail said "Violetta, hand me the iron poker with the point on it."

Abigail took the poker and jammed it between the wall and the bookcase. "There! I don't want to be trapped a second time."

Abigail descended the curved stone stairs which led to a vast dark hall. It had carved stone walls and vaulted ceilings. Red tile covered the floor. She heard low stirrings in the darkness.

Abigail walked forward, making a series of torches affixed to the walls as she went. The light revealed hundreds of people, men, and women in prison cells, dressed in clothing from all ages. They clutched at the iron bars as she approached. Each had been branded somewhere on their body with the same symbol, jagged S-shaped lines within a circle.

These were the people that Jacquis had brought to Eymerich, the source of his strength. He'd branded each with his mark to identify his herd, and Abigail suspected for his own pleasure. Hundreds of eyes fell on her, some in wonder, and others in fear.

"I've come to rescue you. Your suffering is over." The crowd erupted in commotion with the sounds of different languages all speaking at once.

With a wave of her hand, Abigail dissolved the iron bars and then erased the brands that Eymerich had inflicted. Both actions took only moments with no more effort than simply willing it to be so. Lord Eymerich's former captives stared at her in wonderment. Some were joyful, other in shock, and some fell to their knees in tears.

Abigail raised her arms to silence the crowd. "Please, hear me. We need to take you to a different place where Eymerich can't find you. You will be safe and comfortable there."

"Who are you? Where is this place?" shouted a man in the front wearing a black waistcoat and derby hat. The people became still awaiting Abigail's answer.

"My name is Abigail. Like you, I've been trapped in Gehenna. You are in a dungeon beneath Queen Lilith's castle. Load Eymerich has held you captive here to feed on your strength, to sap your will. I've been sent to help you, to free you from Lord Eymerich's grasp."

"Why are we here?" asked an old woman in the crowd. "Why have we been cast into the pit? We did not deserve such a fate."

"You were trapped by evil at the moment of your deaths. Demons rule this existence. Lord Eymerich, the one who brought you here, is one of the greatest demons. He collects souls the way a miser collects gold coins. None of you deserves to be here. Indeed, it is your inner strength and goodness that made you a target for abduction."

Abigail scanned the faces that looked back at her. Each had a story. Each had an expectation of her. "I need your help."

"How can we help?" asked a young man dressed as workman.

"You can help by denying Eymerich your vitality. The queen's plan is to destroy all human life on earth, and I intend to stop her. I need you to give me your energy when the time comes. Strength given is far stronger than strength stolen." The crowd looked to each other for understanding and then back at Abigail for explanation.

"I know this is hard to understand, even harder to believe, but everything you see about you is an illusion, both what you can see and touch, and what is in your mind. The illusion of the mind is the most devious. You've been made to believe that your only hope comes from your captor, Lord Eymerich. Eymerich is as powerful as he is evil. He has trapped you here because you are strong souls. He has been feeding on your energy like a parasite."

A tall, thin man with a gaunt face stepped forward. "It's true. I've longed for the times when Lord Eymerich would appear. I rejoiced when he brought new prisoners. I would have done anything for him. How could I have had these feelings?" His face flashed between anger and misery.

Abigail went to him and touched his shoulder, letting her energy flow into him. She read the vision of his life. He'd been a sheep herder in the western United States, a father of six children and a loving husband. He'd been killed by a cattle rancher in a conflict over grazing rights. His body shivered as Abigail's energy cleansed his soul of the sadness he felt. Abigail let him see a bit of who she was.

"Thank you, I understand," he said softly.

"Come. I will take you to a place of safety. Follow us, walk single file and remain quiet. Eymerich may have spies along the way, and we must not be discovered. Also, there are many distractions on the path. Ignore them all. They are meant to trap you. If you get lost, you may never find your way out."

At the top to the stairs, Abigail explained to Violetta and Wendlandt what she'd found and the need to bring all the souls back to the chamber.

"Violetta, stay here with me by the door. I want you

to listen to the thoughts of everyone who passes by. Let me know if you feel anything strange, anything that's not right."

"Yes, of course. What are you looking for?"

"I don't know, but I think you'll know it when you feel it." Violetta took up her post beside the door to the hidden chamber. Fifty or more people passed by. As with the streets of the castle town, there were people from all ages in all manner of dress, and all looked relieved to be leaving Eymerich's dungeon.

Violetta stepped back from the door, wide eyed, hand to her mouth and pointed wildly at a stooped, elderly woman walking with a cane. A flowered shawl obscured her face.

Abigail stepped in front of her. "Grandmother, can I speak with you?" Instantly, the image of the old woman transformed into a child-sized demon with black, scaly skin, horns, and gyrating tail. It leaped at her with outstretched claws and a piercing shriek. The people walking through the cottage pinned themselves against the walls at the sound. Abigail grabbed it by the throat, stunned it with a bolt of energy, and tossed its limp body into the fireplace.

"Everyone who passed was happy, excited to be leaving. Then this woman came and her thoughts were black, evil, searing with pain," explained Violetta, calming herself with a deep breath. She returned to her station by the door. The people in the room glanced at one another, fear draining from their faces, and resumed their exodus.

"Keep your guard up, there may be others." Violetta smiled hesitantly. Indeed there were three more demons hidden in the crowd, all disguised as captives. As the last demon passed, Violetta simply nodded at it, and Abigail disposed of it in the fireplace with the others. The dead demons had shriveled, cracked, and crumbled to black dust by the time they'd left the cottage.

Abigail followed the last souls out of the cottage. She took the branding iron that Eymerich had used to scar his captives, and dissolved it in a wisp of smoke, ensuring it would never be used again. Abigail sensed her confrontation with Eymerich was close at hand. Surprise was her advantage this time. She'd stolen his source of power. When he searched for it during their coming battle he would not find it. She looked forward to seeing his face when he realized his fate.

Abigail put Violetta in the lead to follow the tracks out of the labyrinth, and sent Wendlandt with her in case anything on the way out had changed. She worried that liberating these people had seemed too easy. Anything easy in Gehenna had turned out to be a trap.

Before leaving the cottage in the back garden, Abigail moved her hand and created a large, green, flowering mountain laurel like the ones from her family's farm. It glowed like a beacon of life and hope within this place of death.

Into the Breach

"Let me not pray to be sheltered from dangers, but to be fearless in facing them." – Rabindranath Tagore

The stewardess brought Sarah and David hot towels. "We are level at forty-five thousand feet. It will be eleven hours flying time to Idaho."

"Thank God," said Sarah. David agreed. They had eleven hours to relax, to not worry about being shot at, to gather their strength. David had a hard time relaxing. The emotions he'd had when they'd flown to Germany came rushing back. They were rushing headlong into a dark abyss where an unseen, inconceivable danger awaited them, a feeling heightened and made all the more real by the ambush. The Lilim played for keeps.

The stewardess' name tag said *Kimie*. She looked slightly Asian, trim, with enticing brown eyes, and black hair pulled back in a tight bun. She wore a tight blue skirt and a white blouse. "We have steak au poivre, chicken Kiev, or salmon almandine for dinner, and a breakfast before we land. Would you or Dr. Austin care for a cocktail before dinner?" The normalcy of her question made David realize he was still running on adrenaline. He took a deep breath.

"I'd love a Manhattan." He said, with a weak laugh.

"Make that two, thanks," Sarah added.

"Is Maker's Mark all right?"

"Yes, thanks." David said. *Much better than my usual Old Crow bourbon.*

'I'll get those right way." She handed David a bulky envelope. "This is for you from Miss Vindex. She has an additional transmission coming in. As soon as the satellite signal stabilizes, I'll print it off for you."

David moved to the couch and beckoned Sarah to sit beside him. He wanted to feel her warmth. David touched her shoulder, and she wrapped her arms around him, her hand on the back of his head. He savored the sensation of her breathing, feeling her chest rising and falling and her warm breath on his neck. The overwhelming terror of the nighttime attack came rushing back. David's eyes flooded with tears and his chest tightened. Sarah was everything to him. Sarah pushed him away holding onto his shoulders. Her eyes were red. She kissed him full on the mouth.

"Me too," she said.

Kimie came back with their drinks. She pressed a tab on the arm of the couch and drink holders popped out. "Is dinner in an hour all right?"

"Yes, perfect. Thank you again," said Sarah.

"There is a shower in the bathroom if you care to freshen up. We have some additional clothing in your sizes. Not much of a selection, though, only slacks and shirts. Our preparation time was short, and we didn't know your destination till just before departure." She was very matter-of-fact about what seemed like amazing service.

"I could use a shower and a change. We'll finish our drinks and then clean up. Can you hold dinner for an hour and a half?"

"Yes, madam, very good. I will lay out some towels on your bed. It's through the door past the galley." Kimie walked to the galley and drew a curtain, leaving them with the hint of privacy.

Sarah took a sip of her drink and raised an eyebrow at David.

"Me as well." David replied. The Manhattan was excellent. The first gulp burned all the way down, relaxing him as it went. David sat back on the couch and opened the envelope. Sarah rested her head on his shoulder and looked on. He dumped the contents in his lap. There were two US passports, a credit card, a letter, two mobile phones, and $5000 in a bound bundle of $100 bills. Sarah reached for a passport.

"David, this has your picture on it but the name is David Fortis from Evansville, Illinois." She opened the second. "Same for mine. What's the letter say?"

"Oh, my god. It's from Shlomo." Sarah squeezed his arm as her eyes went wide.

"It says, 'Dear Dr. and Mr. Austin. If you're reading this, then I am dead. After the attempt on our lives in Damascus, I thought it wise to make plans for this eventuality. The Brotherhood has been alerted to your presence and your importance. David, you are the speaker, the messenger of the goddess. You are the fulfillment of the prophecy. The Brotherhood is at your disposal. They will fight to the death for you.'"

"David. The Brotherhood. This started with Moses, and now ends with us?" Sarah spoke as though she didn't believe her own words.

David thought of Abigail and touched the case under his shirt where he carried her picture. She was there. The psychic tether between them held fast. She knew they were on their way to the Idaho forest where Falcon held the chalice and where David intended to destroy it.

"David, are you with me? You're getting that faraway look again." Sarah shook his arm.

"I'm here." David stroked her head, letting his hand linger on her face. "It's up to us and Abigail now. Abigail has changed. She is not the young girl in the white dress you met in our living room. She's taller, immensely strong, braver, a true warrior. I've felt it. Her strength is in me."

Sarah sat up on the couch facing me. "You've spoken with her again haven't you? Did you summon her? In the hospital? Did anyone see?"

"No, no one saw her. I don't need to summon her anymore. She's there all the time. Even now, it's like she's standing an arm's length away. I can talk to her at any time." David turned to face Sarah. "It's more than hearing her. It's like we're connected by a wire with energy flowing across. I can feel it; it tingles, makes the hairs on my arms stand up."

"Jesus, what's going on with you? This stuff keeps getting more out there all the time. Are Scully and Mulder flying the plane?" Sarah rubbed his hand and looked worried, lost in her thoughts. David continued reading Shlomo's letter aloud.

"'I've taken the liberty of creating new identities for you, since you are now known to the Lilim.

These identities will pass first level scrutiny but not a detailed search. They should suffice while you continue the hunt for the chalice. The phones are preprogrammed with the number for Miss Vindex. She is your conduit to the Brotherhood. The credit card has almost unlimited funds.

"'I wish you well, my friends. Yours is a dangerous quest but one I know you are capable of. The goddess is with you, trust in her.

"'Your friend, Shlomo.'"

David stared straight ahead. He ached at the loss of Shlomo, his friend.

"Goddess?" said Sarah. "I'm struggling to get my head around thinking of the young girl in the white dress as a goddess."

"I'm not sure," David replied softly. She might be.

The energy coming from her was unlike anything I could imagine. "Maybe..." He stood up. The thought was more than he could handle.

"I'm going to shower and change. The last time I washed it was a sponge bath by an unpleasant German guy who smelled like cigarettes." David reached for his drink and downed it in a single gulp.

"I'll join you," said Sarah.

The couple luxuriated in the small but surprisingly robust shower. Kimie had laid out plush white robes for each of them. They stretched out on the double bed to rest before dinner. The tension of the last few days fell away like ice warming on a spring day.

"Mr. Austin, Dr. Austin, it's time to wake up." A gentle hand touched David's shoulder. "We have three hours to go till we land in Idaho. You should wake up now." They were side by side on the bed covered in a blanket and still in their white robes.

"Huh? I thought you said it was eleven hours?" David said, trying to focus his eyes on Kimie.

"It is. You've been asleep for eight hours. I thought it best to let you and Dr. Austin sleep. You've had a rough time, from what I hear. But I have breakfast ready, and there is a transmission from Miss Vindex which she suggests you read before landing."

"What time is it?" asked Sarah.

"It is eight o'clock Mountain Daylight Time, the time zone of our destination. We are in US airspace now. I'll wait for you in the main cabin."

"I feel like I've been asleep for a hundred years," Sarah said as she sat up and swung her feet on the floor.

"I guess we needed that." David reached for the

clothing that Kimie had laid out.

In the main cabin, Kimie had set a table with a white table cloth and two large glasses of orange juice. As soon as they were seated, she served scrambled eggs, sausage links, roasted tomatoes, and toast in a silver caddy. She returned with two carafes, coffee in one hand and tea in the other. David couldn't recall savoring a breakfast more.

After they'd eaten, Sarah went to the couch to read the material Miss Vindex had sent. David sat across from her in a swivel chair. She read for a few minutes and then looked up.

"Holy Cow. If you had any doubts that we're on the right path, they're gone now. Listen to this." She bit her lower lip so as to contain her excitement.

"'In Idaho, there is a furtive organization called the Babylon Woods. It's been in existence since 1862. It started as an explorer's club and has become a gathering place for the rich and powerful, military leaders, and captains of industry. They assemble every year at this time for two weeks deep in a thousand-acre wilderness. Little is known about what goes on, but there are persistent rumors of ceremonies performed late at night in front of a giant owl statue. There are unconfirmed reports of men and women dancing naked in front of the statue flanked by flaming cauldrons.'"

"Abigail mentioned an owl statue in Lilith's castle," David said.

"Yes, I remember you said that." The report says that the gathering has grown both in size within the last few years. There are reports of hundreds of people arriving by bus late at night.

"'The entrance is five miles away from Vice President Connolly's ranch. He is said to be a frequent visitor. The entire compound is patrolled by a private militia. Security is extremely tight." Sarah read furiously, dropping pages as she went.

"Get this. The name of the private surveillance company is Black Sun Security."

"This is it. The chalice has to be there," David said leaning forward as Sarah continued reading.

"The next official meeting is two days away. Connolly has invited many world leaders under the pretext of creating a new global warming initiative. He's always been an ardent critic, and this is seen as a possible new start for an accord, like 'only Nixon could go to China.' Only a critic can make something happen. It's supposed to be the largest meeting ever.

"The report says the Brotherhood has had the Babylon Woods under surveillance for years but it was one of many suspected locations where the Lilim had operations."

"How does this figure into the plague Abigail told us about?" David wondered out loud.

"Makes sense. The Lilim intend to send the world leaders and the military home infected with the plague. Governments will be crippled from the top down, delaying any effective response. Damn. It's a brilliant plan."

"We've got to get in there somehow." He looked out the window at the clouds speeding by and the farmland below.

"We're not invited. We can't just walk in. It's heavily patrolled, so we can't sneak in."

David thought for a few seconds. "Sarah, there are hundreds of the rich and powerful there. You don't suppose they're making s'mores over a campfire do you?"

"No?" Sarah chuckled. "What are you getting at?"

"We're going to sneak in, not through the woods, but through the kitchen. They must have a huge kitchen to feed all these people in the manner they are expecting. We'll be mice in the pantry."

"I like it. How do we pull it off?"

"We'll get Miss Vindex to work another miracle for us." David got up and went to the curtain surrounding the galley.

"Kimie?" The curtain opened.

"Yes, Mr. Austin?"

"Can you get a message to Miss Vindex?"

"Yes, you can do it yourself. I'll get you the laptop." She went to a closet in the forward cabin.

"Good. Thank you. I need to make some special arrangements."

Concealed Enemies

"It is easier to forgive an enemy than to forgive a friend."
– William Blake

Violetta and Wendlandt followed Eymerich's footsteps out of the garden with a long procession of the rescued souls behind them. Abigail brought up the rear with Ilona. They'd been walking for some time when Violetta came running back.

"Lady Abigail, the trail has led us back to the fire pit, but our way is blocked. I fear we're lost, there is no way around." She spoke rapidly, grabbing her hand and pulling Abigail forward.

They ran past the line of people to the opening to the lava pit where a crowd had bunched up. A tendril of molten rock from the pit had spread out on the length of the walkway and blocked the procession. The end of the tendril flopped around like a cat's tail, as though it were searching for a victim.

Ilona threw a stone at it, which only served to frustrate her more. "Lady Abigail, I don't know what to do. The rock is too hot to approach. What can we do to get it to move?" She picked up another stone and threw it. "Ahhh, get thee out of here. Return to your pit below," she yelled. The rock missed and bounced down the cliff face, landing in the bubbling lava below.

"Ilona, this isn't some old dairy cow you can move along with a switch. It's a creation of the labyrinth. We need to find a way of moving it or a way around it."

She stepped aside. All eyes were on Abigail. The crowd murmured, looking frightened and unsure of what was happening next. Abigail had brought them this far.

They expected—she expected—to get them to the relative safety of her chamber.

This blockade was no accident. The living rock had deliberately placed itself so as to prevent their escape. Abigail suspected Eymerich was behind this. Somehow he knew where she was. *How else could Frank Robinson have set a trap for me?* Now he sought to block their path out of the labyrinth.

"Abigail, what's happening? Your body is glowing again like it's lit from within." Ilona's face looked awestruck, as did the people behind her. Abigail hands glowed as the now familiar surge of energy flowing from the people they'd rescued into her. The souls that Eymerich had hidden away were now her source of energy. Anticipation rose in her at the thought of using his own trove to defeat him.

The first time Abigail experienced the surge of energy it was like a wild beast coming to life within her. Now it was natural. The energy was an essential part of her. Abigail understood what to do.

She stepped forward feeling the immense heat radiating from the living rock. It remained inert with red molten rock visible through cracks in its black crusty skin. Without warning, it shot out like a coiled snake trying to reach her. Abigail extended her arm and engulfed it in a swirl of white energy. Instantly, it lost its form, turning into a pool of molten rock that cascaded over the edge and splashed into the pit below.

Just as the last of the molten rock washed away, a searing pain shot through the middle of Abigail's back as though she'd been pierced by a spear. She staggered forward a step, stunned by the unexpected attack. Abigail spun around and saw Wendlandt pointing a small round red jewel at her. It glowed with a pulsing light, smoke rose from Wendlandt's hand.

"D-die, die, you-you-you must die." Wendlandt spoke in a whisper. Her head twisted to the side along her shoulder. Her face contorted. Her arm faltered, and she grabbed her forearm with her other hand and raised the glowing jewel. A bolt of lightning shot from the jewel, striking her in the center of her chest. Abigail was prepared this time, and it dissipated as it struck.

"W-Why won't you die?" she pleaded. "I c-can't be free unless y-you die." She dropped to her knees, her arms drooping by her sides. Her body convulsed with sobbing.

Abigail went to her, grasped her by the wrists and raised her to her feet. She still held the pulsating jewel in her hand. Abigail flicked her wrist and the jewel flew from her hand. It bounced down the chasm walls into the boiling rock, and exploded with a loud crack and puff of smoke. Wendlandt became invisible. An instinctive reaction but Abigail held her wrists firmly. She had not sensed any deceit within her, only fear when they eluded the three-headed dog earlier. Wendlandt's life was defined by waves of fear. She was awash in a sea of terror.

Abigail streamed energy into her and again sensed a frightened young woman whose only desire was to run to a dark corner and hide. Abigail pressed further into her, overwhelming her with a flood of energy. She cried out, threw her head back and arched her back. Abigail was hurting her, but she had to know why Wendlandt had attacked her. As Abigail's will took hold of her, Abigail felt a wall within Wendlandt crumble and new images rushed forth. Her ability to be invisible was not only physical, it was mental as well.

She had hidden her true nature from Abigail, from everyone. Wendlandt was a spy, Eymerich's spy. He'd placed her within the countess's chamber to spy on the countess. Eymerich trusted no one, not even the countess, his closest confidante.

"Why? Why, Wendlandt? Why did you try to kill me?"

"Lord Eymerich p-promised to free me, to send me to a p-place where I wouldn't be afraid any longer. I'm so t-tired of being afraid. He told me that if I didn't help him he'd lock me in the l-labyrinth forever." Wendlandt stared at her feet. "W-when you defeated the countess, Lord Eymerich was worried, worried about who you were. I think he's afraid of you. He g-gave me the jewel and told me I could summon his powers with it. When I held it I could hear him. I could speak to him." Wendlandt let out a wail that resounded in the cavern and collapsed in a heap.

"I'm s-sorry. Y-you were kind. I w-wasn't afraid of you." Her sobbing took her again. She took Abigail's hand and held it to her cheek. "I'm sorry, L-Lady Abigail. It's been s-so long since I felt safe with anyone." She sat up straighter. "Lord Eymerich knew that you'd escaped his trap. He told me to use the jewel to summon the molten rock and block your way out. When that failed, he told me to kill you." She searched Abigail's face for a sign of forgiveness. "I didn't want to kill you, but Lord Eymerich filled me with such fear that I couldn't refuse him." She broke down crying again. Abigail released her arms and stood over her.

"Wendlandt, I forgive you. It wasn't your fault. Eymerich tortured you into helping him."

"Y-you forgive me?" Wendlandt looked up at Abigail. For the first time since she'd known her, her face was relaxed. Abigail helped her stand.

"Yes, I forgive you. Eymerich is a master at discovering a person's weakness and using it to his advantage."

"Yes, you're right. He knows my weakness. He

knows how to control me." Wendlandt had lost her stutter. Her voice sounded clear and calm and her face had a faraway look. "Lady Abigail, I've not had peace, ever since I can remember. In life and then in this horrible place, I've existed in absolute terror, until this moment, until I met you. Your strength has freed me. I am afraid no longer." She smiled at Abigail, a soft loving smile. "I will never betray you again."

Wendlandt dropped Abigail's hand. She turned and threw herself over the edge of the chasm into the bubbling lava. Abigail gasped. Violetta screamed. The rescued souls who had been watching from the entrance way peered over the edge to confirm her fate.

Ilona came and stood beside Abigail. "Why did she do that? Is she dead? I mean is her soul lost?"

"She did it because she didn't trust herself. She feared that Eymerich would gain control of her again. And yes, her soul is gone. I hope she finds the peace she never knew." Abigail thought of Ehyeh sitting beside her flaming pyramid and prayed she would rescue Wendlandt's soul. Abigail grasped Ilona's arm. "Are you okay?"

"Yes, I'm ready." Ilona's face was strong and calm. Abigail saw the vision of her by her side dressed in armor, sword in hand, the two of them charging into battle together, fighting demonic hoards back to back.

"Lady Abigail, what is it? You looked at me in such a strange way?" Abigail snapped out of her daydream.

"Nothing, just a remembrance." Abigail knew Ilona would give her life for her, and she for Ilona. Their friendship transcended time and place. She didn't know where or when, but this was not their first campaign together. "Ready to continue? You and Violetta lead and I'll follow."

Eymerich knew she was coming. He knew she'd captured the souls which were the source of his powers. He waited for her like a frightened beast ready to attack at the sight of her. Abigail was ready for him, and their next encounter would be at a time and place of her choosing. She was the hunter now.

Into the Forest

"Let me not pray to be sheltered from dangers, but to be fearless in facing them." – Rabindranath Tagore

Miss Vindex responded immediately. The Babylon Woods compound employed a large number of temporary staff when in session. She would arrange for them to be hired on. It would take a day to create the appropriate opening; details would follow.

"David, what's your plan after we get in? Do you have a plan?" He heard anxiety in Sarah's voice.

"I don't have a plan. We know almost nothing about what goes on inside the Babylon Woods compound. We don't know the schedule. We don't know the layout. We don't know who's there. We know nothing about the internal security. All we know is that the chalice is there, and the second most powerful man in the world, the leader of the Lilim, has it." David patted her leg. "The chalice is the target. The only thing we can do is to keep moving toward it."

Sarah sat back on the couch. She started to say something but stopped, then pulled her knees to her chest and wrapped her arms around her legs.

"I hate this, just hate it. I don't get out of bed in the morning without a plan. And here we're sneaking into to a gathering of the children of Satan with the fate of the human race in the balance and we have no plan. Fabulous."

"I know, honey, but what else we can do? We have to stay focused on the chalice. It's the key to everything."

"You're right, you're right, but I don't have to like it." She rolled her head back and looked at the ceiling. The engines slowed and the Gulfstream nosed downward. Kimie emerged from behind her curtain.

"Mr. Austin, Dr. Austin, we've begun our decent. We'll be landing in fifteen minutes at the Magic Valley Regional Airport. Please fasten your seat belts."

"Is someone meeting us?" David asked, thinking of the reception they'd had in Germany.

"Yes, Miss Vindex has made arrangements." David started to ask another question when Kimie stopped him. "That's all I know, Mr. Austin. Someone will meet you. I have no other information for you." She nodded her head slightly and took up her position in the jump seat by the door. The jet shook as it banked sharply through the clouds. Sarah gripped the arms of her chair. They were about to be evicted from their sanctuary, alone on an unknown battle field.

A wide river plain with mountains in the distance came into view as the Gulfstream dropped below the clouds on its final approach. The wheels squeaked on touchdown, and the jet decelerated rapidly. They taxied into a large open hanger where the engines shut down, producing a sudden silence.

"Please remain seated for a minute while we make preparations for your disembarkation," said Kimie as she looked out the cabin door window. An electrical motor whined, and the hanger slid closed with a dull thud. There was a double knock on the cabin door, and Kimie flipped the latch and pushed open the door. Humid air rushed in.

She stepped back and bowed with her hands clasped together. "It has been my honor to serve you, Doctor and Mr. Austin. Go with grace and courage."

"Thank you, Kimie," said Sarah. David nodded as they descended the stairs.

The Gulfstream looked small inside the massive

hanger. The painted floor gleamed, reflecting the bright ceiling lights. At the foot of the stairs, a weathered looking man waited. He had a bushy, discolored white mustache and wore blue jeans with a large silver buckle, a western shirt, and boots.

"Morning, folks." He handed David the duffle and an envelope. "Your supplies are in the bag. There's a satellite phone, two mobile phones, new identity papers, and credit cards to match. There a letter from the boss explaining what's what. Please give me your other documents." Sarah and David handed over the passports Kimie had given them.

"Thank you. Now you'll find your vehicle outside that door over there. It ain't much to look at but that's kind'a the point, ain't it?" After giving them a quick grin visible under his mustache, he turned and started to walk away.

"Hey, wait a minute—" David yelled.

He waved his hand in the air and kept walking without turning around, his words barely audible, "It's all in the letter." He disappeared through a far door. David turned to Sarah. Her face reflected his feelings. They were on their own again. Yes, we had the Brotherhood behind us, but they were alone nonetheless, a sensation reinforced by the emptiness and silence in the hanger.

David took her hand. "Come on, let's get out of here."

"Yes, let's." Sarah looked back at the Gulfstream. David wondered if she wanted to get back in and fly to any place other than here. A few days ago he would have, but not now. Abigail's vision of Moloch's chalice on a pedestal before the owl statue kept coming back to him. David's impulse was to drive directly to the Babylon Woods, find the chalice, and destroy it. The chalice was calling to him, drawing him to it. He felt invincible; nothing could stand in his way.

David caught himself. He had to resist the impulse. Acting without thinking was a recurring theme in his life. There were a thousand traps between him and the chalice, a thousand opportunities for him to screw things up. David couldn't afford to be rash.

"I guess we'd better read the letter," David said handing it to her. His shoes squeaked on the shiny floor as they walked to the back door.

David squinted as he stepped outside. The sky was bright blue, cloudless, and the air was warm, humid like a July day in Maine. Parked outside was a dirty black KIA Rio with a dent in the front fender and a cracked windshield. Crusty the cowboy was right — it wasn't much to look at.

"What a POS," he said. The back door creaked as David opened it, tossing the duffle in the back seat. There were two backpacks already there.

Sarah sat in the passenger seat, her nose in the letter. "That old guy was right. This car is part of their new identity. We're part-time kitchen staff." Sarah handed him a wallet containing a driver's license, a bank ATM card, a credit card, and a library card from the Salt Lake City public library.

"This is the new you, David Jolley, and I'm Sarah Jolley. Thank God we're still married. We're Mormons from Salt Lake. We've been homesteading here for two years, cabin in the woods. We both graduated from the Salt Lake City Community College culinary program. There's a few paragraphs of background here which you can read later. Miss Vindex suggests we check into the Parklane Motel on route forty-five for the night and wait for her call. We need to be at the Brinkerhoff Employment Agency at eight a.m."

"What's in the backpacks?" David asked.

"I don't know, she doesn't say. Let's go to the motel.

We need to get into our new identities and be ready for tomorrow. I hope you still like to cook." David had done the majority of the cooking since they'd been married. Sarah never ventured beyond the occasional meatloaf.

The Parklane Motel was a dump, with lumpy mattress, worn carpets, and mold in the shower—but their car matched the other wrecks in the parking lot, assuring their anonymity. They ordered a pizza and spent the evening reading Miss Vindex's materials and embracing their new identities. They turned in for the night, and David scratched Sarah's back the way she liked it, long and slow along her shoulder blades. After a few minutes, she stripped off her clothes and pulled him toward her. They made love frantically like it might be the last time. Their passion fueled by their apprehension about tomorrow when they would enter the locus of evil on earth, the Babylon Woods.

The mobile phone rang at six a.m. "Hello, is this Mr. Jolley, David Jolley?" It was Miss Vindex, cool and crisp as expected.

After a noticeable pause David answered. "Yes, this is David Jolley."

"You've got to be better than that. That pause is enough to draw someone's attention, and attention is exactly what you don't want. You need to be faceless, ignored, and invisible."

"I understand. Are we set for gaining entry?"

"Yes, we've arranged for two prep cooks to come down with salmonella. They were hospitalized last night. The employment agency will be eager to replace them. The Babylon Woods guests have already arrived. You've studied the briefing materials?"

"Yes, we quizzed each other last night. We're good. Do these people really exist?"

"Yes, we're holding them till this operation is completed."

"You kidnapped them?"

"Of course. We couldn't chance that someone would notice two David Jolleys walking around. Besides, if this operation fails, a minor kidnapping will be the least of our worries," advised Miss Vindex.

David didn't answer. Miss Vindex' offhand comment reminded him that failure was the likely outcome. David took a deep breath feeling tension across his shoulders.

"Can I call you on the mobile phone if we need help?"

"No, you'll be searched when you enter the compound. They'll confiscate any electronic devices. I'm afraid there is no secure channel. The phone lines are guarded and the radios are all encrypted. We can't listen in. The woods are quite dense, which prevents most remote observation with the exception of the main stage with the owl statue. We have a single observer watching that location. Our forces are staged some distance away, so don't expect an immediate response. If you look like you're in danger, we'll attempt to move in, although it is unclear what action we could take."

"I guess we're on our own, more or less."

"I'm afraid so." Miss Vindex's voice sounded unexpectedly soft and comforting. She had clearly made her own calculations regarding their odds.

The Eve of Battle

"Lay this unto your breast: Old friends, like old swords, still are trusted best." – John Webster

The last of the rescued souls walked into the chamber and through to the secret room made by the twins. Ilona closed the large wooden door with a thud. Abigail thought the room would be crowded but it wasn't. The twins, Contessa and Constanta, ran up to her.

"Lady Abigail, we made the room bigger with some tables and chairs. All set with food and drink like you did for us when you defeated the countess." They were clearly proud of themselves.

"Thank you, girls. That was thoughtful of you. I'd like you to continue to look after everyone's needs. These people have had a terrible time and they need special care." They curtsied in unison and skipped away, intent on fulfilling their charge.

"Ilona, no other problems on the way back?" Abigail asked.

"No, none. I was worried about being discovered in the hallway when we got close to the chamber, but it was clear, thank the stars."

"Yes, fortune is with us. The time to confront Eymerich, and eventually the queen, is near, but I would like it to be on more advantageous ground, not in a hallway filled with terrified people."

"How do you intend to defeat him?" asked Ilona.

"He knows I have the advantage now. Wendlandt told him that I've taken his souls, his source of strength. He'll be desperate. Desperation breeds fear, and fear leads to rash, unthinking actions. He will attack me the first chance he gets. He will use the last of his energy in an effort to cast me into the void."

"You sound like you're ready for him."

"I am ready, truly. I'm counting on his desperation to help defeat him." Abigail took Ilona's hand, and a sense of longing swept through her.

"Ilona what are you feeling? Are you remembering?"

"I don't know. I'm remembering something—emotions, feelings, vague sensations. You're my sister. I feel like we've planned for battle before, discussed tactics and strategies. I've stood by your side many times. These feelings came to me as a set of images when we marched off to the labyrinth. I've been trying to put these memories back together, but it's hard. It's like pictures from a lifetime that have been all mixed up." Ilona clasped Abigail's forearm. "But I am by your side now, as I've always been." Her face was resolute. No matter what came their way, Ilona would not leave her.

"Too much of our past is hidden by the chaos of the void. It's a veil that obscures who we were and how we lived. We are left groping in the dark for hints, for fragments of our former selves." Abigail let her energy flow into Ilona, and Ilona's energy flowed back to her. Their thoughts, their emotions, and the fragments of their memories intermingled. A vision of them as warriors running across a vast empty plain came to Abigail. She didn't know where they were, only that they were running toward danger, not away from it. Abigail opened her eyes and looked into the face of her friend. She'd been a comrade, closer than a sister, for longer than she knew.

"Abigail, though I know that is not your true name, it does not matter. All I have is yours to command." She knelt down on one knee with her head bowed and took Abigail's hand. Abigail stroked her head and brought forth the image of her as her warrior companion. Her peasant dress vanished, replaced by the leather armor and long pants of a warrior. Abigail took her by the hands and pulled her to her feet. She had not thought it possible to change another's physical form. Maybe she hadn't. Maybe she'd simply helped Ilona remember who she was.

"This is your true appearance." Ilona had been transformed. Her body was taller, stronger, with taut, sleek muscles. Her skin was fair. Her hair hung in a long braided ponytail bound with gold bands. On her hip was a gleaming sword, and a small round shield was affixed to her forearm.

Ilona looked at herself and smiled. "My whole life I resented the constraints of my sex, the weakness I felt, the limitations placed on me by my family, the condescension of men. I knew I was more. I knew I was stronger. I knew I was not meant to be afraid." She drew her sword, sweeping it back and forth, testing its weight.

"I have a thousand images in my head, all fragments, all fleeting glimpses of the past. Some are with you, my fellow warrior. In others, I am alone fighting desperate battles against fearsome enemies." Ilona returned her sword to its scabbard. She took a deep breath.

"We are alike. My past is a broken mosaic with its pieces scattered. And like me, you are beginning to know your true nature. We are both warriors, and it is not the first time we've fought together. In the past, we've always won, but this time the stakes are incredibly high. Our enemy is impossibly strong. Their plan is almost complete, and their victory nearly won."

Ilona's face lost its confidence. Her brow furled. "What shall we do?"

"I'm counting on Queen Lilith's one weak point, Moloch's chalice. It is her bridge to the land of the living, without it she will lose her ability to awaken and guide her children, the Lilim will forget who they are. The Queen will be trapped forever in Gehanna."

"Where is this chalice? Show me where it is? How can I destroy it?" She drew the sword partially out of its scabbard. She would have charged off on her quest if Abigail had given the word. Abigail gripped her arm.

"The chalice is beyond our reach in the land of the living. Our plan, more of a hope really, is a desperate one. There is a man in the land of the living who has tracked down the chalice and the place where the Lilim are gathering. He is there now, but the chalice is heavily guarded. His chances of destroying it are slim. Our only hope is to challenge the queen, and in the ensuing chaos of battle, give him the opportunity to destroy it. The chalice is the nexus of Queen Lilith's power. Without it she is nothing."

"This man must be a mighty warrior," said Ilona with some confidence. Abigail smiled at her and wished it were so.

"No. No, he's not. He's merely a man, perhaps with more self-doubts than most. He was reluctant to even begin the quest. But he is a good man with a warm and kind spirit. He will give his all to see this through." Abigail released her arm. "I hope it will be enough." Ilona nodded, but the doubt remained on her face.

"Come, let's sit down. I need to talk to you about what's behind the door guarded by the three-headed dog."

The Gates of Babylon

"When you can't find a way out, it's best to find a way further in"
– Abdelrahman Ashraf Abuzied

It was five minutes to eight, and Sarah and David waited at the door of the employment agency. The lights were out.

"Do you think they'll open on time?" Sarah asked. She folded her arms across her chest to ward off the cool morning air.

"Who knows," David replied, and then, right on cue, an old faded red pickup truck pulled up in a cloud of red dust. A wiry man wearing khakis, a western shirt, and cowboy boots hopped out and walked briskly to the door. He had a lean, weathered face with black, slicked hair in an unconvincing comb-over.

As he fumbled with the lock, he glanced at Sarah and David. They were dressed in somewhat worn mismatched clothing supplied by Miss Vindex. Sarah was always a careful dresser, very aware of styles and colors, and was not happy with her current wardrobe.

"You lookin' for work, I guess. Know anything about cookin'? I need a couple of cooks pronto." He spoke rapidly with an underlying tension in his voice.

"We both are. Been cooking for six years, ever since we graduated from the Salt Lake City Community College," David said.

He stopped with his hand on the open door. "You ain't shittin' me, are ya? I'm going to check on you, ya know. We don't send just anybody out on this job I'm staffing, not with these folks. They ain't got no sense of humor."

"Hey, sure, go ahead and check. Use these." David

handed him the one page resumes supplied by Miss Vindex. David had corrected Sarah several times for referring to the papers as her CV, "curriculum vitae," not something a community college graduate would say.

"It's all there, dates and places. Call them up if you want to. And we don't work for less than twelve dollars an hour." David added assuredly, raising his chin for emphasis.

The man narrowed his eyes and looked at him. "Well, that won't be a problem," he said softly. He flung open the door and resumed his loud voice tinged with a western drawl.

"Come on in and sit while I make a few calls." He pointed to a line of metal chairs with brown vinyl seats lining a wall covered with fake wood paneling. A yellowed print of a mountain range hung on another wall, and in the corner, a small table held year-old magazines. He entered an office with a glass window and closed the door. Sarah and David watched him work the phone for several minutes. Then still holding the phone, he stood up and opened the door.

"Okay, yeah, they check out and they have the experience you're looking for. I'll send them right over." He hung up.

"Okay," he said, sounding pleased. "My name is Gauthier by the way. You two kind of caught me off guard. I had an emergency call from my best client. Two of their cooks came down sick, both in the hospital right in the middle of their big event. I was rushin' in to start callin' everyone and his brother to find two cooks, and wouldn't you know it, here you two is waitin' for me. How good is that?" He looked smug.

"The pay is twenty an hour plus a hundred cash for you both if you start today, right now in fact. How's that do ya?"

David looked at Sarah. She nodded. "Okay, we'll take it. This sounds like temp work. How long is the job?"

It's a two-week job, but the catch is you gotta live at the site. They have a bunk house for men and one for women. I see you two is married. That won't be a problem will it? You can hold off dippin' your wick for two weeks, I expect." His eyes flickered between Sarah and David.

Sarah's steely glare answered his question. Mr. Gauthier patted David on the back. "Good. Good. Now here's the address. You got your toothbrush and stuff with you, I hope."

"Yeah, our bags are in the car," David replied.

"Great. You don't need a lot; just take your toiletries and some changes of underwear. They'll supply uniforms." He reached into his pocket and peeled off ten twenty-dollar bills. "Here's your starting bonus. Go to this address and wait for the bus. It'll take you to the job." He turned to walk back to his office.

"Wait a minute. Where are we going?" Sarah asked in her professorial tone. Mr. Gauthier looked surprised that Sarah had a voice.

"Well, dearie, it's the Babylon Woods. Your employer is called Black Sun Logistics, if that means anything to ya. I wouldn't worry your pretty face about any of that. It's good pay for these parts. Just get on out there and do what you're told. They'll be waiting on ya, best get a move on."

As they walked to the car, David smiled at Sarah. "Come on, dearie."

Sarah rolled her eyes. "He never mentioned where he was sending us. I wanted to make sure we didn't wind up at Denny's. Then she smiled. "I thought you played that well. Staying focused on the money kept him from asking any other questions."

"Thanks. And Miss Vindex did her part with making sure our backgrounds checked out."

Without speaking, they drove to the address, a parking lot with a chain-link fence and a guard shack. A panel van idled nearby as they pulled in. The guard checked their papers. "Park it over there, lock it up, and take only what you need to the van. No cell phones or cameras, nothing electronic."

The driver waited by the van's open door. "IDs and paper work." His voice and demeanor, like those of the guard, were flat. Both wore black uniforms with the black sun logo on the shoulder. David shivered when he recognized it, remembering its history, and the attempt on their lives. David feared he'd delivered himself and Sarah into the hands of people who had tried to kill them—which, of course, they were.

"Okay, get in. It's a forty-minute drive to the compound. You'll get your orders there."

They sat on the bench seat behind the driver. The windows were deeply tinted, making it hard to see outside. The van drove north into a vast expanse of forest and little else. David gave Sarah's leg a squeeze and she returned a forced half smile. She remained motionless, her eyes fixed on the road ahead, and gripping her arms as though holding in her fear.

David suppressed his fear, a distraction he couldn't afford. He felt excitement mixed with uncertainty, an unsettling combination. Every minute he was a mile closer to the chalice. His palms sweated and his heart pounded. He was closing in on his prey. He had to wait for his moment, a moment neither he nor Abigail knew when to expect.

The bond between Abigail and David had continued to grow to the point where it was now almost continuous. He didn't have to concentrate to hear her. They were almost one person. It was too crazy a thing to tell Sarah, who was still trying to cope with the reality of their psychic connection.

The addiction to Abigail's energy was new, and unlike the bond, it had come on instantly like a switch being thrown. David felt like a speed freak, craving the rush. His senses were heightened. Colors were more vivid. His night vision had improved. He heard faint sounds at a distance. He had little need for food or sleep. He was stronger with lightning reflexes. David was completely wired. Abigail's energy tingled on his fingertips.

The van pulled off the main road, turned onto a forested drive, and stopped at a guard house with a yellow and black mechanical barrier. Two guards stood poised with assault rifles. Their faces were blank, but their eyes were fixed on the van. One wrong movement would result in a hail of bullets.

A guard checked their paperwork against his clipboard. After shining a flashlight in their faces, he waved at the guard house, and the steel barrier lowered into the ground. The van drove off the main drive onto a dirt road, and in a few minutes, stopped in front of a large, dark green metal building with stainless steel ventilators on the roof. The smell of cooking filled the air.

Another armed guard opened the door. "Out, take your bags." We stepped out, and the guard pointed to a gray steel door. "In there," he ordered, and watched them enter.

Inside, a woman sat at a desk. She wore the same Black Sun uniform but with only a pistol on her belt. Her blonde hair was pulled tightly into a bun. She looked at a paper on her desk. "David and Sarah Jolley?"

"Yes, that us. Ready for work," David replied, trying to sound chipper.

"Paperwork." She held out her hand, and David gave her the papers from the employment agency. "Place your right hand on the palm reader." David put his hand on the glass, and a light rolled across it. "You next," she said pointing at Sarah.

"You will change into your uniforms and report to work while we check your identity. If there are any discrepancies, you will be detained." She typed something on her terminal. "You will work a twelve-hour shift or as directed by your supervisor. Extra time should be expected. You will not leave your assigned workspace unless directed by your supervisor or a uniformed Black Sun official. Is that understood?" We both nodded.

She took their photos in front of a white background and produced two clip-on badges. She slid two keys across the desk.

"These badges must be worn at all times, no exceptions. Failure to do so will result in loss of position and loss of pay. Understood?" She scanned their faces for acknowledgement again. "The badge will allow you access to your work area and your assigned barracks. There is no fraternization allowed. You will only enter your assigned barracks. The key opens your locker where you will find your uniform. Clean uniforms are supplied daily. Swipe your badge on that door and a guard will escort you to your barracks. Change into your uniforms and report to the kitchen." It was clear that no questions would be entertained. David looked at Sarah and nodded toward the door.

Inside, a guard led them through a long corridor filled with the sounds and smells of a large commercial kitchen in full swing. The signs for the barracks led them to six low metal buildings, each with a prominently-displayed number. The accommodations were Spartan: rows of bunk beds and a communal washroom. David changed into his uniform, a light yellow jumpsuit with a matching brimless cap. He felt silly.

He waited for Sarah until she appeared in the same getup. The guard led them back to a small kitchen workroom filled with crates of produce.

"Wait here till your supervisor returns." He placed his hand on his sidearm for emphasis and left.

Sarah pulled at the excess fabric of her jumpsuit around her hips. "Not very flattering for a girl's figure. We won't be out wandering around in these. We stand out like a beacon in a dark night."

"It's going to be a problem if we can never leave the kitchen. I'd hate to have come this far only to be trapped," David agreed.

Sarah looked out the kitchen door. "Someone's coming."

A tall man with a pot belly, long salt-and-pepper ponytail, and a face that reflected a life in the sun and weather. He wore a similar ill-fitting yellow jump suit. "Replacements? You're the Jolleys, Sarah and David?"

"Yep, that's us."

"I'm Rodney, and this is the prep area. It's our busiest night. A thousand VIP meals, everyone with special requirements, and a thousand meals for Black Sun and the staff. It's good you two could come on such short notice." He looked up from his papers.

"And no jokes about this bird suit they make us wear. It's a security thing. Security is crazy tight here. You can barely go to the washroom without some blackbird checking on you."

"Blackbird?" asked Sarah.

"That's what we call the guards; inside joke. We're the canaries because of the yellow. There are bluebirds, people in blue uniforms that do ground maintenance. And penguins, the staff in white coats and black pants that handle the service. Lastly, there are the peacocks, the guests." Rodney gave Sarah and David a quick smile.

"We were waiters before we switched to the back of the house," David added, trying to sound like he was making small talk. Rodney raised an eyebrow but didn't comment.

"Okay, kiddies, you know what we do in a prep room, right?" He paused to stare at their blank faces. "We wash, peel, and chop to order depending on the ticket. The tickets are printed here. I take 'em off the printer and post 'em on the board. When you're done with a ticket, you tape it to the lid of the box and ask me for another. You gotta question, you ask me. You gotta take a piss, you ask me. Don't mess with my system. Got it?"

After an infinitesimal pause, he continued, "Okay, here's a ticket for you, twenty-two quarts of julienne carrots, and thirty quarts of half-inch diced Yukon gold potatoes for you."

David stared at the slip of paper. He hadn't a clue how to do the work expected . They each took their tickets and went the empty tables. David started looking for crates of carrots while Sarah hauled out boxes of potatoes. He began to wash bunches of carrots and chop the tops off. When he had a pile of carrots, David looked around for a peeler.

"Hey Rodney, you got a peeler?"

"In the far corner," he said without looking up.

In the corner were metal carts with mysterious stainless steel machines. David was clueless. He'd been looking for a hand vegetable peeler, with the expectation of spending the next few hours peeling and slicing carrots.

"You don't have no fucking idea what you're doin', do ya?" said Rodney wiping his hands and glared at David. Busted.

"No, not really." At best he expected to be tossed out of the compound, at worst, locked up.

"How about you, pretty eyes? You ever done any commercial cookin'?" he yelled at Sarah.

"Sure," she replied confidently. "Just not with these machines," she added more sheepishly.

"Greenhorns, goddamn greenhorns." Rodney cuffed David on the back of his head.

"You going to turn us in?" Sarah asked.

"No, no I ain't, ain't got time to find anyone else today. We're behind already. Get over here."

We stood in front of Rodney like two school children.

"Now I'm gonna show you both what do to. I'm only gonna to do it once. If I gotta do it twice, I'll have your sorry asses thrown out. You got me?" They nodded.

Rodney pulled over two carts. One, David quickly learned, was a peeler, and the second julienned carrots. Within five minutes, David was cranking out julienne carrots by the quart. Sarah had a similar lesson in dicing potatoes. The day became a whirlwind of crisp instructions and fast learning as Sarah and David prepped hundreds of pounds of vegetables.

The clock on the wall indicted five p.m., and no more tickets appeared on the printer.

"Well we made it through," said Rodney. Good thing you two can do what you're told. I don't think they take kindly to people who ain't what they say they are."

"Thanks Rodney, we needed the work. We'd be sleeping in our car otherwise." Sarah was playing to his soft side. David nodded.

"Well, you seem like good folks. I got a sense about who's good and who ain't. There are too many around here who ain't. Us good folk got to stick together."

Just then, four guards entered. "You two come with us."

Rodney walked around from in back of the table he'd been working at. "Hey now, just one minute. We got lots of work to get done, and you're going to leave me shorthanded." Without speaking, a guard doubled Rodney over with a punch to the gut and left him gasping on the floor.

Sarah looked terrified. David threw his towel on the bench. Two of the guards took up positions behind them, handcuffed Sarah and David, and put black hoods over their heads.

Jailed

"This must be what a fly felt like when it was caught fast in a spider's web." – R.K. Lilley

Sarah and David were placed in separate cells facing each other across an aisle. A female guard addressed the captives bluntly. "Your fingerprints don't match those of the Jollys on file. You will be detained till until we verify your identities."

"You can't hold us. This is against the law!" David yelled, knowing as soon as he said it that it was a useless outburst, but he felt the need to continue playing his role.

The woman faced me. A deep malevolence showed in her eyes and a slight smile on her lips. "Mr. Jolly, or possibly Mr. Austin, is it? Once we confirm your true identity, we will ensure that you can no longer threaten our organization." She struck at the bars with her truncheon just as David pulled his fingers away. The iron bars rang out in the concrete room. She turned and left with the other guards.

David looked at Sarah across the aisle. The single overhead light cast a half shadow in her cell. The room smelled like damp concrete making David think they were somewhere underground.

"David, I want you to know I've loved you since the day we met."

"I love you too, sweetie. Don't say it like it's a last goodbye. We're not done yet." David said. He believed it, but at that moment, he was out of ideas.

"My fingerprints are on file with the feds. It won't take them long to ID me, and by inference you. This is the same bunch that tried to kill us before. I hope you've got some ideas, because now is the time." Sarah sounded dejected, as she sat on her cot half-covered in shadow.

"I'm thinking. Don't worry." David thought but drew a blank. He couldn't believe that they'd been caught this close to finding and destroying the chalice. This wasn't the way he'd seen their quest playing out. He believed, and still did, that they'd succeed. He knew they'd find a way.

Sarah curled up on her cot, and David let her be. She couldn't help. It was up to him. He sensed Abigail's progress toward the queen. She was close and expected him to be ready at the right moment. The power coming from her was immense. David touched the iron bars. They seemed to vibrate at his touch. For a moment, David wondered if he could bend them, but they remained cold and straight.

David thought they were alone in this armed compound, when he realized that wasn't entirely true. They had one friend, maybe. Not a longtime friend, but someone who believed they were "good folks." Rodney.

David pictured him in his mind. He called Rodney to come rescue them. David told him that they were trapped in an underground jail and that the fate of the world depended on their escape. David had no idea if his wishful thinking worked or not. He felt himself zoning out again and pulled himself back to the reality of his cell. Wishing for a rescue seemed farfetched. He thought of Abigail, but she was out of touch as well. David was cold. He had to find a way out. Time passed slowly as David despaired at being ready when Abigail made her move.

After what seemed like an eternity, David heard voices outside the door followed by a crash. The door opened and Rodney sprang in with keys in his hand.

"David, Sarah? Are you all right?" He fumbled with the keys, first unlocking Sarah's door and then David's.

"I don't know what's go'in on but I had the strangest feeling you two were trapped down here someplace."

"Thanks, Rodney. I'm glad you came," David exclaimed.

"I felt like I had to come and let you out, strangest thing."

"Ya, we've been getting a lot of that lately. How did you find us?" asked Sarah.

"There's a big basement under the building, I knew you was down here someplace. So I made up a tray of food like I was bringing it to someone so I'd have an excuse to be roamin' around. Then I found this guard where I'd never seen one before. I told him the food was for the prisoners and I put the tray on the table. When he turned his back, I clobbered 'im with the rollin' pin I'd stuffed in my pants."

"Good thinking." David replied.

"Come on. I can sneak you out," said Rodney. Sarah shot David a glance, wondering what his plan was.

"No, we're not leaving. Can you get us to where the owl statue is?"

Rodney gawked at David like he was crazy. "How did I know you were going to say that? No fool in his right mind would want to go there. Ain't nothin' good happening there. I'd want to get as far away from there as I could."

"That's why we have to go. Something really bad is about to happen, and we have to stop it."

"Ever since I signed on too this gig, I've been afraid, just not sure of what. I know this ain't just some bunch of big-wigs blowin' off steam. Some bad shit is about to go down." Rodney paused and ran his hand through his hair. "Okay, I can help you get into the amphitheater. They keep waiter uniforms down here. We can dress you up. It's comin' time for dinner service, and it's gonna be crazy busy. I don't think the guards will check your badges. Do you feel lucky?"

"You wouldn't believe the lucky streak we've been on. I hope it holds out a bit longer." David looked at Sarah, checking that she was willing to go on. Looking grim, she nodded toward the door.

Enemy of My Enemy

"Nothing is easier than to denounce the evildoer; nothing is more difficult than to understand him."
– Fyodor Dostoyevsky

Ilona and Abigail finalized their plan. When the time was right, Ilona would go into the labyrinth and release the souls of the children, the sacrifices to Moloch, who were hidden behind the doors guarded by Cerberus. The massive three-headed dog was a formidable obstacle. She would need Contessa's and Constanta's help to keep the beast at bay. The timing was critical. If she released the souls too soon, the queen would know, and Abigail would lose the advantage of surprise. If she were too late, the queen would be too strong.

David's thoughts came close, his body almost tangible, very little separated them. He was trapped, close to being discovered. Abigail shared his determination, but like David, she didn't see a path forwards. Abigail could only push ahead and hope that events would playout in their favor.

Trumpets resounded throughout the castle. The queen summoned her minions to her vision time. Abigail readied herself, focusing on the impending confrontation, pushing aside all doubts, all worries, all nostalgic thoughts. For everyone else in the castle, the trumpets were a gathering call. For her it was a call to battle.

Abigail cracked open the chamber door and saw the men and women from the salon walking to the great hall. When the last of them had passed by, Abigail followed at a distance. Luck was with her. Any plans Eymerich had for confronting her in the countess' former chamber had been diverted by the queen's summons. If he attacked with the strongest demons from the salon, Abigail would be hard-pressed to defeat them all. All pretext gone, he intended to destroy her. He would come at her with all the strength he could muster once the queen's vision time was over. Abigail could not allow him to choose the time and place of their conflict. She had to seize the initiative by attacking first.

She eased open the door to the hall and slipped into the first gallery, hiding herself in the shadows. The other galleries were filled. The courtiers crowded the railings, all in a near frenzy. Many were gyrating between human and demonic forms. A putrid, sulfurous smell filled the chamber. Screeches and shouts echoed in the great hall.

The hall grew silent as the queen entered and descended to the dais. She wore the same shimmering white dress and necklace of glowing red jewels. Her sad Greek chorus of children lined up behind her. The same small boy clutched at her skirt, his piercing black eyes scanning the galleries. The queen stepped forward and raised her arms as if to embrace the transfixed onlookers.

"Come close, my brethren. It is the gathering. The Lilim have awakened. They await us in our forest sanctuary. We must let them be in our presence, feel our touch. They hunger after us. We must feed them. They yearn for our touch. We must caress them. They long for our voice. We must sing to them." The queen's soft, comforting voice filled the hall. The demonic souls strained at the railings, quivering, with an undertone of snarls and muffled cries. Lord Eymerich assumed his demonic appearance. His boyish face was covered with scales, and horns protruded from his forehead.

Abigail had seconds to act. Eymerich would not expect a challenge now. Abigail ran to the top of the stairway as the queen readied herself.

"My queen," Abigail shouted, "you have a traitor in

your midst." Her voice resounded in the chamber and everyone froze. The hall was silent. The queen looked at her, startled, then inquisitive. The demons in the galleries peered over the railings to see who had caused the break in protocol.

"Who are you, and who is this traitor of whom you speak?" The boy poked his head out from behind her and scowled.

"I am Abigail, Lady Abigail." She stood erect, her hands on her hips.

"Ah yes, we remember you. You were most unusual, unexpected as I remember. Lord Eymerich was your teacher, was he not? Why has he not presented you himself?" She glanced around the galleries.

"Because, Your Majesty, Lord Eymerich is the traitor. He schemes against you. He seeks to destroy you and usurp your throne."

The queen returned to the center of the hall with her hands resting on the shoulders of the boy. "Come, my child, tell us of your suspicions."

Abigail ran down the stairs and stood by the dais with the owl statue to her back. "Lord Eymerich has intercepted new arrivals before you've seen them and has hidden them in the labyrinth. He is hoarding their energy in order to challenge you."

"Where is Lord Eymerich? He should be here to address these charges." The queen looked to the gallery.

"I am here, my queen." Lord Eymerich's voice boomed from the top of the stairs. He plodded down the steps, still in his demonic form.

"What say you? Are you guilty of Lady Abigail's accusations?" Eymerich stared at Abigail seething with rage. If not for the queen, he would have been on her in a second.

"This one has her own plots, my queen—"

"What Lady Abigail says is true." A shout came from across the hall. All heads turned in unison to see Jacquis stepping out of the shadows.

The queen pivoted as Jacquis approached. "What Lady Abigail says is true. Please forgive your humble servant, Your Majesty. Lord Eymerich arranged that I would meet him at the entrance to the great hall when I brought new arrivals. If they were strong and their energy pure, Lord Eymerich would take them to a secret place in the labyrinth. There can be only one reason for this; Lord Eymerich means to depose you when his well of power from the captured souls is strong enough."

Lord Eymerich emitted a demonic cry and hurled himself at Jacquis, knocking him to the floor, and digging in his claws. Jacquis did not resist. He lay on the floor with his arms outstretched like a man being crucified, unmoving except for the silent prayers that fell from his lips.

Within moments, Jacquis' body began to fade, losing color, and then become transparent as Eymerich drained his strength. She thought of rescuing Jacquis, but realized that he had planned this. He hadn't resisted Eymerich's attack.

By provoking Eymerich, Jacquis had sacrificed himself, and had forced Eymerich's public confession, thus sealing his fate. Jacquis' sacrifice was also his penitence. Only by allowing himself to be cast into the chaos, to drift forever between realms, could he atone for his sins and rid himself of his last demon, the need for revenge. Jacquis' face became serene as he faded to nothing with a final prayer on his lips.

A gray mist rose from the place where Jacquis had been. The demon Eymerich remained on all fours, still snarling and pawing at the floor as though he wished to pursue Jacquis into the chaos. Then he became silent as the realization that his actions confirmed Jacquis' statements. His snarls turned to low grunts. Finally he stood, his chest heaving with every breath.

"Eymerich, you are one of our greatest servants. You would have ruled with us in the coming times, but your actions have revealed your treachery." The silent children formed a semicircle in front of the queen and the boy.

Eymerich, still in demonic form, raised his arms above his head. "My followers, it is time. It is our time to rule. Time to depose this child and his shill, this marionette called the queen. Focus on me, give me your strength, and let's be rid of them once and for all." Eymerich's voice was not the simpering, babyish tone of his human form. He was pure beast.

Four people in the first gallery stepped forward looking down on him.

"That's all, only four of you." Eymerich shook his fist in the air. "You cowards, you wretched beings. I will have my revenge on you once Anon and the queen are gone." His voice resounded throughout the great hall.

Eymerich turned to face Abigail. "But first, I think it is time you joined Jacquis in the void."

He leapt at her with his arms outstretched reaching for Abigail throat. She materialized a sword in her right hand and plunged it into his chest as he landed. It seemed to have no effect. He remained strong, seemingly unfazed. He whipped around trying to dislodge her.

"You don't understand do you? I am not like the countess. She had her tricks but, in the end, she was a novice in the ways of Gehenna." Eymerich laughed, though he remained impaled on Abigail's sword. He flung her about like a rag doll as she hung on.

Abigail had lost the advantage. Her only hope was to

weaken him quickly. She tried to pull energy from him as she had with the countess. Abigail forced her energy through her sword into Eymerich, searching for the energy within him. Abigail began to pull, but what came was not energy, but crushing emotions.

Guilt shot through her like an icy knife. She saw her mother from Maine. She had been horribly beaten. Her face was bloodied. Abigail saw her mother through Eymerich's eyes. He held her down with his demonic hands and raped her. She screamed, calling out for Abigail to save her. The vision overwhelmed her sight. Abigail experienced his pleasure and her mother's pain at the same time. She was powerless to stop his attack. Abigail felt like she was collapsing in on herself, crumbling under the emotional pain.

"No!" she shouted. *I will not be tricked again.* Eymerich was powerful, but worst of all, he was a master of illusion. Abigail had been searching for energy within him, and he'd sent a vile, crushing vision back.

She shot a burst of white hot energy down her arm, and heard Eymerich scream. The vision vanished. Her head cleared, and she was once again standing with her sword in his chest.

Eymerich looked stunned for an instant, but then his face contorted in rage. He grabbed Abigail with both arms, causing her sword to push into him up to the hilt. His claws dug into her arms. A bolt surge through Abigail and another vision flooded her mind. She saw her mother and father as demons, naked, laughing and dancing over her grave.

"We've killed her, we've killed her. The bitch is dead," they sang over and over again as they danced frenetically atop her grave in the woods. Abigail was prepared this time. She used her own power to obliterate the vision and loosened Eymerich's grip on her. The rage on his face was replaced with wide-eyed fear.

She'd taken his best and he had failed to subdue her. Two can play at this game.

Abigail pondered why this evil man had the face of a small boy, a face and head that appeared too small for his large frame. Eymerich had a deep, malignant hatred of women. This was his flaw, his weakness, his blind spot. Abigail understood now that his appearance reflected his innermost fear. Abigail created her own vision for Eymerich that played on this fear.

She envisioned him as a small, fat little boy, weak and immature, sitting naked, and surrounded by beautiful women who were laughing and ridiculing him. They called him names and bullied him. His emotions crushed his fragile ego. The demon in front of Abigail began to cry and snivel. He felt weak, vulnerable, and insignificant. Eymerich was unprepared, and the vision consumed him. He was completely immersed in the momentary reality Abigail had spun for him. The vision had pierced his most tender and vulnerable spot. He crumbled and Abigail saw her opening.

She pulled his energy with all her might while keeping the vision foremost in his mind. He began to weaken. The loss of power fed his vision of him as a helpless child which further reduced his defenses. The power flowed easily now, without effort, unwittingly helped by Eymerich himself. He began to lose his form and became transparent.

Abigail released the vision she'd placed in his mind. She wanted him to see that she, a woman, had defeated him, and that a woman was about to cast him into the void. Abigail wanted revenge for all the women he had tortured and killed. Rage replaced the child within him, as he realized that he'd been fooled by an illusion. The deceiver himself had been deceived.

Eymerich fell to the floor with her sword still

embedded in his chest. He was almost gone. Abigail felt the last of his energy draining away. He quivered with terror, knowing that in moments he would fall into the void and drift forever.

"Who are you that you could do this to me? You are no mere girl," he gasped.

"I am Abigail, your student." she whispered bending, low speaking into his ear. Abigail released her defenses and let him see into her.

He stared at her in wide-eyed terror.

"Astarte!" he shouted. The name echoed several times throughout the hall as though chanted by a distant chorus. He became still, completely transparent, and finally vanished, leaving behind a residue of gray smoke.

A barrier within her fell, and the memories from thousands of years exploded into Abigail's consciousness.

On the Mountaintop

"A farewell to my shadow is not my death; it's my rebirth in darkness."
– Munia Khan

The memories of a hundred lifetimes washed over Abigail. The demon-filled hall faded, replaced by thousands of images of people she had loved, the mothers who had borne her, the lovers she'd taken, and the battles she'd fought. As quickly as the rush of memories came, the sensation receded like a wave on a gently sloping beach leaving her, Astarte, restored, and whole. She began to breathe again.

She was Astarte, Arcadia's warrior, and the daughter of Eve. She'd fought countless battles, some against men and some against demons, sometimes leading vast armies and others in solitary combat. Throughout it all was her opponent, her nemesis, Anon, the one common thread of her existence. Anon was the reason for Astarte's many lifetimes, and why she never rested in Arcadia. Anon had sired the race of the Lilim. He had fought and schemed since the day of their unnatural mating to destroy the children of Eve, as Astarte had fought to save them.

She was the warrior Ehyeh had shown her. Astarte had reached the far peak that she'd seen in her dream. Behind her, Abigail stood on her distant hilltop, afraid and unsure of herself. Further behind were a hundred other women, some young, some old, some fierce, and some meek, all Astarte in her many lifetimes.

The façade of young Abigail evaporated. Astarte turned to face the queen, who stood looking stoically from the dais. The small boy, no longer clutching her skirts, stood erect by her side, his scowl replaced with a knowing smile. Astarte curtsied to the queen in a low bow and held it waiting for her to speak.

"You have done us a great service, Lady Abigail. You have exposed a traitor in our midst, and sent him into the void."

The queen stepped to the side as the boy moved to the front. "Now, we should drop all pretext and call you by your true name, Astarte." His voice was deep, not that of a boy at all.

He paused, gauging her reaction. Every fiber of her being convulsed as the memories of Anon came to the fore. He was a creature of deception, a prince of lies, never who he appeared to be. This cherubic boy who was never far from the queen's side was her true foe. The queen, as Eymerich had suspected was a shill, a front for the Evil One, the greatest demon of all.

"And I should call you Anon." Astarte remained straight-faced. Anon nodded without breaking eye contact.

Astarte leaped, raising her sword to strike, but before she reached Anon, a flash of energy shot from his hand, striking her and sending her tumbling across the floor. She was stunned and knocked unconscious. When she awoke some time later, her hands and feet had been bound with heavy iron chains. Astarte strained against the chains and they grew tighter. She was weakened, drained of energy. It was all she could do to lift herself from the floor as Anon stood over her laughing. The queen remained in the shadows, surrounded by the dull-eyed children.

"Astarte, you are such a fool. Did you think that image of the farm girl would trick us? We have suspected you since you arrived at court. Our spies told us of your actions. You have done us a service. You kept Eymerich occupied while we completed our plans. It's ironic, but it was your defeat of Eymerich that betrayed you. Only Astarte could have defeated him."

"I have bested you in every battle throughout the

ages. This time will be no different."

"You think so? You are bound with chains made from Gehenna's own substance. The more you resist the stronger they will bind you. I've drained your energy, and the souls you had hidden in the countess's chamber are gone. You have no source to draw power from. I am all-powerful here." Astarte reached out with her thoughts to the chamber. It was empty. But the secret room was not. There were still hundreds of souls there. The deception had worked. Her reserves were intact.

As Anon spoke, his body slowly transformed into that of a tall, muscular man, bare-chested in a dark red silken skirt. His black hair hung to his shoulders. His voice was cold and resolute.

"Your defeat is most satisfying, a special indulgence. One I will savor." His head rolled back as a deep, low growl morphed into laugher. A tinge of doubt passed through her which she allowed to show. She was not powerless, but needed to wait for the right moment. Astarte hoped David would be ready when the time came.

"And you thought your friend Ilona would deprive me of my children guarded by Cerberus." He waved his hand and a guard walked down the stairs. As he approached, Astarte gasped in horror. The guard held Ilona's head on a spike, and flanking her were the heads of the twins, Contessa and Constanta. Most frightening of all was that they were not dead. Their eyes looked at Astarte in full living terror. Ilona's mouth moved in silent warning. Tears ran down her cheeks and dripped on the floor.

Astarte shared Ilona's suffering, and seeing the twins filled her with rage. The torture of innocents was almost more than she could bear. Astarte summoned her will, and was now in complete control. Her three sisters had sacrificed themselves to hide the remaining souls. She would not squander their suffering. Astarte pivoted to face Anon, and made a play at straining at the chains, but then slumped to the floor once more.

"We are on the verge of our greatest triumph. The presence of the children of Eve have prevented me from crossing to the land of the living permanently, but soon, the children of Eve will all be dead. I shall rule the land of the living for eternity." Anon leaned over her.

"But don't worry, Astarte. I do not intend to dispatch you into the void. I want you to witness our final victory, and then I will place your head on a pike beside your friends where you may watch my glorious reign." Anon stood with hands on his hips. He looked down on her with the eyes of a victor. Astarte felt his hatred, a hatred nurtured for centuries. She had always stood in his way. She had always defeated his plans, and would do so again. But then, with one sweep of his hand, a bolt of energy struck her, and everything went black once more.

The Forest of the Lilim

"There comes a stage at which a man would rather die cleanly by a bullet than by the unknown terror of the phantom in the forest."
– Tahir Shah

They found the uniform storeroom and quickly changed into loose black slacks that Sarah called harem pants, sandals, and white tunic shirts with black sashes. David supposed they looked like slaves from ancient Babylon. They followed Rodney through the basement corridor and stopped at the stairs.

"These stairs lead to the waiters' servin' station in the kitchen. Tuck your badges into your shirts. It's against the rules, but most of the wait staff do it so they don't drop their badges in the soup," Rodney explained. "There are video cameras in the kitchen so keep your heads down, don't look at the cameras."

"What do we do when we get there? How will we know where to go?" Sarah's eyes darted between David's and Rodney's.

"Get in that line with the other wait staff, take a tray and load up some dinner servings. Then you follow them to the amphitheater. After you get there, you're on your own. Stay away from the guards, or anyone dressed in black. They won't take kindly to you bein' where you ain't supposed to be." David knew what he meant. He figured the guard they'd tied up in the cell would be found sooner or later.

"Thanks, Rodney. This is more important than you could possibly know. You should get out of here if you can." David grabbed his hand to shake it, and Rodney felt something surge into him. His jaw dropped and his eyes bulged.

"Gosh…" Rodney jerked his hand back and rubbed it. He waved David away with his hand. "You go on now before someone finds us lollygaggin' around."

Sarah and David started up the stairs. "What was that?" she asked.

"I'm not sure. If felt like electricity except slower."

David opened the door into the din of a large kitchen in full swing. The kitchen staff was darting in every direction. He saw a line of waiters on the far side and pulled Sarah toward it.

"Whatever the person in front does, you do the same. There is a camera pointed at the line so hide your face." Sarah nodded. David saw that she was breathing hard.

They each took a tray. The waiter in front of him took eight covered dishes, hoisted the tray onto his shoulder, and hustled out the swinging door. David took four for fear of dropping everything and blowing his cover. He lifted the tray like the other waiters, and walked briskly outside to the forest. He smelled pine needles mixed with a hint of acrid smoke. Music, loud voices, and the sounds of glassware clinking came from beyond the bushes. A woman shrieked, followed by husky male laughter.

"Sounds like a bad frat party," Sarah whispered.

They turned by some bushes and the full vista of the Babylon Woods came into view. They stood at the top of a tiered amphitheater. Each ring was lined with tables filled with boisterous men, and a few women. Everyone was dressed in long multi-colored robes with hats, crowns, and turbans. David supposed the costumes were Byzantine, more or less. A small orchestra beside the stage played Middle Eastern music. In the center of the stage was a colossal owl statue with man-sized flaming cauldrons on either side. The smoke from the cauldrons hung over the clearing. The acrid smell from the flames was like malevolent incense masking the pure scent of the forest.

The scene was a frenzy of drinking, laughing, and dancing. Each table had a small national flag. David recognized many of the world powers: France, Germany, Spain, China, and Japan. The tables toward the back had signs listing the names of major corporations, mostly defense contractors. Judging from the state of the crowd, the drinking had been going on for some time. A few men were walking about unsteadily.

"Oh my God!" Sarah paused as she surveyed the revelers.

"Hey, move it," shouted the waiter behind Sarah. They scurried down the aisle and found a table without food. The people were drunk, talking wildly, and gesturing with their hands. They were oblivious to the plates of food placed in front of them.

One man held up a bottle of wine and waved it at David. He nodded. "Yes, sir, right away." The drunken man turned back to the conversation.

David walked to the waiter's station where beer, wine and liquor were kept. He made a pretext of looking for wine. "David, that's the president of France who asked you for wine." Sarah looked around. "Over there are a group of Germans I've seen on the news. I think that woman is the chancellor."

Young women in similar black harem pants, some bare-breasted or nearly so, were flirting with the men. A waitress at a nearby table screamed. She was being groped by a fat man whose robes had fallen away to reveal his pink rolling flesh. David reached for her hand and yanked her away. The fat man flashed with anger that he'd been denied, but then broke out into laughter, his rolls of flesh jiggling.

"Thanks," said the waitress adjusting her clothing. "They've got these rovin' lap dancers, and the drunks can't tell the difference between us and them. I fuckin' hate this job. I waitress at a truck stop and come here once a year 'cause the money's good, but I ain't comin' back. I don't need this shit." She looked at Sarah. "Watch out for yourself, hon. This is grab-ass central." She took her tray and stalked away.

"David, do you feel something? This place gives me the creeps. I feel waves of coldness washing over me. I'm angry for no reason. I thought of Abe and Louie, about kicking them. Why should I feel like this? I would never hurt the dogs. They're like our children." Her eyebrows knitted together and she shivered.

"Sarah, it's the owl statue."

"Yes" She grabbed his hand for reassurance.

"That's the statue that Abigail showed me. The chalice is here someplace. Queen Lilith will appear on that stage. You're feeling her presence, or at least her residual presence. This place is the nexus of evil on Earth." David looked around. "And by the looks of it, these people are feeling her presence too. They're all drunk, any inhibitions they have are gone, and the queen's proximity is affecting them."

"David, I hate these feeling. I'm repulsed by my own thoughts."

"You need to focus. You're strong-willed. You can resist. These people have been drinking for hours. They've let their guard down. You haven't. Keep focused." David held her hand tightly, hoping she could feel his strength, his resolve, even his excitement at being this close to completing their quest.

Sarah took several deep, gasping breaths, and her face

became placid. Her look of confidence returned. She held up their clasped hands.

"What did you just do? It was like water flowing into my hand and up my arm. I'm not tired anymore. I could run up a mountain right now." She looked at David with her head cocked to one side.

"It's Abigail. I've sensed her presence becoming stronger the closer we came to this place. She's very close now. There is little separating us, almost like we've become one. Her energy flowed through me into you."

Sarah glanced at David with a half-smile and shivered. "If you say so. Is it cold here? I'm chilled."

"No, it's warm, humid. Are you sure you're all right?"

"We'd better get to work before they throw us out." Sarah walked ahead of him looking grim.

David went through the motions of working, but all he could think about was the Lilim. There were hundreds, if not thousands, of Lilim in black uniforms on the grounds. They would launch their plan tonight, and he had no idea how to stop them.

David spent the next few minutes clearing tables and had returned from dropping off a load of dishes when Abigail's thoughts crashed over him. He clutched at his chest, gasped for breath, and fell to his knees. Abigail, and his connection to her, had changed in a blinding flash. Vast energy flowed between them. It was still her but immensely more powerful. She had changed from human to goddess, and her name was Astarte. David saw hundreds of lifetimes and battles flash by like an improbably fast movie. He raised himself to his hands and knees. His body shook as he struggled to manage the psychic connection with this far more powerful being.

David held onto a chair, and took a deep breath. The bond that joined them didn't have a valve. Whatever she felt, he felt. Astarte was accustomed to wielding such energy. He wasn't. Then just as quickly as the torrent began, it subsided. David was now joined to Astarte the goddess. Abigail remained but Astarte outshone her like a candle out shown by the sun.

David looked at his hands in the dim light. They were different. Astarte's hands appeared overlaid on his. Oddly, this made sense, somehow expected. He was moving in unison with her. What had started as a distant emotional longing was now a union, an overlap of thoughts and sensations, two beings entwined.

Astarte stood before the queen and the boy he'd seen in her thoughts, but he wasn't a boy any more. Through Astarte's eyes, he saw a taller, darker, more maleficent figure. Whoever this man-child was, he was immensely old. The evil within him seemed boundless. The boy stepped closer to Astarte, smiled, and then the image disappeared.

David leaned against a tree. He didn't know what this meant or what might happen next. Before he could worry about it, the section captain shouted at him to get moving.

David continued clearing dishes and glasses from the many dinner courses. Much of the food remained uneaten but the drinking continued throughout. David was amazed that more people hadn't passed out.

Coming back from dropping off a load of dishes, David saw Sarah being manhandled by a drunken Brazilian. He had pulled her onto his lap and grabbed her breasts. David gripped him by the shoulder and yelled, "Stop!" Energy shot down his arm. The man's back arched, and he fell forward onto the table unconscious. His fellow Brazilians stared blankly, and then burst out in laughter.

"What did you do to him?" asked Sarah as she

adjusted her clothing.

"I'm not sure. I saw that jackass molesting you. I got angry and something shot down my arm. Boom. He's passed out."

"I don't understand what's happening to you." Sarah looked at him like he'd grown another head. "I guess I shouldn't be surprised, given everything else that's gone on." Her voice was quick and sharp. Her face looked pained.

The forest was completely dark when they'd finished the final clearing, and set out fresh bottles of wine. The sky and surrounding forest were pitch black with no moon or clouds to obscure the stars. The flickering light from the cauldrons danced across the weary, besotted guests. Sarah and David waited with the other servers at the side of the theater. The band stopped playing and a trumpet sounded. The crowd slowly became quiet, focused on the stage as a line of ceremonial guards in costume marched across it.

A spotlight shone on center stage as a tall, naked woman walked on wearing a black bird mask that covered her entire head with only her mouth exposed. Black wings were attached to her shoulders. The boisterous voices and clinking glassware became silent in anticipation, and for the first time David heard the wind in the trees. She raised her arms and scanned the crowd.

"Good evening presidents, prime ministers, cabinet members, captains of industry, and honored guests. Welcome to the opening ceremonies of this year's Babylon Woods retreat, the greatest gathering of global leadership ever held. You are the elite of the world. You are here to spend time with your peers, to relax, and to have some harmless fun reliving the ceremonies of ancient Babylon. We stand here tonight before the statue of Ninurta, the Sumerian god of war and wisdom." The flames in the cauldrons rose. Spotlights shone on the gleaming statue, and its eyes glowed red. A murmur rose from the crowd.

"Before the opening ceremony can continue, we ask an indulgence. Beneath your chairs are boxes; each contains a mask made especially for you. Please retrieve your mask and put it on. If you so desire, you may remove your clothing, but it is not required." The women who'd been flirting with the men earlier were now naked and wearing bird masks similar to the woman on stage. They moved throughout the audience encouraging people and helping them on with their masks. In a few minutes, a thousand black feathered faces faced the stage. Many stood bare-assed.

"Very good. I now give you the leader of the Babylon Woods, the queen's supreme leader on Earth, Falcon." The woman held up her left hand and backed off stage to the right. Accompanied by a trumpet fanfare, a naked man wearing a black bird mask with a golden beak walked on stage. That he was an older man was evidenced by his thin legs and pot belly. He stood in the center of the stage, hands on hips, looking side to side. After a dramatic pause, he spoke.

"Good evening my honored guests. Our presentation will take you back in time, to a time before ancient Babylon, to when the Garden of Eden rested between the nurturing arms of the Tigris and Euphrates rivers. We know this area today as the Fertile Crescent, the very cradle of civilization. Tonight we bring you Adam's first wife, Lilith, now Queen Lilith, the sovereign of Earth. She is all powerful and submits to no man. And we are her loving children." There was a slight murmur at the "loving children" remark, but the audience stood in rapt attention.

"She has waited patiently for five thousand years, and her time is almost at hand. In a matter of hours from now she will be with us. She will walk the earth and live among us. She will reign over the nations." Falcon paused. The audience was silent as though waiting for the punch line to be delivered.

"Bring her on," cried a drunken voice, followed by sporadic laughter which broke the solemnity of the moment. The leaders of the industrial world were becoming a frenzied mob.

"Yes," shouted Falcon. His long full tone was replaced by a harsher, stern voice. "Yes, it is time you met your new queen. It is time for the children of Lilith to arise." The momentary frivolity evaporated as the crowd wondered why the entertainment had unexpectedly turned dark.

"Bring the girl back," cried the same voice as before, but no laughter followed.

Falcon pointed offstage. "Bring out the chalice."

David's heart skipped a beat. He looked at Sarah. Her face was contorted, her fists clutched at her side. Her eyes were laser-focused on the stage.

"Sarah, its here." He could barely contain his excitement. After searching for months, putting their lives on hold, the death of Shlomo, and almost being killed themselves, they'd found the chalice.

But again, Sarah remain inert, her eyebrows furled with a stern, pained looked.

"Are you okay?" David shook her arm.

"Get your hands off me!" she yelled. Her voice was cold, filled with anger. She tried to slap him but he blocked her hand. Whatever had affected the guests had gotten to Sarah. She looked frightened, desperate, like a wounded animal. She ran off into the crowd. David wanted to chase after her but he didn't dare take his eyes from the stage. He couldn't miss his moment.

The orchestra played a quiet processional march.

From the dark edge of the stage came two men dressed in red robes with black sashes around their waists and the requisite bird masks. A pole stretched between then with a gleaming golden box shaped like a house suspended in the middle. The men stopped in front of the statue, placed the box on the stage, and took up positions beside the statue. This was the replacement for the Chiemsee Cauldron they'd seen pictures of in Germany.

The amphitheater was silent except for the crackling fire in the caldrons. Falcon opened the top, and removed a bronze bowl. It was simple with handles on either side. He held it aloft to the audience. The audience rustled, and glasses clinked. The audience was unimpressed, but the black-uniformed Lilim looked on in awe. David was exhilarated. The chalice was exactly as Abigail had shown him. It was deceptively simple, unadorned, almost commonplace. This simple object was the linchpin of Lilith's entire scheme to rule the land of the living, and their key to victory. His first thought was to rush the stage, but there were too many guards. This wasn't the time. He had to maneuver to a better position, and wait for the right moment. But time was his enemy; there was little left.

Falcon placed the chalice on a pedestal in front of the statue. As he removed his hands, the wings on the owl statue moved as though the giant bird were readying for flight. The audience gasped and became silent once more, mesmerized by the events on stage. The men in red took the box away.

Falcon pointed to the right of the stage. "Bring out the canisters." A line of uniformed Lilim carried out nine white foot tall canisters and lined them up on stage.

Falcon faced the statue with his arms outstretched. "Queen Lilith, I summon you. Come and bestow your blessing on us your children. Give us your strength, your power that we may serve you."

The statue's wings opened, spreading across the stage and its eyes glowed red. A woman in the front row shrieked, and number of people ran up the aisles knocking over chairs in panic.

"Come to us, my queen," shouted Falcon, his commanding voice echoing off the trees. He stepped backwards and dropped to one knee.

In midair at eye level in front of the chalice, a sparkling point of light formed in the dark night like a small ball of lightning. It grew slowly at first then quickly formed a circle behind the chalice. A gray swirling mist filled the circle. The crowd was riveted to the stage. The mist cleared, and a tall woman in a radiant white gown glided onto the stage. He'd seen her before through Abigail's eyes. It was the queen. A tall muscular man, bare-chested and wearing a silken skirt, stood behind her, and within the circle a line of children stood in the shadows.

She approached the vice president, touched him, and his body arched as though in pain. She stepped past him and raised her arms to embrace the crowd.

"My children, I am Lilith, your queen." Her body glowed as though lit from the inside. David's view of the stage wavered as though he was looking at a reflection on the water. An energy pulse swept over the amphitheater. The guests and the servers were all transfixed, their eyes fixed on the queen. He'd once been seduced by the mere vision of her, but now he saw only the projection of evil.

David saw Astarte through the circle of light in chains, restrained by two guards. Their eyes met. She saw that his path to the stage was blocked by hundreds of frantic Lilim. He needed her help if he was to get to the chalice. She was ready. David felt her strength like a taught bow ready to be released.

"Come, my children, draw near to your mother." The queen's voice was soft and lilting but yet resounded in the night. Then from out of the woods came lines of people in black uniforms, men and women, old and young, each with the black sun design on their shoulder. A few people from the audience also moved to the front, gathering before the stage and facing the line of guards. Their faces were blissful, adoring, as they all gazed at the apparition on stage.

Falcon remained on one knee with his head bowed as the queen glided, back and forth on stage. The queen stopped beside Falcon and spoke to him. David couldn't hear what they said. He rose and stood beside her.

The queen opened her arms and pulses of white, translucent ribbons shot from her into the assembled Lilim. A collective gasp came from them. They gazed at the queen with complete adoration. All the non-Lilim — guests and wait staff — gave a collective moan, eyes open but unmoving as if stunned. The queen's energy enveloped him, danced on his skin searching for a way in, but the energy he shared with Astarte kept it out. David scanned the crowd. Every face was contorted in rage. He was the only human not under her complete control.

A ribbon of energy wrapped itself around Sarah and then melded with her. David pushed his way through the crowd to her.

"Sarah, are you okay?" He grabbed her by the arms, but her eyes remained fixed on the queen. "Sarah!" David shook her.

She ripped her arms free and backed away.

"Get away from me before I kill you!" she screeched. It wasn't her voice. It was that of some other creature. David backed away horrified. His beloved and every other human were infected by the queen's evil presence. He panicked knowing that Sarah would soon be infected with the plague and be sent to spread it throughout the world.

"My children, it is time to set the great plan in motion." The queen's body glowed in the dark forest.

Victory in Death

"Victory at all costs, victory in spite of all terror, victory however long and hard the road may be; for without victory there is no survival." – Winston S. Churchill

Astarte awoke in front of the owl statue with two guards holding her by her arms. Anon and the queen were readying themselves for the bridge to appear.

"Astarte, you have a great privilege, to witness the beginning of the destruction the children of Eve."

Anon grabbed her chin, digging his fingers into her skin. "You were instrumental in bringing us to this point. It is only fitting that you should witness our triumph."

She grabbed for his neck but feigned weakness as though the shackles were too heavy. Anon saw her weakness and gloated. He pointed to the guards holding pikes with Ilona's, Contessa's, and Constanta's heads.

"When the great plan is launched and the vision time is over, you shall take your place beside your hapless friends."

"Anon, you have never won. In all the centuries we have battled, no matter how much you schemed and deceived, you could never win. It is not in your nature to win, nor in mine to lose. Your vision of victory is an illusion. It will evaporate before your eyes like a mirage in the desert of Negev where we first fought." She raised herself on one arm and searched with her mind for the pure souls hidden in the secret room behind the countess's chamber.

A moment of doubt flashed across Anon's face. He still feared her. He could not deny history, his trail of defeats. His outward confidence resumed, masking any misgivings.

"You are unable to raise your arm against me, never mind stop me. No, Astarte, this time it is you who are vanquished, and your defeat is for eternity." Anon's rant was interrupted by a point of light forming in the center of the hall. Lilith was being summoned.

"Watch now as my great plan is set in motion, and your fate, and that of all the children of Eve, is sealed." Anon quickly took up his place behind Lilith, the master behind the puppet.

Defeat loomed, marching toward Astarte with certain, inevitable strides. Anon was right to feel confident. His plan was in motion, and he believed she was powerless to stop him. In a few minutes, Anon and the Lilim would infect the leaders of the industrial world with a deadly virus, and other Lilim would carry the virus to every corner of every continent. Before anyone was aware, the pandemic would spread throughout the children of Eve.

Anon turned away. Astarte's mind reached out to the hidden souls and a powerful stream of energy flowed into her. The vast room was filled with hundreds of souls. They all stood erect, eyes closed, focused on directing their thoughts, and their energy, to her. In an instant she was renewed, but remained limp in the arms of her captors.

Anon's reserves were not depleted. The souls of all the children sacrificed to Moloch were hidden behind the doors guarded by Cerberus, the three-headed dog. Anon held the advantage both in power and position, but he believed David was powerless, which gave her a small element of surprise. It would have to be enough.

The queen positioned herself in the center of the dais, and the dot of light expanded into the circle creating the bridge. The gray mist within swirled and faded, revealing the Babylon Woods with Falcon standing in the center. A great crowd faced the stage, the black-clad Lilim in front, their faces beaming in expectation.

Falcon dropped to one knee as the queen glided across the boundary with Anon behind her. She stroked Falcon's face with her finger. His back arched, his face grimaced, and he gasped.

The queen and Falcon addressed the hordes of Lilim who pressed the stage and became more frenzied as she spoke. He scanned the audience. David was here. Astarte heard his every thought. Astarte saw what he saw. She felt his heart beating, his breathing. Their eyes met. He was midway up the amphitheater on the far right.

Astarte, the plague is here. It's in the white canisters on front of the stage. The Lilim intend to release it tonight.

He was ready to act but had no path through the crowd. The Lilim would rip him to shreds if he attacked the queen directly. He needed a diversion. Their only hope was to coordinate their attack. Neither of them was strong enough to defeat Anon and the Lilim, but together they had a chance.

David, find a weapon, be ready for my diversion, and destroy the chalice when you see your chance. David nodded and looked around for some type of weapon.

Astarte, what are you going to do? David saw a guard with gun and moved toward him.

I'm going to attack Anon. I hope it will give you the opening you need to fight your way to the stage to destroy the chalice. She shared David's resolve.

A large group of demons from the salon descended the stairs and formed a ring around Astarte. They'd come to extract their revenge for sending Eymerich into the void. Several demons raked their claws over her, sending icy pain shooting through her. She was ready to act, but being surrounded by this knot of revengeful demons prevented her from reaching the bridge.

"Abigail!" A shout filled the hall, and all the demons turned to the figure at the top of the stairs. It was Jacob dressed in his green uniform with his rifle, bayonet affixed, at the ready. The demons froze, uncertain who this man was, his strength, or his intent.

"It is I, Tammuz. Make ready. Look for your opening!" he shouted, and sprinted down the stairs with a mighty battle cry. Astarte's beloved charged at the demons surrounding her. Their last encounter had spurred his memory, and he'd recovered his true nature. He was entering into battle with her once again.

He reached the bottom of the stairs and tore into the demons. Shrieks rose, and the demons staggered backwards tumbling over each other. Tammuz leaped onto a pile of demons clubbing and stabbing. They were stunned by the ferocity of his attack. He had given her the moment she needed.

Astarte summoned all her courage. Her sword materialized in her hand, and she leaped to her feet, dissolving the iron shackles. Astarte spun, her sword slicing through the two guards who held her. She charged to the shimmering bridge and bounded across, feeling a cold shiver as she crossed between realms, and landed on the stage. A gasp arose from the Lilim as Astarte appeared. She sprinted toward Anon, and as he turned to face her, she plunged her sword into him. He gaped in amazement at the sword protruding from his chest.

She seized the initiative and immediately tried to weaken him, to drain his energy as she had with Eymerich and the countess, but nothing flowed. He was immensely strong and easily resisted. He looked at her, smiling and making no attempt to withdraw the sword.

Anon's quiet chuckle grew into a throaty laugh. His

shape began to morph. Horns grew as his face change to that of a bull. He quickly became taller, pulling her upwards as she held fast to the sword. In a matter of moments, Anon had transformed into Moloch with Astarte dangling from her sword. On his chest was a medallion with the image of the black sun attached with leather straps. His deep resonant laugh echoed throughout the dark forest. He grabbed the sword and tossed her like a rag doll onto the stage. Pain erupted in Astarte's arms and back as she experienced the solid reality of the land of the living. A giant sword materialized in Moloch's hand and he swung it over his head, arching it toward her.

The End of the Game

"Courage is being scared to death, but saddling up anyway."
– John Wayne

David's attention was focused on the stage. The queen smiled, appearing satisfied with the audience's attention. She approached the vice president and stroked the side of his face. His body quivered. He looked up at her and she gestured to the crowd. He rose and faced the audience, naked wearing his bird mask, and spoke. This was the launch of the attack.

"My brothers and sisters. Tonight marks the beginning of the reign of Queen Lilith and the destruction of the children of Eve. What you see before you is the instrument of our victory. In the white containers is the virus that will kill every child of Eve, leaving the way open for our mother, our Queen Lilith to rule the land of the living. The couriers you see before you will leave tonight to carry the virus to every corner of the earth. Our guests will be the vanguard of our attack, taking the virus into the highest levels of government in the developed world. Chaos will begin at the top, effective response will be impossible. Our brothers and sisters in our global media empire will spread fear as the virus takes hold. Panic will rule in the streets and hasten our final victory."

A chant of "Lilith, Lilith, Lilith!" arose from the Lilim in the aisles and forest. They were excited to the point of hysteria.

David looked to Astarte through the glowing circle.

David, find a weapon; be ready for my attack.

She intended to attack the man who accompanied the queen. He was Anon, the true evil behind the plan. The queen was nothing, a diversion. He looked around rapidly for any kind of weapon. A guard standing at the edge of the forest had an assault rifle with a grenade launcher slung beneath the barrel, a formidable weapon. As he'd learned in Germany, the Lilim were nothing if not well-armed. This guard was caught up in the frenzy of the moment. David maneuvered behind him, grabbed a bottle of Champagne and, with one swift blow, launched the guard into dreamland and took his rifle.

Connelly stepped back and bowed to the queen. "We await your benediction and command."

The queen spoke, "Anon, give the command to launch the great liberation of the Lilim that your progeny may rule now and forever more." She backed away and the man took center stage. He looked entirely unimpressive, diminutive below the massive statue.

In a blur, Astarte bounded through the circle and sprinted toward Anon. The Lilim around the stage shrunk back screaming and shouting. Two canisters were knocked over in the pandemonium. He turned just as she plunged her sword through his chest.

Anon gaped at the sword, paused, and then looked up at Astarte chuckling. As his laughter grew louder, he began to change shape. His face elongated into the shape of a bull with large horns sprouting from his forehead. He grew taller than the owl statue pulling Astarte from her feet and leaving her dangling from the hilt of her sword. His legs became goat-like with cloven hoofs. It was Moloch. David had seen drawing of him when they'd researched their trip. A medallion with the symbol of the black sun was strapped to his chest.

He grabbed Astarte and threw her rolling across the stage. A giant sword appeared in Moloch's hand and he slowly swung it over his head and struck at the stage where

Astarte lay. In the last instant, she rolled and jumped to her feet. Moloch's sword crashed into the stage cracking the stones.

Astarte charged at him time after time striking and landing blows. She looked like a mouse attacking King Kong dashing in and out. Moloch seemed slow and ungainly. His giant sword crashed into the stone stage, creating holes and sending shards into the onlookers, but never landing a blow. Moloch roared in frustration, becoming more agitated each time Astarte stung him.

But sting was all she could do. Moloch was immensely strong, and despite his ponderous movements, he defended himself well. And he never moved far from the chalice, never allowed Astarte a clear path. It was his sole weakness. Astarte paused, looking winded and seeming unsure of her next move.

David's attention was riveted on the combat playing out on the stage when someone struck him on his head from behind. He fell and the world went blurry. Someone ripped open his shirt. His eyes focused. It was Sarah, her eyes were crazed. She tore at the case containing the photograph of Abigail David kept in a packet strung around his neck. She ripped it open and ran toward the stage with the photograph in her hand, knocking aside spectators as she went.

"Sarah, come back, come back!" David screamed as he struggled to his feet. "What are you doing?" He stumbled toward the stage trying to clear his vision. Sarah continued to elbow her way to the stage, pushing the uniformed Lilim aside. They were too focused on the battle playing out on stage to stop her. She rushed up the side stairs. A guard tried to stop her but she struck him and ran to Moloch. She knelt and held the photograph aloft.

"Sarah, don't do it, don't!" David screamed in a

desperate plea. The Lilim surrounding David looked surprised, not sure who he was or what Sarah was doing. Moloch raised his fist to strike her when he noticed she offered him something. He took the photograph from her. It looked like a postage stamp in his gnarled hand. Sarah knelt on one knee with her head bowed and arms outstretched.

Moloch studied the photograph and threw his head back with a load roar and snort.

"Astarte, I would have preferred your head on a pike, but I grow weary of this play, and the great plan awaits us. You are of no consequence now. Be gone with you." His voice carried throughout the amphitheater. He threw the picture into a flaming cauldron.

David immediately dropped to his knees, feeling as though a giant hand had reached inside of him and torn out his heart and lungs. He fell forward onto his hands gasping, reeling in pain. An overwhelming sense of fatigue swept through him. The strength and courage from his connection with Abigail, now Astarte, had vanished. David heard a roar from the stage and looked to see what had happened. He pushed himself to his knees and stood on unsure legs.

Astarte was gone. She'd disappeared from the stage and disappeared from his mind. He searched his thoughts for her, but she had vanished, along with her strength. Ever since they'd met in the forest those many months ago, his link with her had sustained him. He had forgotten where he left off and she began. Drawing on her courage had allowed him to pursue the chalice to the very heart of evil on earth.

A minute ago, he witnessed Moloch in the flesh, and felt no fear. His only thought was how to attack.

Now he was terrified. He faced the greatest demon of all and was surrounded by his minions. Panic closed his throat, and he looked around for any escape. In losing Astarte, he'd lost her courage as well. Now, it was only

David, alone, frightened and scatterbrained.

From the stage came the booming voice of Moloch. "My children, I am Anon your father. Your mother, Lilith came to me centuries ago after she refused to submit to Adam. We mated and you are the results. For centuries the Lilim have struggle to achieve their rightful rule over the land of the living. Tonight the restoration of our rule will begin. Nothing can stop us now. My nemesis, Astarte, is gone. None stand in our way." A great cheer went up from the Lilim. Moloch stood on stage, hands on hips, basking in the adoration.

Hearing Moloch's voice filled David with rage. He couldn't let him succeed. For once in his life, he needed to face a challenge. To try when there was no hope of success. His foe was as big as a house and possessed all the evil in the universe. He and his children were threatening to kill everyone he loved, to destroy everything he held dear. With rage came the will to fight. It was a fight David doubted he could win. It was a million to one shot, but he'd take the bet.

David shook his head and took a deep breath. The Lilim were still cheering the monster on stage. He was at least a hundred feet from the stage, and his way forward was blocked by black-uniformed Lilim. He had to clear the way to the stage to get a shot at the chalice.

David picked up the assault weapon he'd liberated from the guard and yanked on the grenade launcher leaver positioning a large round shell in the chamber. He held it to his shoulder and fired at a tree adjacent to the stage. The kick sent him backwards and hurt like hell, but it did the trick. The shell exploded on the tree, showering the Lilim with debris. The cheering turned to screams. The tall pine wavered and then fell across the Lilim gathered in front of the stage. Those not crushed by the tree scattered. Smoke drifted across the stage.

That worked well. David fired again at a stand of trees on the opposite side. Another tree exploded. Wood splinters wounded a number of guards, and the tree toppled onto the crowd, again pinning more Lilim. Shots rang out and whizzed by his head. A guard behind David's had seen his second shot. David flipped off the safety, pulled back the bolt and pulled the trigger. The burst cut into the guard and he went down.

Confusion reigned. The Lilim raced in all direction. The VIP guests remained fixated on Moloch, unmoving and unaware of the chaos unfolding around them. The way to the stage was partially cleared. David fired at the ground as he ran toward the stage. The Lilim in his path fell as the bullets tore into their legs. On stage, Moloch turned toward the gun fire. David was twenty feet away when Moloch held out his arm and a bolt of lightning shot out. David jumped to the side and the bolt struck the ground, cutting down a row of Lilim with shards of rocks.

David fired a grenade directly at Moloch which exploded dead center on his chest. The black sun medallion shattered and the leather straps fell away. Moloch staggered back one step. He was unhurt, and became even more enraged, if that was possible.

David jumped on stage within ten feet of the chalice. He pulled the level on the grenade launcher moving another shell into the barrel. As he raised it to fire, the vice president jumped in front of David. His rage-filled eyes gleamed through his mask. David took a step toward him and raised his rifle. But before he could pull the trigger, he saw Moloch swing his sword in a wide arc toward him. David dropped and rolled off the stage. He looked up and saw Falcon's head, still wearing the bird mask, fly into the crowd. His headless body wavered and collapsed.

Moloch shot another bolt of energy at David who

jumped to one side. The bolt struck the stone stages and the explosion killed several Lilim. David fired again into the feet of the Lilim to the right and another batch went down with shrieks and blood. He needed to get a line of sight to the chalice. Moloch lumbered to the other side of the stage to get a clear swing at him. David jumped on the fallen tree and ran up its trunk looking for a shot; a bad idea. Bullets tore into the tree by his feet and several Lilim close to him dropped in pools of blood. A bullet struck him in the calf. David fell off the tree and landed on the bodies of black-uniformed victims. Pain radiated up his leg.

David turned and saw the man who'd shot him. He was short with a thin mustache, dressed in a suit with a bright pink tie. His face was wild with rage. David was pretty sure he was cursing him in French. He struggled frantically to reload his assault rifle. David leveled his gun at him and fired. Three red dots appeared on his shirt beneath his pink tie, and he flew backwards.

David's wound burned like fire, and there was some blood, but his leg still worked. He turned to the stage. He had a clear shot. He raised the rifle with his finger on the trigger of the grenade launcher. Then Sarah jumped in front of the chalice. She'd seen him maneuvering for the shot and had placed her herself between David and the chalice. Her face was wild with anger. If she was any closer she would have ripped his lungs out. David was frozen. Part of him wanted to fire knowing the explosion would likely destroy the chalice but also kill the person he loved most in the world. His momentary indecision cost him. The guards with the black sun insignia surrounded him with assault rifles trained on him. David glanced up. Moloch snorted through his great bull nose, and roared. His pleasure was obvious. He appeared to revel in David's defeat caused by not killing the woman he loved.

David couldn't fire at the chalice without killing

Sarah. Firing at Moloch had done nothing. Firing at the owl statue would likely kill Sarah as well. Then it came to him, he had one shot. A shot foretold over a hundred year ago in the Nadeau letter, *look to the owl in the window.* David didn't know if this shot would do anything. He didn't know if his target was real or an illusion, or if the grenade would find its mark. In so many ways, it was a shot in the dark—a shot between realms.

In the instant before he fired, David wondered if he'd feel the bullets ripping through his body as the Lilim fired. Then he heard a loud explosion behind him. The guards all turned in unison toward the sound, and David saw his moment. He fired through the circle of light that marked the boundary between realms at the matching owl statue on the other side. He expected to die, but no one fired. They all watched together as the grenade shot through the boundary. The image of the other owl statue wavered as the shell exploded dead center on the matching statue.

Immediately, Moloch arched his back with a deafening roar sounding as though it had erupted from his very core. Through the bridge David saw a bright red glow spreading out from the center of the owl statue. A fissure revealing a red glow appeared on the matching owl statue on stage in the Babylon Woods. More cracks appeared, and the statue began to break apart. Everyone on stage, Sarah included, ran to avoid the falling pieces. Moloch became more frantic. His roars became high pitched screams. He kicked a flaming cauldron, sending it flying off the stage to where the Lilim in red were huddled and setting several of them on fire. They ran screaming in flames into the forest, lighting the trees from below. Moloch stepped toward the chalice. David locked his sights on it and fired another grenade. The explosion sent the chalice flying high into the darkness, and the blast knocked him down. When David cleared his head and looked up at the stage, the smoke drifted away. The portal to the other realm, the queen, and Moloch had vanished. The Lilim in black lay unconscious at his feet.

David saw Sarah passed out on the edge of the stage and hobbled up the steps to where she lay. He hoisted her over his shoulder and limped toward the back of the amphitheater where he set her in a chair and looked for injuries. There were none. Her head rolled and she moaned softly. On stage, pieces of the owl statue continued to fall. A hush settled over the forest punctuated by the low cries of the wounded. David took a deep breath and realized that the atmosphere of the place had changed. Since the day they'd entered the Babylon Woods, he'd had an unsettled anger, almost a touch of madness. He'd resisted this pernicious influence with the help of Astarte's energy. Sarah and the assembled world leaders had no such help. They'd been overcome by Anon's presence. Now his presence and the invisible evil mist that had covered the Babylon Woods had vanished.

The guests, who had stood like statues while the battle with Moloch raged, began to recover. Voices came to life, quietly at first, then louder as reality became apparent. David heard shouting in every language as the delegations began to flee to the exits. The Lilim in their black uniforms looked stunned. The Lilim guards had dropped their weapons and wandered about aimlessly as though they'd just awoken, not knowing where they were, which was probably close to the truth. Without Anon, the Lilim had become dormant.

Sarah came around.

"David?" She took his hand. "What happened? My head's all foggy. I feel like I had a bad dream." She met his eyes. "Was it a dream? Did I hit you?"

"Well actually you did give me quite a whack, but I'm

fine. How do you feel?" He felt her forehead more out of instinct than anything.

"I'm good, I think. I feel like I can breathe again." David stroked her head. His eyes welled up with relief.

The smoke cleared on the stage. Chunks of the owl statue were scattered about; only the feet remained. Many Lilim lay dead or wounded. Vice President Connelly's headless body lay amid the rubble. The small pedestal was shattered. There was no sign of the chalice. David thought of going to look for it, to make sure it had been destroyed, but he didn't want to leave Sarah. He sat next to her and put his arm around her. She started to cry as he held her. It was over. They'd won. They'd stopped Anon's plan to destroy the children of Eve. The evil that had been invading their world was gone. He sensed its absence. Before, the woods had appeared dark and foreboding, a place where pain and suffering reigned. Now the natural beauty of the forest shone through.

Rodney emerged out of the forest and put his hand on David's shoulder. "Are you okay? Nobody hurt?"

"We're okay I think, banged up a bit, lump on my head, a small gunshot wound. Otherwise fine," David said. He looked at Rodney closely. "I thought you were leaving."

"I was until you shook my hand. I don't know what that was, but a whole lot of pictures flashed through my mind. I couldn't put it all together but I knew you was fightin' some real bad hombres, and you might need some help, so I stuck around." Rodney folded his arms across his chest and raised his chin. "So, did you like my little diversion? You looked like you was in a tight spot." He grinned.

"Was that you? What did you do?" David asked.

'Well, when I saw you was trying to get a shot off but

there was too many of the guards running toward you, I took some cans of Sterno and put them in a microwave, punched thirty seconds, and ducked. I saw someone do it in a movie, made a hell of an explosion. I always wanted to try it and see if it worked. I guess it does."

A group of armed men ran into the amphitheater. A soldier looked at David and spoke into a microphone strapped to his throat. "We have the Austins. Canisters in sight." He signaled and other soldiers formed a circle around them with their guns at the ready. A squad of men in moon suits rushed in and began gathering the white canisters and placing each in a drum-like container.

The soldiers guarding them stepped aside as Miss Vindex entered the circle. She wore the same combat uniform as the soldiers minus the assault rifles, but with a handgun on her hip. As she approached, David stood still clinging to Sarah's hand.

"You've had a busy night, Mr. Austin." She looked at the hazmat team securing the virus. David heard voices crackling in her ear piece.

"I guess I did. It's all kind of a blur really."

"What was it you fired at? We were too far away to make out your target. To us it looked like you had no good targets unless you wanted to kill Dr. Austin."

"I fired at the owl statue I saw through the bridge. It was my only shot."

Sarah crushed his hand in that familiar way she always did. "David," she asked, her voice trembling, "were you going to kill me?"

"No, honey, you were in the way and I had to find something else to shoot at."

She rolled her eyes. "Always the impulsive one, even now with the fate of the world hanging by a thread."

"Dr. Austin. What you called an impulse, I would call battle instinct. Your husband was incredibly brave facing overwhelming odds. He made a split-second decision that saved you and most life on earth. I'll go with his instinct any day of the week." Miss Vindex nodded to David, high praise from her, and an acknowledgement of a job well done.

Sarah looked up at David, her mouth agape, and then smiled and patted David's hand.

"That's my husband, Miss Vindex. He's quite a guy."

Home

"A birth is not really a beginning. Our lives at the start are not really our own but only the continuation of someone else's story."
– Diane Setterfield

David sat at the counter at Uncle Moe's Diner savoring eggs over easy, sausage, home fries, and whole wheat toast. The breakfast was simple, normal, and unremarkable in every way. It was pure joy. Every mouthful told him he was home.

"Hey Austin, ain't seen you around. Where ya been? Outta town job?" It was Roland Labonte, sitting at the far end wearing his old camo jacket and grease-stained NASCAR cap. David had grown up with him, gone to grade school and high school with him. Roland had been a loudmouth ever since first grade. Nothing had changed.

David laughed inside. Yes, you could say he'd been doing an out of town job. "My wife went on sabbatical and I tagged along."

"Sabbatical, ain't that when you get paid for doin' nothin'? Shit, I want me a friggin' sabbatical." Roland laughed at his own joke and looked around to see if anyone else thought he was funny.

"You gotta get yourself a real job, something important that a man should be doin', not shaggin' around after yer missus." Part of David wanted to smack him, but he let it pass. He'd saved the world, and no one except Sarah and the invisible members of the Brotherhood would ever know. He'd made his peace with it.

"Yeah, you're probably right, Roland, and I think you could use a sabbatical yourself. We all think you could." The regulars in the café chuckled. Roland joined in but seemed uncertain about what was funny. David paid up, leaving

Rosy a nice tip for always keeping his coffee topped up.

It had been a year since the events in the Babylon Woods. At the time, a news story reported the death of Vice President Connelly of a heart attack while hosting his annual summit in Idaho. He had been buried in an unusually quiet ceremony, no honor guard, no caissons rolling down Pennsylvania Avenue. There would be no future Babylon Woods summits.

They'd been whisked away by Miss Vindex and flown to Portland Maine in the Brotherhood's jet, with Kimie attending to their needs. A limo took them home. When they arrived, their house was lit up. There was food in the refrigerator, and Abe and Louie greeted them at the door. Their bank account had been replenished with enough funds to carry them for a year. There was a letter on the counter from Sarah's dean saying that her absence had been explained by a State Department official and her job would be waiting for her next semester. The college had graciously increased her leave when she'd asked for a maternity extension. They never heard from Miss Vindex or the Brotherhood again. David missed Shlomo.

He walked in the house, and Abe and Louie greeted him with snorts and wiggling rumps. Sarah rested on the couch nursing their six-month-old baby girl. With her on the couch were Sarah's friend, Betty, and her baby boy, Jacob. They'd met in Lamaze class and had their babies two days apart. Despite being only six months old, the babies were best friends. They napped together, played together, and became fussy when Jacob left for the day.

"How's Abigail? Hungry?"

"She is the feistiest little thing. Knows what she wants and when she wants it. She eats like a stevedore. She's going to be one strong-willed little girl. You're going to have your hands full with her." Sarah looked radiant.

"You know what I can't figure out is where she got those gray-blue eyes. Neither of us have blue eyes in our families."

Ehyeh

"I thought I had won, but my folly was that the game had not ended." –
Astarte

Panya sat on the cushion in the dark forest with the stars and
galaxies swirling overhead. He placed his hands on the stone
pyramid and the cold flame rose creating an intricate dance.
He heard the voices from millions of worlds rise and declare
their existence: "I'm here. I exist. Why am I here? Why am I
alone?" The cry in the night was always the same. Panya
never answered.

Someone approached. Panya changed shape. Ehyeh
now sat on the cushion, wearing only her grass skirt. Her
fingers danced with the flame as the visitor came into view.

"Mother. It's Anon, your son."

"Yes, Anon, come sit with me and watch the stars."
The man sat across from her facing the pyramid.

"Mother, I'm angry with you. We've struggled
against you since the first stars were born from clouds of
dust. I always lose and you will not tell me why."

"I'm sorry, Anon, but you did well this time. You
took Astarte by surprise and you almost won."

"Yes I did, but Astarte cheated."

'Ah, yes, the man. You didn't expect the man. He was
flawed and you dismissed him, but his heart was pure. That
was your mistake."

"Tell me how to win," Anon demanded.

"I cannot. You must learn for yourself. All the souls
you had trapped in Gehenna have been released. All those
you hurt have been restored. The castle you built over the
mouth of the labyrinth is gone. The Owari game board has

been cleared. Would you like to begin again?"

Anon stood and started for the forest. He stopped and looked over his shoulder at his mother. "I will win this time." He disappeared into the darkness to begin the game anew. Ehyeh was pleased. For souls to grow stronger, they must be tested by evil. Anon's purpose was to be that test; by resisting evil the good grew stronger. Souls could not reach Arcadia without him.

Ehyeh placed her hands beside the base of the pyramid, then raised them over her head pulling a sparkling flame to the heavens. A new galaxy came into existence, and she listened for the songs.

References

Arcadia

https://en.wikipedia.org/wiki/Arcadia_(utopia)

Arcadia (Greek: Ἀρκαδία) refers to a vision of pastoralism and harmony with nature. The term is derived from the Greek province of the same name which dates to antiquity; the province's mountainous topography and sparse population of pastoralists later caused the word Arcadia to develop into a poetic byword for an idyllic vision of unspoiled wilderness. Arcadia is associated with bountiful natural splendor, harmony, and is often inhabited by shepherds. The concept also figures in Renaissance mythology. Commonly thought of as being in line with Utopian ideals, Arcadia differs from that tradition in that it is more often specifically regarded as unattainable. Furthermore, it is seen as a lost, Edenic form of life, contrasting to the progressive nature of Utopian desires.

Astarte

https://en.wikipedia.org/wiki/Astarte

Astarte (Ancient Greek: Ἀστάρτη, "Astártē") is the Greek name of the Mesopotamian (i.e. Assyrian, Akkadian, Babylonian) Semitic goddess Ishtar known throughout the Near East and Eastern Mediterranean from the early Bronze Age to Classical times. It is one of a number of names associated with the chief goddess or female divinity of those peoples.[1] She is found as Ugaritic ('ṯtrt, "'Aṯtart" or "'Athtart"); in Phoenician as ('štrt, "Ashtart"); in Hebrew עשתרת (Ashtoret, singular, or Ashtarot, plural); and appears originally in Akkadian, the grammatically masculine name of the goddess Ishtar; the form Astartu is used to describe her age.[2] The name appears also in Etruscan as Uni-Astre (Pyrgi Tablets), Ishtar or Ashtart.

Elizabeth Bathory

Countess Elizabeth Báthory de Ecsed (*Báthory Erzsébet* in Hungarian; 7 August 1560 – 21 August 1614) was a countess from the renowned Báthory family of nobility in the Kingdom of Hungary. She has been labelled the most prolific female serial killer in history, though the precise number of her victims is debated. Báthory and four collaborators were accused of torturing and killing hundreds of girls between 1585 and 1610.[2] The highest number of victims cited during Báthory's trial was 650. However, this number comes from the claim by a woman named Susannah that Jacob Szilvássy, Countess Báthory's court official, had seen the figure in one of Báthory's private books. The book was never revealed, and Szilvássy never mentioned it in his testimony.[3] Despite the evidence against Elizabeth, her family's influence kept her from facing trial. She was imprisoned in December 1610 within Csejte Castle, Upper Hungary, now in Slovakia, where she remained immured in a set of rooms until her death four years later.

Baal Shem

https://en.wikipedia.org/wiki/Baal_Shem

Baal Shem (Hebrew plural: Baalei Shem) in Hebrew meaning "Master of the Name", refers to a historical Jewish occupation of certain kabbalistic rabbis with knowledge of using names of God in Judaism for practical kabbalah healing, miracles, exorcism and blessing. The unofficial title was given by others who recognized or benefited from the Baal Shem's ability to perform wondrous deeds, and emerged in the Middle Ages, continuing until the early-Modern era. Baal Shem were seen as miracle workers who could bring about cures and healing, as well having mystical powers to foresee or interpret events and personalities. They were considered to have a "direct line" to Heaven evoking God's mercies and compassion on suffering human beings. In Jewish society, the practical theurgic role of Baalei Shem among the common folk was one mystical institution, contrasted with the more theosophical and ecstatic Kabbalistic study circles, who were isolated from the populace. The Baal Shem, the communal Maggid preacher, and the Mokhiakh preacher of penitence were seen as lower level unofficial Jewish intelligentsia, below contract Rabbis and study Kabbalists.

Black Sun

https://en.wikipedia.org/wiki/Black_Sun_(occult_symb ol)

The term Black Sun (German *Schwarze Sonne*), also referred to as the *Sonnenrad* (German for "Sun Wheel"), is a symbol ofesoteric and occult significance. Its design is based on a sun wheel mosaic incorporated into a floor of Wewelsburg Castle during the Nazi era. Today, it may also be used in occult currents of Germanic neopaganism, and in Irminenschaft or Armanenschaft-inspired esotericism—but not necessarily in a racial or neo-Nazi context. Despite its contemporary use, the Black Sun had not been identified with the ornament in Wewelsburg before 1991, although it had been discussed as an esoteric concept in neo-Nazi circles since the 1950s

Bobovers

https://en.wikipedia.org/wiki/Bobov_(Hasidic_dynasty)

Bobov, (or **Bobover Hasidism**) (באבוב חסידות) is an Hasidic community within Haredi Judaism originating in Bobowa, Galicia in Southern Poland and now headquartered in the neighborhood of Borough Park in Brooklyn, New York. Bobov has branches in the Williamsburg section of Brooklyn; Monsey, New York; Montreal; Toronto; Antwerp and London. In Israel, Bobov has large branches in Jerusalem, Bnei Brak, Ashdod, the settlement of Betar Illit and an enclave *Kiryath Bobov* in Bat Yam.

Bohemian Grove

https://en.wikipedia.org/wiki/Bohemian_Grove

Since the founding of the club, the Bohemian Grove's mascot has been an owl, symbolizing knowledge. A 40-foot (12 m) hollow owl statue made of concrete over steel supports stands at the head of the lake in the Grove; this Owl Shrine was designed by sculptor and two-time club president **Haig Patigian**, and built in the 1920s. Since 1929, the Owl Shrine has served as the backdrop of the yearly *Cremation of Care* ceremony.]

Catharism

https://en.wikipedia.org/wiki/Catharism

**Catharism** from the Greek, "the pure [ones]") was a **Christian dualist** movement that thrived in some areas of **Southern Europe**, particularly **northern Italy** and **southern France**, between the 12th and 14th centuries. Cathar beliefs varied between communities because Catharism was initially taught by **ascetic priests** who had set few guidelines. The Cathars were a direct challenge to the **Catholic Church**, which denounced its practices and dismissed it outright as "the Church of Satan".

Chalice

Bronze Age Chalice

Chiemsee Cauldron

The Chiemsee Cauldron was discovered in 2001 by a local diver at the bottom of Lake Chiemsee, about 200m from the shore near Arlaching, Chieming municipality. It was initially suspected to be some 2,000 years old, judging by its Celtic-style decoration and its similarity to the Gundestrup cauldron. However, when the artifact was passed along to Ludwig Wamser of the Bavarian State Archaeological Collection to be analyzed, it was identified as a 20th-century creation, possibly made during the Nazi era. This seemed to be confirmed by a witness; the senior director of the Munich jeweller's company Theodor Heiden stated that the company's goldsmith, Alfred Notz, before his death in the 1960s, had told him about a "golden cauldron weighing more than 10 kg, with a figurative ornament and manufactured by means of the paddle and anvil technique" which had been manufactured in Heiden's workshop between 1925 and 1939.

China, Maine

https://en.wikipedia.org/wiki/China,_Maine

China is a town in **Kennebec** County, Maine, United States. The population was 4,328 at the 2010 census. China is included in the **Augusta**, Maine micropolitan New England City and Town Area.

Ehyeh

The word *Ehyeh* is used a total of 43 places in the Hebrew Bible, where it is often translated as "I will be" — as is the case for its first occurrence, in Genesis 26:3 — or "I shall be," as is the case for its final occurrence in Zechariah 8:8. Used by God to identify himself in the Burning Bush, the importance placed on the phrase, as it is, stems from the Hebrew conception of monotheism that God exists by himself for himself, and is the uncreated Creator who is independent of any concept, force, or entity; therefore "I am who I am" (ongoing)

Gehenna

Gehenna, Gehinnom (Rabbinical Hebrew: גהנם/גהנום)

and Yiddish Gehinnam, are terms derived from a place outside ancient Jerusalem known in the Hebrew Bible as the Valley of the Son of Hinnom (Hebrew: ‎גֵּיא בֶן־הִנֹּם‎ or ‎גיא הינום-בן‎); one of the two principal valleys surrounding the Old City.

In the Hebrew Bible, the site was initially where apostate Israelites and followers of various Ba'als and other Canaanite gods, including Moloch (or Molech), sacrificed their children by fire. Thereafter it was deemed to be cursed.

Lilith

https://en.wikipedia.org/wiki/Lilith

In Jewish folklore, from the 8th–10th century *Alphabet of Ben Sira* onwards, Lilith becomes **Adam's first wife**, who was created at the same time (**Rosh Hashanah**) and from the same earth as Adam. This contrasts with **Eve**, who was created from one of Adam's ribs. The legend was greatly developed during the **Middle Ages**, in the tradition of **Aggadic midrashim**, the **Zohar**, and **Jewish mysticism**. For example, in the 13th century writings of Rabbi Isaac ben Jacob ha-Cohen, Lilith left Adam after she refused to become subservient to him and then would not return to the **Garden of Eden** after she coupled with the archangel Samael. The resulting Lilith legend is still commonly used as source material in modern Western culture, literature, occultism, fantasy, and horror.

Lilim

http://www.themystica.com/mystica/articles/l/lilim.htm
l

Lilim are the children of Lilith according to Jewish folklore and Kabbalistic teachings

Moloch

http://bibletruthsandprophecies.com/index.php?title=Moloch

Moloch, also known as Molech, Molekh, Molok, Molek, Melek, Molock, Moloc, Melech, Milcom, or Molcom, a

Semitic root meaning "king") is the name of an ancient Ammonite god. Moloch worship was practiced by the Canaanites, Phoenicians, and related cultures in North Africa and the Levant.

As a god worshiped by the Phoenicians and Canaanites, Moloch had associations with a particular kind of propitiatory child sacrifice by parents. Moloch figures in the Book of Deuteronomy and in the Book of Leviticus as a form of idolatry (Leviticus 18:21: "And thou shalt not let any of thy seed pass through the fire to Moloch"). In the Old Testament, Gehenna was a valley by Jerusalem, where apostate Israelites and followers of various Baalim and Canaanite gods, including Moloch, sacrificed their children by fire.

Moloch has been used figuratively in English literature from John Milton's Paradise Lost (1667) to Allen Ginsberg's "Howl" (1955), to refer to a person or thing demanding or requiring a very costly sacrifice.

Momento Mori

https://en.wikipedia.org/wiki/Memento_mori

Memento mori (Latin: "remember that you must die") is the medieval Latin theory and practice of reflection on mortality, especially as a means of considering the vanity of earthly life and the transient nature of all earthly goods and pursuits. It is related to the *ars moriendi* ("The Art of Dying") and related literature.*Memento mori* has been an important part of ascetic disciplines as a means of perfecting the character, by cultivating detachment and other virtues, and turning the attention towards the immortality of the soul and the afterlife

Nazi Symbolism

https://en.wikipedia.org/wiki/Nazi_symbolism

The fascination that runes seem to have exerted on the Nazis can be traced to the and author Guido von List, one of the important figures in Germanic mysticism and runic revivalism in the late 19th and early 20th centuries. In 1908, List published in ("The Secret of the Runes") a set of 18 so-called "Armanen Runes" on the Younger Futhark, which were allegedly revealed to him in a state of temporary blindness after a cataract operation on both eyes in 1902.

In Nazi contexts, the *s*-rune is referred to as "Sig" (after

List, probably from Anglo-Saxon *Sigel*). The "Wolfsangel", while not a rune historically, has the shape of List's "Gibor" rune.

Nicholas Eymerich

https://en.wikipedia.org/wiki/Nicholas_Eymerich

Nicholas Eymerich (Catalan: *Nicolau Aymerich*) (*c.* 1316 – 4 January 1399) was a Roman Catholic theologian and Inquisitor General of the Inquisition of the Crown of Aragon in the latter half of the 14th century. He is best known for authoring the *Directorium Inquisitorum*.

Sicarii (Dagger Men)

https://en.wikipedia.org/wiki/Sicarii

Sicarii (Latin plural of **Sicarius** "dagger-men", in Modern Hebrew rendered *siqariqim* סיקריקים) is a term applied, in the decades immediately preceding the destruction of Jerusalem in 70 CE, to an extremist splinter group of the Jewish Zealots, who attempted to expel the Romans and their partisans from the Roman province of Judea. The Sicarii carried *sicae*, or small daggers, concealed in their cloaks, hence their name. At public gatherings, they pulled out these daggers to attack Romans or Roman sympathizers, blending into the crowd after the deed to escape detection.

Shlomo Halberstam

https://en.wikipedia.org/wiki/Shlomo_Halberstam_(first_Bobo ver_rebbe)

Shlomo Halberstam (1847-1905) was a Hasidic Rebbe, founder of the Hasidic dynasty of Bobov. He was the son of Rabbi Myer Noson Halberstam (1827-1855). Rabbi Shlomo was a grandson of the Divrei Chaim of Sanz (1793-1876), a Hasidic sage of the 19th century whose influence established the groundwork for many other Galician Hasidic movements.

Titi Villus

https://en.wikipedia.org/wiki/Titivillus

Titi Villus is a demon said to work on behalf of Belphegor, Lucifer or Satan to introduce errors into the work of scribes.

Thule Society

https://en.wikipedia.org/wiki/Thule_Society

The **Thule Society**: *Thule-Gesellschaft*), originally the *Studiengruppe für germanisches Altertum* ("Study Group for Germanic Antiquity"), was a German occultist and völkisch group in Munich, named after a mythical northern country from Greek legend. The Society is notable chiefly as the organization that sponsored the Deutsche Arbeiterpartei (DAP), which was later reorganized by Adolf Hitler into the National Socialist German Workers' Party (NSDAP or Nazi Party). According to Hitler biographer Ian Kershaw, the organization's "membership list... reads like a Who's Who of early Nazi sympathizers and leading figures in

Munich", including **Rudolf Hess**, **Alfred Rosenberg**, **Hans Frank**, **Julius Lehmann**, **Gottfried Feder**, **Dietrich Eckart**, and **Karl Harrer**, However, **Nicholas Goodrick-Clarke**, contends that while Hans Frank and Rudolf Hess had been Thule members, other leading Nazis had only been guests of the Thule or entirely unconnected with it. While the ideology of the Thule Society and that of Hitler's regime agreed in philosophy, according to Johannes Hering, "There is no evidence that Hitler ever attended the Thule Society.

Tzadikim Nistarim

https://en.wikipedia.org/wiki/Tzadikim_Nistarim

The Tzadikim Nistarim "hidden righteous ones" or Lamed Vav Tzadikim often abbreviated to*Lamed Vav(niks)*, refers to 36 righteous people, a notion rooted within the more mystical dimensions of Judaism. The singular form is Tzadik Nistar.

Ugarit

https://en.wikipedia.org/wiki/Ugarit

Ugarit was an ancient port city, the ruins of which are located at what is now called Ras Shamra (sometimes written "Ras Shamrah"; Arabic رأس شمرة, literally "Cape Fennel"), a headland in northern Syria. Ugarit had close connections to the Hittite Empire, sent tribute to Egypt at times, and maintained trade and diplomatic connections with Cyprus (then called Alashiya), documented in the archives recovered from the site and corroborated by Mycenaean and Cypriot pottery found there. The polity was at its height from ca. 1450 BC until 1200 BC.

Johann Heinrich Westphal

http://www.biblicalarchaeology.org/daily/biblical-sites-places/jerusalem/rediscovering-jerusalem-in-the-1820s/

In 1818, Johann Westphal visited Jerusalem and produced the first now map of the city. His sketch was recently discovered in a Berlin archive.

Wewelsburg Castle

https://en.wikipedia.org/wiki/Wewelsburg

Wewelsburg is a Renaissance castle located in the village of Wewelsburg, which is a district of the town of Bürez, Westphalia, in the Landkreis of Paderborn in the northeast of North Rhine-Westphalia, Germany. The castle has a triangular layout - three round towers connected by massive walls. After 1934, it was used by the SS under Heinrich Himmler and was to be expanded into the central SS-cult-site.[1] After 1941, plans were developed to enlarge it to be the so-called "Center of the World". In 1950, the castle was reopened as a museum and youth hostel. The castle today hosts the Historical Museum of the Prince Bishopric of Paderborn and the Wewelsburg 1933-1945 Memorial Museum.

Werner Heisenberg

https://en.wikipedia.org/wiki/Werner_Heisenberg

Werner Karl Heisenberg ; 5 December 1901 – 1 February 1976) was a German theoretical physicist and one of the key pioneers of quantum mechanics. He published his work in 1925 in a breakthrough paper. In the subsequent series of papers with Max Born and Pascual Jordan, during the same year, this matrix formulation of quantum mechanics was substantially elaborated. In 1927 he published his uncertainty principle, upon which he built his philosophy and for which he is best known. Heisenberg was awarded the Nobel Prize in Physics for 1932 "for the creation of quantum mechanics". He also made important contributions to the theories of the hydrodynamics of turbulent flows, the atomic nucleus, ferromagnetism, cosmic rays, and subatomic particles, and he was instrumental in planning the first West German nuclear reactor at Karlsruhe, together with a research reactor in Munich, in 1957. Considerable controversy surrounds his work on atomic research during World War II.

Vindex

http://www.latin-dictionary.org/Vindex
defender, protector, deliverer, liberator, vindicator

About the Author

Charles Griswold is an avid reader and writer. His writing combines supernatural and historical events with real world locations that blend the boundaries between reality and fantasy. Mr. Griswold's current work, Arcadia's Daughter, is the middle book of an eventual trilogy.

Mr. Griswold splits his time between Massachusetts and Maine. When not writing, he can be found hiking with his two standard poodles, kayaking, cooking, woodworking, and exploring mid-coast Maine on his Vespa.

Made in the USA
Middletown, DE
10 December 2016